WHALE ADVENTURE

'Sorry, kid,' said third mate Brown. 'Your brother dived to help a chum who had just been pulled down by a shark. That's the last we saw of either of them.'

'But you don't really know that he died,' Roger insisted.

'Look, kid,' Brown explained patiently, 'when a man goes down and doesn't come up, there's only one answer . . .'

AFRICAN ADVENTURE

There was a rushing through the grass just outside the zone of firelight. Hunt put his .375 Magnum to his shoulder. He lowered the gun when he saw that what was emerging was no wild beast but the headman of the village with three of his men.

'*Bwana*, quick, help us,' he called as he came running. 'The leopard. It has taken one of the children.'

Other Red Fox Story Collections

THE CHARLIE MOON COLLECTION
DOCTOR DOLITTLE STORIES
COOL SCHOOL STORIES
BALLET STORIES
ANIMAL STORIES
COMPLETELY WILD STORIES

THE ADVENTURE COLLECTION

WILLARD PRICE

RED FOX

A Red Fox Book

Published by Random House Children's Books
20 Vauxhall Bridge Road, London SW1V 2SA

A division of Random House UK Ltd

London Melbourne Sydney Auckland
Johannesburg and agencies throughout the world

3 5 7 9 10 8 6 4

Whale Adventure first published in Great Britain by Jonathan Cape Ltd 1960,
African Adventure first published in Great Britain by Jonathan Cape Ltd 1963

This Red Fox edition 1998

Printed and bound in Great Britain by
Cox & Wyman Ltd, Reading, Berkshire

Papers used by Random House UK Limited
are natural, recyclable products made from wood grown in
sustainable forests. The manufacturing processes conform to
the environmental regulations of the country of origin.

RANDOM HOUSE UK Limited Reg. No. 954009

ISBN 0 09 926592 3

Contents

WHALE ADVENTURE

1
The Bird with Twenty Wings

On all the hills of Honolulu people looked to the sea. Spectators crowded the docks lining the harbour.

They were all gazing in the same direction. They paid no attention to the steamers and yachts, cargo vessels and tugs. They did not bother to glance at the helicopter passing overhead, or the plane setting out for San Francisco.

These they could see any day.

They looked at something that seemed to have come from another world. It was the kind of ship that used to take men sailing and whaling a century ago.

It had no funnels, no black smoke, no grinding, growling machinery. Its three masts towered more than a hundred feet high. From them hung its twenty great sails, drying in the still, sunny air. It looked like a huge bird about to fly away.

'A fine sight!' said someone.

'Didn't think there were any of those old beauties left,' said another.

'Beauty my eye,' said a man who looked like a sailor. 'You wouldn't think she was such a beauty if you knew what happens to the men who sail on her.'

'Hope it isn't too bad,' said a new voice, 'because *we're* going to sail on her.'

'I'm sorry for you,' said the sailor, and looked up at the newcomer. He saw Hal Hunt, tall, well built, nineteen years old, his deeply tanned face lit by a pleasant smile.

'Well,' admitted the sailor, 'you look as if you could take care of yourself. But I hope this kid isn't going too.'

Roger bristled up and tried to look as big and tough as his thirteen years would permit. He was about to make a smart reply when Mr Scott cut in.

'I don't think we'll have any trouble,' he said as he and the two boys pressed on through the crowd.

The sailor shook his head doubtfully. But Hal and Roger felt confidence in their older companion. Everything would be all right so long as they were accompanied by the scientist, Arthur Scott of the American Museum.

Still, the sailor's remarks left them a bit uneasy.

Reaching the edge of the dock they climbed down a ladder into a waiting launch and were taken out towards the great bird with the twenty white wings. The closer they came the more uneasy they grew. For the ship itself was not white and beautiful like its sails. It was a black evil-looking hulk, and from it drifted the strong smell of whale oil and rancid blubber.

Now the name of the bark could be seen on the stern and it was not a pretty name. *Killer* was the name, and the home port was St Helena.

'She's named after the killer-whale,' said Mr Scott. 'That's the most vicious and deadly of all the whales.'

'Where is St Helena?' asked Roger.

'It's an island far down in the South Atlantic. It has always been a great whaling port. Only fifty years ago you could see as many as a hundred whaling ships in the harbour at one time. And there were hundreds more in northern ports.'

'Only fifty years?' said Hal. 'I thought it was centuries ago.'

'No — whaling under sail was not as ancient as you might suppose. As late as 1907 New Bedford had a fleet of twenty-two whalers. Of course, today the business has been taken over by the big factory ships — but with the new demand for whale products a few of the old sailing vessels have been put back into service. That gives us a chance to see how whaling used to be done. And that's why the American Museum wants me to make a complete record of the operations and take motion pictures for the museum's library.'

'Has the captain really agreed to take you?'

'Yes. But he says he won't sail until he can get two more men. Two of his crew deserted — he has to fill their places.'

'And that's where we come in,' said Hal.

'Exactly. You've never sailed in a square-rigger, but he probably wouldn't be able to find anybody who has. You know something about the sea, after sailing your own boat all over the Pacific.[1] Even Roger is not too young to be useful as a mess-boy or look-out — there are dozens of jobs he could do on a sailing ship.'

He glanced up at the savage black hulk of the *Killer.*

'The only question is — do you want to go? I'm not going to press you, and I don't want any quick answer. It's up to you. I can tell you it's hard work — so hard that crews accustomed to the soft duties on a steamer won't touch it. I can tell you, too, that

[1] For the previous adventures of Hal and Roger Hunt, see the books *Amazon Adventure, South Sea Adventure, Underwater Adventure,* and *Volcano Adventure,* by Willard Price.

the captain looks to me like a bully and a brute. That's another reason he has trouble finding men. I'm glad you cabled your father and got his consent, because I can't be responsible for you. You're on your own. After you've seen the captain and looked over the ship you will still have time to back out if you want to.'

The launch hugged in under the black counter of the *Killer.* Looking up from this point the sight was dizzying. Up they looked to the gunwale over which a rope ladder dangled. Up to the bottom of a lifeboat swinging from its davits. On up the three masts, the mainmast and foremast, square-rigged, the mizenmast carrying fore-and-aft sails in the manner of a bark. Up past mainsail and foresail, topsails and topgallant sails, royals and trysails, up to the look-out's cage at the very tip of the mainmast a good hundred and ten feet above water.

Loving the sea as they did, they had many times studied pictures and descriptions of the old square-riggers, but this was the first time they had seen one. It gave them stomach-butterflies to think of climbing those ratlines that went skyward like narrow spider-webs, up, up to where the gently swaying masthead seemed to scrape the clouds. If it made them dizzy to look up, how would they feel looking *down* from that unsteady basket, say in a storm, when the sway of the mast would be anything but gentle?

'Oh, a sailor's life is a jolly life,' sang Roger, but he was quite out of tune and didn't sound very convincing.

'All right, over you go,' said Scott.

The boys came out of their trance and scrambled up the rope ladder, Scott following. They tumbled over the rail on to the deck.

Was the ship on fire? Red flames shot up and white steam filled the air. Men seemed to be fighting the fire. The boys came closer. Now they could see that the fire was confined inside a brick wall. Huge black pots, each big enough to hold several men, rested in the flames. Men hauled great chunks of meat as big as themselves across the deck and dumped them into the pots.

'Just trying-out,' said Mr Scott. 'That's blubber. Blubber is the whale's overcoat. It's very fat. They put the blubber into the pots and cook the oil out of it. It's called trying-out.'

The men, in ragged blood-and-oil-stained clothes and unshaved beards looked as rough as pirates. The roughest and biggest of them gave orders. He noticed the newcomers and walked growling towards them as if prepared to throw them bodily off his ship. His eyes were large and bulging, like big marbles; his mouth had a mean twist to starboard; and his chin, covered with black bristles like porcupine quills, projected forward like the prow of a pirate ship.

'What do you want — ' he began gruffly, then recognized Mr Scott. 'Oh, you're the scientific fellow.' He made an obvious effort to be more polite. 'Welcome aboard. Are you ready to pay me for your passage?'

'I am,' said Mr Scott, producing from his breast pocket a large roll of notes. 'I believe that's the price you asked for three weeks' passage.'

'All that,' exclaimed Hal, 'for passage on this?' At once he realized he should not have said it. After all, it was none of his business.

The captain glared. 'Who's this smart alec? What does he know about the cost of running a ship? And how about all the trouble I'm going to have with the science fellow stumbling around in our way?' He stuffed the money into his trouser pocket and advanced upon Hal. 'By the Holy Harry, I wish I had you in my crew. I'd trim you down to size!'

Hal did not flinch. He was as tall as the captain, not so heavily built but perhaps just as wiry and strong.

'Start trimming,' he said with a smile, 'because I think I'm going to be in your crew.'

Mr Scott hastened to pour oil on troubled waters.

'It's my fault,' he said. 'I should have begun with introductions. Captain Grindle, this is Hal Hunt and his brother Roger. You are short of two men — perhaps they will sign on. They've had some sea experience. Of course, they don't know much about square-riggers.'

'Nobody does,' growled the captain.

'But they will learn as fast as anyone you could pick up. They're used to roughing it. Their father is a famous collector of animals for zoos and circuses. He has sent his boys on various trips to collect wild animals, and on scientific expeditions to teach them something about the world we live in. They'd learn a lot on your ship.'

'They would that,' agreed the captain sourly. 'I'd learn them things they'd never forget. But I don't know about taking on a couple of gents.'

He spat out the word 'gents'.

'They'll want special favours,' he went on. 'Believe me, they won't get them. They'll sleep in the fo'c'sle with the rest of the crew. They'll eat what's put before 'em. They'll step lively or smart for it, and I don't care if their father is the King of Siam.'

'Don't worry,' said Hal. 'Our father isn't the King of Siam. And we're not "gents". We want no favours.'

'Like as not too soft for this kind of work,' grumbled the captain. 'Let me see your hands.'

The four palms held out for his inspection were hard and tough. The captain may have been surprised but he wouldn't admit it.

'Soft as butter,' he said scornfully. 'You'll have blisters as big as plums before you're on this ship a day. Oh well, if I can't get what I want I have to take what I can get. Come down and sign on.'

2
Two 'Gents' on a Whaler

Captain Grindle clumped down the steps to his cabin. Hal and Roger, about to follow, were stopped by Mr Scott.

'I like this fellow less and less,' said Scott in a low voice. 'I've got to go with him — but you don't have to. I'm sorry I got you into this. Why don't you just back out now before it's too late?'

Hal looked at Roger. He felt he could take what was coming, but it would be harder on his young brother.

'It's up to the boy,' Hal said.

Roger, whose heart had sunk into his shoes at the thought that they might after all miss this great adventure of sails and whales, was suddenly happy again.

'If it's up to me,' he said, 'let's go,' and he led the way down the steps.

On a table in the captain's cabin lay the papers. Hal began to look them over.

'Come, come,' said Captain Grindle impatiently. 'Do you think I have time to stand around while you read all the small print? Sign and have done with it. I'm paying you a one-three-hundredth lay.'

Hal knew the system of lays. Whalers got no wages. Each got a share of the profits of the voyage. This share was called a lay. Hal's lay of one three-hundredth meant that if the ship came back with three hundred gallons of whale oil Hal would be paid the price of one gallon. It was a very small lay.

'And my brother?' asked Hal.

The captain's eyes flashed. 'You don't expect me to pay a child! He goes as an apprentice. He gets nothing but his food and bunk — and won't be worth that.'

It didn't seem fair to Roger. But he held his tongue. After all, he was taking this trip for experience, not money. What bothered him most was being called a child. Wasn't he thirteen years old and so big that some people took him for fifteen or sixteen? He itched for a chance to show this contemptuous captain that he was no child.

When the papers were signed the captain showed Mr Scott his cabin, a small room next to his own. 'Really the first mate's,' he said. 'But since I've got no first for this trip, you may have it.'

He turned to the boys. 'Go up and ask for Mr Durkins. Second mate. He'll tell you the difference between a clove hitch and a donkey's breakfast. And mind you learn fast. You'll be no use to me on a three weeks cruise if it takes you three weeks to learn which end your head is screwed on. Get your gear aboard this afternoon. We sail before dawn.'

'Thank you,' said Hal, going out of the door.

'Wait a minute, young fella,' bawled the captain.

'The first thing you want to learn is to say "sir" when you speak to an officer.'

'Thank you, sir,' said Hal, and went on deck followed by Roger.

They found Mr Durkins waiting for them. He was as rough as gravel but he had a ready smile.

'I usually get the job of showing the greenies the ropes,' he said. 'First you might like to see where you bunk.'

He led the way forward and down the hatch into the fo'c'sle.

It was dark. There were no portholes. The only light came from two sputtering whale-oil lamps. They also sent out black smoke and nauseating fumes.

There were other smells, walls of them, waves of them, smells so strong that they seemed like something solid that could only be cut through with a hatchet or a knife. Clothes hanging from pegs stank of dead whales. There was no ventilation except through the half-opened hatch. That would be closed in rough weather. There was a smell of mouldy rags and mildewed boots and unwashed bodies and decayed food. And the heat made all the smells more suffocating.

'Here's where you doss down,' said the mate, indicating two bunks, one above the other.

Hal examined the bunks. The thin pad lay on wooden boards. There were no springs, no bedding, no pillow.

'How about blankets?' Hal asked.

'Blankets! Man alive, this is the tropics. You're lucky to get a donkey's breakfast.'

Roger remembered the captain had said something about a donkey's breakfast.

'What's a donkey's breakfast?' he asked.

'This pad.'

'Why do they call it a donkey's breakfast?'

'I don't know. Because it's stuffed with straw, I guess.'

'A pretty slim breakfast,' said Hal, pinching the edge of the pad. It was not quite an inch thick. The boards would feel pretty hard through it.

'Good for your back,' laughed the mate. 'Why, they tell me the best people sleep on boards these days. The doctors are all for it. 'Course, nothin' but the best would satisfy Cap Grindle.' He laughed again. 'The best boards, the best brig and the best cat.'

The brig, Hal knew, was the jail, and the cat must be the cat-o'-nine-tails or whip used to flog unruly sailors.

'You're joking about the cat,' Hal said. 'I suppose that isn't used any more. The law doesn't allow it.'

This struck the mate as very funny.

'The law,' he said, between gasps of laughter. 'The law, you say! Believe you me, the captain makes his own law on this ship.' He stopped laughing and his face suddenly took on a look of savage ferocity. In an instant he was changed from a carefree sailor into a snarling animal. He glanced up at the open hatch, then lowered his voice to a harsh whisper.

'You may as well know about it now,' he said. 'You'll learn soon enough. Why does ol' man Grindle have trouble getting men? Why did those two desert? Why is he willing to take on greenies like you? Because he needs new feed for his cat, that's why. Scarce a man on board who hasn't felt it. Even the first mate — that's why he quit. See here.'

He switched off his shirt. His back was ribbed with purple welts standing up a quarter of an inch high. At points the skin was still broken and festering.

'But why do you stand it?' asked Hal. 'You could report it to the Honolulu police. Why don't you all desert?'

'Listen, chum, you don't understand. We been out a year already from St Helena. We get no wages — just a lay — and that isn't paid till we get home. Them as desert now lose everything they've earned. D'ye wonder a man thinks twice before he deserts? No, there are only two things we can do. One is to be patient-like till we get home.'

Hal waited for him to go on. When he did not, Hal prompted:

'And what's the other thing you can do?'

Durkins cast a look round at the empty bunks. 'Walls have ears,' he said. 'And you have ears, and how do I know I can trust 'em? What's the other thing we can do? Use your imagination. No harm in that — but remember I didn't say anything.'

Mutiny. The word stood out as plainly as if he had shouted it at the top of his lungs. Not for nothing had the boys read innumerable stories of mutiny on the high seas. Here conditions were prime for mutiny. The captain, without a first officer to back him up, stood alone against a disgruntled crew. If he were put out of the way they might sail the ship to some smugglers' lair, sell the whale oil and the ship itself and divide the proceeds.

But could such a thing happen in this day and age? The boys knew it could happen and did happen. Even during their own brief voyaging of the Pacific, from San Francisco to Japan and back through the South Seas, several mutinies had been reported.

The Pacific, they knew, is a still unconquered ocean. It is bigger than the whole land surface of the globe. It is sprinkled with more than twenty-five thousand islands, half of them uninhabited.

It is the paradise of both honest men and rascals. So much of it is so far from police stations and law-courts that men do as they please or as they must. And men who choose to disappear may hide in its vast distances more effectively than in the thickest jungles of Africa.

Hal reflected that this voyage might turn out to be even more of an adventure than he had expected.

'Now I'll show you topside,' said the mate, and they climbed to the deck. The clean fresh air seemed like a tonic after the hot stink of the fo'c'sle.

'You've got to know the names of things,' said the mate, 'so when you're told to man the down-haul you won't lay hold of a halyard, and all like that. Now then, you know the three masts — the foremost, mainmast and mizenmast. The horizontal spars the sails hang from are the yards. When you roll up the sails that's reefing 'em, and you tie them tight with those little strings called gaskets — '

He went on to point out and describe all the complicated gear of the most complicated of sailing ships — lifts, clews, bunts, braces, tacks, sheets, shrouds, ratlines, rings, crosstrees, foot-ropes, buoy-ropes, wheel-ropes, belaying pins, catheads, fore-stays, backstays, booms, sprits, davits, and so on and on, concluding with twenty different sails, each with its own particular name.

As he talked he kept glancing at them with a sly grin. He was having a good time at their expense. He thought they didn't know what he was talking about. Finally he said:

'There, I'll bet you can't remember half of what I've told you. What's that sail?'

'Spanker.' The boys spoke together.

'And that one?'

'Gaff-topsyl.'

'What's the difference between a martingale boom and a whisker boom?'

He got the right answer.

He went on with a complete cross-examination. The boys made some mistakes, but thanks to their keen interest in sailing, their schooner experience and much reading, their percentage of error was small.

'Not bad,' Durkins had to admit. Then, as if fearing that the boys might be too pleased with themselves, he went on:

'But it's one thing to name 'em and another thing to use 'em. Wait till you try reefing sails in a storm a hundred feet above deck — or rowing one of those little boats out and tackling a whale that can smash your craft to smithereens with one flick of his tail. Then you'll find out what it takes to be a whaler.'

3
Captain Grindle Amuses Himself

Roger floated above the clouds.

They seemed like clouds, the twenty white sails that billowed beneath him.

He was in the 'rings', a sort of basket or crow's-nest at the top of the mainmast. A hundred feet down was the deck of the *Killer*, but he could not see it. He could see nothing below him but the white clouds of canvas. For a while he was alone, soaring through the sky like a bird or a plane, white clouds below him and more white clouds, real ones, above.

Not quite alone. One man shared his heaven. In the rings at the head of the foremast stood Jiggs, one of the crew. He, too, could not see the ship beneath. But he was not there to look at the ship. Both he and Roger were posted as look-outs to watch for whales.

There they stood, only thirty feet apart, but with an impassable canyon between them. It was as if they were each perched on a mountain-top separated by a deep valley filled with cloud. The cloud ended only a few feet below them and it was easy to imagine that you could walk across this white floor from the head of the mainmast to the head of the foremast. But when you remembered that the floor was not reliable and would treacherously let you plunge to your death on the deck a hundred feet below, it made your head swim and hands grip the rail of your dizzy basket.

Of course, it was the basket that was dizzy — Roger wouldn't admit that he was. The basket was going around in circles. The sea was fairly smooth, but there was enough of a swell to roll the ship slightly from side to side and make it lazily heave and pitch.

Those on deck might not notice the motion, but a movement of a few inches there was exaggerated to many feet at the masthead. So it was that Roger was spun round and round until he began to have a distinctly uncomfortable feeling in the pit of his stomach.

This was his first day of whaling. The *Killer* had left Honolulu at dawn. After their interview with Captain Grindle the boys and Mr Scott had gone ashore for their gear. There Scott had said goodbye to his colleague, Sinclair, who had been unable to go with him on the *Killer* because the captain had insisted that one 'science fellow' was enough to bother with. Hal and Roger had said their own goodbyes to their friends on the schooner *Lively Lady*, on which they had sailed the far Pacific. The schooner was still under charter by the American Museum, and the skipper, Captain Ike, and the

Polynesian man, Omo, would look after it until the return of the *Killer* in three weeks.

The first night on board had not been too happy. The first surprise came at dinner-time.

There was no dining-saloon for the crew, not even a table. The men formed in line and walked past a small window in the wall of the galley (kitchen). Through this window the cook thrust out to each man a pan of meat and beans and a chunk of hard-tack (ship-biscuit).

Then you could look for a place to sit down. Of course, there were no chairs. You might sit on the fo'c'sle head, or on a hatch cover, or on the deck itself.

Or you could eat standing up. This was not too bad because the eating did not take long. It was not the sort of food you would linger over. You got it down as fast as possible. In five minutes it was stowed away.

As for the hard-tack, it was well named. It was so hard that the best teeth could scarcely make a dent in it, and most of the men threw their biscuits overside or tried to hit the gulls and terns that wheeled above the ship.

Having emptied their pans the boys were about to take them back to the galley when a sailor prompted:

'Clean 'em first.'

'Where's the water?' Hal asked.

'Water my hat!' exclaimed the sailor. 'What do you think this is, a bloomin' yacht? You'll be lucky if you get enough water to drink — there's none to spare for washin'.'

He pulled some rope-yarn from his pocket. It was a tangled mass almost as fluffy as absorbent cotton. He wiped his pan, then threw the sticky wad into the sea. He gave some of the yarn to the boys and they followed the same procedure. Then they returned their pans at the galley window.

'You'll soon get the hang of it,' said the sailor who had supplied them with the rope-yarn. 'My name's Jimson. Any time you get stuck, perhaps I can help out.'

'Thanks a lot,' said Hal, and introduced himself and his brother. 'But I don't understand it. Here we are still in harbour — there surely ought to be plenty of fresh water on board.'

'And so there is,' agreed Jimson. 'But you never know when you leave port on one of these sailing tubs how long it will be before you make port again. You're pretty much at the mercy of wind and weather. 'Course, you could fill up the hold with tanks of water, but then what would you do for space to store your whale oil? And, believe me, the skipper puts whale oil before water. Whale oil means money, water only means lives. If it came right down to it, I'm sure he'd rather have a few of us go raving mad o' thirst than crawl back into port with a light load o'oil.'

'But you must use water to wash your clothes,' Hal said.

'We do — but not fresh water. Come back and I'll show you. There's our clothes-line.' He pointed to a coil of rope beside a barrel. 'Once we get moving we'll soak our dirty clothes in that barrel — it contains a weak acid solution — then we'll tie them to the end of that line and throw it overboard. We'll drag that bundle of clothes through the sea for two or three days, and when we haul it out I'll bet the clothes will be as clean as if you had put them through one of those newfangled washing-machines. Of course, there may be a few holes in them where the sharks have closed their jaws on them.'

'Do the sharks ever tear them off that line?'

'No. One taste, and they let them go. That's what usually happens. But a couple o'months ago one fool of a shark swallowed the whole bundle. Probably there was some blood on the cloth that made him think it was edible. That shark must have been real surprised when he found he couldn't get away. He was towed behind the ship nobody knows how long until someone noticed him floundering about and hauled him in. We opened him up and there were our clothes. They had to be dragged another three days to get the shark-smell out of them.'

The boys did very little sleeping that night. They could not make their bones comfortable on the hard boards of their bunks, and they were excited by their new surroundings and the trip before them.

There were about twenty other men in the room, some trying to sleep, others sitting on the edges of their bunks talking and smoking. The smoke from their cigarettes and pipes, the fumes from the whale-oil lamps, the smell of blood and blubber and bilge-water — all this plus the heat made breathing difficult. The boys were not sorry when at four in the morning the second mate bellowed down through the hatch:

'All hands on deck!'

In the grey light of dawn the *Killer* sailed from Honolulu. On the right lay Pearl Harbor, scene of death and destruction when Japan entered the Second World War. As if to balance this place of terrible memory, on the left was one of the loveliest and happiest spots in the world — the long curve of Waikiki Beach and bold Diamond Head wearing the pink halo of approaching sunrise.

Roger, standing by the rail enjoying the view, was roused by a kick in the rear that almost lifted him from the deck. He turned, fighting mad, clenching his fists for battle. The bulging eyes of Captain Grindle glared down at him.

'I'll have nobody loafing on this ship,' growled the captain.

'Sorry, sir, I was just waiting for orders.'

'You'll get your orders in the seat of your pants if you don't step lively.'

He looked round with a sly grin.

'I'll find you something to do.' He scanned the deck for a job that would be hard enough, something that would tax the strength and courage of a young boy. Finally he glanced up the swaying mast.

Roger hoped he would not be sent aloft. Not just now. Some other time he would like it, but now he felt a little faint for loss of sleep and his breakfast of overripe meat had not agreed with him. The captain seemed to guess the boy's uneasiness.

'That's the place for you,' he laughed savagely.

'Up in the rings, and be quick about it. Jiggs is up the foremast. You shinny up the main. All the way to the peak. And you're not going up there to look at the view. Watch for whales, and if you see a spout sing out. Let's see how sharp your eyes are. If you spot a whale before Jiggs does I'll let you come down. If you don't, you'll stay there until you do, and I don't care if it takes a week. Got no use for babes on deck. Get up there into your cradle, and I hope it rocks you sick.'

Roger was half-way up the ratlines to the first platform before this speech was finished. He had never climbed anything so unsteady as this wobbling rope ladder. He would be glad to reach the solid safety of the first platform, or 'top', as it was called.

He was about to go through the opening in the platform when another bellow came from below.

'Not through the lubber's hole,' roared the captain. 'I'll have no lubbers on this ship. Up around by the futtock shrouds.'

Perhaps he hoped to confuse the boy. But Roger knew that the hole he had been about to pass through was called the lubber's hole. And he knew the futtock shrouds were those iron rods fastened at one end to the mast and at the other to the outer edge of the platform. To climb them he must leave the rope ladder and go up hand over hand with the skill of a monkey, while his feet dangled in space.

Half-way up a lurch of the vessel loosened his grip and he hung suspended by one hand, swinging like a pendulum in a grandfather's clock.

A roar of laughter came from below. The captain was thoroughly enjoying himself. Several of the crew had gathered now, but they did not join in the laughter. Hal started up the ratlines to the relief of his brother. A sharp order from the captain stopped him.

Every time the windjammer swayed to starboard Roger was directly over the try-pots in which blubber from the last whale catch was still boiling. If he fell into one of those great steaming vats the comedy would turn to tragedy. But it would still be comedy to the warped mind of Captain Grindle. A wide grin made the porcupine bristles on his chin and cheeks stand out like spears as his eyes passed from the clinging figure to the try-pots and back again. The steam curled up like a snake around the hanging body. Hal edged close to the pots. If the boy fell he might catch him, or at least yank him from the boiling oil in time to save his life.

There came a gasp of relief from the crew and a disappointed grunt from the captain when a list to port swung Roger against the shroud, which he was now able to grip with both hands and his feet as well. He clung there trembling for an instant, then slowly inched his way up over the edge of the top and collapsed on the platform.

A cheer rose from the crew. It was checked at once by the harsh voice of Captain Grindle.

'You varmint! Is this a time to take a nap? I'll wake you up.'

He seized a belaying-pin and flung it upward with

all his great strength. It struck the underside of the top with a resounding whack.

Roger struggled to his feet. He stood swaying dizzily, one arm round the mast.

The crash of the belaying-pin had brought Mr Scott up from his cabin. He turned to Hal.

'What's going on?'

'Just a big bully having some fun,' said Hal bitterly. 'Grindle ordered Roger into the rings. Wouldn't let him go through the lubber's hole. Nothing would have pleased the brute better than to see him drop into the try-pots and get boiled in oil.'

The captain, cursing, grabbed another belaying-pin and hurled it aloft. His aim was good. The heavy wooden club passed through the lubber's hole and struck Roger on the elbow.

Hal and Mr Scott at once began to force their way through the crowd, determined to overpower the captain. The men opened a path to let them through. They were eager to see someone challenge the authority of the master.

The captain saw the two men coming. His eyes shone with evil pleasure and his hand went back to his hip where a revolver rested in its holster.

Then the way was suddenly blocked by the sailor called Jimson. Hal and Scott found themselves held firmly in the grip of the big seaman.

'Stop it, you fools!' said Jimson in a voice just above a rasping whisper. 'You'll get yourselves killed. You'll only make it worse for the kid.' Then he leaned close to Hal's ear, making sure that the captain should not overhear him. 'This ain't the time. The time is coming, but it ain't now.'

Captain Grindle, seeing that he was not to be attacked, roared with laughter.

'What's the matter, gents?' he cried scornfully. 'Why don't you come on? The welcome mat is out. Reception committee is waiting. Step right up, gents — tea will be served.' He spun his revolver around two fingers. 'Pink tea. Will you have lemon or cream? I'll send a cup aloft to your baby brother.'

He fired a shot into the air, not directly at Roger but close enough so that the boy, who was once more climbing the ratlines, heard the whistle of the bullet.

Again Hal and Scott struggled to get at the captain, but several of the crew held them back. Again Jimson whispered harshly: 'This ain't the time. The time is coming, but this ain't it.'

'Cowards and softies!' cried the captain. 'I got nothing but cowards and softies on my ship. The whole pack o' ye wouldn't dare face up to a real man. Now get for'ard and be quick about it.' He fired two shots over their heads. The men retired sullenly towards the fo'c'sle.

Roger, leaving the top behind him, was climbing higher. For the platform called the 'top' is not the top. It is only the head of the lower section of the mast. Two-thirds of the mast rise above it.

Roger thought the mast would never end. He felt like Jack climbing the beanstalk that reached all the way up to another world. He could not use his right arm. The blow from the belaying-pin had not broken any bones, but it had so bruised the elbow that he could not straighten or flex the arm without acute pain.

He tucked the hand within his belt and held to the ratlines with his left hand only. At every rise he must release his grip and transfer his hand to the next higher rung. This might have been easy to do on a wooden ladder, but on a ladder of rope that swung here and there like a loose cobweb at every motion of the ship he was in constant danger of clutching at a rung which was no longer where he had just seen it.

Every near-miss brought a snort of laughter from Captain Grindle, who was now Roger's sole audience. Nothing would so tickle the captain's distorted sense of humour as to see the young 'gent' come to grief.

Roger was determined not to give him that satisfaction. He would not fall, and he would not fail. He was going to reach the rings.

Every time he looked up at them they seemed as far away as ever. It was as if the more he climbed the more an invisible hand drew them a bit higher. At times he must stop and do nothing but cling for his life, as a gust of wind caught his cobweb and whipped it about.

At last he crawled up into the rings, and felt as if he had returned to a solid world when he gripped the iron hoop tightly bolted to the mast. True, the whole basket made dizzy circles in the sky, but it was firm ground compared with the rope ladder.

He looked down at the disappointed master, now almost completely hidden from view by the sails.

Captain Grindle shook his fist as if Roger had deliberately offended him by arriving safely in the rings.

'Remember,' yelled the captain, 'you'll sight first, or stay there till you do.'

Of course, that was not fair. Sighting the spout of a whale is not easy. Experience helps, and Jiggs had had experience, plenty of it.

The beginner is apt to think he sees the spout of a whale when it is only the spume of a breaking wave. Later he gets to know the difference. The spray from a wave-crest is irregular and quickly loses its force. The spout of a whale is like the spurt of water from a high-pressure hose.

And yet it doesn't quite look like water, because it isn't water. Whalers of the nineteenth century supposed it to be water. They supposed the whale to be spitting out water it had taken in by mouth while under the sea.

Now we know that the column of white is steam, not water. The giant of the deeps is letting off steam. The air that he has held in his lungs during his half-hour or more beneath the sea is forcibly expelled. Having been retained so long within the warm body of the whale the air is at the blood temperature of whales and humans, about 98.6 degrees Fahrenheit. It is full of moisture because it has been inside a moist body.

When the whale blows out the warm wet air it condenses to form a mist, just as a man's breath does when exhaled on a frosty morning. So a whale's spout is just a magnificent column of mist rising twenty, thirty, forty feet high. From the rings or crow's-nest of a whaler it can be seen as far as seven miles away.

The spout comes from the whale's nose, located on top of his head. Roger, clutching the rail and looking out to sea, tried to remember some things Mr Scott had told him about whales. Mr Scott had for many years made a scientific study of whales and their habits.

'If you ever have to watch for whales,' he said to Roger, 'keep your eye out for a white palm tree. That's what it looks like, the whale's spout. It goes up in a column and then branches out at the top. And it isn't straight up and down. It leans a little. When you see the spout you can tell which way the whale is going, because the spout always leans forward.'

'Do all whales have the same kind of spout?' Roger had asked.

'No. The palm-tree spout is made by the sperm-whale. His nose has only one nostril, so his tree of steam has only one trunk. If you see two trunks you are probably looking at a rorqual. They have two nostrils and send up twin jets that divide at the top and fall over in two branches like the boughs of a willow. And this twin willow doesn't lean forward, it stands straight up.'

4
The First Whale

Roger now scanned the sea, looking for a white palm with a single trunk, or a willow with two.

He knew he was more likely to see the palm than the willow. The two-nostril whales were best hunted far down in the seas of snow and ice near the South Pole. But the sperm-whale is a tropical animal and loves the warm waters near the Equator.

Whalers of the past hunted it there so relentlessly that it became scarce. Now, after a half-century of rest, sperm-whales were once more fairly plentiful in the warm seas between Hawaii and Tahiti.

And so many new uses have been found for all the parts of this great animal that no richer treasure can be discovered in the sea than a big sperm-whale. So Roger felt a thrill of importance at the thought that the winning of such a treasure might depend upon him.

Of course, Jiggs would probably sight one first. But just now Roger noticed that Jiggs was not looking out to sea. He was looking at Roger. Presently he called across to the boy:

'Cap was a bit rough on ye.'

'Is he always so mean?'

'You haven't seen the half of it yet. My advice to you is, keep your eyes skinned for a whale.'

For an hour, and then for another hour, Roger searched the sea. What a hopeless task it seemed. You couldn't look everywhere at once. While you were staring in one direction a whale might be spouting to high heaven behind you.

He revolved like a radar screen trying to cover the whole circle of the sea every ten seconds. His own revolving, plus the wheeling of his high basket, did not help that uneasy feeling at the pit of his stomach. His eyes became tired and blurred. When he closed them for a moment he could still see nothing but leaping blue waves. His nerves were tight and his arm pained badly.

What was so hard for him seemed to be easy for Jiggs. The sailor had had long practice. A quick glance about him every few seconds was all he needed.

He looked at the boy with sympathy, remembering his own hard experiences as a lad on a whaling ship. He had heard the captain's threat — that if Roger did not sight a whale he would stay there until he did.

They had been watching for three hours when Jiggs, in one of his quick surveys, caught sight of a white jet rising from the sea on the starboard bow.

He was about to sing out when he remembered Roger. The boy did not see the spout. He was looking in exactly the opposite direction, but he was turning and soon would be facing towards the whale.

Jiggs still had a chance to make the first call. There was always keen competition between look-outs. Jiggs was not used to letting any look-out beat him, if he could help it. But now, sympathy for the greenhorn held his tongue.

The whale spouted again. It was barely two miles off. Someone on deck might see it. In that case both look-outs would be disgraced, and might even be in for a flogging.

Jiggs could have told Roger where to look. He did not, because he had already seen enough of the boy's courage to know that he would refuse to sing out for a whale if he knew that Jiggs had seen it first. No, the lad must discover it for himself.

Roger was now facing directly forward. Now his eyes turned to starboard. He was looking straight towards the whale, but that beast, hidden in the waves, chose this instant to be contrary and was sending up no spout. Roger's gaze turned farther to starboard. Jiggs gave up his generous plan and opened his mouth to call 'Thar she blows' as the whale sent up another white palm tree.

He never did let out that call. Roger, though not looking directly towards the whale, saw the jet from the corner of his eye.

He had known for years that the look-out sighting a whale is supposed to call 'Thar she blows!' But now he was so excited that he could not think of the words. He jumped up and down and yelled: 'Whale! Whale!'

The captain came running from the afterdeck calling:

'Where away?'

'Over there,' yelled Roger, forgetful that the canvas between him and the deck would prevent the captain from seeing where he was pointing.

'Where, you young fool? Weather or lee?'

Roger tried to collect his wits. 'Four points on the weather-bow, sir. About two miles off.'

'What kind?'

'Sperm-whale.'

Captain Grindle came swarming up the ratlines. When a whale is sighted the captain belongs in the rings. In an amazingly short time Grindle made the masthead and stood beside Roger.

He looked away, four points on the weather-bow, and saw — nothing. He fixed an icy stare upon Roger.

'If you got me up here on a fool's errand — '

'I'm quite sure I saw something, sir.'

But was he sure? He had seen it only out of the corner of his eye. When he had looked straight towards it, it was gone. The breeze had freshened and every once in a while the white crest of a wave would burst into spray. Perhaps this was what he had seen.

The same thought had evidently occurred to the captain. He gazed to starboard for a few minutes, then his patience snapped.

'White water, that's what you saw. I'll teach you to waste my time,' and he swung a heavy fist at the boy's head.

Roger ducked just in time to avoid the blow, and the captain's fist crashed into the mast. He yelped with pain and looked at his bleeding knuckles. Of course, he put the blame on Roger. Muttering curses, he was about to thrash the greenhorn when Jiggs, seeing what was likely to happen, interrupted with a ringing shout:

'Bl-o-o — o-o-ws!'

The captain and Roger turned to look. There was no mistake about it this time. The boy's report had been right. The jet was four points on the weather-bow and it was the spout of a sperm-whale.

'All hands on deck!' roared the captain.

The call was repeated by the mate below: 'All hands on deck! Back the main yard! Stand by to lower!'

5
Nantucket Sleigh Ride

At once the ship came alive. There was the sound of heavy sea-boots on the deck as the men ran aft to the boats. The mate kept shouting orders. Again the captain turned upon Roger.

'Well, what are you doing here? Get down to the boats.'

Very willingly, Roger left the captain and scrambled down to the deck as fast as his gammy arm would permit. Durkins, the second mate, caught sight of him.

'You — I can use you in my boat. Third oar.'

The men leaped into the whale-boats. The lashings were cast off.

'Lower away!'

The falls raced through the sheaves. Down went the boats. The men bent to the oars. Three light cedar whale-boats, six men in each, streaked away towards the spouting whale.

'All right, boys,' shouted the mate, 'give way now and spring to it. Put some beef in it.'

Roger felt the mate's eye on him. He could guess what the mate was thinking. This greenhorn would probably catch a crab — get his oar fouled with the others.

Durkins relaxed when he saw that Roger knew how to handle an oar. The kid kept his eye on the stroke-oar and timed his own stroke with it. What the mate could not guess was how painful this was for Roger with the right arm singing from the blow of the belaying-pin.

The mate stood at the steering-sweep. He could not see the whale, and even the spout was hidden by intervening waves. Yet he knew where to steer. He kept glancing at the ship, which had turned its prow towards the whale.

He knew, too, when the whale was on the surface and when it dived. This information was signalled to him by the captain at the masthead. When the whale broke water the captain ran up a flag; when it 'went flukes', plunged beneath the surface, the flag was lowered.

Roger saw his brother in one of the other boats. Hal was pulling lustily. His boat was edging ahead. But Durkins was not to be easily beaten.

'Pull, boys. Pull like steers. Pull. Pile it on. Long and strong. Pull — every son of you. What's the matter, kid?'

This last remark was addressed to Roger, who was in such pain that he could no longer pull the fourteen-foot ash oar.

'My arm,' said Roger.

'And I don't wonder,' said Durkins, 'after the rap that pig gave you. Ship your oar.'

Roger took in his oar. He felt like a deserter. With only four oars working the boat steadily lost ground. Both the other boats passed it. Durkins still urged his men on, but it was hopeless. Roger knew how disappointed the second mate must be. Then his eye lit on the mast, which lay across the thwarts.

'I could put up the sail,' he suggested.

'No good,' said the mate. 'We're too close to the wind.'

Roger knew nothing about whaling, but a good deal about sailing. He did not want to argue with the mate. Testing the wind on his face, he felt that the sail would draw enough air to be worth while. They might even be able to overtake the other boats.

'Please, sir, may I try it?' he ventured.

The mate hesitated. 'Guess it will do no harm,' he said, and added rather bitterly: 'You're no good to us, anyway. You may as well be doing that as sitting there like a lump on a log.'

Roger lost no time in stepping the mast. Lifting it, he placed it erect in the hole in the forward thwart. The boom dropped. The triangular sail opened and hung like a tired dishcloth. The men muttered in disgust.

Roger hauled in on the sheet-rope. The sail suddenly filled with air and began to pull.

Roger handled the sheet like the rein of a racehorse, drawing a little, giving a little, to suit every changing whim of the breeze. The boat gained speed. Presently it was racing away like a scared cat. It was rapidly overhauling the other boats.

'The kid's got something,' said Durkins.

The whale was now in plain sight. Its great black

hulk blocked the sky. To Roger it looked as big as the ship. This little twenty-foot boat was only as long as the monster's lower jaw.

He realized fully for the first time the risk men take who go out in such an eggshell to attack the greatest living creature on the face of the earth. Excitement raced up and down his spine. He had to confess to himself that he was scared. He almost hoped that one of the other boats would get there first.

And that was what happened. The boat in which Hal was pulling shot up alongside the whale a split second before the mate's. The harpooner standing in the bow hurled his iron. In his hurry to be first he threw at too great a distance and the harpoon fell into the water.

At the same instant the mate's boat, propelled by both oars and sail, slid into position beside the whale just behind its enormous head. The harpooner was Jimson. Dropping his oar he leaped to his feet in the boat's bow, raised his harpoon and plunged it into the black hide.

The monster hardly felt it, for the iron 'boned' — that is, instead of penetrating deep into the flesh, it struck a bone, and with such force that the iron was bent. Then it dropped away into the sea.

At once Jimson snatched up his second iron and threw it with all his might. It sank in up to the hitches.

A tremor like an earthquake ran through the giant body.

'Stern all!' yelled the mate, and the men lost no time in rowing the boat backward out of reach of the whale's flukes. At the same time the enormous two-fluked tail, bigger than the screw of any vessel afloat, rose thirty feet into the air and came down again upon the water with a resounding crash not six inches from the gunwale of the boat. The wave made by this gigantic blow washed into the boat and half filled it.

Away went the sea giant, towing the boat behind it. The line from the harpoon to the boat was as taut as a tightrope. The boat was flying through the spray at a good twenty knots. Wave-tops kept tumbling in. The men shipped their oars and bailed for their lives.

A picture of the whole exciting operation was being taken by Mr Scott in the third boat. But it was only a few moments before the whale and the towed boat had disappeared behind the blue waves, tearing across the sea on what whalers choose to call the 'Nantucket sleigh ride'. Roger wondered if it was the last picture that would ever be taken of him. If they couldn't get the water out of the boat faster than it came in, they would all very soon be on their way down to visit Davy Jones.

6
Man Overboard

Suddenly the whale changed direction. The boat was yanked round to the right so forcibly that a man who had stood up to bail a bucket of water into the sea went over the side.

Roger was amazed that no one did anything about it.

'Man overboard!' he yelled.

Surely they would cut the tow-line, turn the boat about and go back to the rescue. But the mate gave no such order. He stood, gripping the steering-oar, gazing straight ahead at the speeding whale. The other men were equally silent. They kept on scooping out the water. The mate noticed that Roger had stopped work and was staring at him in astonishment.

'Bail, boy, bail!'

'But the man — '

'One of the other boats may pick him up. If not, it's his bad luck.' Seeing the shocked look on Roger's face the mate went on: 'You'll soon learn, boy. Whaling is a serious business. That big bull has a hundred barrels of oil in him. What d'ye think the captain would say if we let him go just to pick a man out of the water?'

Roger went back to bailing. He felt he was in a world of a hundred years ago. The whaling ship *Killer* stuck to the old traditions. Human life was cheap. What mattered was barrels of oil. Today, men who work are protected by many safety devices. In the old days a man must look out for himself and devil take him if he didn't look sharp. Today, we are quite careful not to kill one man at a time — we only plan to kill a hundred thousand or a million at one blow with a hydrogen bomb. Roger gave up trying to figure which were more cruel, the old days or the new.

Suddenly the line slackened. The whale had again changed direction. It was now coming straight for the boat.

It had not been able to get rid of its enemy by running away. Now it was going to attack.

It opened its enormous jaws, revealing a cavern big enough to take boat and all. It was like looking through the door into a room twenty feet long and twelve feet wide.

But it was not a comfortable-looking room. The floor was paved with sharp teeth a foot long and weighing as much as four pounds each. The upper jaw had no teeth, but a row of sockets into which the teeth of the lower jaw would fit when the mouth was closed. It would be too bad for the man or the boat that happened to get ground into one of those sockets like meal in a mortar.

Roger had learned enough about whales to know that the sperm is a man-eater and a boat-eater. It is quite different from the toothless baleen, or whalebone-whale, that has nothing in its mouth but a big sieve to catch the small creatures of the sea that are its food. Such a whale couldn't swallow a man, and wouldn't want to. It could take a thousand crayfish but wouldn't know what to do with a shark.

But the big sperm has no use for the little titbits that can be found on the surface of the sea. His favourite food is the enormous cuttle-fish sometimes fifty feet long and equipped with a great savage beak that may kill the whale or wound it so badly that it will carry the scars for the rest of its life.

Such a whale can swallow a man as easily as a man may swallow a pill. Many times whalers have found a shark twelve feet long or longer in the stomach of a sperm-whale.

'Lay to the oars!' yelled the mate.

The men left bailing to row. The boat had not yet lost the momentum of its swift flight over the sea. This, helped by the rowing, carried it forward fast enough, so that when the whale arrived the boat was no longer there. It barely missed the jaws, which closed on the steering-oar, crunching it to bits.

Away went the whale, only to turn and come back again towards the boat. This time it dived, as if planning to come up beneath the boat and toss it into the air.

'Hang on!' shouted the mate.

The men clutched the gunwales and waited for the shock.

Now all could look forward to being dumped into the sea. Blood from the wound made by the harpoon had stained the water and attracted sharks. Roger suddenly realized that the man who had fallen overboard back there where there were no sharks and no angry whale was the lucky one after all.

The blow from beneath did not come. Instead, the line began to sing out of the tub in which it was coiled.

'He sounds!' said Durkins.

Roger heard no sound. Then he realized what Durkins had meant. When a whale 'sounds', it means that he dives deep. A strange word, when you come to think of it. A sounding whale makes no sound. On the surface he may have been blowing and splashing and champing his great jaws, and even groaning with pain, but when he dives you hear nothing. Nothing but the whirr of the line out of the tub as the great beast carries the harpoon deeper and deeper.

'Look out for that line!' commanded the mate. The flying line lashed about like an angry snake. If an arm or leg got caught in it the limb would be nipped off as neatly as if amputated by a surgeon's saw. Either that, or the man would be snatched out of the boat by the whizzing line and carried down after the whale.

How deep would the whale go? The sperm-whale is the best diver on earth. With the greatest of ease he can go a quarter of a mile or more straight down.

A man would be crushed to a pulp long before

he could reach such a depth. The pressure of the water upon his body would squeeze all the flesh out from between his bones and crush his skull. Even if he could descend to such a depth he could not rise again to the surface without getting a terrific case of the 'bends' that would cost him his life.

The line was nearly all gone from the tub. But there was a second tub of line, and a sailor hastily tied the two ends together. In a few seconds the first tub was empty, and the line was whirring out of the second so fast that the eye could not follow it.

'He can't go much deeper,' said one of the men.

'Can't he, though?' retorted the mate. 'Ever hear what happened down near Panama. A submarine cable broke and a repair-ship was sent out to fix it. When the ship hauled the two broken ends to the surface a dead sperm-whale was found in the coils. That cable had been lying on the bottom of the sea, and the sea at that point is half a mile deep. To get caught in the cable, the whale had to dive half a mile straight down.'

'We can't afford to have this one dive so deep,' said the man who had spoken before. 'We have only three hundred fathoms of line.'

'Better start snubbing,' said the mate.

A sailor threw two loops of the line around a loggerhead, or post. The line still ran, but it was slowed by friction against the post and this increased the drag on the whale. The monster might even be discouraged from his downward dive.

This snubbing could be dangerous. If the line

was too tight round the post the whale might drag boat and all beneath the sea. The bow was already much lower and the gunwales were awash. Men bailed lustily as waves broke into the boat.

There was still another danger — fire. The friction of the line against the loggerhead sent up a curl of blue smoke and presently a yellow flame sputtered.

'Douse it!' ordered the mate.

The man nearest the loggerhead emptied his leather bailing-bucket over the flame. It disappeared, and so did the smoke. But it was only a few moments before the heat of the passing line started a new blaze. Again and again the loggerhead had to be baptized with sea-water.

7
A Quarter of a Mile Down

The line went slack.

The big bull had ended his dive. Perhaps he thought he had gone deep enough to be safe, perhaps he had been slowed down by the pull of the line. He lay there more than a quarter of a mile deep while five men in a boat anxiously waited.

'How long can they stay down?' Roger asked.

Roger remembered his own underwater experiences. When diving in the pearl lagoon he had been able to hold his breath for three minutes. No human diver could do much better than that.

'No telling,' said the mate. 'Usually fifteen to forty minutes. But they've been known to stay below for an hour and a half.'

'How can they do without air for so long?'

'You saw all that spouting,' replied the mate. 'Every time he spouted he blew out dead air and took in fresh air. He did that about a dozen times. That wasn't just to fill his lungs – it was to put oxygen into his blood. That's where it counts. And a whale can do about five times as good a job of oxygenating its blood as a man can do. No other breathing animal can do as well. A living submarine, that's what a whale is.'

The other whale-boats had come up, ready to help if they were needed. The man who had tumbled overboard had been rescued and now climbed back into the mate's boat.

He was soaking wet and worn out, but he got no sympathy from the crew. Whalers had no kind words for a man who was too clumsy to keep his balance in a boat.

He shivered with cold. Roger stripped off his sweater and gave it to him. The men laughed at him for taking clothes from a boy. Angrily, he gave the sweater back to Roger. He would rather shiver than be laughed at.

For more than three-quarters of an hour they waited. The men sat idly in the bobbing boats. One would think they would be glad of the rest. But every moment was full of suspense.

No one could say where the monster would come up. He might rise beneath the boats, tossing them high into the air and spilling their occupants into the shark-infested waters.

'The longer he stays down the faster he'll come up,' said the mate. 'He'll be crazy for fresh air.'

The sea began to boil. It was as if a great fire had been lit under it. It rose in a high bubbling hump, and up through this hill of water shot the whale as if he had been fired from a gun.

He rose clear out of the water and seemed to be standing on his tail like a black tower eighty feet high — about the height of a seven-storey building.

Imagine seeing a skyscraper suddenly appear on the open sea. It was a spectacle to remember, and Scott operating his ciné-camera was making sure that it would be remembered.

Down came the skyscraper, sending out waves that dashed the boats into each other and made the men bail furiously. The whale threw up one white palm tree after another as he breathed out stale air and took in fresh. It would take him many minutes to restore oxygen to his blood, and during that time he would think of nothing else. This was the whalers' chance.

'Lay to it, boys,' shouted the mate. 'Pull! Come in just behind his left eye.'

He left the stern and stepped over the thwarts to the bow, while the harpooner came back and took his place in the stern.

It was the old custom. The officer must have the honour of killing the whale. Durkins took up the lance. It was an iron spear five feet long and as sharp as a razor. It was quite unlike the harpoon. The harpoon was made to go in and hang on, like a fish-hook. The lance was made to go much farther in, and kill.

The mate stood in the bow, the lance held high in his right hand.

'Closer,' he ordered.

Roger would have been willing not to get any closer to the great black boat-slasher. His heart was in his mouth. The enormous hulk of the whale loomed above the small boat and shut off half the sky. The fountains of steam blasted off into the sky like the exhaust of a jet plane.

Now the bow actually touched the black hide. The mate leaned forward and plunged the lance in just behind the eye.

'Back her, back her!' he yelled.

The boat pulled away. The whole body of the whale was trembling and twisting. A deep groan came from the monster, reminding those who listened that this was no fish, but a mammal like the man who was killing him. The groan began on a low tone, but rose to a high wailing bellow.

Then again he spouted. This time the palm tree was not white, but red with blood. This the whalemen called 'flowering'. And it did look like a gigantic flower, thirty feet high. It was evident that the lance had pierced the lungs. Roger shrank as the rain of blood fell on the boats, but the men were cheering.

'A hundred barrels if he's a pint!' exulted Jimson.

The whale was dead. The sea was blood-red and the sharks were already tearing at the carcass.

A line was put over the tail and the three boats joined forces in hauling the prize back to the ship.

It was a long, slow job. Fifteen oars dipped and pulled. Each pull won only an inch or two. The captain could have brought the ship closer, but he seemed to take a perverse delight in seeing the oarsmen sweat it out. It was long after dark before the whale was alongside the ship. There the cable round the tail was passed aboard and secured. It was as if two ships lay side by side.

The boats were hoisted to the davits and the men collapsed on deck, quite exhausted. The cook

brought them meat and coffee. Roger said to Jimson:
'Boy, won't that bunk feel good!'

8
The Wolves of the Sea

There was great turmoil in the water around the dead whale. The sea was alive with sharks rushing frantically about, taking bites out of the carcass and out of each other.

'That won't do,' growled the captain. 'By morning we won't have any whale left. Somebody's got to get down there and fend off those sharks. Who volunteers?'

No one volunteered. Even if they had been fresh none of them would have chosen to spend the night on that slippery carcass fighting off the wolves of the sea.

Captain Grindle walked about among his weary sailors. His eye lit on Roger. The captain's fist was still sore from the whack against the mast when Roger had dodged his blow.

'You — you young squirt!' snapped Grindle. 'Get down on that whale.'

Hal spoke up. 'Let me go.' Mr Scott also ventured to protest. The mate said:

'The kid's pretty well whacked, Captain. He pulled a good oar. He deserves to rest.'

'Who gives orders on this ship?' roared the skipper. 'Did ever a ship have such a pack of softies! The next man who talks back at me will be put in irons.'

He gave Roger a hard kick in the ribs.

'Get down there, you lazy loafer. This ought to be good — a gent dancing on a whale's back. You may find the dance-floor a bit slippery. One good thing about it —if we lose you, we won't lose much. I can't spare a real man. Get along!'

He kicked again, but since Roger had already moved away the captain lost his footing and sat down hard on the deck. Some of the men laughed. That did not improve the captain's temper. Hurling curses about him like belaying-pins, he strode off to his quarters aft.

Roger stood at the rail looking down on the dead monster besieged by sharks. An almost full moon lit the weird scene. The mate was looping a rope around Roger beneath the arms. The other end of the rope would be held by a seaman on deck.

'If you slip, he'll pull you up,' said the mate.

The seaman, whose name was Brad, did not willingly accept the job.

'Look here,' he complained. 'This ain't my watch. I'm tired. I've done my bit.'

'So has everybody else,' replied the mate. 'You know well enough there aren't any watches when we catch a whale.'

'But suppose I fall asleep?'

'Don't,' warned the mate.

He gave Roger a whaling-spade. This was a flat razor-edged knife about the same shape as a spade fastened to the end of a fifteen-foot pole.

Tomorrow, spades like this would be used to cut the blubber from the whale. Tonight, the spade would be Roger's only weapon against the sharks.

'Try to punch them in the nose,' the mate instructed. 'That's where they kill easiest. Or rip them in the belly when they turn over.'

Roger, trembling with weariness, but stimulated to new strength by this new challenge, climbed over the rail. Brad eased out the line and Roger was lowered to the whale's back.

Roger's first act was to fall flat on his face. The captain had not been fooling. The whale's back was slippery. It was more slippery than any dance-floor.

The whale's skin is not wrinkled like an elephant's or rhino's. It is not hairy like the hide of a buffalo or lion. It has no scales like those of a fish. It is as smooth as glass.

Worse than that, it is like greased glass. Oil from the blubber beneath it oozes up through it, filling the pores so as to keep out the cold and enable the monster to slide through the water like a streamlined submarine. Roger heard a low chuckle from the sailor Brad, watching him from the deck above. He crawled to his feet, clutching the spade. The ocean swell rolled the whale gently from side to side. At each roll Roger slid, and Brad chuckled.

If Roger slipped down on the off-side he would be promptly finished off by sharks. If he slid down on the other side he would be crushed between the ship and the whale. The danger terrified Roger, but the man above him couldn't care less.

Brad resented being posted on this dreary night

duty. He was already tired of holding the rope-end. Glancing round to make sure that no officer was looking, he made fast the end of the line to a stay. Then he settled himself to enjoy the acrobatics of the moonlit figure on the rolling dance-floor.

Roger was not going to give him much amusement. The boy was learning how to keep his footing. With his sharp spade he cut two footholds in which he could sink his heels. Now he swayed with the role, but did not slip. With his feet firmly planted, and the rope to hang on to, he could stay upright.

Brad was disappointed. It had promised to be a good show, but the boy had spoiled it. Disgusted, Brad slumped down to the deck and went to sleep.

The jar made by a big wave sent Roger sliding and he got back to his footholds with difficulty.

'Hi,' he called. 'Will you hold that line a little tighter?'

He got no answer. He called again, without effect. He saw that the line had been looped to a stay. He supposed that Brad had sneaked off to his bunk.

The silence terrified Roger. The silent sky above with stars racing back and forth as the whale rolled, the silent ship, the silent sea hiding mystery and death.

Only the dorsal fin of each shark could be seen. It stood up like a little black sail in the path of the moon. There were at least a dozen of these small black sails speeding here and there, now rushing in to the whale's flank, now sailing away again as

the shark swam off with a chunk of meat in its teeth to swallow at leisure.

As one sail approached, Roger plunged in his spade and felt it go deep into the living ship beneath that sail. At once blood poured from the injured shark while its tail savagely thrashed the water in an effort to escape. But the other sharks were upon it at once and, like the cannibals they were, proceeded to tear their companion to bits and devour him.

When they had done dining upon their brother they turned their attention once more to the whale. Another sail came flying in, but disappeared at the last moment as the shark turned upside-down before taking its bite. Some sharks prefer this upside-down way of attack. Roger's cutting-spade plunged into the brute's throat. Again the sharks forgot the whale to turn upon their injured companion.

Why did they prefer to eat each other? It was because they were blood-lovers. Blood is to sharks what alcohol is to men. They go wild over it, drunk even at the smell of it. And it is much easier to get through the skin to the blood of a shark than to penetrate a whale's coat of blubber a foot thick and reach its arteries and heart.

If Roger could just keep these cannibals feeding upon each other he could save the whale. He tried every time to strike the sensitive nose. Often this was impossible and he sliced into the shark as it was swimming away. When the cut was far back towards the tail where the shark could reach it by turning its head back and tail forward, this strange devil of the sea would actually tear at the wound with its teeth, drink its own blood and devour its own flesh.

The red sea attracted more and more sharks. Many of them attacked out of reach of Roger's fifteen-foot spade. He must be able to run forward towards the whale's head, or back towards its tail. Two footholds were not enough — he had to cut a row of them, both forward and aft, each hole cupped two or three inches deep into the hide. Along this curious path on a whale's back Roger ran this way and that as far as the length of his rope would permit, and stabbed every attacker he could reach.

Once as the whale rolled he slipped out of the tracks and slid far over until his feet were in the sea. With a rush the savage beasts closed in on him, snapping at his boots. Fortunately they were tough and strong, and not easily crushed.

Then one boot was yanked off together with the woollen sock beneath it.

Roger felt teeth closing upon his bare leg. He jerked it out of the way and hauled himself up on to the whale by means of the rope.

Blood streamed from his leg. Should he climb on deck and have it attended to? There was no surgeon on board. It was usual for the captain to have some skill in first aid. But Roger would rather suffer the pain and risk of blood-poisoning than submit himself to the tender mercies of Captain Grindle.

He scrubbed the wound with sea-water, tied his

handkerchief round the leg and went on with his work.

Midnight came and went. Roger had trouble in keeping his eyes open. A ghostly haze lay over the sea. It was the time of night for men to sleep and ghosts to walk. Roger was not superstitious, but he could not help but be affected by the mystery of the night.

And then he saw something that sent a chill of fear down his spine. It could not be true. He must have gone to sleep and he was having a terrible nightmare.

For the dorsal fins that cut the water, each of them about a foot high, had suddenly grown into great black sails as tall as a man. Taller — they were certainly seven or eight feet high.

No more did they skim along gently like sail-boats. They shot by at furious speed. They ploughed up the water and sent spray high into the air.

One of them came straight towards the whale. It struck the great eighty-foot monster with such force that Roger felt the vibration throughout the huge body. No shark, not even the great white shark, could strike such a blow.

9
Fighting Killer-Whales

Then one of these impossible monsters raised its head six feet above the surface of the sea. It looked like a great black torpedo standing on end. It was as big as a dozen sharks. Evidently supported by the moving tail and fins beneath, it continued to stand up like a statue for many seconds. And it looked straight at Roger.

The moon in its westward journey was now in position to light the beast's eyes. Roger had never seen such eyes. They were not small like those of a whale. They were as big as saucers, and round and staring. Roger felt as small as a midget under that terrible gaze.

And he realized that he was not dreaming. He was looking at a killer-whale.

The killer-whale is the most dangerous creature of the sea. Curiously enough it is not really a whale. It is the largest of the porpoise family. But sailors of the early days gave it the name killer-whale, and the name has stuck.

A famous scientist has called it 'the most terrible flesh-eating creature on our planet'. A full-grown killer-whale is about thirty feet long. It is shaped like a torpedo and can flash through the water at a speed of thirty-six miles per hour. It has a dozen huge sharp teeth in the lower jaw and another dozen in the upper. The teeth are curved inward, and whatever they take hold of has very little chance of escape.

The big eyes have keen vision and behind them is an intelligent brain. In fact, the brain of the killer-whale is said to be better than that of the chimpanzee, better than that of any other living thing except man.

But unhappily that wonderful brain has only one ambition — to kill. It is the brain of a devil. No wonder the Eskimos who believe in evil spirits call this beast a wicked god that can take on the form of a killer-whale in the water or a wolf on land.

Killers are clever. When they see walruses or seals lying on a floating cake of ice, they will come up under the floe and break it to bits so that the animals will fall into the water. They will go after men in the same deadly fashion. Cherry Garrett in *The Worst Journey in the World* tells of what happened on an Antarctic expedition when a man and two dogs on an ice-floe were attacked by seven killer-whales: 'The next moment the whole floe under him and the dogs heaved up and split into fragments. One could hear the booming noise as the whales rose under the ice and struck it with their backs. Whale after whale rose under the ice setting it rocking fearfully. Luckily Ponting kept his feet and was able to fly to security. By an extraordinary chance also, the splits had been made around and between the dogs so that neither of them fell into the water. Then it was clear that the whales shared our astonishment, for one after another, their huge hideous heads shot vertically into the air through the cracks which they had made. As they reared them to a height of six or eight feet it was possible to see their tawny head markings, their glistening eyes and the terrible array of teeth, the most terrifying in the world. But the fact that they could display such deliberate cunning, that they were able to break ice of such thickness, at least two feet, and that they could act in unison, was a revelation to us.'

Sometimes instead of coming up under the ice a killer will slide up on top of it, clear of the water, grab its prey, then wriggle off into the sea. In the same way it may come aboard a raft, a whale-boat or a small ship.

Recently a tuna-boat off the California coast was visited by a killer. It circled round and round the boat until the ship's cook got annoyed and potted the beast with a rifle bullet.

Instead of killing it or scaring it away, the bullet only made the killer furiously angry. He swam straight for the ship, shot up into the air and crashed head-on into the galley, the great jaws chopping the cookhouse into kindling. Luckily the cook saved himself by diving head-first into the hold.

The killer thrashed savagely about, breaking all the dishes and crunching the iron pans and buckets until they looked as if a tractor had run over them. He chewed up the galley stove, fire and all, but when a huge pot containing enough soup for twenty men spilled its boiling contents on his nose he flipped back into the sea and swam off.

The cook crawled up, green and shaking, from the hold and looked at the ruins of his galley. The crew ate cold salt pork that day. The cook never again fired a bullet at a killer-whale.

One after another the killers sat up in the sea and looked at Roger. He knew they could easily slide up on the whale's back. Then — one crunch — and Hal would have no brother.

Perhaps he had better swarm up to the safety of the deck while there was still a chance. But if he ran away the killers would devour the whale. Already they were making savage lunges at the body and swimming off with great chunks of flesh. Several of them were attacking the head. Roger remembered hearing, on his Pacific voyages, of the killer's habit of forcing the whale's mouth open to get at its tongue.

Luckily this was a sperm whale, not a baleen.

Nothing tasted so good to a killer as a baleen's tongue. It was also valuable to the whaler, since it contained fifteen barrels of the finest oil.

The sperm's tongue was small and dry by comparison. Yet if Roger allowed these thieves to get away with even that, he hated to think what would happen to him at the hands of Captain Grindle.

The great carcass quivered and shook as the savages knocked their noses against the lips in an effort to open the mouth and get at the tongue. Whatever Roger was going to do he would have to do quickly. His rope was not long enough to allow him to get to the whale's head.

With more courage than common sense he threw off the rope and started forward. He cut holes for his feet. Even with the help of these footholds he had trouble in keeping his balance. The big whale rolled with the waves and trembled under the attack of the killers.

Roger was now on the whale's head. The head of a sperm-whale is an enormous box some ten feet high. The nose is on top of it and the mouth is under it. So Roger stood many feet above the killers as they battered against the whale's lips. Fortunately they were too busy trying to break into this big food-box to pay much attention to the small morsel of boy above them. So long as he left them alone they might leave him alone.

He could not afford to let them alone. But what could he do with a spade when even a rifle bullet would have no effect upon such a beast?

He believed that the spade could do what the bullet could not. The spade would let out blood. If these monsters had as bad table manners as the sharks, they would attack their bloody brother. He hoped it would work. There was nothing else he could do.

With all his strength he drove the sharp spade down into the head of the nearest killer. The tremendous thrashing that resulted scared him out of his wits. The animal he had wounded backed off, raised his head man-high out of the sea and stared full at Roger. Then he submerged and came in with a rush. Close to the whale he shot up out of the water and on to the big head.

Roger had not waited for him. He had lost no

time in running aft. The killer's jaws clamped upon emptiness.

With one wrench of its body the angry beast twisted its head close to the boy. Blood spurting from the wound sprayed upon Roger. He hunted for the rope by which he could pull himself up to the deck. Dawn was now greying the sky and in its light he could see that the precious rope had swung out of reach against the side of the ship.

He shouted for help. Brad woke, rose and looked sleepily over the rail. He could not believe what he saw. His mouth hung open stupidly as he tried to clear the mist of sleep from his brain.

'Throw me a line!' yelled Roger.

The big killer was squirming like a fish out of water, trying to get near enough to close its jaws upon its enemy. Then a line came whistling over Roger's shoulder. It was not the stupid Brad who had thrown it, but the second mate, Durkins.

'Latch on to it, boy!'

Roger immediately gripped the line and had his arms almost pulled out of their sockets, so powerful was the pull of the mate's strong arms as he hauled in on the line. Roger's swinging body crashed into the ship's side, but how good that felt in comparison with the crunch of the killer's teeth! A moment later he was spilled on the deck. He got unsteadily to his feet.

'Are you all right, boy?'

'I'm all right,' said Roger, but he was still dizzy from the nerve-racking experience of the last few moments. 'The killers are after the tongue,' he said.

'Don't worry about that,' said the mate. 'You fixed it so they won't get it. Good job, kid.'

Roger was not so sure that he had fixed it. Five killers were still struggling to get their heads into the whale's mouth. In the meantime the wounded killer twisted himself off the whale's back and fell heavily into the sea. The blood spread out over the waves. It attracted his companions. They rushed in upon the wounded animal, churning the sea, gulping the blood, taking great bites out of the flukes, the fins, the lips. They would not stop until there was nothing left but the skeleton.

'It will keep them out of mischief for an hour,' said the mate with satisfaction. 'That will give us time to get the stage out.' He turned towards the fo'c'sle and bawled: 'All hands on deck!'

The men came tumbling up. With them was Hal, who had spent a sleepless night worrying about his young brother. Scott came from his cabin aft. Both of them would have been glad to spend the night helping the boy, but their interference would only have got him as well as themselves into trouble. Now they were eager to hear about his experiences. They talked, over the brief breakfast of coffee and hard-tack.

Their conversation was cut short by the appearance of Captain Grindle.

'Everybody loafing as usual,' he snarled. 'And a whale waiting to be cut in.'

He fixed his eye on Roger.

'I thought I posted you on the carcass. Who told you to come up?'

'I hauled him up, sir,' said the mate.

'Well, get him down again.'

Durkins ventured to object. 'It isn't necessary, sir. He sliced a killer. That will keep the other killers busy. As for the sharks, the killers scared them away.'

The captain peered over the rail at the surge of savage beasts enjoying their blood breakfast.

'Then what are you waiting for?' shouted the captain. 'Get out the cutting-stage. Hop to it!'

He had forgotten about Roger. Durkins spoke in the boy's ear.

'Get to your bunk. Quick, before he spots you.'

Roger slipped forward and down into the fo'c'sle. The boards of his bunk felt like feathers. He promptly lost himself in beautiful, delicious, heavenly sleep.

10
Cat-O'-Nine-Tails

Captain Grindle turned upon Hal.

'Well, if it ain't the Gent!' he sneered. 'Your softie brother got his. Pretty soon I'll be getting around to you.'

'I hope you do,' Hal answered. 'That would be better than taking it out on the boy.'

Grindle glared. 'Do you question my authority?'

'I question your intelligence.' Hal knew he was unwise to say it but he was too angry to guard his tongue.

Grindle's always prominent eyes now seemed to stand straight out from his head. He could not believe what he had heard. He pushed his face close to Hal's and said in a low, rasping voice:

'Do I understand you proper? You say that I don't know how to handle my crew?'

'Of course you don't,' Hal replied. He knew that he had waded in too far. He would have been glad to wade out again, but it was too late. He might as well go deeper. 'A man who would do what you did last night to that boy is not fit to give orders to anyone.'

The captain started back as if he had been struck.

He stood like a man turned to stone. Then he came to life and bawled: 'Mr Durkins!' in a voice that made everybody jump.

The mate came running.

'String this fellow up,' ordered the captain. 'Strip him to the waist. We'll put a pattern on his back that will stay there if he lives to be a hundred.'

The order took the mate by surprise, but he did not dare object.

'Aye, aye, sir,' he answered, 'right now, if you say so. But perhaps you'll be wanting us to get in the blubber first before the killers make off with it.'

Grindle looked over the rail. The cannibals were still breakfasting on their companion, but soon they would be done with him and free to attack the big whale.

'Of course,' he said. 'Business first, then pleasure. And what a party we'll have when the work is done! Something to look forward to, eh, Gent?' He turned and strode aft.

The mate scowled at Hal.

'Now you've done it. Why in the devil's name couldn't you keep your mouth shut? Don't expect me to get you out of this.'

'I won't,' Hal said. 'I got myself into it.'

He could not be sorry. The captain's brutality towards Roger was enough to make anyone rebel. And yet perhaps he had only made things worse for Roger by speaking up. As for himself, he could already feel the cut of the cat-o'-nine-tails into his flesh.

The cutting-stage was now lowered. This was a sort of platform that was lashed to the rail of the ship when not in use. When let down it projected about ten feet from the ship like a balcony. Directly under it was the whale.

The cutters went out on the stage. Each was armed with one of the long-handled spades. With these sharp tools they cut a foot deep into the whale's hide, making a lengthwise slit. Then one man descended to the whale's back and fixed a large 'blubber-hook' in the hide. A line ran from the blubber-hook up over a block in the rigging and down to the windlass.

The man who had fixed the hook clambered back to safety and the mate shouted: 'Haul!'

Then men heaved on the windlass. The rope tightened. The strong pull of the hook lifted the whale an inch or two higher in the water. It had a greater effect upon the ship. The weight of the monster made the vessel lean farther and farther to starboard until it was hard to keep a footing on the slippery deck.

Then there was a tearing sound and the hook went up carrying a great strip of hide with it. As the whale rolled the hide peeled like the skin of an orange. Whalers called this the blanket. It was a good name. This hide, a foot thick, consisting mainly of oily blubber, wrapped the whale as in a blanket and kept it snug and warm when it sank into the chill depths of the sea.

The piece of blanket was hauled inboard and dropped on the deck. The process was repeated and, piece by piece, the entire blanket of the whale was brought aboard.

The hardest job came next. The head must be

cut off. The spades attacked the neck, cutting deeper and deeper through muscle and nerve and flesh. Every once in a while the blades, dulled by bones, had to be resharpened. They must be so sharp that they would slice through the bones and even through the backbone itself.

At last the head and trunk parted company. The carcass was now cast loose and drifted several hundred feet off, where a company of sharks attacked it.

Now it was a race with the killers. They had almost finished off their dead friend. They began making passes at the whale's head, trying again to get at the tongue.

The head, still floating in the sea but secured by hooks, was turned upside-down. Cutters neatly removed the lower jaw. And there, exposed to view, was the elephant-size tongue.

It was severed at the root, a hook was fixed in it, the windlass creaked, and the great spongy morsel so loved by the killers began to rise. It was none too soon. Already the killers were nipping at it feverishly. Several large bites were torn out of it. Even when it was eight feet above the sea three killers stood up on their tails snapping at it. Then it was drawn out of their reach and hauled aboard.

It would have done Roger good to hear how the men cheered. The rich fine oil of the tongue would put more money into the pocket of every man aboard. 'Don't forget,' said Jimson, 'we owe it to the kid. Fifteen barrels in that tongue if there's a pint!'

The disappointed killers turned upon the floating carcass. They scared away the sharks, but they could not scare away the frigate birds, albatrosses and gulls that had come in swarms to this royal feast.

The cutters were not done with the head. It contained another rich prize. Having turned it right side up a cutter with a rope about his waist stood on the head and poked about with his spade, hunting for the soft spot. When he found it he cut a round opening about two feet across.

A bucket was let down through the hole and came up full of clear oil as sweet-smelling as any perfume. Bucketful after bucketful was hoisted to the deck and poured into casks. For this oil was so pure that it did not need to be boiled in the try-pots.

When the job was finished the mate did some adding up.

'Two thousand gallons of oil we got out of that head!'

Now the head itself was hoisted aboard. Even without the tongue and empty of oil it was so heavy that its weight listed the whaler far to starboard. When it lay at last on the deck it seemed as big as a cabin. Hal had to look up to see the top of it. He had known that a sperm-whale's head is one-third of the entire body, but it was hard to believe such a thing without actually seeing it.

Then came the dirty, greasy job of trying-out. The head and hide were cut into small pieces and dumped into the try-pots. As fast as the oil was boiled out of the blubber it was ladled out into casks.

Then the scraps of blubber from which the oil had been boiled were thrown out on deck. Hal wondered why they were not tossed overboard.

He soon saw why. When the fire burned low no more wood was put on it. Instead, the scraps of boiled-out blubber were thrown in. Thus blubber boiled blubber. The whale was actually cooking itself.

This saved both money and space. There would not be room on a ship for the wood required to boil down all the whales captured on an average voyage. Besides, it would be costly. But the scraps were supplied free of charge by every whale that came aboard.

Because of their oiliness they made an extremely hot fire. But it was not as pleasant as a wood fire. It sent up a greasy smudge of rank-smelling black smoke that made the men choke and gag and cover their faces with grey masks. Sweat running down their cheeks made rivers of white through the grey.

As the knives attacked the blubber, spurts of oily blood spattered the shirts and trousers of the workers. Some of them saved their clothes by taking them off and stowing them, and worked almost naked. Their bodies were rapidly covered by layers of grease and grime and blood. It got into their unshaven whiskers and uncut hair.

They were the sort of creatures one might see in a nightmare. They were pictures no artist could paint. If one of them had appeared suddenly in a Honolulu street women and children would have run screaming to their homes.

And the crew could not look forward to soap and

a hot shower when the job was finished. Water was too precious to be used to clean bodies that would only become dirty again. Most of the mess could be scraped off with the back edge of a knife, and the rest would wear off.

No, trying-out was not a pleasant job on an old-fashioned whaler. Yet the men went at it with a will, because every additional pint of oil meant more money in their pockets at the end of the voyage.

Hal, slipping on the fat-slimy deck, hacking at the blubber blanket with a long knife, shutting his eyes when the stuff spurted into his face, coughing in the oil smoke, was as grey, greasy and grubby as anyone else on board.

This was not his idea of a good time. How delighted he and his brother had been when their father proposed to let them go on a number of scientific expeditions, skipping a year of school because they were both too young for their classes. They were thrilled with the prospect of a whole year of hunting, fishing and exploring. And a lot of it so far had been great fun. But Hal had not looked forward to anything like this — drowning in a sea of oil and blood and smoke, with nothing to look forward to when the job was finished but a cat-o'-nine-tails.

Any hope that the captain had forgotten about the flogging was dispelled when Hal heard Grindle say to the mate:

'What man o' yours has the strongest right arm?'

'Well, Bruiser throws the hardest harpoon.'

Bruiser was a great brute with the strength of a gorilla. The mate might have made a different answer if he had known that the captain was not thinking of harpooning.

'Good,' said Grindle. 'He's the one to swing the cat.'

'You mean, you still aim to string up Hunt?'

'Of course!' snapped Grindle. 'Did you ever know me to go back on a promise?'

The mate felt like saying: You never go back on a bad promise. Just on good ones. He did not say it. He only thought it.

'I'll tell Bruiser,' he said.

11
The Great Bull

A cry came from the masthead.

'Whale away! Sparms on the lee bow! They blow! They blow!'

The captain went up the mainmast like an electrified monkey. He had no time now to think of 'the Gent'. Hal must wait for his flogging. Hal was almost sorry. He would rather have had it over and done with than be for ever looking forward to it.

The men piled into the boats. The tackle creaked and groaned as the boats descended from the davits and struck the bouncing waves.

'Cast off!' came the call. 'Oars — all together! Jump to it! Stroke — stroke — stroke!'

The spouts could be plainly seen. It was not just one whale this time, but a whole pod.

Funny, the names we give to various groups of animals. We speak of a flock of sheep, a herd of cattle, a gaggle of geese, a pride of lions, a school of fish — and a pod of whales.

It was hard to tell how many whales were in this pod. Perhaps half a dozen. Two of the spouts were very short, indicating that they came from babies.

Possibly all the animals in the group were of one family.

In Hal's boat the third mate, a small man named Brown, stood at the steering-sweep. At the bow-oar was the big, gorilla-like fellow, once a boxer, whom the men called Bruiser. When the time came he would rise from his seat and throw the harpoon.

Brown was small, but he had courage. He steered the boat into the very centre of the pod of whales.

'Steady now,' he said. 'Quiet with those oars. Don't alarm the beasties.'

The boat crept in between the two largest whales, probably the father and mother of the two youngsters. The other two whales might be uncles or aunts or just hangers-on.

Still unaware of the boat, the mother was giving milk to one of the youngsters. This is done in much the same way as a cow feeds a calf. But it is not quite as easy. If the baby whale were to try to take its breakfast under the whale it would not be able to breathe and would drown. Therefore the mother rolls over on her side to bring the nipples near the surface. The baby takes a nipple in its mouth and at the same time can keep its nostrils above water.

The greatest difference between a cow and a whale is that the cow gives milk only if the calf works to get it, but the baby whale does not have to work. The mother is equipped with a pump — a set of strong muscles which literally pump the milk into the infant.

When the baby's mouth slipped aside for a moment, Hal saw a great jet of white milk shoot out over the waves with the force of a stream from a fire-hose. The baby hastily fastened on again so that no more of the precious liquid would be lost.

Perhaps Nature made this unique pumping arrangement because it would take too long for the infant to get its breakfast by ordinary methods. The baby should have about two hundred pounds of milk a day. The new-born whale may be anywhere from fourteen to twenty-five feet long. It is without exception the biggest baby in the world. A lot of milk is needed to fill such a whale of a baby. If it had to pull for every drop it might easily become discouraged and fail to get the amount of food it needs for its rapidly growing body.

And how fast it does grow on this milk, much like cow's milk but extra rich in minerals, proteins and fats. The weight of the infant whale increases by nearly ten pounds every hour, two hundred and forty pounds a day! Within a year it doubles its length. At the age of four it becomes a mother or father.

The boat crept into the centre of this family group. The eyesight of whales is not very good and the monsters were still unaware of their danger. Their extremely keen ears did not detect any sound, for the men did not speak and dipped their oars silently.

Then Bruiser took up the harpoon. The haft of it touched the gunwale of the boat and made a faint click.

That was enough. At once the mother threw a protecting flipper over the baby, gave a spout of alarm, and turned to face the boat. The great bull struck the water with his flukes.

'Harpoon!' yelled Brown. 'Quick!'

Bruiser was both quick and strong. The harpoon went from his hand as if shot from a gun. It sank deep into the neck of the enormous male.

Bruiser, who looked like a giant among other men, was a dwarf beside this monster. And yet his arm, as big as a pin in comparison with one flipper, had made an earthquake go shivering through the huge black mountain of flesh. Man can move mountains, it is said, and Bruiser had done it.

12
The Giant Nutcracker

Hal braced himself for a sleigh ride. Surely the beast would take off on a wild race, towing the boat behind it as the previous catch had done?

But this bull had a family to take care of. He was not going to desert them. He wheeled about and came for the boat. He sent up a spout that reminded Hal of the launching of a satellite. The roar was like the blast of a jet when it breaks the sound barrier. Up and up went the column, house-high, then spread out like the leaves of a palm, and the spray falling from it sprinkled the men in the boat.

Now the two monsters both came head-on towards the boat. The two enormous heads were like the jaws of a giant nutcracker. Between them the stout cedar whale-boat would be crushed as easily as a walnut.

'Pull, pull!' shouted Brown. 'Pull for your lives!'

Five men pulled as they had never pulled before. Hal's oar cracked with the strain he put upon it.

The boat slid out from between two oncoming battering-rams. The forehead of a sperm-whale is straight up and down and some ten feet high. Now these two black cliffs met in a crash that sent a shiver through both great bodies and must have resulted in two whale-sized headaches.

The mother whale lay trembling, sheltering her babies under her flippers, one on each side. The big bull, infuriated by his failure to smash the boat and maddened by the pain of the harpoon in his neck, thrashed the water into white foam. The two who might have been uncles, for they both seemed to be males, swam round and round, blowing furiously and keeping the other two boats from entering the circle. Mr Scott, standing up in one boat, was getting a picture of the whole great show.

The big bull submerged and the water was suddenly quiet. Hal could see the long black body like a submarine passing just below the boat. He saw the tail whipping upward.

Then the world flew apart. The boat rose into the sky as if being hauled up by unseen cables. It turned upside down. Hal and his companions were flung out into space and whirled round and round together with oars and tubs and spars and gear of every sort.

Then he struck the water and went deep into it. Clawing his way upward he collided with the underside of a whale. Hal's breath had already been knocked out of him and if he could not get to the surface very soon he would drown.

Which way should he go? He should try to come out on the flank, but he could not tell how the whale lay. If by mistake he went towards the rear a whip of the tail might knock him senseless. If he went forward it would be an even greater mistake.

He swam, his back brushing against the whale's hide. He kept groping for a flipper. If he found one he would know that he was on the whale's flank and could come up to breathe.

Presently his hand grasped something that might be a flipper. He was about to pull himself up when he realized that this was no flipper — it was the edge of the whale's lower jaw. He was practically inviting himself to dinner. One snap of that great mouth and Hal Hunt would go to join his ancestors.

He backed off at once and came up at the whale's right side behind the fin. He had never thought to see the boat again, but there it was right-side up. It had landed luckily and had very little water in it. Oars and gear floated all about. Hal, after a deep breath or two to replenish his starved lungs, joined with the other men in collecting the floating articles, chucking them back into the boat and climbing in after them. Third mate Brown counted heads. Not a man was missing.

'All right, boys,' said Brown, raising his voice to be heard above the spouts and splashes of the whales. 'You're lucky to be alive. Oars! Let's get out of here.'

'Easier said than done!' growled Bruiser.

The boat rammed head-on into a whale.

'Try backing up,' commanded the third mate.

A few strokes backward and the way was blocked by an uncle.

The boat was trapped in whales. It lay in a bit of water no bigger than a swimming-pool, with whales all round it. They closed in upon it. The big bull,

smarting from his wound, began to rush off across the sea, and all the others with him. The whole pod moved like one animal, and snugly packed in the centre was the whale-boat, in peril of being crushed at any moment between the great flanks.

And yet even at such a time a whaleman thinks of barrels of oil. Brown seized the lance and went forward. The boat was snugged up tightly to the side of the big bull. It was a perfect set-up for a killing. A perfect chance for Brown to kill the whale, an equally perfect chance that the whale and his pals would kill every man aboard.

Brown stood in the bow with lance raised. He was enveloped in spray thrown up by the speeding boat and thrown down by the spouting whales. He looked like a statue in a fountain.

The lance went home. Deep, deep it went, and the whale in one convulsive movement struck the water with its head and tail, raising its middle so that it looked like a great black arch over the waves.

'Back away!' yelled Brown.

But there was no room to back away. The eighty-foot arch came down with a thunderous crash, barely missing the boat. The wave produced by the fall of some one hundred and twenty tons of whale washed the boat high up on to the flank of an uncle, from which it slid back into the sea, still right side up but full of water to the gunwales.

The men bailed furiously, expecting another attack at any moment. But they looked up to see with astonishment that the big whale had left them. It was swimming away from the pod.

The reason was plain. The ship had drawn nearer, and the great whale in its agony was about to attack it.

If that rock-hard head collided squarely with the keel below the water-line the timbers would be stove in. Many a sailing ship had been sunk in this fashion, and occasionally a vessel under steam power or diesel.

Grindle in the rings could be heard bawling orders to the helmsman. The ship began to veer to port. The whale was ploughing ahead at a good twenty knots. The men watched anxiously. Would the ship turn in time?

Whale and ship met. Men breathed again. It had not been a square hit. The whale struck the vessel's side a glancing blow and slid off towards the stern. The vessel shook itself like a dog and the sails shivered, but her hull was still sound beneath her.

The whale did not try again. He seemed to remember that he had some unfinished business to attend to. Back he came towards the boat, whose deadly irons were already draining away his life. He was still spouting, but now his spout blazed blood-red.

'His chimney's afire!' yelled one of the men.

The monster sank out of sight.

'He's done for!' shouted one.

'No such luck!' came the voice of the second mate whose boat was still held off by the circling uncle. He called to Brown:

'Look out below!'

'Aye aye, sir!'

Brown and his crew looked over the gunwales

into the depths. Hal at first could see nothing. Then he made out a small white spot. It seemed only as big as a hand, but it was rising and it rapidly grew in size as it rose.

Then he could make it out plainly. It was the open mouth of the bull whale. The enormous teeth, each as big as Hal's head, were ready for action.

'Full astern!' yelled Brown.

The men pulled, but it was no use. A whale blocked the way, and there was another ahead. With terrible speed the open jaws rose towards the middle of the boat. The men tumbled out of the way, some aft, some forward.

One man was not quick enough. He was caught between the two twenty-foot jaws as they closed in, one on either side of the boat, and crushed it like an eggshell.

The two ends of the crippled craft drifted apart, men in the water clinging to them, and thanking their stars they had something to cling to.

What had happened to the man who had been caught? There was just a chance that he lay unharmed in the beast's mouth and would be thrown out when the jaws opened. Hal watched anxiously.

But when the great mouth sprang open it was empty. The monster that could attack and devour a cuttle-fish almost as large as itself had had no difficulty in swallowing this human morsel.

If the man had escaped being injured by the closing teeth, was he still alive? It was a fantastic thought. However, there was the story of Jonah and the whale, a story that was supposed to be based upon fact. The stomach of a whale was as big as a good-sized cupboard. There might possibly be enough air in it to sustain life for a short time. Now and then a shark, still alive, has been taken from a whale's stomach. But a man is not so tough as a shark.

The mad bull thrashed about among the wreckage, his great jaws crunching everything within reach. The men had to let go their hold upon the pieces of the boat and swim to one side. There was always the danger of an attack by the other whales. Sharks had been drawn by the smell of blood and Hal splashed vigorously to keep them off.

He yelled a warning to one of his companions as he saw a shark about to seize his foot. The man, numbed by fear and cold, did not act in time. The razor teeth closed on his leg and he was drawn down.

Hal at once dived down in the hope of rescuing him. He explored the blue depths in vain. There were plenty of sharks about, but no sign of the man and the shark that had taken him.

He battled his way back through the gleaming silver bodies to the surface and came up by the rolling flank of the big whale.

13
Wild Ride

His hand struck something hard and cold. It was the harpoon in the whale's neck. Instinctively he grasped it and felt himself lifted out of the water and carried away at high speed.

The bull, having destroyed the boat, had now changed his tactics and was trying to run from the pain that tormented him. The rest of the pod followed at a slower pace. Sharks snapped alongside and Hal drew his feet up out of their way. He was thankful to the big bull. The monster that he had been helping to kill was now saving him.

He looked back and saw with relief that the two other boats were now able to come in and pick up the survivors.

Would anyone think about him? Some of them must have seen him dive, but perhaps no one had seen him rise again, because he had come up on the off side of the whale. They could not know what a wild ride he was getting.

Many a man had ridden horseback, camel-back, elephant-back and even ostrich-back, but who had ever gone for a ride whaleback?

In other circumstances he might have thought it

was great sport. It was like riding on the bridge of a submarine before it submerges.

Submerges. That was an unhappy thought. If this living submarine took a notion to dive, what would happen to its rider?

The bull, as if the same idea had just occurred to him, slid below the surface. Hal caught his breath as his head went under, and held on grimly. Perhaps this was just a surface dive. On the other hand it might be a 'sound', a dive far down to a depth of as much as a quarter of a mile. The whale might stay down for an hour. Three minutes of that would be quite enough to exhaust Hal's air, and the terrific pressure would crush him as flat and dead as a pancake.

But he had no sooner thought of these things than his head rose again above the waves. The whale sent up a terrific spout of blood and steam. And Hal remembered being told that a whale spouting blood never sounds, perhaps because its pierced lungs and drained arteries cannot retain enough oxygen for a long stay under water. However this may be, the big bull made only brief dips below water, coming up within a minute or so.

Every time he emerged he blasted more blood into the air which showered down upon Hal until he was so plastered from head to toe that his own mother would not have known him.

Wherever this deposit touched his skin it stung like fire. It was not the blood that caused this violent irritation, but the poison gases expelled from the monster's lungs. The wind blew these vapours back upon Hal along with the blood.

During a whale's stay of a half hour or an hour beneath the sea the pure air with which it has filled its lungs gradually changes, much as it does in the human body. Perhaps if a human could bottle up his breath for a half-hour or an hour it would, when expelled, be poisonous too.

The whale's spout is not kind to any living thing that gets in its way. A sailor who looked over the gunwale of his ship just as a whale below happened to spout got the blast full in his face; the skin itched terribly and a day later peeled off so that he looked as if he had come through a fire. Fortunately his eyes had automatically closed when the jet struck him. Eyes fully exposed to the fumes may be seriously damaged or even blinded.

If the healthy whale's spout is poisonous, the breath of a wounded whale is much more so. Again, the whale is like you and me. When we are sick or suffering or badly worried, the breath is not apt to be as sweet as when we are healthy and happy.

Hal, feeling the smart on his skin, was learning the hard way about the breathing of a whale and prudently closed his eyes whenever it spouted.

He looked back anxiously. No one was coming to his rescue. The two surviving boats had gone back to the ship. His mad race had covered more than a mile and every moment he was being carried farther and farther away.

Should he slide off into the sea and try to swim back? He would never make it. The water was alive with sharks. On both sides of the blood-spouting whale their long silver bodies flashed through the water as they kept up with the monster that they hoped soon to devour. The picture of the seaman hauled down by the shark was still fresh in Hal's mind. He had no desire to go to Davy Jones's locker by that route. His only chance was to hang on, and hope.

Would this great bull ever give up? He still ploughed along like a speed-boat. As the distance lengthened the ship gradually sank below the horizon. Now the hull was gone, the deck had disappeared. He could still see the masts, but they were steadily growing shorter.

He strained his eyes, hoping to see someone at the masthead. There was no look-out in the rings. Captain Grindle had gone down when the whale had attacked the ship.

Probably right now, thought Hal, they're holding a funeral service for those two poor fellows.

He was almost right. A funeral service was being held, but it was for three poor fellows, not two. Hal was counted among the dead. Roger was roused from his bunk to hear the sad news.

'Sorry, kid,' said third mate Brown. 'Your brother dived to help a chum who had just been pulled down by a shark. That's the last we saw of either of them.'

'But you don't really know that he died,' Roger insisted.

'Look, kid,' Brown explained patiently, 'when a man goes down and doesn't come up, there's only one answer. The boats that came in to pick us up — they rowed all over the place to make sure they weren't missing anybody. No use fooling yourself.

The sharks got him. We looked everywhere. You can trust us. We know our business.'

'But you don't know my brother. He's met sharks before and he didn't let them take him. I'll bet he's alive. Couldn't we go out and look again?'

'It ain't no use,' said Brown. 'But if you want to ask the Captain — '

Roger at once went to Captain Grindle.

'Captain, may we take out a boat and look for my brother?'

The captain looked as indignant as if he had been asked to send a boat to the moon.

'You impudent young squirt, what do you think we are? Do you suppose we have nothing to do but hunt for gents who don't know enough to take care of themselves?'

'But that's just it,' said Roger. 'He does know how to take care of himself. That's why I feel he's still alive.'

'And where d'you suppose he'd be?' sneered Grindle. 'In a mermaid's palace at the bottom of the sea, I suppose. He wasn't afloat, or he woulda sung out when the boats went looking. Or perhaps you think he got flung so high in the air that he hasn't come down yet.' He grinned his evil sarcastic grin, then turned harsh again. 'We've done all we can for your fool brother. We gave him a nice funeral service, some pretty words from Holy Scriptures, and a watery grave. Your brother just wasn't tough enough for this life. It should be a lesson to all gents who think they're real he-men.'

He gripped Roger by the shoulder and brought

his porcupine beard uncomfortably close to the boy's face.

'And if you really want to know what I think happened to your brother, I'll tell you. He knew he was going to be flogged within an inch of his life if he came back to this ship. That put him in a funk. When a man is scared he can't defend himself. Your brother was scared and the sharks got him.'

14
Alone

In the meantime, Hal, very much alive, was beginning to face the possibility that he would not be alive much longer.

The whale was steadily losing blood. In due time it must roll over, 'fin out', as whalers say when a whale dies. Then the sharks would close in and make a dinner on the carcass, with Hal as dessert.

Even if the whale lived the prospect was not bright. It would plough on far away into unknown seas. Its rider would bake in the heat of the tropical sun by day and, always wet to the skin, would shiver in the cold night wind that sweeps across the ocean after dark even on the Equator. He would endure the agonies of hunger and thirst until his mind would fail, his grip on the iron would loosen and he would slip off into the sea.

The masts of the *Killer* had disappeared. There was nothing to be seen but a million humping waves. He felt terribly alone.

Then he remembered that he was not alone. Beneath him, inside this animal submarine, there was another human being.

Suppose this modern Jonah was alive. What

dreadful thoughts he must be having as he found himself imprisoned in this living tomb.

Was he fighting to get out? If he could escape from the stomach through the gullet into the mouth, what were his chances? The muscles of swallowing would force him back into his prison. Or he would be crushed by the huge teeth. At the very best he might slip out of the mouth whenever it opened, but then he would only be the helpless prey of the sharks.

More likely there was no breath of life left in him, and Hal was truly alone.

He was startled to hear a deep groan.

Had he really heard it, or was his own mind beginning to give way? Then it came again, a sad and painful sound. He realized that the mournful voice he heard was the voice of the suffering whale beneath him.

He felt at that moment that he would never want to kill another whale.

Hal was not merely imagining that he heard the voice of the whale. Whales are not dumb. They have no vocal chords, yet they make a great variety of sounds. Some naturalists believe that whales 'talk', or at least signal to each other by means of sounds. The Woods Hole Oceanographic Institution has recorded the sounds by tape recorder. The zoologist Ivan T. Sanderson says in *Follow the Whale*: 'It is now known that all whales, and especially porpoises and some dolphins, keep up a tremendous racket underwater, lowing like cows, moaning, whistling, and making chuckling sounds . . . Belugas have an enormous vocabulary of different sounds, which gives rise to their popular name among seamen of "sea canaries". They twitter, whistle, scream, gurgle, chuckle, hoot, and make strange popping and puffing noises.'

And it is not surprising that the whale has a voice. After all, it is not a fish, but a mammal like a cat or dog or the reader of this book.

Some millions of years ago it had four legs and waddled about on land. Perhaps it could not get enough to eat on shore to fill its great body and took to swimming after food. It became more and more used to the water, and after thousands of years its useless legs dwindled away.

The remains of them are still there. The front legs have changed into flippers, but inside each flipper may be found five toes left over from the time when whales walked the earth. And deep in the rear part of the whale are two useless bones, the remains of what were once hind legs.

So, thought Hal, this fellow is my cousin.

It helped a little. He did not feel quite so lost

and lonely in this watery waste when he remembered that the creature below him was, like himself, warm-blooded, breathed air, had a skeleton, brain, heart and blood vessels much like his own, and could feel pain, grief or joy as he could.

15
How to Steer a Whale

The big bull frequently changed direction. When south did not get him away from his misery he tried west, then east. If only he would head back towards the ship!

Hal wondered if there was any way to steer a whale. The whale is one of the most intelligent of beasts. Hal had seen, on his father's animal farm, how less intelligent animals than the whale could be guided here and there.

A horse even without a bridle could be steered by pressure of the rider's knees. A camel could be turned to the right or left by the rider's bare toes tickling his neck on one side or the other. The mahout on an elephant's back could make this mountain of flesh go to one side or the other by touching one of the big ears with his pole. And Hal had seen a rhino mother push her young one along ahead of her and direct its course by pressing her horn against its withers on the left side or the right.

But how to apply this knowledge to the problem of steering a whale was quite beyond him. Perhaps if he pulled out the lance and used it to stab one of the whale's ten-foot cheeks it would turn the other way.

It was not a bad idea and quite possibly it might have worked — but Hal couldn't do it. The big bull had become a person to him, almost a friend. He could not add to its suffering.

'The Cap is right,' he said to himself. 'I'm a softie.'

Hal still held on to the harpoon with one hand. His other hand held the rope which trailed away from the harpoon back over the waves, its end having been torn loose from the broken boat.

Could he use this rope? The idea appealed to his sense of humour. He laughed aloud at the notion of putting a bridle on a whale. His laugh frightened himself, it seemed so out of place in this desolate silence.

Well, anyhow, he could try it. He gathered up several fathoms of the line, looped it as he had so often done for lassoing animals on the farm, and threw it twenty feet forward so that the bight dropped just beyond the animal's head and was drawn tight at the mouth. Hal held two reins in his hands. He felt like Neptune, lord of the sea, driving his chariot over the waves.

According to the sun, he calculated that the ship was a little east of north. He must pull on the right rein. As he began to do so the bull, annoyed by this thing like the tentacle of an octopus that rubbed across his lips, opened his jaws and took the line firmly in his teeth.

Hal pulled manfully on the right rein. It might have worked on a one-ton horse, or even on a seven-ton elephant. It had no effect whatever on the one-hundred-and-twenty-ton bull of the sea.

No effect except to annoy still more the whale which now savagely bit the rope in two. Hal hauled in the rope and looked at the place where it had been cut apart as if with a knife. He had had no idea that a whale's teeth could be so sharp.

All right, that was no good. But Hal's inventive mind did not give up. He must try, and keep on trying — his life depended upon it. What else could he do?

He might entangle the left fin in the rope so that it could not work properly. He had once seen in the aquarium a fish with a disabled ventral fin. Because only one fin was working the fish tended to turn in one direction.

But a whale does not swim like a fish. A fish uses its fins as well as its tail to propel it through the water. The whale uses only its enormous twenty-foot-wide tail. The fins are used merely for balancing. Hal saw that they were quite motionless. He gave up the idea of lassoing a fin.

What else did a whale have that might influence his direction? It had ears.

Hanging on to the harpoon rope he slid down to one of the ears, very small for a brute of such size. He plugged the ear with rope and waited for results. There were none. The whale continued steadily in the same direction. Hal removed the rope from the ear.

But the eyes. Why hadn't he thought of them before?

A whale's eyes are planted in the sides of the

head, not the front. The whale can see nothing behind him and very little ahead. He sees to the left with the left eye and to the right with the right eye.

Like a bird, thought Hal. Or a horse.

He had once owned a horse named Right. He was called that because he always had a tendency to go to the right. He was blind in the left eye. Any animal likes to see where it is going, and since this horse could see right he went right.

It was always necessary for the driver to keep a tight left rein if he wished to go straight. A normal horse would continue straight even if the reins were dropped. Not so Right. As soon as the reins went slack he would begin to shy away slightly from the world he could not see and which might contain any number of dangers and edge over into the world that his good eye told him was safe.

The ocean, too, has its dangers. The sensible whale would want to avoid them — dangers such as rocks and shoals, schools of sharks or swordfish, the giant cuttle-fish with his horny beak, and men in boats. If the whale could see only to one side, his instinct for safety should cause him to favour that side.

Hal put his theory to the test. He stripped off his blood-caked shirt and let it hang from his hand so that its folds covered the whale's left eye.

The great bull seemed to take no notice. He had been going due west and he kept going due west. Hal persisted for a good five minutes, but there was no change.

Bitterly disappointed, he was about to haul up

his shirt when he happened to glance again at the sun. It was not quite where it had been. Yes, the whale was veering ever so slightly to the right. His direction was a shade north of west, then a definite west-north-west, then full north-west.

Hal was in an uncomfortable and dangerous position. Huddled part-way down the whale's left flank, he was hanging on to the harpoon rope with one hand and with the other operating his blinder. It was hard to block the whale's vision continually because gusts of wind kept blowing the shirt aside. Hal was so close to the water that the sharks took a great interest in him and frequently thrust their jaws above the surface in an effort to reach a leg or an arm.

But the whale was steadily edging towards what he could see and away from what he could not see. From north-west he slowly swung to north. When he had turned a few degrees east of north Hal was satisfied that his black chariot was now headed for the ship. He took away the blinder and climbed up the rope to the higher and safer point beside the harpoon.

But his work was not done. Every once in a while the bull would take a notion to charge off towards another point of the compass. Then Hal would have to slip down and cover sometimes the left eye, sometimes the right, to get his speed-boat back on course.

And wasn't the speed-boat slowing down? That was new cause for worry. The tips of the *Killer*'s masts were now above the horizon. But there was still a long way to go. The whale's enormous flukes beat less rapidly, his groans were more frequent, his spouts more thick with blood and only half as high as they had been. At any moment he might give up and roll over fin out, throwing his rider to the sharks.

Hal focused his tired and poisoned eyes upon the mastheads of the whaling ship. He thought he could make out a black blob near the head of the foremast. Soon he was sure, and his discouragement and fear gave way to new hope. There was a look-out in the foremast rings. Hal shouted for joy. His own voice frightened him, it was so quickly soaked up by the great silence.

Perhaps the look-out would not see the whale after all. The man at the masthead watches for a white spout, but the spout of this whale was a dull red and now so low that it would scarcely appear above the wave-tops. The whale's body might be seen, or it might not, for the dying bull was not swimming as high out of the water as before and his tiring flukes made no splash.

Hal could not see who was in the rings. He hoped it was a good man, one with keen eyes. Hal's fate depended upon those eyes.

The whale was weakening fast and the throb of his twenty-foot propeller almost stopped at times. Then with a savage grunt he would make a new spurt forward. These spurts became slower and shorter until at last the monster lay without motion, wallowing in the waves. As a last gesture of defiance, the great bull sent up a column of red mist into the sky.

16
Rescue

Hal thought he heard a cry across the sea. It might have been only the scream of a gull — but it might have been the call of the look-out. He listened intently. Now he heard it again and there was no mistake. It came faint but clear:

'Blows! Blows!'

Thank the Lord for the sharp eyes of that look-out, thought Hal. He had been seen. No, not he, but the whale. He himself would not be visible at that distance, especially since his colour was exactly the same as that of the whale's back, both painted dull red by the bloody spouts.

He saw another figure climb into the rings. That would be the captain. The look-out went down out of sight.

'Bless his hide, whoever he is,' said Hal fervently.

It seemed a very long time before the boats appeared. The men in those boats were coming after a whale — they could have no idea that a man was aboard.

Hal prepared to give them the surprise of their lives. He lay flat on the far side so that he could not be seen by the men in the approaching boats.

What a pleasure it was to hear human voices once again, so much more cheering than the groan of a perishing whale.

'All right. Pull up alongside.' It was the voice of the second mate. 'What in Heaven's name do we have here? Look, he has a harpoon in him! And a lance! I'm staggered if it isn't that same old bull — the one that gave us all that trouble and then ran out on us.'

Other voices chimed in.

'Whatever brought him back!'

'Perhaps he came back to do us in. Look out for him!'

'No, he's done for. He'll roll over any minute.'

Hal thought it was time to make his appearance. He crawled up so that just his head showed above the whale's back.

'Am I seeing things?' cried someone. 'What's that?'

They might well be puzzled. Hal's face and head were caked over with half-dried blood.

Hal stood up, red from head to foot.

The men stared in disbelief.

'It's the divvil himself,' muttered one, crossing himself.

'It's Hal!' cried Roger leaping to his feet. Hal grinned a bloody but happy grin to see his brother whom he had almost feared he would never set eyes on again.

He slid down into the nearest boat. At once he was bombarded with questions.

'Where you been?'

'We saw you dive but you didn't come up. What happened?'

'How far did he take you?'

'How did you get so stinkin' bloody?'

The questions were interrupted by the big bull. Irritated by the presence of the boats, he turned to attack them. He opened his great boatsize jaws. But he was not his old self. His movements were sluggish, and the oarsmen easily pulled their craft out of his way.

The huge jaws came together with a thunderous crash. The bull sent up a last brave spout that fluttered like a red banner in the wind. A low groan came from the depths of him and he rolled over, belly up.

'Throw a line over that tail,' ordered the mate, 'and we'll tow him to the ship.'

'Wait a minute,' said Hal. 'First we'd better try to save the other chap.'

'What other? Were there two of you?'

'Yes.'

The men looked at each other understandingly. Hal's terrifying experience must have affected his mind.

'Try to calm down,' the second mate said. 'There isn't any other.'

'I don't have time to explain,' Hal said, snatching a knife. 'If we're quick we may get him out alive.'

Avoiding the men who tried to stop him, he leaped out on to the dead whale's white belly. He began to make a lengthwise cut over the region of the stomach. The men looked on in astonishment, wagging their heads.

'Crazy as a loon,' one said.

The skin on a whale's underside is more tender than elsewhere. Hal had soon made an opening eight feet long. If the men wanted any further proof that he was crazy, they got it when he dropped through the opening into the stomach of the whale.

He found himself in a chamber some fourteen feet long and five across, lit only by the light coming through the slit above. He felt the sting of gastric juices on his face and his bare trunk.

He wondered if anybody had ever before gone inside a whale. Probably. In Africa when an elephant is killed the hungry men go inside to get the heart, kidneys and other choice portions of meat. And there is much more room in a whale than in an elephant.

Groping about, his hand struck something that might be the horny beak of a cuttle-fish. Then he found his companion. He lifted him so that his head emerged from the slit along with his own.

When the men in the boats saw this strange sight they could well believe it was not Hal who had gone crazy, but they themselves. Their amazement grew when Hal climbed out, and pulled the other man out after him.

Now several men leaped up beside him and willing hands eased the still form down into the boat.

The mate tested for respiration and heartbeat. Hal hoped desperately. If a shark had been brought out alive from the stomach of a whale, why not a man? The mate finished his examination, and shook his head.

'It was a bit too much for him.'

Two men had paid for this whale with their lives. The high cost of cold cream, Hal thought. Whale oil was used to make cold cream as well as many other useful products. But did the young woman who sat before a mirror applying cosmetics to her face realize what they had cost — not in money, but in struggle, strain and life itself? Did the person washing his hands with soap containing whale oil realize what it had cost to put it in his hands? The users of glycerine, margarine, paints, varnishes, textiles, fertilizer, cattle fodder, vitamins made with whale-liver oil, hormones obtained from the glands of the whale, many life-saving drugs, gifts from the whale to man — did the people who made daily use of these things ever think of the men who had fought and died to provide them?

Not to mention the monarch of the sea that had perished so that his human cousins might be a little more healthy and happy.

The line was out over the tail and the long job of towing the monster back to the ship began. Meanwhile the questions continued.

Hal told how he had steered the great whale.

'Now you're spoofing us,' said one man. 'Steer a whale, my grandmother!'

But the other men were inclined to believe Hal. After all, there was the whale. Durkins turned to the expert on whales, Mr Scott. 'What does the professor say?'

'Hal was lucky enough or smart enough,' Scott

said, 'to hit on something that has been known to zoologists for a long time — that any animal with eyes in the sides of its head instead of in front will tend to favour the side with better vision. It's a scientific fact. More than that, it's just common sense. You take more interest in what you can see than what you can't. Suppose you had eyes in the back of your head instead of in front. Would you want to walk forward?'

'No, backward,' said Durkins.

'Right. And it's the same way with the whale. If his view is cut off to one side, he'll edge over to the other. But not everybody would have thought of it. I think you owe Hunt your thanks for bringing home a fine whale.'

'Bet your life!' agreed Durkins, and the rest of the men chimed in. They began to speculate on how many barrels of oil the monster would yield and how much extra pay it would mean for every man.

'But,' Hal said, 'the fellow you really ought to thank is that look-out. Without him, you wouldn't have had a whale. He must have been pretty sharp, because the whale was low in the water and wasn't spouting white.'

'Do you want to know who the look-out was?' asked Durkins.

'I certainly do.'

'He was your kid brother.'

Hal grinned at Roger and his heart was pretty full. There was a lot he wanted to say, but all he could say now was: 'Good job!'

'The kid wouldn't believe us when we told him

you were dead,' the mate went on. 'Guess he knew you were a hard nut to crack. He pestered the Captain till Grindle let him go up in the rings and watch.'

'I thought I might see you hanging on to a piece of wreckage somewhere,' Roger said. 'Then this whale came along. I didn't see you on its back but I had a sort of hunch you weren't far away.'

'You sure surprised us when you popped up over that whale's back,' Durkins said. 'I hope to see the Cap's face when his eyes light on you. He thinks you're at the bottom of the sea.'

A sudden shadow fell upon the boats. The men looked up to see that a dark grey mist had swallowed the sun. From the cloud-bank long tails of mist spiralled down to the sea.

'Fog!' said Durkins. 'In ten minutes we won't be able to see a thing. Pull, boys, while you can still see the ship.'

Heavy wet curtains of fog settled down until they brushed the wave-tops. Seen through the curtains, the ship came and went as if it was only a dream, not an actual vessel on a real ocean. The men looked uneasy. Sailors are superstitious, and to their minds the sea is never so mysterious as when veiled in fog. It is at such times that the Flying Dutchman is seen, or imagined. And such ghostly visions appear as those described by Coleridge in *The Rime of the Ancient Mariner.*

A sighing sound came from the heavens. Some of the men fingered charms that hung round their necks, and their lips moved as they repeated silently magical words that were supposed to fend off the evil eye. Now the ship was gone and the fog closed in like a smothering blanket over the boats.

The mate tried to pep up his men: 'It won't last long. Keep at it, boys. Only a cable's length to go.'

At one moment there was nothing ahead. At the next moment the boats were ramming their noses into the hull of the *Killer.* A man clambered up the ship's forechains with the whale's tow-line and made it fast. The boats were eased back to the rope ladder that rose to the deck.

The fog was so heavy that the men in the boats could not see Captain Grindle at the top of the ladder, nor could the captain see them. But he could hear their voices and the clugging of the oars in the oarlocks.

'Ahoy, down there!' called the captain.

It was the second mate who should have called back. Instead, he put his finger to his lips, signalling his men to be quiet. Then he whispered to Hal:

'Let's give the old geezer the scare of his life. You go up alone. I'll bet he'll think you're a zombie.'

17
The Ghost in the Fog

Hal climbed the rope ladder. He tried to move without making a sound. He raised his face and saw Captain Grindle looking down. The captain's eyes were great balls of terror. He tried to speak, but could not. He backed away from the rail as Hal rose before him.

The fog-blinded captain could see very little and could not believe what he saw. This thing, plastered with red from head to foot, looked more like a demon than a man. It reminded Grindle of the Gent. But it could not be. The Gent was drowned and a funeral service had been said over him.

This vision, appearing and disappearing through the fog, must be his ghost. It had come back to take revenge. The captain suddenly regretted that he had ever insulted the Gent or threatened him with a flogging.

Hal stood up on the gunwhale. His burning eyes looking out from the mask of blood terrified the captain. Grindle backed away, muttering: 'No, no!' And again: 'No, no! Don't.'

The other men were now climbing to the deck to see the fun. Hal spread his arms as if he were about to take off from his perch on the gunwhale and fly at his enemy. The captain, still backing up, stumbled against the rim of a pan of porridge that the cook had put out to cool and sat down in it, splashing the pasty stuff in all directions.

He was up again in a hurry and retreated to the companionway that led down to his cabin.

At this distance he felt safer and began to bluster.

'You, whoever you are, get down off that rail. If you don't, I'll shoot you down.' He began to reach back for his revolver.

Before he could touch it, Hal was swinging towards him at the end of a clew-line from the mainsail yard-arm. The fog hid the line. All the captain could see was an indistinct something flying straight towards him through mid-air like an angel of Satan.

With a bellow of fear he started down the companionway, lost his footing, tumbled and bumped all the way to the bottom, scrambled into his cabin and locked the door.

He lay trembling in his bunk, fearfully watching the door. A phantom that could float through the air could certainly come through a locked door. Or through a porthole. One of the portholes was open and he crawled over to close it, but before he could do so he heard a strange sound.

Roars of laughter drifted down from the deck. All his men were screaming with joy. What was so funny? He listened to catch any words. He heard shouts of: 'Good boy, Hunt!' 'You gave him a proper fright.' 'That will teach the old bully.' 'Three cheers for Hunt!'

The captain stopped trembling. He wiped the sweat from his forehead and a cold rage crept over him.

So they were laughing at him. The thing he had seen was not a ghost, it was Hunt himself. But how could that be? He had buried Hunt and logged him as dead. The log-book lay open on the desk and there was the entry:

> Seaman Hal Hunt, losing his life through his own carelessness and stupidity, was this day consigned to the sea with all due rites of funeral, though undeserving of such honour.

There it was. He was dead and gone and buried, but he was alive and on deck at this very moment. There should be a law against this sort of thing. A man once logged dead had no right to come back. It was a breach of discipline and ought to be punished.

The captain had so enjoyed writing that item in that log — now he regretfully crossed it out. This spoiled the appearance of the page: that was Hal's fault and he would have to suffer for it. The captain was now boiling with resentment and injured pride. They would laugh at him, would they? Well, he would have the last laugh.

He took out his revolver and made sure that every chamber was full. He was the only man on board with a gun. That thought made him swell up with importance. It did not occur to him that only a coward would use a gun against unarmed men.

Thanks to his gun he could command obedience.

He would make an example of this Hunt, such a terrible example that no man on board would ever forget it. This fellow must be flogged within an inch of his life. Forty strokes of the cat was the usual punishment on the *Killer* — this time it would be eighty. With what pleasure he would write it down in his log!

Why not write it now? Then he would be bound to carry it through. Nothing could stop him. He would have to do it because it was already written. He wrote:

> On this day, Seaman Hal Hunt, guilty of defying established authority, received eighty lashes.

There it was, in black and white, and this time he would not have to cross it out. It was going to be done, and at once.

Gritting his teeth on this resolve the captain unlocked the door and went up the companionway, gun in hand. At the top, he peered round the door-jamb to see what was going on.

The men were marching round the deck carrying Hal Hunt on their shoulders. They were laughing, cheering, shouting: 'Hooray for Hunt!'

With a grim smile on his porcupine face, Captain Grindle aimed his revolver just above the head of the man who had returned from the grave.

He fired. The bullet whizzed above the crew and thudded into the mainmast. The men stopped cheering. Hal was dropped to the deck. Some of the men ran to the fo'c'sle. Others hid behind the masts.

Captain Grindle, much pleased with the effect of his shot, strode out on to the deck. He was every inch the master, and he gloried in the feeling.

'Bruiser!' he bawled. 'Come forward!'

The ex-prizefighter stepped out, cringing like a small boy. 'I didn't do anything, sir,' he said, his eye on the captain's gun.

'Spread-eagle that man!'

'What man?'

'The Gent.'

An angry murmur ran through the crowd. Bruiser stood irresolute. Second mate Durkins cast about for a way to gain time.

'Begging your pardon, sir,' he said, 'the man the whale got — his body is in the boat. Shouldn't we give him a funeral first?'

'He's already had his funeral. Tell Sails to stitch him up in a piece of canvas and dump him overboard.'

The man nicknamed Sails because it was his job to look after the ship's canvas, retired to perform this unhappy duty.

The captain would not let himself be side-tracked from his purpose. 'Bruiser, did you hear my order?'

The second mate tried again.

'Sir, this man Hunt has given us a big whale. It's well over a hundred barrels, sir. He brought it back single-handed.'

The captain flew into a rage. He fired twice and men dropped to the deck to get out of the way of the singing bullets.

'What!' he cried. 'Am I to be questioned and

corrected by my own officers? The next time I fire it won't be for fun. And you,' he pointed the gun at Bruiser, 'will be my target if you don't carry out my orders. Spread-eagle the Gent!'

Bruiser still hesitated, and the captain might have carried out his threat if Hal had not stepped forward.

'Better do as he says,' Hal said, and placed himself with his face against the mainmast and his arms stretched forward around the mast, his legs braced apart. Bruiser bound the two hands together, thus tightly securing the victim to the mast. From a utility chest the captain pulled out the cat-o'-nine-tails and put it in Bruiser's hand.

'Eighty lashes!' he ordered.

Again an angry growl went through the crew. Then Scott, the scientist, pushed his way through the crowd and faced Captain Grindle.

'Captain, may I have a word with you — in private?'

'Can't it wait till this is done?'

'I'm afraid not,' said Scott. Placing his hand on the captain's arm he led him back out of earshot.

'Captain, I am a passenger on this ship and not one of your crew, so you may allow me to speak to you frankly. I would earnestly advise you not to flog this man. Flogging belongs to the old days — it is forbidden by modern maritime law.'

'Now let me tell you something,' said the angry captain. 'This ship belongs to the old days. So do I. I've always made my own law aboard ship and I intend to keep right on making it. If that's all you have to say to me, you're wasting your time.'

'It's not quite all,' said Scott, trying to keep his voice polite and reasonable. 'Hunt may have been impertinent — but I think you might excuse him since he has just done you a very great service.'

'Done me a great service? How?'

'By bringing in this whale. It was really a very remarkable feat. The whale, as you well know, is worth round about three thousand pounds, and a good proportion of the profit goes to you. The rest will be divided among the men. Naturally they are very happy about it and Hunt is very popular with them. If you have him flogged, I don't think they'll stand for it.'

The captain's face behind the black bristles flushed an angry red. 'You threaten me with mutiny? Do you know I could clap you in irons for that? You're a passenger, but remember I'm master over passengers as well as crew. You'll do well to keep a civil tongue in your head.'

'I'm trying to keep a civil tongue,' said Scott. What else could he say to influence this stubborn bully? He would try flattery. 'I know you're the master, and I know you're a strong man and I know that even without a gun you're the equal of any man on board.'

'Equal?' snapped the captain. 'I'm better. There's not a man in the crew who could stand up to me in a fair fight.'

'Not even Hunt?'

The captain fell into the trap.

'Hunt? Why, I could take him apart with my bare hands.'

'Now you're talking!' exclaimed Scott, pretending to be lost in admiration. 'That sounds like a real man. No gun. A man like you doesn't need a gun. You could leave it in your cabin. You wouldn't be afraid to do that. Not you.'

'Afraid?' scoffed Grindle. 'I'll show you how afraid I am of that young squirt.'

He took out the revolver and went down the companionway to his cabin. He came back without the gun. He strode up the deck to the mainmast.

18
Grindle Takes a Blubber Bath

'Loose that man,' he ordered.

Bruiser, wonderingly, unbound Hal's hands. Hal turned about to face the captain.

Grindle's pop eyes swept haughtily over his crew like a pair of searchlights.

'Breach of discipline,' he said, 'don't go on the *Killer*. It has to be punished. Yesterday this man made insulting remarks about my ability to run a ship. Today he has the impudence to come back from the dead and try to scare me with a pack o' ghost tricks. He didn't scare me a bit. I'm so little scared of him I'm going to give him a choice. A choice between the cat and these two hands!'

He stopped for a moment to let the idea soak in.

'It ain't fair,' came a voice from the crowd. 'You got a gun.'

'No gun,' said Grindle. 'It's below decks. A man like me don't need a gun. The science fellow says so, and he's right. Don't need a cat neither. Just my own bare hands, that's enough. And when I get done with this varmint he won't have one bone connected to another.'

He turned to Hal. 'Or perhaps you'd rather have the eighty? Whichever you prefer. Our aim is to oblige.' He bowed in mock courtesy.

It was not easy for Hal to decide. Eighty lashes would, he knew, leave him an unconscious bleeding heap on the deck. Men had died under the blows of the cat-o'-nine-tails. The alternative was a hand-to-hand fight with Grindle. That could be tough too. Hal was tall and powerful for his age, but Grindle was enough taller so that he could look straight over Hal's head. He was heavier and more solidly set. Long years of sea life had put muscles that bulged like sausages under the skin of his arms and back of his shoulder-blades. His hands were as big as meat-hooks.

'Come on, Gent!' demanded Grindle. 'Cat or hands?'

'Hands,' said Hal and closed with his opponent. At once he felt the hands that he had invited locked round his own throat. Hal ducked and plunged his head into the big fellow's stomach. Grindle let out a grunt of surprise and relaxed his grip just enough so that Hal could tear loose.

Hal backed off a few feet.

'Hah!' exclaimed Grindle. 'Running away already!'

He came fast, his big gorilla-like hands outstretched.

Hal let him come. He even helped him to come. He seized one of the hands and pulled, twisting to the right at the same time. The captain went over

Hal's shoulder, turned a somersault and came down on his back on the deck. The breath was knocked out of him, and some of the conceit too.

Hal had not visited Japan in vain. While there, his Japanese friends had taught him some of the moves of judo (ju-jitsu). The principle of judo is to let your opponent destroy himself. You conquer by yielding. If he plunges at you you let him come, but step out of the way at the last moment and let him plunge into the wall. If he comes running you may trip him and give him a bad fall. His own speed is his undoing. If he swings a fist at you you may seize him by the wrist and increase his swing so that he throws his shoulder out of joint. If he exerts a nerve or muscle you may increase the strain to the danger-point by striking that nerve or muscle. At such a moment of strain, a slight tap on a sensitive spot may have a crippling effect. The judo-fighter is taught the location of these sensitive spots; for example the elbow, or funny bone, where a nerve is partially exposed, the armpit, the ankle, the wrist-bones, the liver, a tendon below the ear, the nerves of the upper arm and the Adam's apple.

In judo the man with the big muscles may be beaten by the man with the quick brain. Hal was no expert in judo, but he knew more about it than his opponent. His might not be as strong as the captain, but he was wiry, swift and intelligent. If Grindle was a lion, Hal was a panther.

The captain never knew where to find him. He lowered his head and charged like a bull, hoping to strike Hal in the solar plexus — he found himself butting the capstan instead. He shot his great fist towards Hal's face, but Hal moved his head to one side and the fist caught Bruiser an ugly crack on the jaw.

'Look out what you're doing,' growled Bruiser.

The men were laughing. The captain got the painful impression that he was making a fool of himself. Was he going to be beaten by this gent? Not if he knew it. He would bash the fellow's head in. He seized a belaying-pin.

'Not fair,' yelled the crowd. 'Hands only.'

Grindle swung the heavy club, but at the moment when it should have made contact with Hal's head he felt a sharp rap on his wrist that spoiled his grip and the weapon went overboard.

With a savage curse he pulled a knife from his belt. His crew booed him but he paid them no heed. He rushed at Hal, who retreated swiftly until he backed up against one of the try-pots. Grindle came on at a dead run. At the last moment Hal ducked, seized one of the captain's ankles and heaved. Grindle was lifted in the air and came down head-first into the pot.

Luckily for him the blubber was not boiling. The try-pots had been neglected when the big whale came in and the fire had burned low. The contents of the pot were like a rank-smelling jelly or paste, and when the captain's head finally popped up out of the mess it was completely covered with half-solid blubber. The men rocked with laughter.

The captain rubbed blubber from his eyes and spat blubber from his mouth. 'Get me out of here!' he screamed.

Hal and Bruiser pulled him out and he collapsed

on the deck in a puddle of grease. He still held his knife, but all the fight had gone out of him.

He stood up, dripping blobs of fat. He wobbled aft to his cabin and left a river of blubber behind him.

After he had stripped, cleaned himself as well as he could and put on fresh clothes, he sat down heavily to think things over. Before him on his desk was his open log-book. His eyes fell on the entry:

> On this day, Seaman Hal Hunt, guilty of defying established authority, received eighty lashes.

He crossed it out.

19
Grindle Shakes Hands

Grindle took up his revolver.

He balanced it on the palm of his hand. This gun was his only friend. It felt good. Courage flowed from it up his arm and into his chest.

Much of the conceit had been cooked out of him by his plunge into the pot of whale grease. The gun made him feel better. He was still master, so long as he possessed the only firearm on the ship.

He could hear them still laughing on deck. His friend, the gun, would stop that. A gun has no sense of humour.

'I'll show them,' he muttered.

His anger grew as he looked at the spoiled page of his log. What would the ship's owners think when they read this page? A man was logged as dead, but wasn't dead. The same man got eighty lashes, but didn't. What kind of nonsense was this? The owners would think the captain a fool for writing such things and then crossing them out. Didn't he know his own mind?

He knew what he was going to do now, but he wouldn't write it down this time until it was done. As soon as he felt a little less wobbly he was going to go on deck with this gun and fill the Gent's carcass with bullets. Then he would write in his log that he had been compelled to use the gun in self-defence against an unruly seaman who had tried to murder him.

He thought this over. He began to see that it would not work. The crew was against him. If he shot Hunt they would report it to the police as soon as the ship reached port.

A sly grin came over his bristly face.

I've got it, he thought. I'll fool 'em. Make 'em think it's all right between me and the Gent. Pretend we let bygones be bygones. No hard feelings. We had a fight and it's all over and now we're as friendly as two kittens in a basket. And after I get them thinking that way they won't blame me when the Gent has an accident.

He settled back happily into his chair. A real bad accident. I'll fix it for him so he won't come out of it alive. But nobody'll be able to pin anything on me.

He got up and tried his legs. They still felt like two ribbons of spaghetti. His back was bruised where it had thumped the deck, his solar plexus ached where Hal had dived into it, and his head was battered where he had bashed it against the capstan.

He looked in the mirror. His skin had been blistered here and there by the hot blubber. He could be thankful it had not been hotter. But he was not thankful — only possessed by a terrible hate and passion for revenge.

To think that a nineteen-year-old boy had done

all this to him! Wrathfully he blew his nose; blubber filled his handkerchief. He wiped the last traces of blubber from the corners of his eyes, and dug blubber out of his ears. Despite all his cleaning, he still smelled like a dead whale.

He went up on deck. The fires had been built up again and the blubber in the try-pots was boiling. The black smoke rising from the whale-scraps that were fed into the fire, and the white steam rising from the try-pots swirled and swooped through the rigging like great black and white birds. Men dumped chunks of blubber into the pots and other men drew off the oil into barrels. At the same time men out on the cutting-stage were beginning to peel off the hide of Hal's great whale. Everyone was in great good humour, still laughing at what had happened to the captain.

'There he is!' someone warned, and they all quit work to see what would happen. 'He'll be hopping mad,' said one. 'He'll probably shoot the place up,' said another, and looked for something to hide behind. 'He'll kill Hunt,' said someone else. 'I'd hate to be in Hunt's shoes now.' Another said: 'If he lays a hand on Hunt, we'll finish him.'

But the captain did not pull his gun and he did not seem to be in a rage. In fact there was something almost like a smile behind the porcupine bristles.

'Hunt,' he called. 'I have something to say to you.'

Hal stepped forward. He was as wary as a cat, and ready to move fast if the captain drew his gun. But Grindle only stretched out his hand.

'Put it there,' he said. 'Let's shake hands and forget it. Nobody can say I ain't a good sport. It was a fair fight and you beat me and that's that. Shake.'

Hal did not remind the captain that it was not a fair fight. Instead of fighting hand to hand as agreed, Grindle had taken up a belaying-pin and then a knife. No good sport would do that. But Hal was so grateful for Grindle's change of heart that he impulsively shook the hand of the captain of the *Killer.*

'It's very handsome of you to feel that way about it,' Hal said. 'I was afraid you might be sore.'

'Me, sore!' Grindle laughed. 'Boy, you don't know me. Sore? On the contrary, it's a pleasure to find I've a real man on my ship. To show you how I feel about you, I'm going to promote you. From now on you're master harpooner.'

'But I've never thrown a harpoon,' Hal protested.

'Listen, boy,' said the captain, thrusting his evil-smelling bristles among which bits of blubber still remained close to Hal's face, 'anybody who can throw me can throw a harpoon.' He laughed loudly at his own joke. 'Yes sir, you're a harpooner from now on. Shake again!'

Hal shook again, but a little uncomfortably. He had the slightest suspicion that the captain was putting on an act. But he brushed it aside, for he was always inclined to believe the best about others and perhaps even the brutal Grindle had a good streak in him.

During the next few days the captain was persistently kind to Hal. This was not easy. Inside the captain's barrel chest was a churning rage and it was hard to turn this into smiles and pretty talk. The rage had to get out somehow, so he vented it upon other members of the crew. He counted them all as his enemies, for they had laughed at him.

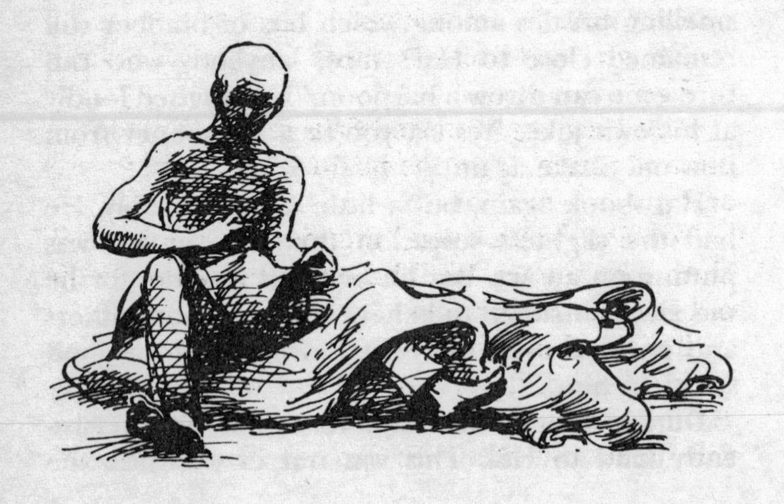

20
The Mako Shark

One whose laugh especially stuck in his memory because his cackle was high and shrill was Sails, who looked after the ship's canvas.

Sails had always been a thorn in his flesh. He was older than the captain and sometimes failed to conceal the fact that he had more sense. Having been at sea most of his sixty years he was weather-beaten and wise and did not hesitate to differ with his chief.

A split developed in the mainsail and the captain ordered Sails to patch it up.

'No, no,' said Sails. 'It would only break again.'

'I say patch it up.'

'And I say not,' retorted Sails testily. 'That sail is old and rotten. It's done its duty. I'll chuck it away and put in a new sail.'

'You'll do as I tell you,' thundered Grindle. 'Sail-cloth costs money. We'll have no new sail while the old one can be patched.'

'But it will only bust — '

'If it busts, I'll bust you — so I will by the Holy Harry! I know you, you old fossil. You'll fix it so it will break and then you can say "I told you so".

Well, I'll tell you something. If that sails breaks, you'll take a ride.'

To 'take a ride' was to be tied to the end of a line like a bundle of dirty clothes, heaved overboard and dragged behind the ship.

'You can't scare me,' snapped Sails. But he said no more, for he knew the captain was quite capable of carrying out his threat. Muttering, he set to work on the sail, applying the patch with all the skill of long experience. He didn't want to 'take a ride'. At last he was satisfied that he could do no more. The patch was strong and was stoutly stitched to the canvas; but the canvas itself was thin and brittle.

'It ain't no use,' he said to himself regretfully. 'It will break.'

And so it did. The patched sail had not been up for an hour before a sudden burst of wind split it along the line of the stitching. It broke with a sound like a pistol shot. The captain came running. He found Sails mournfully regarding the whipping rags of canvas.

'I told you it would bust,' he said.

'Yes, you told me,' sneered the captain. 'Then you made sure it would do just what you said. All right, I warned you. I told you what I'd do, and I'll do it. Bruiser! The dragline!'

Angrily Sails turned upon the captain. 'You dare to lay a hand on me and you'll be in irons before the day is over.'

The captain's face burned red. 'You dare to threaten me? You'll feel different about it after you've had a bath. Bruiser!'

Bruiser hesitated. 'He's not as young as he used

to be,' he said. 'I don't know that he could stand it.'

'Who asked you for advice?' stormed the captain. 'Get a bowline on him.'

'It could be murder, sir,' objected Bruiser. 'I want no part of it.'

'Whose murder?' retorted the captain, drawing his gun. 'Perhaps it will be yours if you don't carry out my orders. Now will you tie that line?'

Bruiser looked coolly into the barrel of the captain's revolver. 'No sir, I won't.'

The men had gathered solidly around Bruiser. The captain's angry eyes surveyed them. They said nothing, but he didn't like the way they looked at him. He realized that there was not a man among them who would put a dragline on the old sailmaker.

He seized Sails by the arm and walked him to the aft rail. Deftly he fitted the loop under Sails' shoulders. The proud old sailmaker did not struggle or cry out. The men were coming aft.

'Stop where you are,' commanded the captain. 'I'll shoot the man who takes another step.'

The men stood still, growling, irresolute. Before they could decide what to do the captain stooped, threw his arm round Sails' legs and heaved him over the rail. There was a dull splash as the sailmaker, still silent, dropped into the sea.

Like so many of the older seamen Sails could not swim. His body at once sank out of sight. The line ran out fifty, sixty, seventy feet and then snapped taut on the bitts.

The drag on the line yanked Sails to the surface

and he was hauled along through the wave-tops at a speed of about four knots. He choked and gasped for air but did not cry for help. The captain watched him with grim satisfaction.

'That will teach the stubborn old fool.'

The men anxiously watched the sea for sharks and killer-whales. There was no sign of the two-foot triangle of a shark's fin, nor the man-high fin of the killer. But just when they began to believe that this part of the sea was free of dangerous fish the surface exploded close to the unfortunate man and up went something blue and white like a fountain, on up twenty feet high, then turned and dived into the sea.

'Mako!' yelled the mate, and the men made a rush to the after rail in defiance of the captain's gun. They seized the line and began to haul it in.

There are sharks and sharks. Many of them are quite harmless. People who have gone in swimming

among harmless sharks without being attacked may foolishly believe that all sharks are harmless.

But there are three kinds that are man-eaters. They are the mako, the white shark and the tiger-shark.

The white shark is the largest, reaching a length of forty feet. The tiger-shark is the smallest, about twelve feet long. The mako is the worst and best of the three.

The best because of his blue and white beauty, his amazing speed because he is the swiftest of all fishes, and his spectacular habit of leaping twenty feet into the air (twice as high as the tarpon).

The worst because of his enormous, razor-edged teeth and his utterly savage nature. He is afraid of nothing, always hungry, and always spoiling for a fight.

Twice more the man-eater soared into the sky.

He seemed to be playing with his victim as a cat plays with the mouse that it intends to devour. If he would only continue playing for a few moments the man could be hauled to safety.

The thousand-pound fish went up as if he were as light as a balloon. He was as big and round as a barrel, and as long as three men laid end to end. Each time he came down he dived into the water a little closer to Sails. The sailmaker uttered no

cry and now could not, for the battering waves had shut off his breathing and he was unconscious.

'Pull boys, pull!' yelled Durkins. 'Break your backs!'

A few more pulls and the man would be safe. Now he was actually being lifted out of the water.

But the wily fish knew when to stop playing. Again it leaped, so high that the men had to look up to see it. Gracefully it turned in the air and headed downward. Its great jaws opened. Its huge teeth flashed like ivory in the sun. The jaws closed upon Sails. The line snapped. The shark, with its victim in its teeth, dived deep and was seen no more.

21
Mutiny

The men hauled in the line and looked at the broken end.

Then they turned upon the captain. They were no longer afraid of his gun.

Grindle tried to back away. His face was an ashen grey behind the black bristles. His eyes which usually bulged in anger now bulged with fear. He waved his revolver.

'I'll blast you if you come closer! Get forward, every man of you. It's an order.'

'You'll give no more orders,' said the mate. 'I'm taking your place as master of this ship.'

'That's mutiny,' shouted Grindle.

'It's mutiny,' agreed Durkins, and took another step forward.

'Get back. I'm warning you. I'll report you. I'll have you all hanged.'

'Go ahead and report. And suppose we report what you've just done. Murder, that's what it was.'

'Murder, nothing! Just discipline. He had to be taught a lesson.'

'It was murder. You knew Sails couldn't swim. You knew he was too old for that sort of treatment.

You knew there were sharks about. You threw him out to drown or be killed by sharks. That's the last brute trick you'll ever pull.'

'Mutiny!' again cried Grindle.

'Sure! But any court will say we done right — to arrest a killer. You're under arrest, Grindle.'

The crowd roared its approval.

'Grab him!'

'Clap him in irons!'

'Throw him to the sharks!'

'Tear him apart!'

'Boil him in oil!'

'Give him eighty lashes!'

Every man had some punishment to suggest, each worse than the last.

The captain could not retreat farther; his back was against the rail. Desperately he looked about for a way of escape. His eye caught sight of a vessel on the horizon.

A plan formed swiftly in his mind. He would leap into the sea and pretend to drown. After the *Killer* had gone he would come to the surface. The ship was coming this way. He was a good swimmer and could last out until it picked him up.

But first he must get these hounds back so they would not catch him as he went over the rail.

'Stand back!' he roared. 'I'll count three. If you're not out of the way by that time, I'll fire.'

He counted three. The men kept closing in.

Grindle fired. Bruiser went through the rest of his life with one ear. Grindle fired again. The bullet lodged in the mate's arm. Once more Grindle pulled the trigger. Nothing came from the gun but a futile click.

He hurled the gun with all his might. It caught Jimson a stunning blow on the forehead. Grindle tried to leap the rail, but hands, many hands, were already upon him. He struggled and bit like a wildcat.

Soon he was held so tightly that he could not move a muscle. He could still roar, and roar he did while they dragged him forward and pushed him into the brig.

The door clanged shut and the key turned in the lock. He gripped the bars and looked out between them, raging and roaring like a captured gorilla.

The brig was a miniature jail. Many a ship had a brig, but surely there was no other quite like this one. It looked like a cage intended for a wild animal.

Grindle himself had had it built and had made it as uncomfortable as possible, so that the prisoner would repent of his sins. There were no solid walls, only iron bars all round, and iron bars above. A man could not stand up in it, since it was just four feet high. He must crouch like an animal, or sit.

There was no protection against the weather. The scalding tropical sun beat down upon the inmate during the heat of the day. Cold night winds chilled him and sudden storms soaked every rag on his body.

There was a bunk, but it afforded no rest. The malicious Grindle had ordered that it be made only four feet long. A man could not stretch out on it but must lie humped up in a ball. The men in the fo'c'sle might complain of the boards on which they lay but the prisoner in the brig fared worse. Instead of boards set close together, the bunk was made of slats with three inches between slats. To lie on these slats for an hour was torture, to lie there all night was impossible.

There were no blankets. No food was allowed, except bread and water served once a day.

Grindle had always been extremely proud of his brig. He had enjoyed standing on the outside and looking in at the unlucky prisoner. Now he was on the inside, looking out. For some reason this did not give him as much pleasure.

'I'll have you all hanged, hanged, hanged!' he screamed through the bars. 'See that ship coming? The captain is a friend of mine. He'll come aboard and see what you've done. Mark my words, I'll be out of this thing in an hour. Then I'll have every blasted one of you logged for mutiny.'

Some of the men half believed him. Nervously, they watched the oncoming ship. Grindle saw that he had them scared. He followed up his advantage.

'I'll give you one more chance,' he said. 'Let me out and I'll promise to say nothing about this business. It'll be as if it hadn't happened.'

The men turned to the mate, Durkins, for advice.

'Do you think we ought to turn him loose?' said one. 'I'm not hankerin' to be hanged.'

'Don't let him fool you,' said Durkins. 'He don't know the captain of that ship from Adam. Besides, they ain't comin' to gam with us. See, they've already changed course.'

Sure enough, the motor vessel had turned and was now sailing parallel with the *Killer*, still about three miles off. Durkins studied it through binoculars.

'It's a catcher,' he said.

'What's a catcher?' It was Roger who asked the question, and Mr Scott who answered.

'A ship sent out to catch whales,' he said. 'We do it the old way — they do it the modern way. They kill the whale with a harpoon fired from a cannon. Then they tow it to the factory ship.'

'Factory ship?'

'Yes. You can see it — away beyond — just on the horizon.'

Where sea and sky met Roger could make out not one but a number of ships. One was very large, the others much smaller.

'The small ones are catchers, just like this one,' said Scott. 'The big one is the factory ship.'

'Why do they call it a factory ship?'

'Because it's equipped with all kinds of machinery to turn whales into oil. It takes us all day, sometimes two or three days, to process one whale. A factory ship can put through four dozen whales a day. A large factory ship can keep a fleet of eight or ten catchers busy, combing the seas in search of whales.'

Hal, too, was listening and was as interested as his younger brother.

'It would be great if we could get aboard a factory ship or catcher,' he said, 'and see how the new way compares with the old.'

'Perhaps with good luck, you will,' said Scott.

Hal was to remember that remark. 'With good luck,' Scott had said. It was to be bad luck, not good, that would introduce the boys to modern whaling.

22
Escape — Almost

Night closed in over the ship of the mutineers.

The breeze held steady, the sails needed no trimming, the men were idle. Down in the fo'c'sle they ate and talked over the events of the day.

On deck all was quiet. The helmsman dozed over the wheel. The caged captain tried the four-foot bed of slats that he had designed for the discomfort of his men. He gave it up and lay on the deck. The deck was wet with spray, and cold. His dinner had been bread and water.

Grindle was sorry for himself. It did not occur to him to be sorry for all the others he had put into this wretched little prison.

Outside of the brig stood a guard. This was the seaman Brad.

Brad spent half his time watching his prisoner and half regarding the lights of the catcher that had stopped sailing for the night and lay hove to a few miles off.

'Brad,' whispered the captain hoarsely.

Brad came close to the bars.

'Listen,' Grindle whispered. 'How about getting me out of here?'

'Me, get you out? Shut up and go to sleep.'

'It would be worth your while.'

'Why?'

'It would save your neck.'

'I don't know what you're talking about.'

'Heavens, man, don't you know what happens to mutineers? Every man will be hanged by the neck until dead. All except you. If you stick with me I'll see that you get off scot free. Besides, there'll be some cash in it for you. Say two hundred pounds. How does that sound?'

'It sounds crazy,' said Brad. 'Suppose I let you out of there — what would they do to me? They'd slaughter me.'

'They won't have a chance. We'll be off the ship and away before they know what's going on. We'll slip the dory into the water and row over to that catcher.'

'Mmm,' hesitated Brad. 'I dunno. I'll have to think it over.'

'You haven't time to think it over,' urgently whispered Grindle. 'We'll be leaving the catcher astern. You gotta act now, or never. Never mind thinking it over. Just think of your neck.'

Brad felt a noose tightening round his throat. Yes, anything was better than that.

'I'll get the key,' he said.

He slipped aft and down the companion to the supply-room.

At the other end of the ship Roger looked over the edge of his bunk. Hal in the bunk below was fast asleep. The other men had turned in. Only one sputtering, smoking whale-oil lamp had been left burning. Dark shadows crept about the room.

Roger had something on his mind. He would have liked to talk to his brother about it, but didn't want to wake him. Probably everything was all right. But he couldn't help wondering about Brad.

Brad had been posted to guard the brig. Roger had reason to distrust Brad. Brad was the one who had been detailed to hold the lifeline when Roger had spent the night on the dead whale, fighting off the sharks. Brad had gone to sleep on the job. It was no thanks to him that Roger had come out of that night alive. Could such a man be depended upon to guard the brig?

'It's none of my business,' said Roger to himself. The mate had picked Brad and what the mate did was usually right. Roger turned over and tried to go to sleep. He found himself more awake than ever.

'It won't hurt just to take a look.'

He slid down from his bunk, pulled on his trousers and, without bothering to put on his sea-boots, slipped quietly up the companion to the deck.

Hiding behind anything that came handy, the galley, the capstan, the masts, Roger crept close to the brig.

He could make out a black shadow. That must be Brad. He could hear a slight scraping sound as of metal against metal. A key was being slowly turned in the lock.

Then the barred door of the brig was being opened very gradually so that it might not squeak.

Another shadow appeared. That must be the captain.

What should Roger do? He must slip back and rouse the mate.

He left his hiding-place, but before he could gain another he found himself gripped firmly from behind and a great hand clapped over his mouth.

'So, my fine lad,' it was Grindle's hoarse whisper, 'you'd spy on us, would you?'

Brad was already regretting what he had done. 'I told you it wasn't safe. We'll have the whole pack of them on us in a minute. You better get back in the brig.'

'Don't lose your nerve,' retorted the captain. 'As for this young sneak, he won't trouble us long. I'll hold him while you slip your knife into him. A little higher — just over the heart. That will do it.'

Roger felt the prick of the steel point on his bare chest.

'Wait a minute,' said Grindle. 'I have a better idea. He can help row us to the catcher. Keep your knife out. If he hollers, let him have it. Now listen, young fella. I'm going to take my hand off your mouth. If you make a squawk, it'll be your last. Got that clear?'

Roger managed to nod his head.

The hand over his mouth fell away. Grindle pushed him towards the dory. Brad kept close, the point of his knife tickling Roger's back.

'Mind you move quiet,' ordered Grindle. 'And keep outa sight o' the wheel.'

The dory hung from the davits. It was a light cedar craft, half the size of a whale-boat. The two

men and the boy climbed aboard. The falls were released and the boat was eased down slowly and noiselessly to the sea.

The surface was smooth. The wind had dropped and the ship was barely moving. The boat did not slap and bump — all was quiet, and Grindle could congratulate himself on a perfect getaway.

'Cast off!' he whispered.

The boat floated free. Roger stooped to find the oars.

His hand touched the plug.

Each of the ship's boats had a hole in the bottom. It was a round hole about two inches in diameter. It was not meant to let water in, it was there to let water out. The hole was filled by a round wooden plug, like a large cork. When water washed into the boat it was bailed out, but it was impossible to get rid of all of it in this way. So when the boat returned to the ship and was hauled up to the davits the plug was removed from the hole to allow the rest of the water to drain out. Then the plug was replaced.

Roger pretended to be still groping for the oars. His fingers were working to loosen the plug. Finally with a twist and a pull he got it out of the hole and slipped it into his pocket. Then he unshipped his oars and prepared to row.

Water was boiling up into the boat. Roger could already feel it up to his ankles.

'What the Holy Harry!' came Grindle's harsh whisper. 'Where's the water coming from? Those all-fired deck-hands musta forgot to put in the plug. Find it, quick!'

He and Brad searched the boat's bottom for the

missing plug. Roger seized a leather bucket and pretended to bail. The boat was now half full.

Scrambling about between the thwarts the men could not avoid making considerable noise. They bumped into oars and gear. Roger could hear running feet on the ship's deck, then the voice of the helmsman rousing the mate.

The boat was now completely awash. Slowly it rolled over and its occupants were spilled into the sea. They clung to the overturned boat. Grindle obstinately remained silent, but Brad began to yell.

'Help! Help! Help!'

The ship was slowly passing. Soon they would be left behind in the great silent waste of waters. Brad yelled again.

There was a commotion on deck. Men were running, shouting. A whale-boat hit the water.

'Where away?' came a voice.

'Over here,' screamed Brad.

Grindle proudly held his tongue. He held it until he felt a nudging against his leg. A shark? All at once his pride left him and he yelled bloody murder. He kicked and splashed and bellowed. He seemed to go crazy with fear.

Roger watched him with a sly grin. For it was Roger, not a shark, that had nudged him. Again Roger gave him a poke. Again the big bully exploded with terror. Grindle would have been very happy at that moment to be back in his safe little jail.

He began to sob and wail like an oversized baby. His behaviour showed Roger once and for all that a 'tough guy's' bold front may have nothing but jelly behind it. He was seeing Grindle in his true colours — several shades of yellow.

The whale-boat came alongside and the three were hauled aboard. The dory was taken in tow and the whale-boat started back to the ship.

'Who was doing all that blubbering?' asked the mate.

'It was the kid,' said Grindle. 'Scared out of his wits.'

Roger opened his mouth to speak, but decided to say nothing.

Grindle was tempted to make a bigger story out of it.

'We were attacked by sharks,' he said. 'Must have been a dozen of them. I beat them off with my bare fists. Punched them right in the nose. That's a shark's most sensitive point you know — the nose. Lucky for these fellows that they had me along.'

The mate was not fooled. 'Sounds too good to be true,' he said sarcastically.

Back on deck, Grindle was marched to his cage.

'Now you're not going to put me back in there,' complained Grindle. 'Not after me savin' the lives of two men!'

'Not only you,' said the mate, 'but Brad also.' He turned to Roger. 'And I'm afraid we'll have to lock you up too.'

'What for?'

'For desertion. And for helping a prisoner to escape. I never would have thought it of you, kid.'

'Will you let me tell you just what happened?'

'Yes, but you'd better make it good.'

'I saw Brad unlock the brig and let the Captain

out. I started to get you, but they grabbed me. They made me help row the boat. I pulled out the plug so the boat filled with water.'

Grindle laughed. 'The young rascal — he's just trying to save his own skin. Now you'd better let me tell you the truth. The kid was in it with us from the start. He sneaked down and got the key and let me out.'

'Then what did he do with the key?' demanded the mate.

'I don't know — put it in his pocket, I suppose.'

'Search them,' the mate said to Jimson.

Before Jimson could move to do so, Brad was seen to draw something from his pocket and throw it away. He had meant to cast it into the sea, but it struck the rail and bounced back on deck. The mate picked it up. It was the key to the brig.

'Now we have a pretty good idea who unlocked the brig,' the mate said to Roger. 'But that still doesn't prove that you weren't in league with them. How can you prove that you tried to stop them by pulling out the plug?'

'He can't,' snorted Grindle. 'I can tell you all about that plug. I forgot — now I remember. Yesterday I took it out of the boat myself. I put it down in my cabin.'

'Why did you take it out?'

'I had good reason. Some of the men were getting unruly. I suspected some o' them might grab the boat and try to desert. So I hid the plug. Makes sense, don't it?'

'It makes sense,' admitted the mate and turned again to Roger. 'You're in a tough spot, chum. You claim you were loyal to us — that you pulled out the plug so these fellows couldn't get away. The captain says he removed it himself and took it below, then forgot about it. Do we have to search his cabin to find out which of you is telling a straight story?'

'I don't think so,' Roger said. He drew the plug from his trouser pocket and put it in the mate's hand.

Grindle's eyes bulged with surprise. The men cheered. They liked the boy and were happy that he had been able to clear himself. The mate clapped him on the shoulder. 'Good for you, my lad!' he exclaimed. 'You're no lad, you're as good a man as any on this ship. If it hadn't been for you these scum woulda got clean away. Say, we had lemon pie in the officers' mess tonight. Go to the galley and cut yourself a big piece of it. Tell the cook I sent you. And as for you two,' he said to Grindle and Brad, 'since you're so fond of each other's company you'll have plenty of time to enjoy it. Get in there, both of you.' He pushed them into the brig and locked the door.

This time a more reliable man, the big harpooner Jimson, was placed on guard.

23
Can a Whale Sink a Ship?

'Blows! Whale on the lee bow!' shouted the foremast look-out late in the afternoon of the next day.

'Blows! Three points off weather-bow!' came from the look-out on the mainmast.

'Another to leeward!' yelled the first.

'Two straight ahead!' announced the second.

'Whales! A dozen of 'em! Ganging up on us!'

'Whales! Whales! Whales!'

The mate scrambled up the mainmast to the rings. An amazing spectacle lay before him. Ahead and on both sides silver fountains leaped into the sky. At least a dozen whales were sporting in the waves.

They did not behave like the usual school or pod

of whales. This was no family group, quiet and dignified. The height of their spouts showed they were all full-grown monsters, and probably all males.

They flung themselves out of the sea. They soared up like black meteors. They arched above the waves like curved bridges. They threw their enormous tails into the air and brought them down with a gigantic slap.

It was one big wild party.

They seemed to have noticed the ship and were closing in on it — ganging up on it, as the lookout had said.

'Bulls on a rampage!' muttered the mate. 'I only hope they leave us alone.'

Mr Scott on deck was watching the whales through binoculars. Hal and Roger stood beside him.

'What do you make of it?' Hal asked.

'Bachelors out on a binge,' said Scott. 'Whales are like men. Sometimes they leave the ladies and children and go off and raise Cain. The ringleaders may be young bulls that have no families or old bulls who have lost theirs. Sometimes the leaders are ones that have been injured by harpoons or lances, and their suffering makes them wild and dangerous. Usually an old or wounded bull will go off by himself. When they gang up this way it's bad. Just like men. One teddy-boy or hoodlum may lack nerve, but get a dozen of them together and they'll try anything.'

'Why doesn't the mate order the boats lowered?'

'It's too late. The sun has set and it will be dark

in fifteen minutes. It would be risky enough by daylight to run a boat into that pack of rowdies; at night it would be suicide. You'll have to wait until morning.'

'We'll leave them far behind before morning.'

'I doubt it. They're coming closer. They seem to be taking a lot of interest in the ship. Chances are they'll go right along with us. It won't be too pleasant.'

'Why not?' Roger asked. 'I think it will be fun to see them playing around.'

Scott smiled and shook his head. 'They may play rough.'

'But we're safe enough,' said Roger. 'They couldn't do anything to the ship.'

'I hope not,' said Scott doubtfully.

When it was too dark to see more the mate and the look-outs came down from the rings. Mate Durkins and his men stood by the rail, listening.

The whales were now all about the ship. Their spouts whooshed up like rockets.

'Keep out of the way of those spouts,' the mate warned. 'You'll get gassed.'

Hal had already learned this lesson. Most of the men prudently retreated when a whale came too close. One man whose curiosity got the better of him looked down on a whale's head just as the column of gas and steam rose into his face. He was half blinded and went to his bunk with medicated compresses over his eyes.

The whales were a talkative lot. As they dipped, swooped and slid about, they grunted like rhinoceroses, squealed like elephants and bellowed like bulls. Hal remembered the groans of the suffering whale that had carried him so far across the sea. But he had not imagined that the monsters could make so many different sounds.

Evidently they were highly excited. They were having fun with the ship. Perhaps they instinctively knew that they were terrifying the humans on board. They dived beneath the vessel on one side and came up on the other. One shot up so high that his great box of a head was above the deck. His skull was twice as big as the crate that is used to pack a grand piano. He dropped again into the sea with a thundering splash that sent a shower of spray over the men on deck.

One took to butting the rudder. The wheel was jerked out of the helmsman's hands and went spinning. Luckily the playful beast desisted from this game before completely wrecking the steering-gear of the ship.

There was a crackle and crash up forward.

'There goes the bowsprit,' exclaimed the mate.

He went to investigate. The bowsprit was gone, probably swept away by one flirt of a big bull's tail. The flying jib, the jib and the staysail, previously made fast to the bowsprit, hung in rags.

A monster coming up from beneath lifted the ship a good three feet, then let it drop. The masts shivered and cracked, the sails shook, men sat down hard on the deck, and there was a great clatter in the galley as all the pans on the walls tumbled down on the surprised cook.

'If this is their idea of fun,' said the mate, 'I only hope they don't get serious. Last year a whale gave us a crack that stove in two strakes. Luckily we were near land, but the bark was half full of water before we made port.'

'But a whale can't actually sink a ship, can it?' asked Roger.

'Not only can, but does. There was the *Essex.* She was struck by a big sperm just forward of the fore-chains. It busted her wide open and the pump couldn't save her. The crew had only ten minutes to abandon ship. They got away in three boats. One boat was lost. One got to Chile. One landed on an uninhabited island where the men managed to live on birds' eggs until they were picked up five months later.'

'What an experience!' Hal said.

'Oh, there've been lots of others like it. A whale hit a Peruvian sloop so hard that the men were shaken out of their hammocks and the captain was thrown out of his cabin. Everybody thought the ship had struck a rock. They sounded, but found only deep water. Then the whale came back to finish the job. This time he cracked open the hull just above the kelson and sank the ship.

'And perhaps you've heard of the *Ann Alexander.* A whale they had lanced attacked the ship just abreast the foremast. One whack was enough. The men only had time to tumble into the boats and row clear before the ship went down.'

The mate was rudely interrupted by a whale that thrust its head out of the waves and said 'Rrump!' before sinking back into the sea. Durkins continued.

'Then there was the *Parker Cook.* A mad whale had

to hit it three times before he smashed it. And the *Pocahontas.* Her captain was only twenty-eight, and that's pretty young for a master, so the crew called him the boy-captain. He was pretty smart. After a whale stove in his ship, he kept the pumps going at two hundred and fifty strokes an hour and set out for the nearest port. It was Rio, seven hundred and fifty miles away, but the boy-captain made it.'

'Is it always the sperm that does the damage?' Roger wanted to know.

'Oh no. A finback hulled a hundred-foot craft, the *Dennis Gale,* off Eureka, California. And along the same coast in 1950 a large yacht, the *Lady Linda,* was smashed by a blue whale.'

'I suppose,' Hal said, 'those were all wooden ships. Could a whale do anything to a steel hull?'

'I can tell you something about that,' Scott said. 'Not so long ago a steamer with a steel hull had its plates pushed open by a huge humpback. The break was through the side of the vessel at the coal bunkers. The inrush of water put out the fires and sank the ship in three minutes.'

He paused to smile at the startled look on the boys' faces, then went on.

'You've heard of the great explorer, Roy Chapman Andrews, former director of my museum. He made a study of whales, just as I'm trying to do now. His steamer was nearly sunk by a big sperm, but it lost its enthusiasm when it ran into the propeller and the whirling blades ripped the blubber off its nose.

'Just to give you an idea of the strength of a whale — Dr Andrews tells of the big blue they snagged with a heavy line. That whale dragged the ship forward at six knots, and all the time the engines were at full speed astern! Altogether it towed the steamer thirty miles.

'And he tells of a finback that came at a steamer at high speed and crushed her side like an eggshell. The crew was hardly able to get a small boat over before she went down.

'Of course,' Scott added, 'an ocean liner or a freighter is safe enough. But Dr Andrews reported many cases of whales sinking ships up to three hundred or four hundred tons.'

Hal's eye roamed over the *Killer.* Her tonnage was considerably under three hundred and there was no steel in her sides.

'You'll be scaring the lads,' said Durkins.

'I don't think so,' said Scott. 'They don't scare easily. Anyhow, I think we're in no danger tonight. These rascals are just playing. You haven't hurt them yet. But what do you plan to do tomorrow morning? If you stick one of these rogues with a harpoon I think you are in for trouble.'

'You're probably right,' said Durkins. 'But we'll have to risk that. After all, our business is whaling. There's a lot of oil out there, and we've got to go after it, trouble or no trouble.'

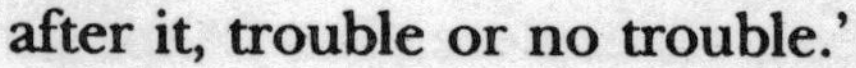

24
The Wreck of the *Killer*

No one on board the whaler slept well that night.

It was an all-night party for the rogue whales. They snorted and squealed like beasts of the jungle. They spouted with a sound like that of a steamer when it blows its stacks, or a steam locomotive when it lets off pressure.

The men in the bunks no sooner began to drift off to sleep than they were roused by the bumping of a mammoth body against the hull or a curious rubbing sound when a monster scraped his back across the keel. Now and then the ship bounced up and down like a wagon going over a rough road. The ship's timbers strained and creaked. Boots on the floor hopped about as if unseen sailors were dancing in them. Whale-oil lamps swung and shivered in their gimbals.

Roger sat up in his bunk with eyes popping when he heard the rush of a whale coming at tremendous speed towards the ship. He waited for the smash of the great head against the timbers.

But the big mischief-maker was just amusing himself. Instead of crashing head-on into the hull, he must have raised his head at the last moment and struck the rail a glancing blow. There was a crackling, splintering sound as the heavy body smashed the gunwales. Roger heard Hal in the bunk below mutter:

'That was a close one.'

Roger lay down again, plugged both ears with his shirt and tried to sleep.

'All hands on deck!' came the call at dawn.

Usually this call brought a chorus of groans and mutterings from sleepy sailors. This time there was none of that. They could hardly wait to get a crack at their night-time visitors. In two minutes every man was on deck. The cook dealt out coffee and hard-tack.

The whales had drawn off about a quarter of a mile from the ship and were indulging in a sort of gigantic leapfrog, playfully jumping over each other in great graceful curves.

'Man the boats!' ordered the mate. 'Lower away!'

The ship had been equipped with four whale-boats and a dory. One whale-boat had already been smashed. The other three now put down and pulled away from the *Killer*'s side.

Hal, in the bow of the mate's boat, was to have his first experience as a harpooner. Scott with his cameras was in the second boat, and Roger in the third. The men all pulled lustily, each crew eager to get there first.

In the excitement of the chase no one worried about the danger. This was no ordinary whale-hunt. They were about to break up a party of gangsters, the world's biggest. So far the gangsters were only playful, but what would they do when they felt the cold iron? But just so long as men, women and children in far cities wanted the things that whales could provide, whalers must take chances.

'We'll make it!' cried the mate. 'Bend your backs. Blister your hands. Three more pulls!'

His boat was the first to break into the circle of monsters. Hugging the steering-oar, he directed the boat alongside the largest bull.

'All right, Hunt! Hop to it.'

Hal dropped the bow-oar, seized the harpoon and stood up. His legs were uncertain under him. His mind was uncertain too. He wanted to succeed in his new task. But he hated to kill. He gritted his teeth, poised the harpoon and waited as the boat slid up to the monster's neck.

'Now!' cried Durkins.

As if in a bad dream, Hal felt his arm fly forward and the harpoon leave his hand. The harpoon went in all the way.

'Couldn't be better,' yelled Durkins. 'Back off!'

As the ship had trembled when butted during the night, so the great whale trembled now. His black hide rippled like water from stem to stern. He seemed to wonder what had struck him. The men waited anxiously. Perhaps he would set off and tow the boat on another 'Nantucket sleigh-ride'. Perhaps he would sound a thousand feet deep and drag the boat after him.

But the big bull did not try to run away. He angled about so that his weak eye could see what had bothered him. Then he came straight for the boat with open jaws.

'Overboard!' shouted the mate.

The men tumbled into the water. The whale took the boat bow on. The mouth from front to back was more than long enough to accommodate a twenty-foot boat. The monster was a good ninety feet, and thirty feet of him was head. Only the sperm among the whales has a head one-third of the length of the body.

So the bow of the boat never tickled his tonsils before he closed his teeth upon its stern. The men who had leaped into the water sank a few feet below its surface, and when they came up again they looked about in amazement.

'Where's the boat?'

There was no sign of it — not even a floating oar.

Then the monster tossed up that mighty head, as big and boxlike as a caravan. He opened his jaws and with a push of his five-ton tongue threw out fragments and splinters of what ten seconds before had been a whale-boat.

Clinging to these scraps, the men anxiously watched the huge black bodies milling about them.

They were used to whales that swim away from danger. These whales did not try to escape. Instead, they seemed about to attack.

They circled around the floating men, snapping their great jaws, thrashing the water into foam with their flukes.

The men looked for the other boats. Surely one of them would come to the rescue.

But they, too, were having trouble. In the third mate's boat the big harpooner Jimson had struck

home. The harpooned whale angrily turned upon his enemies, dived, came up under the boat and tossed it twenty feet into the air.

For a moment the sky was full of flying arms and legs as the men who had been spilled out of the boat fell to the sea. Then the bull savagely smashed the boat with his tail.

He disappeared for a moment, then came rushing back to crunch the floating wood to bits.

The one remaining boat now drew in to pick up the survivors. The big bulls, blowing like thunder, kept circling about, but by great good fortune every man was saved.

With three crews on board the boat was so crowded that any further attempt to capture a whale was out of the question. Loaded to within an inch of the water it laboured slowly back to the ship. The angry whales went along with it. Their beating flukes sent up showers of spray. Again and again they dived beneath the boat and the men held their breath, expecting to be tossed sky high.

What a relief when they were back on deck and the lone whale-boat was swinging from its davits!

The relief did not last long. The whales, instead of taking themselves off, now began to threaten the ship. Boiling with rage they swam round and round, tail-swiped the hull with resounding whacks, scraped beneath the keel.

'Square the yards!' the mate commanded. 'Let's get out of this — fast!'

The sails filled and the ship got under way. For a bark it made good speed, but not good enough.

Its ten knots was insufficient to shake off enemies who could easily go twenty.

Suddenly there was a smashing sound astern. The wheel was usually hard to turn — but now it spun idly in the helmsman's hands. Third mate Brown ran aft to inspect the damage.

'The rudder!' he exclaimed. 'It's gone. One of those brutes has snapped it off.'

Rudderless, the ship fell off course. With her sails slatting, and yards banging against the masts, she slowed to a drift, rocking lazily in the waves.

Now she was a sitting duck at the mercy of the bulls of the sea. It was just a question as to which one would strike the final blow.

A sperm-whale's forehead is straight up and down like a cliff. It is almost as hard and tough as iron. It has been compared to the inside of a horse's hoof, so firm that a lance or harpoon cannot make the slightest dent in it. The eyes and ears are ten feet or more behind the forehead. They cannot be injured if the whale decides to use his head as a battering ram.

So the men went about their work nervously, watching out of the corners of their eyes as a dozen or more of the great black foreheads menaced the ship. The carpenter and some sailors tried to rig a jury-rudder. The mate, well aware of the danger to the vessel, ordered that the whale-boat should be stocked with food and water.

Why was the boat not already stocked? Why were not stores of food and water kept in it at all times, to be ready for any emergency?

For the simple reason that a whale-boat is a boat

to fight whales. It is not intended for storage. There are no lockers or cupboards in it. Boxes and crates of supplies would be seriously in the way, their weight would slow the boat down and they would be lost whenever the boat capsized.

Even at best, a whale-boat is heavily loaded. It must carry not only its crew but oars, mast, sail, harpoons and lances, leather bailing-buckets, wooden tubs for the line and a half mile or more of heavy line.

But now if the whale-boat was to be used not for fighting whales but for escape, the harpoons and lances and tubs of line must be taken out and provisions put in. The men assigned to the job hurried to the supply-room and began to turn up hogsheads of salt pork and tins of hard-tack.

They were interrupted by a cry from the deck followed by a terrific crash and a bursting of timbers. Water thundered into the supply-room and the men in a panic abandoned their work and fled to the deck.

It was the great ninety-foot whale harpooned by Hal that had struck the fatal blow. The men on deck had seen him coming and there was nothing they could do about it. His lashing tail made a wake of foam behind him, and the surf flew up above him like a dozen fountains. His head was half out of water. His speed was terrific. There was no doubt of his intentions. Stung by the pain of the harpoon, he was mad enough to smash his own skull if necessary in order to destroy this floating enemy.

He struck the ship to windward just abaft the

cathead and stove in her starboard bows. Then he floated free, perhaps a little stunned by the blow but otherwise unharmed. His angry left eye was focused upon the ship, and he seemed quite willing and capable of giving it another crack if necessary.

It was not necessary. The ship was sinking. Durkins made a desperate effort to save her.

'Man the pumps! Carpenter — never mind that rudder! Get below. See if you can patch the hole.'

He might as well have cried to the moon for help. The carpenter and his men were not half-way down the companion-way before they were met by a boiling uprush of sea-water which carried them back to the deck.

The pumps had no effect. The ship was settling by the nose. The bow was already under water. Men who hoped to descend into the fo'c'sle to get a few of their belongings found it full from top to bottom.

The water throbbing into the hull made the ship tremble as if terrified by the fate awaiting her and appealing to her crew to save her. And all the time the great bull, with the iron protruding from his neck, lay by and watched, and one could imagine a sardonic grin at the corner of his great mouth.

The masts dipped forward, making their last bow to the relentless sea. The sails shivered as the waves, the fingers of the sea, reached for them. The final dive was now only a matter of moments.

No master, even if he is officially only a second mate, likes to lose his ship. Durkins felt the agony of his vessel, the tremble, the shiver, and it was with the same pain in his own heart that he cried:

'Abandon ship! Into the boats!'

The men made a rush for the whale-boat and the dory. They were filled in an instant, and in another instant were lowered to the sea and cast off.

'Pull away!' ordered Durkins. 'We've got to be well off or we'll be sucked down when she sinks.'

There was a cry from the deck. Who had been left aboard? The captain and Brad in the brig. In the rush of events they had been completely forgotten. They would be drowned like rats in a trap.

'Let them sink!' yelled Bruiser.

'It's what they deserve,' said another.

'We can't leave them without a try,' Durkins said. 'Jimson, you have the key to the brig. Go back and get them.'

'Not me,' said Jimson. 'They ain't worth it. Besides, there's no time. The ship'd go down before I could get them out.'

'And you'd go down with it,' admitted Durkins, 'so I can't order you. Is there a volunteer?'

Silence. It seemed that there was no volunteer. Then Hal spoke up.

'I'll go. Give me the key, Jimson.'

'You're a fool,' said Jimson, and gave him the key.

The boat pulled alongside. The ship was so low in the water that Hal could step from the whale-boat to the deck. He ran to the brig. It looked even more than usual like a cage for wild animals, for the men in it were wild with terror.

'You'd leave us here to drown!' screamed Captain Grindle. 'I'll get you for this.'

The water was already knee-deep on the deck and in the brig. Hal unlocked the door. Without troubling to thank him, the released prisoners ran for the gunwale and tumbled into the boat. Hal followed.

The two boats barely had time to get out of range before the ship with a deep sighing sound, and a trembling and shaking from stem to stern, slid head-first into the sea.

It was a slow dive. Sail after sail disappeared. The foremast was gone. The rings at the head of the mainmast where Roger had stood as look-out sank beneath the surface. The mizenmast struggled for a moment to stay up, but the waves threw their arms about it and pulled it down.

Nothing remained but the stern, standing up like a sore thumb, rudder posts broken where the rudder had been torn away, the name of the ship and its home port visible to the last.

The waves closed in over the painted words, there was a large lazy whirlpool with a pit in its centre from which came a breathing sound, the circling stopped, the surface looked like any other bit of ocean and the sea promptly forgot that there had ever been a bark *Killer* of St Helena.

25
Adrift

The ocean suddenly seemed very large and empty.

The castaways in the two small boats looked in vain for a sail or a plume of smoke. The horizon was bare. There was no sign of the factory ship and its catchers. Even the whales had disappeared.

Some of the men still stared in fascination at the spot where the *Killer* had gone down. It was as if they expected the ship to rise again before their eyes.

The mate counted heads. There were five men in the dory. It was meant for one, or at most two. Only twelve feet long, it was intended merely for use in harbour, by the painter or the carpenter, or a messenger to shore. Now it lay dangerously low and water sloshing into it kept the bailers busy.

Eighteen men filled the whale-boat — it was meant for six. The men stood, shoulder to shoulder. There was no room to unship an oar. They waited, bewildered, doing nothing, knowing nothing they could do.

'At least we can put up the sail,' said the mate.

This was done with difficulty. A line was passed

to the dory, and the whale-boat with the dory in tow began to move sluggishly through the waves.

Captain Grindle was complaining.

'Get off my toes. Quit crowding. Take your elbows out of my ribs. Remember, I'm still master. I'm not going to be jammed in like a common seaman.'

'Stop squawking,' said the mate sharply. 'Don't forget that if Hunt hadn't gone back for you you'd be at the bottom of the sea right now.'

'Small thanks to Hunt,' retorted the captain. 'He did it just to be smart. Just to make himself look big and make me look small. I'm not the man to stand for that. I'll make him suffer for it.'

The mate stared, speechless. How could a man be so ungrateful to the one who had saved his life? Hal Hunt had rescued his worst enemy. The mate was sure he had not done it to be 'smart'. He had done it because it was a job that had to be done. You couldn't stand by and let a man drown, even if that was what he deserved. If Grindle were human, he would appreciate what had been done for him. He wasn't human.

'You're a rat,' said the mate. 'We should have let you go down with the others.'

'Don't be insolent,' snapped Grindle. 'I'm not in the brig now. I'm taking over the command of these boats. I am captain and you will obey my orders.'

Durkins smiled, but did not answer. Grindle's anger rose.

'You think that's funny. I suppose you think it's funny that you lost me my ship. It was your fault. All due to your carelessness and stupidity. I could have saved her.'

'Just how?' asked Durkins.

Grindle evaded the question. 'Never mind that now. Now the thing is to save our skins. I'm the only one who can do that. It's no job for a half-baked second mate. Look at you now — you don't even know where you're going.'

Durkins did not answer. A worried frown creased his forehead. Some of the men looked at him anxiously. Jimson, chief harpooner, ventured to say:

'Mr Durkins sir, begging your pardon, where are we heading?'

'I don't know,' Durkins said honestly. 'I'm just keeping her pointed south. Sooner or later we ought to raise one of the French Islands — perhaps Tahiti, or Bora Bora, or one of the Tuamotus.'

Grindle snorted. 'That shows how little you know about it. The islands are at least five hundred miles away. Loaded the way we are, and what with contrary winds, we'll be lucky if we do ten miles a day. That's fifty days. How can we last fifty days? We haven't a scrap of food or drop of water. In ten days every man in these boats will either be dead or stark staring mad.'

A murmur of agreement ran through the crowd.

'That's right,' said Bruiser. 'The old boy has a point there.'

Durkins realized the uneasy mood of his crew.

'Men,' he said, 'I didn't ask for this job. If you'd rather the Captain would take over, all you got to do is say so. But don't trust his figures. We're closer than five hundred miles to the islands and we might do a lot better than ten a day. Sure, we have no food. But we might snag a few fish, and if it rains we'll catch drinking-water. Some small boats have kept going for six months. We may or may not reach the islands. But we could be picked up tomorrow by a ship. We just have to take our chances. If you think the chances would be better with Grindle, it's up to you. Why don't you vote on it?'

Third mate Brown spoke up.

'The mate has put it to you fair and square,' he said. 'You know what sort of treatment you got from Grindle. If you want to go back to that, vote for him. For Grindle, how many?'

Brad hesitantly raised his hand.

'And for the mate?'

There was a general show of hands, and cheers for the mate. Grindle grumbled and mumbled and cast out dire threats that he would have every last man of the crew hanged until dead.

The hours dragged by. Grindle pushed aside the men who stood close to him and sat down on a thwart. A sitting man took up more room than a man standing, but Grindle had no thought for the comfort of others.

As night came on the men could stand no longer. They slumped down upon the thwarts or in the bottom of the boat, lying across each other, sometimes three deep. In such a case the man in the middle layer was the lucky one, for he was kept warm by the bodies above and below him.

The water that continually splashed into the too heavily loaded boat and the spume from the waves kept everyone wet, and the night wind through wet clothes was chill.

The rising sun was welcome. How good it felt on shivering flesh and cold bones!

But as it rose higher and grew hotter its equatorial fire burned unshaded bodies and parched thirsty throats.

There was no sign of a ship. The only fish that appeared was a hammer-head shark that swam alongside until someone tried to strike it on the nose with an oar. The oar missed its target and the shark swam away.

26
An Albatross Named Bill

Gulls and terns swooped overhead but did not come close enough to be caught. Far above floated a great white albatross.

'I'll bet that's Bill,' said Bruiser. 'He's been following the ship all the way from Hawaii. You'da thought he'da left us when the ship went down, but he's sticking by us. Makes a fella sorta feel better. Good old Bill.'

The greatest of all sea-birds hovered overhead like a sort of blessing. Whalemen have always been fond of the albatross, or 'goney' as they choose to call it.

They are superstitious about it. They imagine the gonies to be the souls of dead sailors, so fond of ships that even after death they choose to follow the vessels day after day across the sea. Antarctic cold does not bother them, nor tropic heat – in fact, three varieties of albatross nest on islands west of Hawaii.

To get closer to living sailors they may perch on the yards, or even on the deck. They have little fear, for they know that sailors will not harm them – dare not, for they might be their own dead comrades. To kill an albatross would bring disaster, as it did to Coleridge's ancient mariner.

The bird the men called Bill had become very tame. He would swoop down behind the ship to pick up scraps. He would come aboard and hang around the galley door waiting for the cook to throw him bits of pork.

He was sometimes in the way when there was work to be done, for he had a wing-spread of twelve feet. But he never stayed long at one time because the motion of the ship made him seasick, and there's nothing more ridiculous or pathetic than a seasick goney.

'He won't stay with us long when he finds we have no food for him,' said Durkins.

Bill lazily circled down until he was just over the whaleboat. He floated, airborne, almost within reach. He held this position without flapping his wings, in fact without the least movement that anyone could see. His great shadow gave the men a little relief from the scorching sun. The men looked up and grinned at the friendly bird. Even when he opened his long hooked bill and gave forth a hoarse 'Br-a-a-a!' like the braying of a donkey, Bruiser said:

'Sounds good, don't it?'

'Just like music,' said Jiggs.

And another man put in: 'Sorta like a protectin' angel, ain't he?'

'You sentimental fools!' roared Captain Grindle. 'Slug him with an oar. Pull him down. That's our dinner — pretty stringy meat, but better than nothing.'

Some of the men protested loudly. Others were not so sure. Their hunger was greater than their respect for a bird, even if it was the ghost of a dead sailor.

'We'll be ghosts ourselves if we don't eat soon,' grumbled one.

'If he'd take a message for us —' said Roger.

Grindle glared. 'What kind of nonsense is that? In my days boys kept their mouth shut and left the thinking to the men.'

'Wait a minute,' said Scott. 'Perhaps the boy has something there. We have several accounts in the files of our museum of just that sort of thing — I mean, a bird carrying a message. Usually it was an albatross or a frigate-bird — because they love ships — and are large enough to be easily noticed. Since we haven't any food for Bill, he will soon leave us. Chances are he'll make for the nearest ship.'

'But who'll pay any attention to a bird?' objected Grindle.

'We paid attention to this one, didn't we?' said Scott. 'Remember, he's half tame. Likely as not, he'll come down on the spars or the rail, looking for a hand-out. He's so big and handsome and friendly — they'll notice him all right.'

'And how'll he give them our message? He can't talk.'

'Hee-haw! Hee-haw!' said the albatross, sounding more than ever like an indignant donkey. 'Can't talk indeed!' he seemed to be saying. 'Just try me.'

'We won't depend upon his talking. We'll fasten a message to his leg.'

'And who is apt to notice a little wad tied to a bird's leg?' scoffed Grindle.

'We'll tie a ribbon to it.'

Grindle roared with laughter. 'Where do you think you're going to get a ribbon? What do you suppose this is — a girls' school?'

Scott looked down at his shirt. It was a sports shirt, and it happened to be red. 'You fellows get the bird,' he said, 'and I'll supply the ribbon.'

'Still think we ought to eat 'im,' objected Grindle, but he was smothered under the scrambling men reaching for one of the trailing legs of the big bird. The goney kept just beyond their grasp. When one man climbed on another man's shoulders the bird rose a few inches and still floated clear.

Hal Hunt's experience in taking animals alive stood him in good stead now. He made a bight in a line, fashioned a slip-knot, threw the lasso into the air and snared the bird's right foot. The goney was drawn down, braying like a dozen donkeys, pecking at the men with his powerful hooked beak and thrashing his great wings, so strong that they packed the kick of a mule. There were several bruised pates and shoulders before the mightiest

of ocean birds, still braying loudly, was held motionless by many strong hands.

In the meantime Scott had torn a page from his notebook and with the help of the mate was constructing a message. He read it to the men:

> Crew of the wrecked ship *Killer* adrift in two boats. Approximate bearings, 150° 5′ West, 3° South. Sailing South. No food or water. Urgent.

The note was wrapped in a piece of sailcloth cut from a seaman's coat and tied to the bird's right leg with a bit of twine frayed from a rope's end. Scott pulled his shirt out of his slacks and tore from the bottom edge a long strip two inches wide. The end of the strip was tied firmly to the bird's leg.

'All right, let him go.'

27
Winged Messenger

The released bird with a final angry squawk soared into the air, the red streamer fluttering behind him. Even at five hundred yards Scott's fiery shirt-tail could be plainly seen.

The goney struck out due west. He seemed delighted to escape from his tormentors.

Nothing could more please the tormentors.

'Disgusted with us, he is,' said Bruiser. 'He's making straight for another ship.' Every hungry and thirsty man had a new spark of courage and hope.

But in an hour the bird was back. He had evidently forgiven his persecutors. Again he hovered over the boat, though he was cautious enough to ride a little higher than before. His red banner fluttered bravely in the breeze.

The men tried to shoo him away. 'Go on — chase yourself!' They made motions of throwing rocks at him, but unfortunately they had no rocks nor anything else to throw. The goney watched with beady eye for any scraps that might be tossed overboard. Afternoon wore into dusk and dusk into night and the bird still floated above.

Again the castaways huddled around and upon each other in the bottom of the boats. Sleep was difficult, due to the nagging misery of hunger and thirst.

But the first man to open his eyes at dawn roused the others with a joyful shout:

'Bill's gone!'

They scanned the sky. There was not a sign of the great white wanderer. Hopes rose high.

'That factory ship we saw can't be more than a few hundred miles away,' Jimson said. 'She had about a dozen catchers. That makes thirteen chances we'll be picked up.'

'Providin' your stupid bird finds the ships,' put in Grindle. 'That goney ain't got radar, you know.'

'Birds have something very much like radar,' said Scott.

Grindle tried another tack. He was determined to turn the men against Durkins. If he could just make a fool of the second mate he might still get back his command.

'If it was me,' he said, 'I'd be makin' straight for Christmas Island. It's due west, and it's a lot closer than your French islands.'

Durkins did not answer. But Bruiser spoke up smartly:

'Shut your trap, Cap. With the wind the way it is we wouldn't get to Christmas by Christmas.'

'Our best bet is south,' said Jimson.

'Our best bet is Bill,' said Scott cheerfully.

But as the fresh morning air gave way to the scorching heat of midday both bets began to seem very poor. The men looked at Durkins with blood-shot eyes, inflamed by sun and brine. Was he doing the right thing? Which would come first, Tahiti or death? And were they idiots to be trusting their lives to a bird?

They splashed sea-water on their clothes. This had a cooling effect, but it did not last. Exposure to sea-water was bringing out salt-water boils.

Hunger was agonizing. Even a belt or a boot began to look good. One man tried chewing a leather bailing-bucket.

A small shark appeared. Jiggs dangled his bare foot over the side to attract it. It was a dangerous experiment, but it would be worth while if he got something to eat.

The shark came closer, eyeing the flashing fish-like thing that trailed through the water. Then it lunged.

Jiggs brought down an oar upon its head, jerking his foot away at the same time.

Perhaps he was fortunate that the shark got only the big toe and not the whole foot. The shark swam away, relishing this titbit, while Jiggs and his companions still went hungry.

Men dying of thirst do not behave like ordinary people. Jiggs felt no pain where the toe had been — he only saw the dripping blood. He caught it in the palm of his hand and drank it. Then Scott bandaged the stump with a fragment of shirt-tail.

Another cold wet night, and another blistering day. Hunger was less, but thirst was more. The stomach had given up its demand for food. But the need for water had become a shrieking pain.

Thirst had cracked the lips and swelled the tongue so that every man talked as if he had a baked potato in his mouth. Some began to drink sea-water.

'Better not,' said the mate, 'unless you want to go off your head.'

But the mate thought that he himself must be going out of his mind when at the next dawn he saw a ship on the horizon.

He poked Hal Hunt.

'Do you see what I see? Over yonder.'

Hal rubbed his sore eyes. 'It's a ship and no mistake. A catcher, I think.'

Some of the men cheered faintly. Others were too weak to raise their heads.

'I'll bet she's looking for us,' the mate said.

Grindle peered at the ship. 'She may be looking for us, but she won't find us. We can see her because she's big, but she can't see our sail at this distance.'

'But she's coming straight on. Pretty soon she *will* see us.'

But as they watched the ship veered slowly to the north and then to the north-west. In half an hour she had disappeared.

'I told you so,' said Grindle.

The men sank into a heavy stupor. They lay as they had lain all night, heaped in the bottom of the boat. Even the mate was ready to give up. He closed his eyes and slept.

Hal never knew how much time went by before he heard that whirring sound. Drowsily he looked

up. Then he shouted — as well as anyone could shout with a mouth full of tongue.

'Look!'

Directly over the whale-boat hovered a small helicopter. It settled to within twenty or thirty feet and the pilot looked down. His grin was good to see.

'How goes it?' he shouted.

The mate tried to answer but could not command his voice.

'Got your message by bird,' shouted the pilot. 'Been looking for you for two days. I'll phone the catcher.'

They could hear him speaking over the radio telephone. Then he looked down again.

'Catcher Seven is just over the edge. Perhaps you saw her a while back. She'll be here in half an hour.' And with a friendly wave and another grin he rose to a safe altitude and waited.

The change in the men was remarkable. A few moments before they had been sunk in misery and resigned to death. Now it was as if they had just had a drink of fresh, cold spring-water.

They strained their eyes for a glimpse of the ship. There is was at last, a small white blob that rapidly swelled as the catcher bore down at a speed of fifteen knots.

Hal estimated that she was a vessel of about four hundred tons — a little larger than the bark *Killer*. She had a single smokestack. There were two masts but they bore no sails. Radio antennae stretched between them. At the peak of the forward mast was a crow's nest and in it stood a look-out.

Now the name, Catcher 7, painted on the bows

could be plainly seen. Above it in the very bow was a platform on which stood something that looked like a cannon. Hal knew it must be a harpoon gun.

And to think that there were a dozen of these catchers, every one of them bigger than Captain Grindle's *Killer.* At the masthead of every catcher was a look-out, watching for whales. Even these twelve pairs of eyes were not enough. Also there were the pilots of the little insect-like helicopters which ranged across the sea more swiftly and widely than any catcher could go. Whenever the helicopter pilot sighted a whale he would radio back the news to the nearest catcher.

And all these catchers and copters were just small chickens compared to the great mother hen, the factory ship. A catcher after killing a whale towed it to the factory ship where it was hauled aboard and cut up. The modern floating factory could process more whales in a day than the old-time whale-ship in a month.

After the castaways had been taken aboard the catcher and given a little water and a little food (too much at first would have made them deathly sick) they were made comfortable below deck in the bunks of the crew. There they slept the day out.

At night they received a little more food and water, then slept again while the catcher's crew who had obligingly given up their quarters got through the night as best they could on benches in the messroom.

In the morning there was a bit more to drink and eat, then more sleep. Sleep! It seemed as if they could never get enough of it.

28
Whaling the Easy Way

The first one to bounce back was the youngest. It was about noon when Roger woke to find that his tongue no longer felt like a large potato, the dizziness and dullness were gone from his head, and he was almost tempted to get up.

Presently he heard a running about on the deck above, much shouting, then the boom of a gun. His curiosity got the better of him. He slid out of his bunk, pulled on his clothes and went up on deck. His legs seemed to want to buckle under him, but he managed to make his wobbly way forward.

Several men were moving about on the gun platform. One of them noticed him.

'Come on up, boy,' he called.

Roger climbed the few steps to the platform. The man at the gun greeted him heartily.

'Well, I'll be danged if the kid isn't the first one to get on his feet. Good for you, lad.'

Roger said: 'I thought I heard the gun.'

'So you did, but we missed. A big sperm. He's under now, but he'll probably be up again in a few minutes.'

Roger inspected the gun with interest. It looked quite like a cannon, except that a harpoon projected from its muzzle.

'Know how it works?' asked the gunner.

'Well, I've heard about it,' Roger said. 'There's a bomb in the harpoon. When the harpoon goes into the whale the bomb explodes – and kills the whale.'

'You're ninety per cent right,' grinned the gunner. 'I mean, about ninety per cent of the whalers still use bomb harpoons. We don't. This is the very latest — the *electric* harpoon.'

'How is that better?'

'Several ways. One trouble with the bomb is that when it explodes it scatters bits of steel through the flesh. When the whale goes into the factory these steel fragments damage the saws. Another thing — a bomb killing is very painful. The whale doesn't die at once. He suffers terrible agony. Why make him suffer if it isn't necessary? And there's one more point: agony poisons the meat. Doctors say it's the same way with humans; if you suffer terrible worry or pain your system becomes toxic — poisoned. Toxic whale meat is no good. But with the electric harpoon it's a different story. It packs a wallop of two hundred and twenty volts, one hundred amperes. The electric shock kills the whale before he has time to get poisoned. In ten seconds he's a dead duck. It's as painless as the electric chair.'

Roger smiled. This gunner made the electric chair sound almost attractive. Well, perhaps it was better than a long-drawn-out death agony.

'If the electric harpoon is so good,' he said, 'why don't they all use it?'

'Because it's new. Some of them are afraid it won't work. The most progressive companies already use it – they all will in time. You'll see for yourself what kind of job it does.'

'Breaches!' came a call from the masthead. 'Five points off the weather-bow.'

The whale had surfaced half a mile away. The two-thousand-horsepower diesel of the catcher sprang into action. The catcher raced towards its quarry. The whale was swimming away at full speed, but the catcher swiftly overhauled it.

How easy, Roger thought, compared with the backbreaking labour at the oars of a whale-boat! And how swift. And safe. The monster that could smash a whale-boat to bits and kill its crew was no great danger to the men on the deck of this four-hundred-ton, steel-hulled catcher. Modern methods were certainly more efficient, but they had taken much of the adventure out of whaling.

The catcher slid up beside the speeding whale. The gunner swivelled his gun into position.

'Want to shoot?' he asked Roger. 'When I say "Fire", pull the trigger.'

He sighted the gun carefully, then said: 'Fire!'

Roger pressed the trigger. The harpoon shot out, trailing a line to which was bound an insulated electric wire carrying the fatal charge. The harpoon sank deep just behind the head.

Without a groan, without a tremor, the whale rolled over on its side, dead.

A line was dropped over the tail flukes. With the seventy-ton monster in tow the catcher ploughed on with scarcely any lessening of its former speed.

29
Marvels of the Factory Ship

Late in the afternoon the factory ship hove in sight. To Roger it looked as big as an aircraft carrier.

'She's a whopper!' he said.

'Thirty thousand tons,' said the gunner who had befriended him.

Roger thought of the three-hundred-ton *Killer*, a ship that would have been considered large in the whaling days of the past century. This vessel was one hundred times as big.

But not as beautiful. Instead of twenty white sails billowing in the breeze she carried two grimy smokestacks. The curious thing about them was that they were not one behind the other, as on an ordinary ship, but side by side.

The most amazing thing about this ship was that it seemed to have lost its rear end. It was chopped off square. Where the stern should have been was a great gaping hole, wide enough for two railway trains.

'They haul the whale right up into the ship

through that hole,' said the gunner. 'You'll see how it works when they take your whale aboard.'

The gunner's words, 'your whale', gave Roger a thrill. Of course, he had only pulled the trigger — yet it was exciting to think that he had shot one of the greatest animals on earth. It was a mixed feeling. Along with the thrill was the regret that the great and wonderful sea monster had had to be killed.

The factory ship was well named. It sounded like a factory. On the *Killer* there had been no sound but the talk of the men. Here the voices of men were drowned by the roar of the machinery.

There was the hum of scores of motors, the rattle of chains, the grinding of gears, the clank of arms of iron that did what human arms had once done. Yet it took men, skilled men, to run the machinery. Roger learned from the gunner that the crew of the factory ship was three hundred strong.

They were close enough now to see half a dozen helicopters perched like ladybirds on the ship's forward deck.

'The others are out looking for whales,' said the gunner. 'We have a dozen altogether.'

The name painted on the bow of the factory ship was *Queen of the South.*

'Why the South?' asked Roger. 'This is the tropics.'

'Yes, but our main business is in the Antarctic. You see, there are international rules that govern whaling. Up here we can take only sperms. Down south, during the season, we can take blues and fin-whales and seis and humpbacks and most any-

thing we like. We're on our way there now. Down there we'll really get busy. We'll be at it day and night. Our factory ship alone processes fifteen hundred whales a year. And this is only one of many. The total catch is over thirty thousand whales a year. Some people think whaling is a thing of the past. On the contrary, it's never been as big as it is today.'

'What kind of a plane is that?' asked Roger, pointing to an indistinct white object floating in the cloud of steam above the factory ship.

'Why, that's your albatross. He's adopted us now. He likes the scraps of blubber that get thrown overboard. We often have an albatross hanging around and wouldn't have paid any attention to this one if it hadn't been for that red rag tied to his foot. We caught him and found your message.'

'Good old Bill!' said Roger fervently.

Catcher 7 snugged up alongside the *Queen of the South.* The twenty-three castaways were taken aboard. Some could walk, others had to be carried, and all were given comfortable quarters in the depths of the great ship. The ship's doctor skilfully attended to their needs.

Roger, still boiling with curiosity, was soon on deck again. There he found Hal and Mr Scott talking to Captain Ramsay of *Queen of the South*.

They were gazing down at the cutting-deck. A whale was being dragged in through the great hole in the ship's stern. A winch groaned as it wound in a steel cable attached to what looked like a gigantic pair of pincers clamped on to the monster's tail.

My whale! thought Roger, but said nothing.

'That was brought in by our catcher,' his big brother informed him.

'You don't say!' said Roger in mock surprise. 'Do tell me all about it.'

Hal was glad to find his younger brother so eager to learn. 'Well, you see, there's a platform in the bow of the catcher, and a gun on the platform.'

'Oh, I see,' said Roger, making his eyes round.

'The gun holds a harpoon instead of a bullet. It fires the harpoon into the whale. There's a bomb in the harpoon — it explodes and kills the whale.'

'Well now, I never!' said Roger. 'Gosh, a kid can learn something new every day if he just has a big brother to tell him things.'

Hal looked at him suspiciously. Just at this moment the gunner of Catcher 7 joined them.

'Well, if it ain't my young friend,' he said. 'That's your whale right there, boy.'

Hal looked puzzled. 'What do you mean — how is it his whale?'

'Why, he shot it, of course.'

Hal stared. 'You young rascal! What were you up to while I was asleep?'

'Oh,' said Roger, 'I was just learning that you can't believe all you hear. Like that about bombs and harpoons. That's old-fashioned. These catchers have electric harpoons. But then — you can't expect to be hep to what's new if you spend all your time sleeping below decks.'

Hal swooped to grab his mischievous brother with every intention of paddling his rear end. But he found himself too weak to move fast and the youngster easily evaded him. The gunner and Captain Ramsay were laughing.

'Yes,' said the captain, 'things change pretty fast nowadays. If you want to see speed, watch the way they put through this whale.'

Roger's whale was already being peeled like a banana. Blubber hooks, operated by machinery, plunged into the hide, took hold and ripped it off in great strips. Knives attacked the strips and cut them into chunks four feet square. More hooks seized the chunks, dragged them to holes in the deck that looked like oversized manholes, and down went the blubber into cookers below deck.

Suddenly there was a shout, a scream from the winches, and the carcass as big as a railway carriage was turned over as easily as one would flip a pancake. Then the other side was peeled in the same way.

Another roar of machinery and the skinned carcass was frisked through a tunnel — Hell's Gate, the captain said it was called because of the rolling steam and deafening noise that came out of it — to the forward deck.

Here there were more machines that sliced off the meat faster than one could carve a turkey. Down went the meat through more holes in the deck. Not just any hole. Each part had a hole of its own, and under each hole was a machine to handle that part of the whale and nothing else.

The liver, weighing a ton, went down to the liver plant. The pituitary gland took a different route, the pancreas another, and so on. Each went down to special pots and special chemists who knew just what to do with them. In five minutes there was nothing left of the whale but the skeleton.

Even that was not to be wasted. Huge power-saws, each fifteen feet long, descended to saw up the great bones and drop the pieces into bone-boilers where the oil would be cooked out of them. What was left would be ground into bonemeal.

It was only half an hour since Roger's whale had come aboard and now it had completely disappeared.

'We can process forty-eight whales in twenty-four hours,' said the captain. 'Thirty minutes for each whale. There are ten thousand tons of machinery on this ship. Most of it you can't see — it's down below. There are two decks under that whale-deck, both of them full of processing plants and laboratories. Also there's a fresh-water plant. The cookers require a lot of water and it must be fresh. We take in salt water and turn it into fresh at the rate of two thousand tons a day. Want to see the bridge?'

They climbed to the bridge. Here there were more wonders. An automatic pilot kept the ship on course. A radar screen showed everything within forty miles. A fathometer told the depth of water beneath the ship. A local phone made it possible to talk to any man anywhere on the vessel. A radio telephone reached far out, so that the captain could chat with the captain of any one of his catchers or the pilot of any one of his helicopters. Not only that — it was just as easy to talk to the owners in London on the other side of the world.

It was even possible to receive messages from whales. When a whale that had been killed could not be brought in at once it was left afloat and a small radio transmitter was shot into its hide. This gave out continuous signals that were picked up by an instrument on the bridge of the factory ship. Thus the location of the floating whale was known exactly and it could be picked up whenever convenient.

The boys were still studying these marvels when another visitor appeared on the bridge. It was Captain Grindle.

'I want to see the captain,' he snapped.

'You're talking to him,' said Captain Ramsay.

'Sir, I am Captain Grindle, master of the bark *Killer.* I have come to demand action. If you don't give it to me at once I'll report you to the police.'

Captain Ramsay gazed with surprise at the bristling Grindle. One of his catchers had saved this man and his crew from almost certain death. He had supposed that Grindle had come up to thank him. Instead of expressing gratitude Grindle was scolding and threatening. At the very least, he was showing very bad manners. However, Captain Ramsay's reply was quiet and polite.

'You have had a very unfortunate experience, Captain Grindle. We are glad to have been of service to you. If there's anything more we can do for you, you have only to let us know.'

'I'll let you know fast enough,' Grindle rasped. 'And if you don't do what I say you'll suffer for it.'

'Now, now, my dear captain,' said Ramsay soothingly. 'I know you've had a rough time of it and it has upset your nerves. Suppose you just relax and tell me what I can do for you.'

'Relax, the man says! Relax!' roared Grindle. 'I'll not relax till this thing is set right. My ship was sunk and we had to take to the boats. You know that much. But I'll bet the skunks didn't tell you the rest of it. They didn't tell you that they mutinied. They didn't tell you that they put me, their captain, in the brig. They didn't tell you that their carelessness sank the ship. They didn't tell you that you have a pack of mutineers on board at this very minute.'

'Well, as a matter of fact,' said Captain Ramsay, 'your second mate has told me the whole story — of course, from his point of view.'

'Then why didn't you clap them in the brig instead of tucking them in soft beds, feeding them pap and having your doctor fussing over them as if they were innocent babes instead of desperate criminals?'

'In the first place,' said Captain Ramsay, 'we have no brig. We don't need it. In the second place, mutiny on your ship is your responsibility, not mine. Of course I'll give you any reasonable assistance. I should say that the first thing for you to do is to notify the owners. Who are they?'

'Kane Whaling Company, St Helena. I'll send Mr Kane a radiogram — and will I make it a sizzler!'

'You can do better than send him a message,' suggested Captain Ramsay. 'You can talk to him.'

'Talk! Do you realize St Helena is half-way round the world from here?'

'Of course.' Captain Ramsay took up the phone and spoke to his radio operator. 'Call the radio station on St Helena. Have them connect with Mr Kane of the Kane Whaling Company. Sunset here — it'll be early morning there. Get him up out of bed if necessary. It's important.'

In an amazingly short time Grindle found himself talking to his boss. True to his word he told a sizzling story. Some of it was true, most of it was not.

He told of the mutiny. He said nothing of the events that had let up to it — the brutalities, the flogging of the men, the harsh treatment of Roger, the death of the sailmaker dragged at the end of a line until he was taken by a shark.

Hal, listening, was astonished to hear his own name mentioned. He was named the chief conspirator. He, Grindle said, had stirred up the men to mutiny, and he should be the first to hang. Grindle, evidently, had never forgiven Hal for telling him he was unfit to command a ship, for beating him in a fight, and, worst of all, for saving him from the sinking ship. Gratitude being an emotion unknown to him, Grindle nursed a grudge because he had had to be rescued by his enemy.

His story told, he listened to Mr Kane's instructions. He nodded and grunted and nodded again, and an evil smile spread over his face. When he put down the phone he seemed highly satisfied.

'My orders are,' he said, 'to place all the mutineers under arrest. Special provision for Hunt — he's to be put in solitary confinement. First chance I get I'm to take 'em all back to Honolulu for a hearing before the British Consul.' He grinned happily and his bristles stood out like black needles. 'They're as good as hanged already.'

'As for arrest,' said Captain Ramsay, 'I can't help you. I can only assure you that they won't escape from this ship. As for transportation, I'll provide it. As soon as your men are able to travel I'll put you all aboard one of my catchers and send you to Honolulu. It's not far — at fifteen knots you should be there in less than two days. You can radio the Honolulu police and have them meet the ship as she docks and jail your mutineers until the time comes for the hearing. I hope you feel that I am giving you every possible co-operation.'

Grindle only grunted. His contemptuous gaze swept over Captain Ramsay and his visitors, and as he stamped his way off the bridge he could be heard mumbling:

'Good as hanged already!'

30
To African Adventure

When the catcher pulled up to the Honolulu docks two days later a row of police-vans were there to meet it.

The mutineers were loaded into the vans and trundled away to enjoy the dubious comforts of the Honolulu jail.

Only two men did not go behind bars — the one who had most to do with the trouble and the one who had least to do with it — Captain Grindle, and his passenger, Mr Scott. Scott took advantage of his freedom to see the British Consul and give him his own honest account of what happened on the *Killer.*

Also he cabled John Hunt at his wild animal farm on Long Island, New York:

'Your boys are in Honolulu jail.'

John Hunt lost no time in winging his way to Honolulu.

At the hearing Grindle told his side of the story and his men told theirs. The result was severely disappointing to Captain Grindle. The Consul in his report to Mr Kane recommended clemency towards the mutineers. The owner cabled back that he would prefer no charges against them.

They were set free.

As for Grindle, who had expected to see his crew hanged, he himself barely escaped the same fate. With all his brutalities exposed to view, he was condemned by press and public all the way from Honolulu to St Helena and back. He was never to command another ship.

John Hunt, famous explorer, collector of wild beasts for zoos and circuses, sat in the garden of the Royal Hawaiian with his two sons and Mr Scott.

They looked out upon the glittering semicircle of Waikiki Beach and the sparkling bay dotted with surf riders, canoes and catamarans. Behind it all rose the grim bulk of Diamond Head.

People strolling by looked at the four curiously. Most of the hotel guests had come from sunless offices on the mainland for a two weeks vacation and looked as pale as if they had lived under stones; but these four were as golden brown as ripe coconuts.

Perhaps some of the passers-by recognized the two boys, for pictures of all the mutineers had appeared in the papers.

Hal said to his father: 'Hope you don't mind being seen with a couple of jailbirds.'

John Hunt smiled.

'No, indeed. Quite the opposite. I'm proud to be seen with you.'

'You have reason to be,' said Scott warmly. 'Your

boys had some tough breaks. When I think of the night Roger put in on that whale fighting off sharks and killers — and the way he prevented Grindle's escape by pulling the plug of the boat — and the way Hal gave Grindle a blubber-bath and later saved him from going down with the ship — I think the boys did you a lot of credit.'

'Anyhow,' said Mr Hunt, 'you certainly packed a lot of experience and adventure into three weeks. It may have been tough, but it's been good education. Perhaps you've had enough of that sort of education for a while and would like to go home and rest.'

The suggestion was not received with enthusiasm. In fact the boys looked as glum as if there had just been a death in the family.

'Who wants to rest?' said Roger. 'We'll have plenty of time to rest when we get to be your age.'

John Hunt laughed. 'And I'm afraid you won't rest then, either. No, the Hunts aren't very good resters. Well, if you don't want to rest, I have another proposition for you.'

The boys perked up immediately. New excitement came into their eyes.

'Whatever it is, we accept,' said Hal.

'Now, don't be in too big a hurry. You may not like it. Africa is quite different from the Pacific.'

'Africa!' exclaimed Roger. His eyes shone like saucers.

'Yes, Africa. Land of the malaria mosquito, the tsetse fly, the crocodile, man-eating lions and leopards and all sorts of uncomfortable things.'

He was trying to scare the boys, but he could see that he was not succeeding.

'Go on,' said Hal. 'What do you want us to do in Africa?'

'Well, we're getting orders for more African animals than we can supply. Some of the zoos want hippos and rhinos and giraffes. A big circus wants elephants and lions. Of course, they all have to be taken alive – and that's a lot harder than taking them dead. I'll go with you and get you started. We can fly from here by way of Hong Kong and Calcutta to Nairobi. We'll engage a good hunter and he'll take us on safari. Think about it until tomorrow morning.'

The boys did not need to think about it — they had already decided. And yet they thought of little else all night. Their dreams were full of roaring lions and rampaging hippos and charging elephants. But they never gave a thought to the most dangerous monsters of the African jungle, the mosquito and the fly.

And how they fared with the creatures of Africa, great and small, will have to be told in another book, *African Adventure.*

AFRICAN ADVENTURE

1
Leopard in the Night

Hal woke with a start. He found himself sitting up in bed, his spine tingling. What had roused him? A cry of some sort.

The play of light and shadow in the tent told him that the camp-fire outside was still burning. It was meant to keep off dangerous visitors. Wild animals were all about – yet the sound he had heard did not seem the voice of an animal.

Still, he could be mistaken. This was his first night in the African wilds. Beside the camp-fire earlier in the evening he and his younger brother, Roger, had listened to the voices of the forest while their father, John Hunt, told them what they were hearing.

'It's like an orchestra,' Hunt had said. 'Those high violins you hear are being played by the jackals. That crazy trombone – the hyena is playing it. The hippo is on the bass tuba. Doesn't that wart-hog's "arnk-arnk-arnk" sound just like a snare drum? And listen – far away . . . you can just hear it, a lion on the 'cello.'

'Who's that with the saxophone?' asked Roger.

'The elephant. He's good on the trumpet too.'

A sharp grinding roar made the boys jump. Whatever made it was very close to the camp. It sounded like a rough file being dragged over the edge of a tin roof.

Roger tried to cover his fright with a joke.

'Must be Louis Armstrong,' he said, and the others laughed rather uneasily. It did sound like the gravel voice of the famous jazz singer.

'Leopard,' said Hunt. 'He sounds hungry. I hope he doesn't come any closer.'

But the sound that had made Hal sit up stiff and startled in his bed was none of these. Now he heard it again — a piercing shriek, followed by the screams of men and women and the barking of dogs. The noise seemed to come from the African village on the hill just behind the camp.

He heard his father's cot creak. Roger remained fast asleep. Thirteen-year-olds do not wake easily.

'Better see what the trouble is,' said John Hunt. He and Hal pulled on their clothes and went out. The African scouts and gun-bearers who had been sleeping around the fire were awake and talking excitedly.

There was a rushing through the grass just outside the zone of firelight. Hunt put his .375 Magnum to his shoulder. He lowered the gun when he saw that what was emerging was no wild beast but the headman of the village with three of his men.

'*Bwana*, quick, help us,' he called as he came running. 'The leopard. It has taken one of the children.'

'Come on, Hal,' said Hunt. 'Joro, Mali, Toto — get your guns and come along.' And to the headman, 'Did you pick up its trail?'

'Yes. It went down towards the river.'

'Get a couple of flashlights,' said the senior Hunt. Hal plunged into the tent to grab the electric torches. A sleepy voice came from Roger's bed.

'What's up?'

'We're going hunting.'

'What?' complained Roger. 'In the middle of the night?'

Hal did not wait to explain. He dived out and joined the men already on their way up the hill. Knowing his adventurous younger brother, he was not surprised when Roger came panting up behind. He was still in his pyjamas, having taken time only to put on a pair of boots.

At the edge of the group of thatch-and-mud huts angry villagers milled about, men shouting, women wailing, children crying.

Here the headman pointed out the leopard's trail. Hunt played his torch on the tracks and led the way down the hill towards the river.

Hal noticed that a woman was accompanying them.

'Why is she coming?'

'It was her child,' the headman said.

Half-way down they came upon the child's body. The leopard, frightened perhaps by the commotion, had dropped it and fled. The bare brown skin was deeply cut by teeth and claws, and oozed blood. The woman, with a little cry, gathered up her child. Hunt felt for the pulse.

'Still alive,' he said. And while the sobbing mother turned back to the village with the unconscious child in her arms, Hunt again took up the trail.

'No time to lose,' he said. 'It could have gone a mile by this time. Or it might be lying just here behind a bush, waiting for us. That's one thing you can always expect of a leopard – it will do the unexpected. Watch out.'

He stopped, puzzled, where the footprints were indistinct. John Hunt, explorer, collector of wild animals for zoos and circuses, had had long experience in tracking animals – yet he didn't claim to know everything. The best tracker in Africa is not the white man but the African, who from childhood has learned to interpret every turned pebble and every bent blade of grass. The official tracker in Hunt's safari was big black Joro, and Hunt now called his name.

'Joro, take a look at this.'

There was no answer. Hal swung his light on the men. There were the headman and the three others from the village, there was Mali, and there Toto. And the camp dog, a big Alsatian named Zulu. But no Joro.

'I thought I told him to come,' said Hunt.

'You did.'

'He acts strangely sometimes. Well, no matter – I think this is the way,' and Hunt led on down the hill.

Hunt's flashlight, strapped to his forehead to leave both hands free in case he had to use his gun, threw a strong shaft of light on the pug marks. Yet John Hunt hesitated. Something was wrong with these footprints. Certainly they had been made by the feet of a leopard. There was no mistaking the imprint of the four oval toes and the large triangular heel. But at the tip of each toe-print was a deeper dent, evidently made by the claw. That was odd, because a leopard has movable claws which come out when he is attacking but are drawn back into the toe when he travels. This looked more like the trail of a cheetah, whose claws are always out.

'But it can't have been a cheetah,' he said to Hal. 'A cheetah would never enter a house and grab a child. These are a leopard's tracks all right. But the claws wouldn't be out — not unless the beast was dead.'

'Dead,' Hal repeated. He wondered. Could the tracks have been made by dead feet? The idea was fantastic. But this was a land where the fantastic was commonplace.

His sharp eyes noticed something else.

'Dad,' he said, 'there are no blood-stains along this part of the trail.'

His father stopped and gazed at Hal thoughtfully. That was curious. After clawing the body, the leopard's feet had left a little of the child's blood in every print. But now, suddenly, there was no more blood. The feet would get dry, but not so quickly. There should be a trace of blood left. He knelt and examined a print at close range. There was not the slightest speck of red. He grinned up at Hal.

'You'll be a tracker yet.'

But Roger wasn't going to let his nineteen-year-old brother walk off with all the honours.

'There's something else,' he said. 'When we were after that jaguar down on the Amazon — remember? — it slid along close to the ground — pressed the grass down flat. Doesn't a leopard do the same?'

'Yes, it does,' admitted his father.

But here nothing of the sort had happened. The grass stood up two feet high between footprints.

Hunt shook his head.

'Beats me,' he confessed. 'But we can't solve the mystery by standing here. Let's get along.'

They went on down the slope at a half-run. The headman came up beside John Hunt and poured out the troubles of his village. This was the third child the leopard had taken in the last ten days. The first two had been killed. Every time the leopard grew bolder. The people of the village lived in constant terror.

'You will kill it?' he pleaded.

'I didn't come to Africa to kill animals,' John Hunt said. 'I want to take them alive. But a man-

eater deserves to be shot. Don't worry — we'll get it one way or another.'

They entered a grove of trees and bushes along the river bank. On they went with tense nerves, knowing very well that the beast might spring out at any moment from a patch of grass or brush, or might drop from an overhanging limb.

'What's that — over there, near the doum-palm?' said Hal. His father directed his forehead light towards the spot. Something was moving, something yellow with dark blotches. Now it stood out plainly, and it was certainly the hide of a leopard. But the thing seemed to be erect like a man. It was leaping for cover. Just before it disappeared from sight it looked back at its pursuers. Its face was a man's face, but so poorly lit that one could not clearly see the features.

Now it was gone. The hunters reached the place where it had been seen, and fanned out in all directions. But the beast, or man, or whatever it might be, seemed to have vanished into thin air.

2
The Leopard-Man

Even the tracks had disappeared, hidden by the tangle of brush and grass. No one knew what to do next. The men from the village plainly did not want to go farther. A leopard was bad enough. But a leopard that could change into a man was an evil spirit. It could appear and disappear at will, and no gun or arrow could hurt it. So they believed, and trembling with fear, they were ready to call it a night and go back to the village.

'But how about your children?' Hunt said. 'Are you willing to let them be taken, one after another?'

'There is nothing we can do,' said the headman. 'And nothing you can do. A leopard can be killed, but not a leopard-man. Come – you will return with us to the village. You have lights – we dare not go back in the dark. Listen, he laughs at us.'

From the depths of the wood came a harsh, grating, coughing sound that only a terrified imagination could interpret as a laugh. It was like the rasp of a saw through coarse wood.

'That fellow, whoever he is,' said Hunt, 'can certainly give a good imitation of a leopard. I'm going after him. You can come along, or stay here, just as you like.'

He and the boys set off in the direction of the sound, and the Africans unwillingly followed. Scrambling through brush, over logs and around trees, they chased the 'evil spirit' and hoped it would not be there when they arrived. The two torches, worn by Hal and his father, cast their beams far in among the trees, searching for something in yellow and black.

Hal stopped. 'I think I see him. Up on a branch, just to the left of that ant-hill.'

Hunt strained his eyes. Yes, he could just make out something yellow and black, probably the skin disguising the figure of the leopard-man.

The dog Zulu growled softly and began to run ahead.

'Wait, Zulu,' Hunt ordered. 'Come back.' The dog reluctantly obeyed, still growling.

'Now that's strange,' said Hunt. 'When we saw the leopard-man before, Zulu was quiet. Now he's all excited. Why the change?'

'If we go straight for the leopard-man he'll run, just as he did before,' Hal said. He took off his light and gave it to Roger. 'Stay here and keep the light shining on him. I'll sneak round and come up behind him. I think I can wrestle him off that branch. And I have a knife I can use if necessary.'

'Don't use it unless you have to,' said his father. 'Remember, this is just a man and we have no warrant to kill him. I must say his actions are suspicious. But all we can do is arrest him and turn him over to the police for questioning.'

The headman objected. 'Your son must not do this. He is strong, but he has no magic. The leopard-man will turn into a leopard and kill him.'

But Hal had already crept out into the dark and was making a wide circle round the crouching figure on the branch. Hunt had little fear for his safety. He knew that his six-foot son, with muscles like steel springs, stood a good chance against any human enemy. As for the notion that the leopard-man might turn into a leopard, he had no patience with any such superstition. He noticed that Zulu had followed Hal. The two of them should be able to give a good account of themselves against the mysterious stranger.

The impatient dog kept pressing on. Hal warned her.

'Easy, Zulu, don't be in a hurry.'

Now they came out on the river bank. The stars glinted down on the smooth surface. Those slow-moving masses on the other shore were hippos. Almost under Hal's feet a crocodile that had been resting with its head on the bank switched about and dived.

They came up silently behind the tree. It was an ancient baobab with a huge trunk, probably hollow inside. They slipped round it until they could see the dark form on the branch. A strong smell penetrated their nostrils. Hal remembered the same smell in a zoo coming from the leopard's cage. But, he reminded himself, this was no leopard but only a man.

The eager dog went into action first. With a savage growl she leaped for the branch. At the same instant

the thing on the branch leaped at the dog and they met in mid air. Hal realized with a sickening shock that this was no human being but a full-grown leopard. Zulu would not last ten seconds under those terrible jaws and claws. The two animals fell to the ground, the leopard's teeth around Zulu's neck.

Hal drew his knife and closed in to rescue the dog. The two bodies whirled about so fast that it was hard to distinguish between the dog and the big cat. Hal's knife might find the wrong animal.

Then a strange thing happened. The leopard, with a howl of pain, released its jaws from the dog's throat. Zulu's collar, covered with heavy, brass studs as sharp as nails, had saved her. The points had stabbed the palate of the leopard and made it relax its hold.

Now it turned on an enemy it could hope to conquer more easily, and Hal felt the full crash of the leopard's body against his own, striking him with such force that he tumbled backwards into the water. The impact had sent the knife flying from his hand. By instinct he gulped a lungful of air, just as he and the beast plunged beneath the surface. He felt the savage claws tearing at his clothing and biting into the flesh. He knew that a leopard's claws can do far more damage than a lion's, because a lion mauls with his front feet only, while a leopard uses all four at once. And teeth as well.

Probably his father and the others were now on the bank, but there was little they could do to help. He must work this out for himself. He hooked his foot under a waterlogged branch that lay on the river bottom, and so held himself and his quarry under water. Could he drown the beast? Or would he himself drown first?

He had had a good deal of experience during his underwater adventures in the Pacific. From his Polynesian friends in the South Seas he had learned how to last a good three minutes without coming up for air.

He had no idea whether a leopard could do better than that, or not so well. He clutched the animal's throat, trying to hold the head well away so that the powerful jaws could not reach his face. But he could do nothing about those ripping claws. Curiously enough, they did not hurt. Later on they would — and plenty.

Staying down three minutes without exertion is one thing. Staying down three minutes while locked in a life-and-death struggle with a big cat is something else. Hal was getting winded. But the leopard was not doing too well either — the fight had almost gone out of it and now it was only anxious to get away. Hal grimly held on. His enemy's struggles grew weaker. If he could just hold the creature down one minute more . . . .

He had forgotten about the crocodiles. The swish of a powerful tail close by reminded him. A crocodile would ordinarily think twice about attacking a man — but attracted by blood it might think only once, or not at all.

Hal loosed his foot and came to the surface. His head emerged and he took air, but he still held the leopard's head under water. A beam of light from the shore struck him and he heard his father's voice. Then both his father and Roger leaped in beside him and hauled him ashore, his hands still gripping the motionless leopard's throat. They dragged the beast up on the bank and Hal put his hand over the heart. The leopard was dead.

'How about you?' Hunt asked. 'Did you get badly mauled?'

'Only scratched,' Hal said, still too excited to feel his wounds.

The Africans were happy and terrified. Happy that the killer of their children was dead, terrified that it might come alive again in human form.

The limp body lay on the river bank. Not one of the Africans would touch it. When Roger went towards it the headman said sharply:

'Keep away. It is still full of magic.'

Hunt studied the worried face of the headman.

'You really believe that, don't you? You went to

a Christian mission school, you speak English, you learned something about science – and you are afraid of a dead leopard.'

'My friend,' smiled the headman, 'not all wisdom is to be found in school. Our knowledge is passed down to us from our fathers and grandfathers. We have always known what you have learned for the first time tonight – you have seen it for yourself. The leopard became a man and the man became a leopard. And all the time it was neither man nor leopard, but an evil spirit.'

Roger, under the spell of the night and the strange things that had happened, was staring at his father with open mouth.

'Perhaps there's something in it, Dad. It's all been so crazy I could believe almost anything.'

His father grinned. 'I don't blame you. But perhaps it isn't quite as mysterious as it seems. I think I'm beginning to see through it. You remember when we were following the tracks from the village and they became lost in the grass, and when we found them again they seemed peculiar. At the point of each toe-print there was a claw mark. But a live leopard doesn't keep his claws out when he walks. Those prints were made by dead feet.'

Roger's jaw hung a little farther open. Was his father going a bit barmy?

'Dead feet,' his father went on. 'The paws of a dead leopard strapped to the feet of a man. You remember that the grass wasn't flattened down as it would be by a leopard. It stood two feet high, as it would if a man's legs had brushed through it. That man was trying to mislead us so that we shouldn't find the real leopard. Later we saw the man — dressed in a leopard skin.'

'But why — why should he try to lead us off — and why does he dress like a leopard?'

'Because he belongs to the Leopard Society. That's a band of killers. It's not so active here in Uganda, but we are very close to the Congo border and it's strong in the Congo and all through Central and West Africa. It's a very secret society. When a man joins it he is given a leopard skin to wear, leopard's paws for his feet, and steel hooks strapped to his fingers so that he can claw his victims. He is taught that he can actually change into a leopard at will. And since he belongs to the leopards, he must defend all leopards. He must kill anybody he is ordered to kill. Especially he must kill anyone who kills a leopard.'

Roger's forehead was puckered with the effort to understand all this.

'So he led us off the leopard's trail,' he said. 'Then we saw him — and he ran. But when we found him again he had changed into a leopard.'

His father smiled. 'He didn't change into anything. He was a man, and is a man. Then we heard the real leopard, and Hal stalked it. And there it is.' He glanced at the dead animal on the bank.

'And where's the leopard-man?'

'Who knows? Probably skulking around in these woods waiting for his chance to do us in for killing his brother beast.'

'A comforting thought,' said Hal. 'Let's get out of here.'

3
Mystery of the Missing Tracker

As they turned to go, a flash of one of the lights revealed two more leopards — but very small ones — emerging from a hole in the trunk of the baobab and running to their dead mother to suckle. Mewing like oversize kittens, they nuzzled against the quiet, wet body.

'Poor little duffers,' Hunt said. 'We'll take them back to camp and see if we can't fix up some substitute for mother's milk.'

'Let me carry them,' said Roger. 'Will they claw me?'

'Not likely. They're too young to be afraid of you.'

Roger, a little gingerly, with proper respect for both claws and jaws, gathered up the two babies, one in each arm.

'And we'll take the big cat too,' Hunt said. 'Some museum will be glad to get that skin.' He signalled to the Africans to take up the body. When they showed no sign of obeying, he did not press them.

'Well, Hal, it's up to us.' He drew some cord from the pocket of his bush-jacket and tied the feet

together, while Hal found a fallen branch that could be used as a pole. The pole was run through between the looped feet, and with Hal at one end and his father at the other, the 100-pound cat was raised from the ground and began its journey to camp. The two lights were kept sweeping here and there, on guard lest the leopard-man should be lying in ambush.

'And how about the male?' said Hal. 'Isn't he apt to pounce on us when he sees us carrying off his family?'

'A male lion would be after us in a minute,' said Hunt. 'But a male leopard isn't a family man. After he's started things off, he lets mamma take care of the children and herself. He's probably miles away, hunting.'

Roger, carrying the cubs, was suddenly startled by a cold nose against his wrist. He expected to feel teeth next, for this must be the father of the cubs. Should he drop the little animals and run? He peered down into the gloom. The animal he saw was not quite like a leopard – no, it was just the big Alsatian, Zulu.

The dog was a handsome female, owned by Mali. Though a lady, Zulu was every bit as strong, courageous and beautiful as a male. And she went beyond a male in her affection for anything small on four wobbly legs. Before coming on this safari, she had had to leave a litter of pups. Unable to mother them, she now seemed to want to mother the leopard cubs, and kept sniffing at them and nuzzling her nose into their fur as she trotted alongside.

It was a relief to come out of the dangerous dark into the warm glow of the camp-fire lighting up the circle of tents.

'Bring a cage for the cubs,' Hunt said. 'A large one, so they'll have plenty of room to play.'

Mali and Toto hauled down a lion cage from one of the trucks. Hunt padded a large clothes-basket with a warm blanket and pushed it into one corner of the cage. Then the cubs were introduced to their new home. Just before the door was closed, Zulu slipped into the cage.

'Come out of there,' commanded Mali. But the dog whined and retreated to the far side.

'Suppose you let her stay,' suggested Hunt. 'Let's see what she has on her mind.'

Mali closed the door. Zulu, with ears cocked forward, studied the two balls of fur. She sat on her haunches and seemed to be lost in thought. Then she came forward and sniffed at each in turn. They did not seem exactly like pups, but they were just as helpless. Certainly they needed somebody to look after them.

She went over by the basket. Looking back at the cubs, she gave out a series of little yipping barks which plainly said, 'Come here!' The cubs did not understand. They lay quiet and frightened on the cold, hard floor of the cage.

With a business-like air, Zulu walked to one of the cubs, gripped the fur at the back of the neck in her teeth, and lifted the squirming animal from the floor. She seemed to find it a bit heavier than she had expected. She carried it to the basket and laid it down on the blanket. Then she brought the other cub and laid it beside the first. There was still room in the large basket for herself. She stepped into it, lay down in a half-circle, and drew both cubs against her. After a protesting mew or two, they snuggled close to her, evidently enjoying the warmth of her body, because an African night, even near the Equator, can be cold.

In the meantime Hunt was treating the scratches on Hal's arms and chest. Luckily Hal's heavy bush-jacket had prevented the claws from going very deep.

'Just scratches,' Hal said. 'Never mind them.'

' "Just a scratch" from a leopard's claw can be serious if it isn't attended to,' his father told him. 'The claws can be highly poisonous, because the leopard eats dead animals and particles of the decaying flesh remain in the claws. Hold steady.'

He cleaned out the wounds with boiled water and applied a strong antiseptic. Mali returned from a search in the bushes with some leaves and roots which he proceeded to pound until they gave out a thick, white milk. This was smeared on as a poultice and covered with bandages.

But one cut in the left arm was too deep and wide for such treatment. It had to be sewn up, and Hunt, searching through his medical kit, discovered that his supply of catgut thread needed for sutures was exhausted.

'We will use ants,' suggested Mali. Hunt had often heard of this art, for it is practised by primitive tribes all over the world, but he had never seen it done. He watched with great interest as Mali poked into one of the ant-hills so common in Africa and stirred up the white ants, better known as termites, until the warriors rushed out. He seized one of these and squeezed it until its jaws opened wide. With skilful fingers he drew together the edges of the cut in Hal's arm, then placed the open jaws one on either side of the cut, where they bit savagely like two pincers, completely closing the wound. He broke off the ant's body, leaving the head in place and the jaws locked. They would remain locked until the wound healed, when the ant-jaw stitches could be removed.

More ants were used in the same way until a row of heads extended the full length of the cut. Hal and his father looked on with admiration as the skilful black fingers put the last ant-clamp in place, then applied the milky poultice and a final bandage.

Wounds so treated generally heal without difficulty, but Hunt took the added precaution of giving Hal a strong hypodermic injection of penicillin.

No one thought it worth while to go to bed, for dawn was already streaking the east with rose and silver.

One of the mysteries of the night had not yet been solved. What about the tracker, Joro? He had been ordered to go along on the hunt. But when he was needed to read the tracks, he was not there. Why had he stayed in camp? Or *had* he stayed in camp?

'Tell Joro I want to see him,' John Hunt told the cook, who was going round from tent to tent with cups of steaming coffee.

'Joro is not here, *bwana*.'

'But he must be here. He didn't go with us.'

The cook seemed surprised. 'He wasn't with you? Where else could he have been?'

'That's exactly what I want to know. There he is now.'

The cook turned and looked across the camp ground. Joro was just coming out of the bushes. Evidently hoping he would not be seen in the half-dark of dawn, he crept like a cat to his tent and slipped inside. As usual, his chest and back were bare, his only garment a well-worn pair of safari pants. He seemed to carry some sort of bundle under his arm.

'Ask him to come here,' said Hunt.

When Joro came, Hunt was impressed by the drawn, haggard face and hate-filled eyes of his tracker. It was not the first time he had noticed this bitterness in the man's face, but it had never been so marked as now. But Joro was a good tracker, and this was the first time he had definitely disobeyed orders.

'Joro,' said Hunt, 'I asked you to go with us last night. Didn't you hear me?'

Joro answered sullenly. 'I didn't hear you.'

'Where were you all night?'

'Here, of course.'

'But they say you were not in the camp.'

'They are mistaken. I was in my tent, asleep.'

'But I saw you come out of the brush just a few minutes ago.'

'Yes, *bwana*. I went out early to look for you.'

Hunt saw that this line of questioning was getting nowhere.

'Joro,' he said, 'what do you know about the Leopard Society?'

That question went home. Joro was visibly shaken. His voice was unsteady as he replied, 'I know nothing of it, *bwana*.'

It was plain that he was deeply disturbed. Hunt was sorry for him. He could not answer this man's hate with hate, for he was not a hating man. He realized that Joro was somehow in the grip of terrible forces and the good and bad in him were struggling against each other. Here was a man to be pitied and helped, not feared or fought. Joro, shifting uneasily from one foot to the other, said, 'May I go now?'

'Joro,' said Hunt kindly, 'you are in trouble. You don't want to tell me what it is. That's quite all right. But remember, in this camp you are among friends. If you ever need us, all you have to do is ask.'

'I won't need you,' Joro said with a sudden flash of anger, and left the tent.

4
Cubs' Breakfast

Hunt went out into the morning sunshine and breathed deeply. The air was sweet with the scent of dew on the grass and all the better for the fragrance of bacon and eggs cooking over the open fire. Hal and Roger joined him. Together they looked at the miracle that is fresh every morning in the African big-game country.

In the low rays of the just-risen sun the animals were coming down to the river to drink.

Animals, animals, animals, of every shape and form, animals by the hundred, by the thousand, were on the move.

'I never dreamed it would be like this,' Hal said.

'No one can believe it until he actually sees it,' said Hunt. 'Every time I come to Africa it strikes me as hard as it did at first. You often read nowadays that wild life is disappearing, and it's true in a way — but you can see that there's a lot of it left.'

'Looks as if all the zoos in the world had just been let loose,' said Roger, as he made a complete turn-about, his eyes sweeping over a sea of bobbing heads, every head containing the same thought — break-fast.

Nibbling at shrubs or high grass as they went, or seizing smaller animals if they were meat-eaters, they ambled down towards the river. On the other side of the river, too, they could be seen coming down from the hills to meet at the river's bank.

Hunt pointed out those that passed close to the camp, and named them. The big eland was cram-full of dignity and majesty. The graceful, streamlined impala was full of fun, jumping six feet high over bushes instead of troubling to go round them. The ungainly wildebeest (in crossword puzzles it is called the gnu) flounced about awkwardly like a fat old lady trying to do the twist. The little duiker (which means diver, because he dives through brush) did not go round bushes like the stately eland, nor leap over them like the impala, but plunged straight through.

And still they came — zebras frisking like horses, long-faced hartebeest, springing klipspringers, dik-diks almost small enough to put in your pocket, waterbuck, bush-buck, kob, oryx and those lovely gazelles which they would see all over East Africa, the Grants and the Tommies.

A giraffe went by, his long neck angling into the sky like a derrick. He paused to pick some tender young leaves from the top of a tree. Then he went on to the river. How would he get that high head of his down to the water?

The giraffe lowered his head, but even when it was as far down as he could get it, it was still several feet above the surface. He knew by instinct how to solve that problem. He spread his front feet wide apart so that his body slanted down from tail to neck like the roof of a house. Then his lowered head easily reached the water. Every gulp ran up his neck in a bulge as big as a cricket ball.

'Lions!' exclaimed Roger. Two big, tawny beasts with heavy manes, who looked as if they belonged in Trafalgar Square, walked along with heads down.

What seemed strange to Roger was that gazelles and waterbuck a few feet away from the lions paid no attention to them.

'Why aren't they afraid?' asked Roger. 'I thought all animals were afraid of lions.'

'See those sagging bellies?' Hunt said. 'The lions have eaten during the night. They are full and satisfied, and the antelopes know it. So why should they be afraid?'

One of the lions let out a sudden roar that seemed to shake the ground. Roger expected to see him spring upon one of the passing animals. Surely his father must be wrong; a roar like that must mean business. But the animals still gave no heed to the King of Beasts. Hunt saw the bewildered look on his son's face.

'A lion roars *after* he has had his dinner,' Hunt said. 'Perhaps it's his way of saying thank you. It means he is satisfied, content with himself and with the world. If you hear a lion roar during the night, you don't need to be scared. It's the lion that doesn't roar that you need to be afraid of. When a lion is hungry he creeps up on his victim without making a sound.'

Until now all the animals had politely gone round the camp, not through it. But suddenly two huge black objects that seemed as big as locomotives came blundering straight into the camp ground. They squashed one of the tents, and two Africans popped out of it shouting with terror. The two monsters went straight on through the camp-fire, kicking pots and pans in all directions and spattering eggs, bacon and coffee over themselves and the astonished cook. Out they went on the other side and down through the bushes to the river. A troop of terrified baboons fled out of their path and went galumphing into the woods where the leopard and her cubs had been found the night before.

It is easy to scare an African, but after the danger is over he just as easily laughs. And now the whole camp rang with laughter over the confusion that had been caused by the two living locomotives.

As they cackled and giggled, they went to work putting up the badly battered tent, and the cook collected his kitchenware, raked together the scattered embers of his fire, and started all over again to prepare breakfast. But everyone kept a sharp eye out for more rhinos.

'Why did they barge through the camp?' Hal wondered.

'They probably didn't even realize there was a camp,' Hunt said. 'Rhinos are just about the stupidest animals in Africa. They have very poor eyesight.

Those two brutes probably didn't see the tents or the fire. They simply knew there was a river down below, and nothing was going to stop them from getting to it.'

A plaintive mew came from the cage of the baby leopards. The dog had been let out earlier to take her morning run. Now she was back, looking into the cage and whining softly. The two cubs stood on their hind feet, with forefeet clawing the wire screen as they looked out at her and mewed.

'How about breakfast for the cubs?' said Roger.

'That's a bit of a problem,' his father said. 'They need their mother's milk, but since she is dead we'll have to mix up some powdered milk. Then we'll warm it a little over the fire.'

This was easily done. But it was not so easy to work out how to get the warm milk into the cubs. Some was poured into a dish and placed inside the

cage. The cubs smelt it eagerly but evidently had no idea of how to lap it up.

'What we need is a couple of feeding-bottles with rubber nipples that they can suck, just as they have been used to feeding from their mother. But I'm afraid we won't find anything like that in camp.'

'Can't we spoon-feed them?' said Roger.

'We'll try it.'

Roger opened the cage and drew out one of the cubs. It wriggled and snarled, but did not try to bite or extend its claws. Roger held it firmly while his father placed his hand beneath the jaw, and pressed his thumb into one cheek and fingers into the other. That would open a cat's jaws, or a dog's. But the leopard's jaws were too strong and remained tightly closed.

Now Hal got into the act. While Roger held the animal and his father poised the spoon, Hal took

hold of the upper and lower jaws, confident that he could pull them apart.

They would not budge. All the strength of the small animal seemed to be concentrated in those jaws.

Suddenly it wrenched its head about and sent the milk flying. Milk dripped from the little whiskers, but the jaws were still clamped shut.

Hal laughed. 'Funny thing, when three big men can't make one small cat take its breakfast.'

Zulu was nuzzling the ball of golden brown fur with her nose and whimpering softly.

'What's the matter, Zu?' said Roger. 'What are you trying to say?'

Hunt studied the dog. 'I think I know,' he said. He called Mali, the dog's owner. 'Mali, didn't you say that Zu has just had pups?'

'It is so, *bwana*.'

'Then perhaps she's still in milk. She seems to have adopted these little rascals. Perhaps she wants to feed them. Put the cub back into the cage, Roger, and let's see what happens. Leave the door open.'

Zu, with a little bark, followed the cub into the cage, put one and then the other into the basket, got in herself, and lay down.

But nothing happened. The small animals turned away from the dog. One of them began to climb out of the basket.

'They need a little coaching,' Hunt said.

He went into the cage on his knees, took both cats by the nape of the neck, turned them about, and pressed their noses close to the food supply that was waiting for them. The cubs tried to wriggle out of his grip. When they found they could not, they relaxed. Their sense of smell gradually won them over to this unfamiliar foster-mother and they began to lick, then to suckle greedily.

Hunt could now let go and crawl out of the cage, and the cubs' breakfast continued with many little gurgling sounds of satisfaction. Roger was about to close the cage door, but his father said, 'I don't think you need to. Now that they know where they can find their dinner, they won't run away.'

When their meal was finished, the two cubs stretched themselves out contentedly and purred like organs. The dog began to lick their woolly hides.

'Getting their morning bath,' Roger said.

'It looks like that,' Hunt replied. 'Actually what it does is to massage the muscles and aid digestion. Many animal mothers do it by instinct, without knowing why — dogs, leopards, lions, antelopes and others.'

Roger admired his two pets — he considered them his. Their fur was like dark gold. They didn't look much like leopards. The circles and spots that mark the grown-up leopard were as yet only soft blurs — they would appear more plainly as the animals grew older. The whiskers, still short, would become long and bristly. The greenish-yellow eyes were fierce, but not so fierce as they would be. The teeth and jaws were already bigger than a grown man's. But the way each little cat staggered around on awkward paws showed that it was still very much of a baby.

'Can we keep them until they grow up?' Roger asked.

'No. They will have to go to a zoo where they can

be cared for properly. Grown leopards don't make good pets.'

'Why not? These little fellows aren't bad-tempered. They haven't put their claws out once. And a leopard doesn't grow very large — like a lion.'

'But they don't keep that sweet disposition when they get older,' Hunt said. 'No matter how kindly they are treated, they finally turn savage. A lion or an elephant can be your friend for life — but not a leopard. Something in their nature makes them suspect and hate everything else that moves. And the leopard is very strong. Zoologists say that it is the strongest animal for its size on earth. A leopard is a wonderful climber. It can run up a tree as fast as you can run on the level. When it kills an animal, it drags the body up a tree and puts it in the cleft of a high branch so that lions and hyenas can't get at it. Many times game wardens have reported seeing a leopard shinny up a tree dragging a waterbuck or a zebra three times as heavy as itself. Sounds impossible, but they've proved it by shooting the leopard and weighing the carcasses. And a leopard is more bold than other animals. Ask the villagers. They are more afraid of the leopard than of anything else. A lion won't come into a house, and an elephant can't — but a leopard thinks nothing of creeping in through a door or window and seizing the first living thing it finds.'

'Then why don't the game scouts go out and kill all the leopards?'

'A good question,' his father agreed. 'The answer is that in the scheme of nature the leopard has its place. For one thing, it keeps down the baboons. The leopard is very fond of baboon meat. If it weren't for leopards, there would soon be such vast numbers of baboons that every farmer's field would be stripped clean of every growing thing, and troops of baboons would become so bold that they would make raids upon village people and kill hundreds of them. That very thing has happened in parts of the country where there were no leopards.'

Roger swatted a tsetse fly that had lit on his hand. He looked at his father with mischief in his eyes.

'Well, Dad, if everything is good for something, tell me what's good about a tsetse?'

Hunt grinned. 'You think you've got me there, you young rascal. All right, I'll tell you what's good about a tsetse. First I'll admit it's the most dangerous fly in the world, because its bite can give you sleeping sickness. That can happen, but usually doesn't — most tsetse bites are harmless. But the good thing about this bad fly is that without it you wouldn't be looking now at thousands of wild animals. They just wouldn't be here.'

'How's that?'

'I remember once I was making a trip through the Tsavo game reserve with the warden and I swatted a tsetse. He said to me, "Don't kill the tsetse. It's our best friend. Without the tsetse we wouldn't have any game park." I understood what he meant. The Africans raise millions of cattle and the cattle roam all over the land eating the grass right down to the roots, so that there is nothing left for the wild animals. But there is one place where the cattle can't go. They can't go into any area inhabited by tsetse flies, because the tsetse bite is deadly to cattle. So those parts of the country are left for the wild animals to enjoy.'

'But don't the flies kill the wild animals too?'

'No. The wild animals have been living with the tsetse for so many hundreds of years that they have become immune to tsetse bite – they are used to it, and it doesn't hurt them. You notice this village has no cattle. That's because this is a tsetse belt. Of course cattle are good to have, but it's also good to have some places left where the most wonderful animals in all the world have a chance to exist.'

Roger looked at the dead leopard which the men were beginning to skin. 'Too bad we had to kill that one.'

'Yes. But when they become man-eaters, we have to do something about it.'

'Who gets that skin?'

'The American Museum in New York has ordered one.'

Breakfast was ready now, and the hungry hunters fell to with a will. Zulu came out of the cage to get her share. Everyone was too much interested in bacon and eggs and hot biscuits and coffee to notice the cubs until Roger cried:

'They're out. They're running away.'

But the little leopards were not running away. Instead, they waddled in pursuit of their foster-mother. They rubbed against her legs and licked her fur. They sniffed at her dish of meat and turned away. This was not their idea of good food. They were friendly little beasts. One of them scrambled up into Roger's lap and licked his face with a tongue that felt like coarse sandpaper. In no time at all it had rubbed off the skin and drawn blood.

'Ouch!' cried Roger. 'You're just too good to me,' and he pushed the woolly ball down into his lap.

But the little bundle of energy showed surprising strength. He threw off Roger's hand and leaped up on the camp table, one paw splashing into Hal's fried eggs and the other into a cup of coffee.

He was captured and placed on the ground, where he set to work licking off his wet paws.

In the meantime the other cub had disappeared.

'It can't be far away,' Hunt said. 'Look in the tents.'

The men dived into the tents and searched in corners and under cots and even in the canvas bath-tubs, but found no cub. They came out and searched the grass and bushes around the camp, with no result.

Then Roger happened to look up into the foliage of a tree that stood just inside the circle of tents. There was the cub, lying perfectly still on a low branch, watching with bright eyes as these silly humans ran here and there hunting for him. Now he really looked like a leopard rather than just a ball of woolly fur. His little claws gripped the branch. There was an almost savage blaze in his yellow-green eyes. He was ready to spring on anything passing below. This was something he had never been taught, but something that leopards have done for thousands of years, and the instinct was planted deep in his nerves and brain.

5
The Unlucky Colonel Bigg

It was just Colonel Bigg's bad luck that he should choose this moment to walk into camp. The leopard, perched high where he could get a good view, was the first to see him. The mischievous little beast crouched low, dug his claws into the branch and prepared to leap upon the newcomer.

Colonel Bigg did not see the ball of fur on the branch. He saw only the tents and a fire and men. And he smelt bacon and eggs. And he was hungry.

While he was still hidden by the bushes, he stopped to spruce himself up. He removed his hat, took a comb from his pocket and combed his hair. He smoothed the kinks out of his hat, replaced it on his head and tipped it at just the right angle. After all, he was a Hunter, or pretended to be, and must look the part. He straightened his bush-jacket and brushed the dust from his safari shorts.

He puffed out his chest like a pouter pigeon and tried to look important. That was not too easy, since he was not important. It so happened that Colonel

Benjamin Bigg, Hunter, was not a colonel and not a Hunter.

He had owned a farm in Northern Rhodesia, but he was not a good farmer. He had gone bankrupt and lost his farm. While he was wondering what to do next, a man suggested, 'Why don't you become a Hunter?'

It was an exciting idea. He, a Hunter!

When a wealthy American, or German, or anybody, wants to go hunting big game in Africa, he hires a Hunter to go with him, a man who knows the country, knows where to find the animals, and knows how to shoot.

When out on safari (a hunting trip) it is the Hunter who bosses the expedition, sees that the camp is supplied with food, tracks the elephant or buffalo or lion, and tells the sportsman when to fire. If the sportsman only wounds the beast and it charges him, it is the Hunter who must save his client's life by bringing down the enraged beast with a bullet in the heart or brain. When the sportsman poses for his picture with rifle in hand and one foot on the dead beast, the Hunter has the right to pose beside him.

It's a proud life, a wonderful life. Who wouldn't want to be a Hunter?

'But it's not for me,' Bigg said. 'I don't know a thing about hunting.'

'Now don't tell me that,' said his friend. 'Haven't you ever shot anything?'

'Only a jack-rabbit. And it got away.'

'No matter. You don't need to be able to shoot. Your client will do the shooting.'

'Suppose he misses?'

'Tell your gun-bearers beforehand to be ready to shoot. Then if your sportsman misses, you and your gun-bearers blaze away all at the same time. One of them is bound to hit home, and who's going to say it wasn't you?'

'But I wouldn't know where to take anybody to find game.'

'What of it? Your Africans will know. Leave it to them. Let them do the work and you take the credit.'

It sounded good. Bigg smiled. 'How do I get started in this racket?'

'Put an advertisement in one of the sport magazines. You know — "Professional hunter, long experience, expert shot, results guaranteed" — then give your name and address. Oh, there's one more thing. You ought to have a handle to your name.'

'Like what?'

'Captain or major or something. Makes it easier to sell yourself. Gives you class.'

Benny Bigg thought it over. If captain would be good and major better, then colonel would be still better. So he became Colonel Benjamin Bigg, Hunter.

His advertisement in *Outdoor Life* brought a radiogram from a wealthy New Yorker: 'State price for thirty-day safari.' He must have been wealthy, since he did not back down when Bigg replied with a quotation of seven thousand dollars for his expert services for one month.

Bigg's offer was accepted. Bigg instructed his client to meet him in Nairobi, where most safaris are outfitted.

The client, Hiram Bullwinkle, together with his wife, arrived at the time set. In the lounge of the Norfolk Hotel they met the famous hunter to whose skill and daring they were going to trust their lives for the coming month.

Colonel Bigg played his part to the limit. He casually referred to his exploits during the war (he didn't say which war) and tossed off the names of some of his former clients, such as the Archduke of Austria and the King of Norway. Mrs Bullwinkle was entranced with this romantic hero of war and wilderness. Mr Bullwinkle was impressed, but a little uneasy. Somehow this professional hunter seemed a little *too* good.

Bigg went to an outfitting firm which did the things he didn't know how to do for himself. They got for him the necessary game licences, experienced African gun-bearers and trackers, food supplies for thirty days, tents, cots and folding bath-tubs, jeeps and Land-Rover.

So the safari took off, the clients guided by the 'colonel', the 'colonel' guided by his Africans.

For the first week everything went fairly well. Mr Bullwinkle bagged an elephant. His own bullet merely wounded the beast, but the gallant Hunter and three black gun-bearers all fired at once and the elephant dropped dead.

It was odd that a monkey in a tree fell dead at the same moment. Colonel Bigg explained that one of his gun-bearers was not a very good shot. But Mr Bullwinkle remembered that the Hunter's gun had most curiously wobbled about and at the moment of firing seemed to be pointed rather above the elephant's back and directly towards that monkey.

A waterbuck, a wildebeest and a zebra were added to the bag, but each time there seemed some doubt about the Hunter's part in the act. Mr Bullwinkle, who had some knowledge of men, began to suspect that his Hunter was a fraud.

Then came the day of the lion. Mrs Bullwinkle ventured a hundred feet from camp to get a shot at a Tommy gazelle. She carried a .275 Rigby, which was just right for a gazelle but not for big game. She was not afraid, for her Hunter was beside her and he carried a .470 Nitro Express, which was tough enough to tackle anything alive.

What should pop up out of the elephant grass but a huge male lion! He gazed for a moment at the two advancing hunters; then, since he was not looking for trouble, he turned to go. Mrs Bullwinkle knew her gun was not built to shoot lion.

'Get him!' she whispered. Colonel Bigg glanced around. His gun-bearers were not close enough to help him this time. Anyhow, there was nothing to fear. The lion must be a coward. He was running away. What a feather it would be in the colonel's cap if he could bag this lion! Bigg raised his heavy gun and fired.

What happened then scared him out of his wits. The lion, wounded just enough to become angry, wheeled about with a savage growl and came straight for his tormentor.

Colonel Bigg dropped his gun and ran for his life. Mrs Bullwinkle stood her ground and fired. With a final leap the big cat was upon her, teeth and claws tearing into her flesh. She heard another explosion, then knew nothing more.

She woke to find herself on her cot in the tent. The senior gun-bearer had just finished treating and bandaging her wounds.

'What happened?' she said.

'This man got in a shot just in time,' said her husband. 'The lion is dead.'

'Where is Colonel Bigg?'

'Gone. I sent him packing. I told him if I ever see him again I'll kill him.'

'But we can't get back to Nairobi without him.'

'Nonsense. Our Africans will get us back. They've been the brains of this trip all along. Do you realize you'd be dead now if it hadn't been for this gun-bearer? Bigg ran like a scared rabbit and left you to the lion. Hunter indeed! He's a fake and we're lucky to be rid of him.'

So Colonel Bigg wandered for three days and nights before the smell of eggs and bacon led him to the Hunt camp.

He did not arrive unobserved. Roger saw him stop to comb his hair, set his hat at a rakish angle, and take on the air of a big Hunter. Roger also saw the crouching cat on the branch. And the stranger saw Roger.

'My boy,' he called. 'I want to see your master.'

Roger didn't like to be called 'my boy' and he didn't care for that word 'master'. With mischief brewing in that innocent-looking head of his, he came forward and stopped just short of the half-hidden leopard. To reach him the stranger would have to pass under the branch.

'Good morning, sir,' Roger said politely. 'What name shall I give my — master?'

The stranger drew himself up to his full height. 'Colonel Benjamin Bigg, professional hunter.'

'Who is it, Roger?' came the voice of John Hunt.

'A very important person, Dad. You'd better come.'

Hunt joined his son, and would have gone on directly beneath the branch to shake hands with the visitor if Roger had not stopped him with a hand on his arm. The newcomer repeated his name and rank.

Hunt thought he knew all the Hunters, but he had never heard of this one. But he only said:

'You are welcome. What brings you out so early in the morning? Is your camp near by?'

'It is not, sir. I was guiding an American fool and his wife, who is a bigger fool. I rescued them repeatedly when their own folly led them into danger. They would not obey my instructions. Therefore I cancelled my contract and sent them back to Nairobi.'

'And you?' Hunt said. 'You struck out alone? No car, no gun-boys, no supplies?'

'Think nothing of it,' replied Bigg loftily. 'I know this country like the palm of my hand. And so long as I have this' — he tapped his rifle — 'I won't go hungry. Plenty of game about, and I'm not a bad shot.'

'Then I suppose you've already had your breakfast?'

Bigg looked beyond Hunt to the fire and the breakfast table, and his mouth watered.

'Well, well, I'll sit with you if you like, but I won't

promise to eat anything. I'm pretty full.' He patted his stomach. 'Nothing like a buffalo steak grilled over an open fire.'

'So you killed a buffalo this morning? Pretty tough customer for one man to tackle.'

Bigg swelled up like a bullfrog. 'After you've been in this business as long as I have, you forget how to be afraid.' He took a step towards breakfast. 'No, no, I don't scare easily.' He took another step. He was almost under the branch. Roger prayed silently, 'One more, just one more.'

Bigg took one more step. Then he let out an unearthly scream as a snarling something came down on his head, making him stumble and fall. He dropped his gun, wildly waving his arms and legs to rid himself of this horrible beast, all the time shrieking and yelling as if his last moment had come.

Hunt picked up the baby leopard and helped the terrified man to his feet. When Bigg saw the size of the wild beast that had attacked him, he turned red. Hunt pretended not to notice.

'You will at least have a cup of coffee,' he suggested, and led the way to the table.

Bigg had little to say as he put away six eggs, eight rashers of bacon, ten helpings of hot breads with butter and honey, and five cups of coffee. Hunt, realizing that his guest was really hungry, had the cook broil a large antelope steak. Bigg made short work of it. Then, after a few more cups of coffee, his self-importance showed signs of coming back.

'By the way,' he said, looking about, 'who is your Hunter?'

'We have none,' Hunt said.

'What? No Hunter? You *are* in a bad way. Where do you come from?'

'New York.'

Ah, thought Bigg, another innocent New Yorker. Bigg had fooled one New Yorker — at least for a week — perhaps he could do better with this one.

'A city man,' said Bigg. 'The streets of New York are hardly the place to learn about big game, are they now?'

'I suppose not.'

'So you know nothing about hunting?'

Hunt smiled. 'A little.' He did not think it necessary to explain that he was not just a city man. He had a house in the city but spent most of his time at his animal farm in the country. There the wild animals gathered in Africa, India and South America were held until they were bought by zoos, circuses or carnivals. And he did not think it necessary to say that after many safaris in Africa he knew more about big game than most Hunters. He could not only shoot animals, he could take them alive, which is much more difficult.

And his sons were also good hunters. In the Amazon jungle, under his direction, they had taken alive many strange creatures, including the giant ant-eater, the tapir, the anaconda (largest of all the world's snakes) and the jaguar. In Pacific waters they had captured the great sea-bat, the giant squid and the octopus, and had gone deep into the sea in search of pearls and the treasure of sunken ships.[1]

[1] For the previous adventures of Hal and Roger, see *Amazon Adventure, South Sea Adventure, Underwater Adventure, Volcano Adventure* and *Whale Adventure* by Willard Price.

'I'll tell you what I'll do,' said Bigg grandly. 'You need me, that's plain, and I won't fail you. It's lucky that I just happen to be free. I'll guide you, and it will cost you very little – let us say only three hundred pounds a week. But mind you, I can't do it for long, I have too many other important engagements coming up.'

'No thank you,' Hunt said. 'I wouldn't think of taking up your valuable time. I hope you have a safe trip back to Nairobi.'

Panic seized Bigg. He dare not go out again into that wilderness full of ferocious animals. If they did not get him and give him a quick death, he would die slowly of starvation and the vultures would pick his bones. As for Nairobi, he had not the faintest notion whether it was north, south, east or west. Somehow he must manage to stay under the protection of this safari.

Hunt saw the anxiety in his visitor's eyes. His heart melted. Hunt was naturally kind to animals, and no less kind to the human animal. He had no liking for this big bluffer, but he could hardly turn him out at the mercy of the risks of jungle and plain.

'We don't need a Hunter,' he said. 'But if you'd like to remain with us as a guest until we get out of the game country, we'd be happy to have you.'

Bigg felt as if a great load had been taken from his shoulders, but he was careful to conceal his relief.

He pursed his lips and nodded slowly, as if giving the matter great thought. 'I'm a pretty busy man,' he said. 'Still, I can't desert you, after seeing the trouble you are in.' He waved his hand airily. 'Forget the fee. I'll stay with you a few days at least if by doing so I can render you a service.'

The best service you can give us, thought Hunt, is to keep out of our way. Aloud he said:

'Make yourself at home. I'll get the boys to put up a tent for you.'

6
Hip-Hip-Hippopotamus

The largest lawn-mower Roger had ever seen was cutting the grass.

Just outside the camp, a huge mouth as broad as a door, backed up by a body as big as a safari tent, moved along, the great jaws champing the grass clear down to the roots and leaving a bare path four feet wide.

'Crazy!' said Roger, hardly believing his eyes.

At the sound, the monster stopped chewing, raised his head and looked at Roger with huge goggle eyes that seemed to stick out like glass balls from his flat face.

He took a step towards Roger, then stopped as if to think. This queer, two-legged thing was not doing him any harm, so why should he bother with it? He did not fear it. He could take it at one bite. But it was not his idea of good food. He liked grass better.

'Look!' Roger had found his tongue at last. Hal and his father turned. The hippo's ears went up, and his eyes seemed to reach out a little farther.

'Steady,' said Hal. 'He's not likely to charge unless we give him cause.'

'He has plenty of room for it,' his father said. 'His stomach is eleven feet long — almost as long as he is. I'd say he measures about fourteen feet over all.'

'How much does he weigh?'

'Probably between three and four tons.'

'See him yawn!' cried Roger.

The hippo, perhaps to show his indifference to these creatures, or because he was still quite sleepy, opened his jaws in an enormous yawn. He revealed a great pink cavern four feet wide and four feet deep. Roger could easily have stepped inside it — but he had no intention of doing so. The yawn was edged with immense teeth. Most of them were grinders, but those in front were canines three feet long.

'Lots of elephants don't have bigger tusks than that,' marvelled Roger. 'Are they as dangerous as they look?'

'They will go through metal. And these tusks are not unusually large. I've seen them four feet long. The upper teeth grind against the lower and that keeps them worn down. But if an upper canine breaks off, the lower has nothing to stop it from growing. The greatest length of a hippo tusk ever recorded was five feet four inches.'

'Are they any good — those teeth?'

'They're extremely hard, harder than elephant's ivory. For many years they were used to make false human teeth. I suppose a lot of sportsmen who have come over here hunting hippos didn't realize that they had hippo teeth in their own heads.'

'Do museums want hippo heads?'

'They do. That head would bring seven hundred pounds. But we can do about four times as well as that if we deliver a live hippo instead of a dead head. I think the Hamburg Zoo would like this baby.'

'Baby!' exclaimed Hal.

'Yes. He's not full grown. He's still young enough to get used to a zoo and not be homesick for Africa.'

The hippo was still yawning. 'I never saw such a long yawn,' Roger said.

His father agreed. 'Yes, he's the world's biggest yawner. Sometimes when he comes up out of the water and yawns, he throws his head back so far that he topples over backwards. But his yawn can be very useful. When he lies at the bottom of the river he points his head up-stream and holds his big mouth open, and sooner or later some fish that are being carried down by the current will find themselves going down his throat.'

The great thick lips were rosy red. 'Wonder what kind of lipstick he uses,' Roger remarked. 'It would take just about a quart for each lip. He must like red. He has it all over him.'

The whole great black hulk was covered with a reddish moisture. 'Naturalists used to say that the hippo sweats blood,' said Hunt. 'But it's just a red perspiration. The hippo doesn't like the heat. That's why he likes to spend most of his time under water. He easily gets sunburned. If he is out in the sun very much he has to use skin lotion. The skin lotion he prefers is mud. You wouldn't think a hide two inches thick would get sunburned — but look at those big cracks in the back of his neck. He'll fill them with mud when he gets to the river. Once I caught a

young female hippo that was suffering so badly from sunburn that we had to give her an injection of forty c.c.s of penicillin. Then we dug a good mud-hole for her to wallow in, and within a week she was all right.'

Eight white tick-birds sat on the monster's back and went about picking at the hide. They paid special attention to the wrinkles, in which they could usually be sure of finding ticks or other biting and burrowing insects. The hippo never shook off the birds. Even when one flew into his mouth after a flitting insect, caught it, and settled down on a great tooth to enjoy it at leisure, the hippo did not clamp his jaws shut to punish the impertinent bird.

'The tick-birds are the hippo's best friends,' said Hunt.

When the bird had flown away, the great red cave

slowly closed and the mammoth beast again looked suspiciously at the three humans. He snorted, tossed his head, and waggled his great rear.

'Just trying to scare us,' said Hunt.

'He couldn't catch us anyhow,' said Roger. 'He's too big and fat and heavy. I could run twice as fast.'

'That's what *you* think,' Hunt said. 'In spite of his weight, he can gallop as fast as a horse. Besides, bushes that would stop you cold would mean nothing to him. He'd go through them like a bulldozer. Never try to race a hippo.'

The hippo had returned to his job of eating a path and was beginning to move off.

Hal turned to his father. 'How are we going to catch him?'

'To catch him I'd need your help.' He looked at the bandages that covered the ant-jaws holding together the cut on Hal's arm. 'And today I think you'd better just rest.'

'Rest, nothing! The arm is O.K. Doesn't hurt a bit. Let's go after that fellow.'

Seeing that his son was determined, Hunt said, 'Very well – but don't be in a hurry.'

'If we don't hurry he'll be gone.'

'If you do hurry you'll be a goner. He's making for the river. If there's one thing a hippo can't stand, it's anything that gets between him and water. Then he goes wild. He can be as savage as a lion and an elephant rolled into one. Don't forget – hippo means horse and potamus means river. The "river horse" loves water, can't bear being shut off from it. Let him get to the river. We'll follow him with the catching trucks and try to haul him out into a cage.'

The plan was perfect, except for one thing. The three Hunts had forgotten about their guest, Colonel Bigg.

The colonel had gone on a little walk down to the river. For a while the grass was only two or three feet high. As he got down into the lower land, where there was more moisture, the elephant grass grew to a height of fifteen feet. Elephant grass is really a grass, though it looks more like a reed or cane. It is very tough and has sharp edges. If you brush your way through it, you are sure to be badly scratched. Often it grows so thick that it is impossible to get through — impossible for a man, but the powerful hippo barges through, making a path that other hippos follow. When many have gone that way, the path is quite smooth and clear, with a wall of elephant grass rising on each side and bending to meet overhead, forming a tunnel.

The 'hippo tunnel' is used not only by the hippos but by many other animals, and man as well.

But when a hippo is passing through the tunnel towards the river, anything that gets in his way is out of luck. The hippo does not change his mind easily. When he is set upon getting to water, he will plunge straight ahead with open jaws and tackle even a rhino or an elephant that blocks his way. And as for a mere man-size creature, such as Colonel Bigg, that would not stop a water-loving river horse for one moment.

The colonel, enjoying the cool morning air and the shade beneath the canopy of grass that closed over his head, was returning from the river. He was thinking about lunch, although he was still full of breakfast. He was reflecting upon what an easy life he had fallen into, thanks to these suckers who had let him join their camp.

There was a rustling ahead, but he paid no attention to it. He walked along with his eyes on the ground. The rustling increased, and he looked up. Two huge bulging eyes stared into his own. Behind them was a great black mass that completely filled the tunnel from wall to wall.

The hippo stopped and so did the man. The animal opened its mighty red mouth full of flashing swords and let out a terrific bellow, a grinding, gritty roar that sounded like the dumping of a load of gravel.

The colonel fired from the hip and, of course, missed. The target wasn't quite big enough for him. The sound further enraged the beast. It came forward at a fast trot, and the colonel promptly turned tail and ran.

He was not worrying too much. Surely he could run faster than this clumsy lubber. This great awkward hulk of fat would never catch him.

A blast of hot air from the big mouth behind him warmed the back of his neck. He dropped his rifle and speeded up. But he could not escape those terrific puffs of hot air. They were like the spurts from a jet engine. One blew off his hat. The beast snorted as if with savage pleasure, and the colonel could feel a great lip, or it could be a tusk, nuzzling against his shoulder.

He stumbled and fell flat. Now the living steamroller would go over him. He would be crushed into the ground by the thousands of pounds of angry fat.

Instead, he felt himself seized by the bush-jacket and tossed up through the grass roof, sprawling through the air, then scratching down through sharp-edged elephant grass to lie at last, gasping and itching, in what seemed like a bed full of razor-blades. He heard the steam-roller thunder by, then splash as it plunged into the river.

Bigg crawled out of his uncomfortable nest into the hippo tunnel. Bloody grass-scratches streaked his face and hands. He was sure all his bones were broken. He felt himself all over and could find nothing wrong except that there were large holes in the back of his jacket, punched by the brute's teeth.

He staggered up through the tunnel, found his gun and picked it up. Then he heard voices and saw John Hunt and Hal coming from the camp. Bigg pulled himself together.

'What's up?' said Hunt. 'We heard a shot.'

'Yes,' said Bigg, trying to collect his thoughts. It never occurred to him to tell just what happened. True to his nature, he must make a big story of it.

'How did you get bloodied up?' Hal wanted to know.

'Hippo,' said Bigg. 'I met him in the tunnel. We had a fight to the finish. But I got the best of him.'

'But these scratches?'

'Made by his teeth. For a while I was practically in his mouth.'

Hunt said, 'Strange marks to be made by teeth. They look more like grass cuts.'

Bigg looked indignant. 'I hope you don't doubt my word, sir. It was a hand-to-hand struggle, against great odds. A thirteen-stone man against a three-ton beast. Finally I managed to get my gun into his mouth and I nearly blew off the top of his head.'

'So you killed him? Where's the body?'

'Oh, he just managed to get to the water before he died. Probably the body has been washed away downstream.'

Hunt smiled. 'Well, suppose we just go and take a look.'

Bigg blocked the way. 'I tell you it's no use. You want live animals, not dead ones. He's as dead as a doornail.'

A thundering hippo snort came from the direction of the river.

'That doesn't sound like a very dead doornail,' Hunt remarked, as he and Hal brushed by the great hippo-killer and went on towards the river. Bigg, still protesting, followed.

They came out on the river bank and there was the hippo, half in and half out of water. Bigg, still unable to believe that he could not fool these 'tourists', insisted that this must be another animal – the one he had shot must have been carried miles away down-river by this time in the current. But the Hunts recognized this to be the same animal that they had studied so carefully as it passed by the camp. The top of its head was not blown off; in fact there was no sign that a bullet had nicked it anywhere.

'We'll go back and get the trucks,' Hunt said. 'Colonel, you might stay here and keep watch. But mind you, no more shooting. You might make a mistake and hit it this time.'

To get the cars to the river, it was necessary for the Africans to hack the hippo path wider with their bush-knives. The largest truck carried a cage eighteen feet long, made of stout two-by-fours reinforced by iron bars.

The young bull hippo was now in deeper water. Only the top of his head was above the surface. He could still hear, see and breathe, because a hippo's ears, eyes and nostrils are not on the front and sides of his head, but on top.

If he wished to go completely under water he could do so quite easily. His eyes remained open, but large valves closed his ears and nostrils. Taking a deep breath before going down, he could stay there from six to ten minutes.

'He's really wonderfully made,' John Hunt said. 'Not only can he stay submerged three times as long as the best human diver, but he can walk along the bottom, eating water-weeds as he goes.'

'He doesn't seem too friendly,' Hal said.

'You can't expect an animal that has just been shot at to be friendly.'

The hippo snorted angrily, then opened his great red mouth and let out a bellow that echoed back from the hills like thunder. Colonel Bigg shivered and kept well behind his companions.

The cage truck was backed up to the shore and a ramp placed, up which the animal might be hauled into the cage. A two-inch nylon rope of great tensile strength was made fast to a powerful four-wheel-drive truck directly in front of the cage truck. The loose end of this cable was drawn back through the cage and down to the water, where it was finished off with a loop large enough to go over the hippo's head.

'But how are you going to get the hippo to put his head in the noose?' Roger wondered.

'We'll have to help him do that,' his father said. 'Joro, bring one of those canoes.' He pointed to native boats drawn up on the shore. 'We'll paddle out and take the noose with us.'

The canoe was brought, and the Hunts along with Joro boarded it. This left Colonel Bigg and the rest of the Africans on the bank. The colonel declined an invitation to join the boating party.

'I think I'd better stay here and help get the beast ashore,' he said. 'You can't depend upon these blacks. Always fail you just when you need them.'

The canoe was a heavy thing, fashioned from a single log of ironwood, and its gunwale was only two inches above the water. The occupants must be very careful to keep their balance or the craft would upset.

Hal tapped the thick side of the boat with his paddle. 'There's one good thing about it,' he said. 'Even a hippo's jaws couldn't make much of an impression on this.'

'I wouldn't be too sure,' Hunt said. 'Up at Murchison an annoyed hippo took the rear end of a car in its mouth and crushed it like a nut.'

'He's gone,' cried Roger. The eyes, ears and nose had sunk out of sight and only a swirl of water remained where they had disappeared.

'He seems to be going towards the other bank,' Hunt said.

'How can you tell?' Roger asked.

'By that line of bubbles. Let's follow him. Not too much noise with your paddles.'

It was several minutes before the hippo broke the surface, snorting and sending up a column of spray like the spout of a whale. He seemed displeased to find the canoe close by. He promptly sank again. This time no bubbles betrayed his position.

7
Canoe, Hippo and Croc

The canoe suddenly rose straight up into the air, teetered dangerously for a moment, then slipped off the animal's back and slumped into the water, the splash wetting everyone aboard. Luckily the canoe did not capsize.

'Favourite hippo trick,' Hunt said. 'He'll probably try it again.'

'I never did see his head,' Hal complained, for he was holding the noose, ready to slip it over the quarry at the first opportunity.

Five, ten, fifteen minutes passed with no sign of the hippo.

'He couldn't possibly stay down all that time,' Hunt said. 'He must have walked off down-river. That's strange. I could have sworn he would attack us again, he seemed so angry.'

Roger pointed to some broad water-lily leaves that lay on the surface. 'What's going on there?' The leaves bulged upwards. Something appeared to be hiding beneath them. As the men watched, one leaf slipped, revealing the hippo's nose. How long had he been concealed there, breathing comfortably, awaiting his chance to attack again?

Two other hippos now broke the surface and glared at the canoe with their great goggle eyes. One of them, evidently a mother, carried a baby hippo on her back.

'They're ganging up on us,' Hunt said.

'But I thought hippos were supposed to have mild dispositions,' Hal objected.

'Generally, yes. But not when they're shot at. Not when they're blocked off from water. Not when they're hunted, and not when they have young ones to protect: I don't like this situation a bit.'

But there was one who did seem to like it. Hal noticed that Joro's eyes were shining with an evil light. A sort of snarling smile tightened the African's lips. He seemed even happier when two crocodiles that had been basking on the shore came off and began lazily circling the boat.

'I was afraid of that,' Hunt said. 'Crocs and hippos often work together. The hippos spill the men out of the boat, then the crocs come in for the kill. Look – the lily pads.'

The leaves no longer bulged upwards but lay flat on the surface. The bull hippo had gone under. The line of bubbles showed his progress. He was coming straight for the boat.

'Paddle!' cried Hunt. 'Let's get out of his way.'

Three paddles dug into the water to propel the boat forwards. The fourth paddle, Joro's, also went into action, but in reverse. Powerfully, he was pushing backwards, holding the canoe exactly in the path of the approaching bubbles.

'Joro!' shouted Hal. But before he could say more, the water exploded by the canoe and the bull hippo shot straight up into the air until half of his body was out of the water, then brought his forefeet smashing down upon the canoe. Hal, watching his chance, got the noose over the animal's head just as the capsizing canoe tossed its occupants into the river.

The four struggled to right the canoe. No, only three. Hal observed that Joro was swimming ashore. He could not understand this. African safari men are not cowards. But Joro was plainly leaving them in the lurch.

There was no time to think about it. The mother hippo had dumped her baby on the river bank and had joined the other two monsters in angry snortings and teeth-clashings, while the two crocodiles, no longer lazy, were swooping closer to the struggling bodies in the water.

It was the bull hippo who put an end to their efforts to right the canoe. His great red jaws opened, his huge teeth glistening in the sunlight closed on the boat, raised it from the water and shook it as a cat shakes a mouse, then crushed it as if it had been an egg-shell. The iron-wood canoe, so hard that you couldn't drive a nail into it, crumpled like paper. Fragments fell to the surface and drifted off.

Roger struck out for shore, Hal close behind, splashing to keep off the crocs. Roger looked back. 'Where's Dad?'

Their father was floating face down. They swam back to him, gripped him by either arm and swam him ashore.

Mali and Toto helped them drag the unconscious

man out of the river and lay him on the sand. John Hunt opened his eyes to find Hal running his fingers over his chest to see if any ribs were broken.

'What happened, Dad?'

'The bow. Came down on my back. Knocked me out for a minute.'

'Are you all right now?'

Hunt tried to move. His face twisted with pain. 'Something wrong back there.'

'We'll get you up to camp right away.'

'Not so fast,' Hunt said. 'First I want to see that fellow safe in his cage. Mali, get going with the forward truck.'

Mali ran to the truck, jumped in, started the

engine and eased the car gently forward. The nylon cable that ran back through the cage to the noose that circled the hippo's neck slowly tightened.

It was going to be quite a pull. Three tons of hippo wanted to go somewhere else. Mali slipped the gears into four-wheel drive.

'Easy does it,' called Hunt. 'Don't choke him. Just persuade him.'

The hippo did not seem to know what to make of it. His enemies had gone, and his anger subsided. Something was around his neck, but it was hardly more annoying than a water-weed. He felt himself slowly drawn across the river. Now and then he struggled and when he did, Mali eased up on the pull. When the struggling stopped, the pull began

again. At last the young bull found himself waddling up on to the bank.

Now he faced the ramp slanting up to the open cage on the truck. This was enough to make any animal nervous. He began to toss his head and bellow.

'Give him the gun,' said Hunt.

Hal knew what his father meant. He took the syringe-gun from under the driver's seat of the truck. It looked like a pistol but it contained no bullets. Instead, it was loaded with a capsule of curare. This is a medicine that can be deadly if too much is used. But a moderate amount shot into an animal only quiets the beast, makes it sleepy and easy to manage.

Hal placed the muzzle against the hippo's thigh and pulled the trigger. The hippo snorted with surprise, pulled at his noose, and performed a heavy dance on the beach. Since no one did anything more to him, he soon calmed down and the men waited patiently for the drug to take effect. After ten minutes the bull's head began to droop as if his huge jaws were getting too heavy for him.

'Go ahead, Mali,' said Hunt.

Mali started his truck and the line through the cage drew taut. The animal yielded as if in a trance. Sleepily he gave in to the pull of the cable and with slow steps went up the slight slant of the ramp into the cage. The cage door was quietly closed behind him.

Hunt tried to get up but sank back with a groan. Hal and Roger, with the willing help of the Africans, picked him up, carried him to the forward truck and laid him on the boards. Then both trucks drove through the hippo tunnel back to camp, very slowly so as not to jolt either the disabled man or the caged animal. Hunt was laid on his cot in his tent. Hal bent anxiously over him.

'It's my back,' Hunt said. 'Slipped disc or bunged-up nerves or something — makes all my left side numb.'

'I think I'd better go and get a doctor,' Hal said.

Hunt grinned. 'You talk as if you'd find one just round the corner. I don't need a doctor. I know what he'd tell me to do. He'd tell me to rest — and perhaps have a little massage. Mali can give me that. He's good at it. I'm sorry to poop out on you this way. If I know these back ailments, it may take a week or two for me to get on my feet. During that time, I'm afraid you'll have to go it alone.'

'Don't worry about that, Dad. Give me your order-sheets so that I'll know what animals are wanted — then we'll go and get them.'

'I know you will. I'm not worried about that. But there's something else.'

He closed his eyes. Hal waited. 'What is it?' he said finally.

'I hate to bother you with this,' his father said, 'but it's something you should know. That leopard-man who tried to lead us away from the trail of the leopard last night — I think I know who it was.'

'Someone from the village?'

'No. Someone from our own camp.'

Hal, greatly surprised, objected. 'Now, Dad, that's not possible. None of our men would do that. Besides, we know where every man was. They're all accounted for.'

'Except one,' said Hunt. 'How about Joro?'

'Well, what about him? You told him to go along with us, but he misunderstood. He stayed in camp.'

'The cook tells me he was not in camp last night. This morning, while it was still quite dark, I saw him creep out of the bushes to his tent. Later, I talked with him. He was very nervous. What he said didn't ring true. He seemed to be a man in torture, torn this way and that. I wanted him to tell me what was troubling him, but he would not. I strongly suspect he was the leopard-man.'

'I can't believe it,' Hal said. 'Joro is a fine man, and a wonderful tracker.'

'Agreed. But didn't you notice anything strange when we were trying to get out of the way of that hippo? We were paddling forwards. What was Joro doing?'

'It *was* a bit peculiar,' Hal admitted. 'He seemed to be paddling backwards. Perhaps he thought we stood a better chance of escape if we backed up.'

'I'd like to believe that,' his father said. 'But I'm afraid he was trying to hold the canoe just where it would be struck by the hippo. To put it plainly, it looked as if he wanted us to be dumped and hoped we would be drowned or killed by the hippos, or the crocs, or both.'

'But he was putting himself in danger too.'

'Didn't you see how fast he got himself out of danger? We stayed to try to right the canoe. Did he help us?'

Hal tried to remember. 'Now that I think of it, he didn't. He set out for the shore as fast as he could go.'

'Right. And when we got ashore, he looked angry and disappointed. His plot had failed. But mark my words, he'll try again.'

'But why in the world should he want to kill us?'

'I don't think he does want to. But that's what he's trying to do.'

Hal looked puzzled. 'Dad, your bump must have affected your brain. You contradict yourself. You say he wants to and doesn't want to. Does that make sense?'

'It makes African sense. It makes Leopard Society sense. This isn't London. A couple of dozen African countries have become independent during the last few years, and they have parliaments and presidents and delegates to the United Nations, and they are making a lot of progress and we hope the best for them. But that must not blind us to the fact that outside the cities, away back in these forests, life can be as savage as it was a hundred years ago. Ninety per cent of black Africans have never been inside a school. Some of them blame everything on the white man. You've heard of the Mau Mau — the secret society that makes its members promise to kill whites. It was at its worst in 1952 but popped up again in 1958, and now it has become more secret than ever and is likely to go on as long as there are white men in East Africa holding land that the blacks think should belong to them. More than twenty thousand people have been killed by this society. Most of the killers don't want to kill — the society makes them.'

'How can they make them want to do what they don't want to do?'

'Simple. They grab a black man and tell him he will be tortured to death unless he takes an oath to kill whites. If he objects, they begin the torture. When he gives in, they make him take an oath to kill, and to make him remember the oath he must eat a dinner of human brains, blood, sheep's eyes and dirt.'

'And the Leopard Society?'

'Like the Mau Mau, but very much older. The Society seizes a good man and makes a bad man out of him. He must promise to kill. He is given a leopard suit and told he can change into a leopard and must defend all leopards. The heads of the Society are usually medicine men. Africans have a deadly fear of medicine men and will do anything they tell them to do. If the new member will not promise to kill, he himself and his wife and children are killed. So what can the poor man do? He is caught in a trap.'

'And you think Joro has been pledged to kill us?'

'It certainly looks that way.'

'Then we'd better fire him, at once. I'll take care of it.'

'Not so fast, Hal. As you said, he's a good man and a good tracker. We need him. What's more, he needs us. He needs somebody to get him out of this horrible trap they've got him into. Now I know it's risky to have a man around who's bent on killing us. But we've run risks bigger than that. Now that we know what to look out for, I'm sure we can take care of ourselves. Tell Roger. And both of you, watch your step.'

'But just what do you hope to accomplish?'

'I don't know yet,' Hunt admitted. 'Somehow, a

way may open up. In the meantime, carry on with Joro as usual. He must not suspect that we know.'

Hal went out, shaking his head. He respected his father's desire to help Joro. But wasn't it pretty dangerous to try to help a man who was out to murder you?

8
The Colonel Dances

Hal counted his troubles.

Some other time he would count his blessings, but just now he was counting his troubles. Number one was his father's accident. Number two was the responsibility that had fallen upon him to take charge of the animal-collecting. Number three was the leopard-man. Number four was Colonel Bigg.

The first thing he saw as he came out of his father's tent was the colonel, posing for a photograph. He had interrupted the men who had been skinning the leopard. The dead animal lay stretched on the grass. Colonel Bigg stood, gun in hand, one foot on the leopard's head. Mali was holding a small camera.

'You are just in time,' the colonel said to Hal. 'Take the camera. Mali is not such a good photographer. It's all set – just get me in the view-finder, then press the trigger.'

'But what's the idea?' asked Hal, quite puzzled.

'Just a picture. Being a Hunter, I have to have a few pictures. Just to show I can kill leopards and things.'

'But you didn't kill this leopard.'

'What of it? I might have done.'

'But you're claiming credit for something you didn't do.'

'Oh, I see, you're jealous, young man. You killed the leopard and you think you did something great. Why, I've killed hundreds of leopards, thousands. Just didn't happen to have a camera with me. Now I have the camera and here's a leopard, and what does it matter whether it's one of mine or not? Tell you what I'll do – you take a shot of me, and I'll take one of you. That way we'll divide the credit, fifty-fifty. That's fair enough, isn't it?'

Hal laughed. 'Thanks, Colonel, I don't want either the credit or the photograph. Hold it.' He snapped the picture and gave the camera back to Colonel Bigg.

Hal walked away, chuckling. He had never met anybody quite like the colonel. The man was harmless enough, so long as he only wanted his picture taken. But a fool was a dangerous person to have along on a safari. This fake Hunter would have to be watched. He might get himself and everybody else into serious trouble.

A scream behind him made him turn round. The colonel was already in trouble. He was dancing and prancing, yelling at the top of his voice, ripping off his jacket, shirt and trousers, slapping his body and stamping his feet.

Hal could guess what had happened. He had seen soldier ants at work during his Amazon journey. Now the ants had been attracted by the leopard's carcass, and when the colonel placed his foot on the animal's head the ants had swarmed up his legs and were puncturing every part of his body with red-hot needles.

Hal ran back into camp. He did not run fast enough to suit the colonel.

'Hurry up! I'm being eaten alive. Do you want 'em to kill me?'

He was astounded when Hal paid no attention to him. Hal had something else to think of besides a dancing colonel.

Soldier ants are one of the greatest terrors of the tropical jungle. They march across the country like an army and devour everything in their path. They swarm over their prey in a thick blanket. They can strip the hide from an elephant.

'Make fire!' he yelled to the Africans. 'A ring of fire all round the camp.'

The ants already in the camp were bad enough. But behind them would be a column of soldiers perhaps a mile long, marching steadily towards the camp.

The colonel would have to take care of himself. Hal dashed into his father's tent. If the ants attacked a helpless man he might be killed.

'Ants!' Hal cried.

His father needed only that one word to get the whole story.

'None here, Hal. The hippo. Quick!'

Hal was out again and racing to the hippo's cage. He would open the cage door and let the animal escape rather than allow it to be murdered by the ravenous ants. The hippo was trembling with fear, for even the largest animals know this danger and dread it. But the ants had not yet climbed the wheels of the truck. Hal jumped into the driver's seat, started the engine, and drove the truck several hundred yards out of camp.

His next thought was for the baby leopards and the dog. He came running back to the camp site, whacking as he ran the few ants that had managed to get on his body.

He found the dog and the spotted kittens huddled together, while Joro thrashed the ground around them with an old shirt, driving away the ants.

To Hal, this was an amazing sight. Here was truly a man divided against himself. Joro was pledged to be a murderer. He was ready to kill men. The savage was strong and fierce within him — yet also inside him was a very gentle heart that prompted him to protect two leopard cubs and a dog.

His own body was not free of the biting ants, but he let them bite as he beat away the danger from the whimpering animals.

Who could hate this good-hearted killer? Hal at last saw clearly that his father was right. Even if it was dangerous to keep Joro, he must be kept and somehow freed from the deadly grip of the Leopard Society.

The ring of fire that the men had made round the camp prevented more ants from coming in, and those already inside were either killed or driven out. The marching army had changed its course to go round the camp and beyond into the jungle. Hal made sure that their path did not take them near the caged hippo.

Now at last he had time to think of the yelping colonel. Bigg had got rid of his last scrap of clothing and was grabbing himself here and there and wherever he felt a new bite. The huge ants, never less than half an inch long, dug their pincers into the flesh and did not relax their hold, even when their entire bodies except the head had been torn away.

The tingling of his own arm reminded Hal of the line of heads that closed his wound beneath the bandage, and he could sympathize a little, not too much, with the cavorting colonel. He pulled out his knife and ran the back of it over Bigg's body, scraping off the heads.

Bigg was not grateful. 'Took you long enough to get to it,' he grumbled. His voice was hoarse from much squawking. He pulled on his clothes. He was still shivering and shaking. Hal turned to the cook.

'Got any coffee?'

'Plenty,' said the cook cheerfully. He had not been bitten, since the ants had kept well away from his fire, so he had been able to attend to his duties as usual. He filled the canteen with strong, hot coffee and passed it to Hal, who poured some of it down Bigg's throat. Hal kept the canteen strapped over his shoulder, in case anyone else needed some of the same medicine.

As Bigg began to feel better, he seemed to expand and grow until he was once more the great Hunter. He surveyed the camp like a general inspecting his army.

'This would never have happened,' he said, 'if I had been running this safari. All this trouble could easily have been prevented.'

'How?'

'With ant-poison. Surely you have some.'

'I believe there are some boxes of it in the supply wagon,' said Hal. 'It's good for ordinary ants. I don't think it would have stopped the soldiers.'

'You don't think? That's what's wrong with you young fellows, you don't think. This camp is still in danger, you know. Those ants are going round us just now, but they may change their evil little minds at any moment and come straight through the camp. But don't you worry — I'll fix them.'

He went to the van that held the supplies, rummaged about among boxes and packets, and emerged with a tin of ant-poison.

He just wants to show how clever he is, thought Hal. Well, let him have his fun.

Bigg stepped over the burning bunches of grass, twigs and sticks with which the men had ringed the camp, and began to sift ant-poison on the hurrying ants, taking good care to keep his feet weil away from the line of march. The ant army came on in a column about a foot wide, the soldiers marching so close together that they touched. They did not seem to mind the poison that sifted down upon them like a miniature snow-storm.

Bigg followed the column back to where it emerged from the forest, sifting as he went. He walked on into the woods until he could no longer see the ants because of the thick underbrush.

Then, well satisfied with himself, he returned to camp. The ants, however, kept marching by. For an hour they kept coming. Then the last of them passed and the protecting fires were allowed to die out.

Bigg, his self-conceit completely restored, beamed upon Hal.

'Well, my boy, it's a good thing I thought of the ant-poison, isn't it? You see how well it worked. Next time you'll know what to do.'

Hal was about to point out that the poison had not worried the ants in the least. But what was the use of arguing? He would never convince Colonel Bigg. So he smiled and said nothing.

9
The Poisoned Baboon

A loud clatter of voices came from the woods — shouts, barks, what sounded like the wail of a suffering infant, and high-pitched screams like the voices of women in distress.

Hal stopped to listen. The sounds were almost human, but he knew they came from the large troop of baboons that inhabited the forest. What was bothering them?

He pulled out his father's order-sheets. Baboons — yes, a travelling circus wanted two of them.

Perhaps if he wandered down to the woods and took a look at the troop, he could think out the best way to capture two baboons. Besides, he was curious to find out what was the cause of all this disturbance.

He walked slowly down to the edge of the forest, following the poison trail laid by Colonel Bigg. As he came in under the trees and saw angry baboons in every direction, he realized that he should have brought a gun, or at least some staunch companions, for these brutes were in anything but a good mood.

Everywhere, on the ground, in the branches, the baboons, sometimes called dog-headed monkeys because of their long, dog-like faces, peered angrily down at him. He made a hasty estimate of their number. There must be three hundred of them.

As a naturalist, he had learned enough about baboons to know that he was in real danger. All the scientific reports on animal behaviour that he had read, and all the hunters he had talked with in Nairobi, agreed that baboons are among the most quick-tempered of animals. At one time they might be as mild as milk, but when they become excited there is no animal more savage.

The big fellows weigh eleven stone, and one of them is a match for a man. Two of them can tear a leopard to bits.

They are more to be feared because they are remarkably intelligent. They react much like human beings. Throw a stone at a baboon and he will throw one back, and his aim is good. He will pick up a stick and use it as a club.

He knows how far an average rifle will shoot and keeps just far enough away to be out of range. He likes to tease the man with the gun. He will put his head down, look at the hunter from between his legs, and make faces at him.

Only the birds have sharper eyes. Scientists credit the baboon with eyes equal to eight-power binoculars.

When they make a raid on the farmer's crops, one of them stays up in the top of a tree to act as a sentinel. He gives warning of any approaching danger.

But he knows the difference between a man and a woman. Also the difference between a man with a gun and a man unarmed. He gives a shrill alarm when he sees a gunman, a mild alarm when he sees a man without a gun, no alarm whatever at the appearance of an unarmed woman.

A ranger had told Hal that the baboons knew his car and kept well away from it. When he wanted to approach them closely he had to use another car. Also the baboons recognized the uniforms of the African game-scouts, who are called askaris. When a farmer saw his crops being ruined by animals, he would call the askaris. They would come in, shoot some of the marauders, and scare off the rest.

That would work very well if the animals were rhinos, buffaloes, hippos, wart-hogs, forest pigs, or even elephants.

It didn't work with baboons. As soon as they saw the uniforms, they didn't wait to be shot at. They disappeared as if by magic. When the askaris had gone, they would return and continue their thievery.

To get close enough to shoot them, the askaris must take off their uniforms and put on plain clothes so that they looked like ordinary villagers. And as they walked towards the baboons they must conceal their guns behind their backs.

Even so, a baboon sentinel up in a tree might catch sight of a gun and give the alarm, whereupon every baboon would promptly vanish.

The baboon is smart enough to know what is good to eat. He is not like the lion who will eat no grass, the elephant who will eat no meat, the crocodile who will eat no vegetables, the leopard who will eat no shrubbery, or the giraffe who eats only the leaves of trees.

The baboon, like the human being, has learned the value of many different kinds of food. He enjoys fruit, berries, sprouts, vegetables, insects, worms, snails, young birds, and when he is very hungry he may kill and eat pigs, sheep, lambs, goats, chickens and dogs.

He has one great advantage over man. A man cannot take more food if his stomach is already full. A baboon can. He stores the extra food in his cheek pouches. He keeps it there until there is room for it in his stomach. Then he takes it out of these storage pockets, chews and swallows it.

A scorpion is dreaded by most animals because of the poisonous stinger at the end of its tail. The intelligent baboon does not worry about that. He knows exactly where the stinger is and how to pinch it off and throw it away. Then he eats the scorpion.

If you let baboons alone they will let you alone. That's a pretty good general rule. But it's not always true. Suppose someone else has made the baboons very angry. Then you happen to come along. They may take out their anger on you.

Hal faced three hundred angry baboons. Certainly he had done nothing to provoke them. Had anyone else annoyed them? Had anyone from the camp been in the woods today?

He could think of no one until his eye happened to rest upon a pale-green dust on the ground. Ant-poison! The blundering Colonel Bigg had been there and left a trail of poison.

But why should that bother the baboons? They were wise enough not to eat poison.

A pitiful wailing like the loud crying of a woman

came from a female baboon whose arms were wrapped round a screaming baby. Suddenly Hal understood. The small baboon's lips were covered with a pale-green foam.

Not as wise as its elders, it had eaten some of the green poison. Now it was suffering terrible pain. It twisted, writhed and screamed in its agony. Death was not far away.

The troop could not punish Colonel Bigg, but here was a man they *could* kill and they showed every intention of doing so. They bared their great canine teeth, furiously barked and screamed, and danced up and down with rage.

Hal knew that one false move on his part would bring them upon him like an avalanche. If he picked up a stone and threw it, that would seal his own fate.

He stood perfectly still and calculated his chances. If he turned his back on them and ran, they would overtake him.

Perhaps he could quietly withdraw. He took one step backward, then another. He heard baboon voices behind him. He turned and saw that his escape was cut off. The three hundred baboons had so distributed themselves that they completely surrounded him.

Now they were beginning to move in on him and their angry jabbering rose to a high pitch. One by one they would leap forward, then back, then forward again. Each of these cavortings would leave them a little closer to their victim.

Hal gave up any idea of escape. He would try

something else. If baboons were so intelligent, he would appeal to their intelligence.

Instead of retreating farther, he took a step forward. The surprised baboons shrank back a little and there was sudden silence.

Quietly, Hal spoke to them. He said anything that came to his mind. It didn't matter what the words were, because they couldn't understand words. But they could understand the tone of his voice. It was gentle and kind, and there was no fear in it.

As he spoke, he looked at the suffering youngster. He loosed the strap from his shoulder and held his canteen out at arm's length. He shook the canteen slightly so that the splash of the liquid could be heard. Then he raised the canteen to his lips as if to take a drink. Again he stretched it out towards the baby, all the time speaking gently.

He took another step forward. Immediately the baboon mother screamed and began to back away. But the baboons behind her did not let her go.

Three grave, wise old fellows seemed to be reasoning with her in a sort of conversation made up of low grunts and barks. They appeared to be saying:

'Perhaps he isn't so bad after all. Perhaps he can help your baby.'

The mother was hard to convince. She clutched her infant more closely and tried to slip away. When Hal took two more slow steps forward, she screamed with terror and that started the baby shrieking once more. Some of the other man-haters in the troop began roaring anew, and their savagely bared teeth did not make Hal any more comfortable.

He stood perfectly still until the noise died down. Then he spoke soothingly and offered the canteen once more.

It was the baby itself that decided in favour of Hal. It watched him with great round eyes, then reached out its hand towards the canteen. Hal did not move. The baby, straining to clutch the canteen, tried to free itself from its mother's grip. It had the curiosity of any child, the desire to get hold of a strange new thing and play with it.

It began a loud whimpering. The mother, losing patience, turned her brat upside-down and whacked its little red bottom. She tried again to escape, but now she was completely walled in.

Hal had only a few feet more to go. He went down on one knee. Now he did not look quite so terrifying.

Little by little he inched forward. His heart was beating wildly. He was quite aware that this was a dangerous experiment. Perhaps this strong, bitter coffee would counteract the poison. On the other hand, perhaps it would kill the patient. If it did, the 'doctor' would promptly be ripped up into small pieces by three hundred sets of savage teeth.

Suspiciously the baboons watched. How could they be sure that the stuff in this thing was not more poison? But Hal's manner and voice quieted their fears.

Like all animals, they respected courage. If Hal had bolted, they would have been on him in a minute. His easy, steady advance had them puzzled and almost convinced.

One last, long reach and the baby had clutched the canteen. Hal did not allow it to be drawn from his hand. He shuffled forward a little closer to his patient in spite of the angry muttering around him. He removed the cap from the canteen.

Then, very slowly, he raised the canteen, tipped it, and let a little of the contents drip out.

The baby, instinctively, opened its mouth to catch the dripping liquid. Hal poured the coffee down its throat. The baby choked and sputtered, then opened its mouth to get more. The rest of the coffee went down the hatch.

Would it kill or cure? The young baboon closed its eyes, then began to twist and cry. The mother was making threatening sounds, other baboons were snarling, and Hal, looking about, could see nothing but row upon row of great yellow teeth crowding in on him.

Hal laid down the canteen. The small baboon suddenly squirmed out of its mother's arms and lay face down on the ground, panting and wheezing. Hal watched every move in an agony of suspense. If the little beast died, he would die too.

Spasms shook the small body, at first in rapid order, then farther and farther apart. Finally the baby lay without movement.

Hal reached beneath and squeezed the baby's belly, hard. Greenish-yellow curds came in a flood from the youngster's mouth. Hal squeezed again and again, until nothing more came out.

Now, still on his knees, he waited. He had done all he knew how to do. It was not a hot day, but he found himself sweating at every pore. The strain had been greater than he realized.

The barking about him had risen to a steady roar. The mother took up her apparently dead baby and began to wail over it.

Suddenly there was a tightening of the small muscles and the little round eyes flickered open.

The barking of the baboons was suddenly hushed. Then there was a low chattering, but there was no longer any anger in it. The apes began to amble off into the woods.

Hal, his heart bursting with relief, picked up his canteen and screwed on the top. For another ten minutes he waited as his small patient steadily recovered its strength. Now there were no baboons left in sight except these two, mother and child.

Hal rose slowly to his feet. The mother's yellow-brown eyes looked up at him with an expression of gratitude that would warm the heart of any doctor. The baby was chattering and stretching out its small brown hand for the canteen.

Hal turned and started towards camp. The youngster raised its shrill voice, struggled out of its mother's arms and pursued the dangling canteen. Its mother gave it a good scolding, ordered it to come back, but when it did not she ambled slowly after it.

So it was that Hal walked into camp with two prize trophies captured only by love and a canteen.

10
Apes Are Smart

The big baboon stopped when he saw the men. Hal took her hand. On the other side he took the hand of the youngster. He strolled in with his two companions as if he were in the habit of going for a walk with apes every day of his life.

The men stood speechless with surprise. Hal enjoyed the sensation he was causing. Now the men would congratulate him on the capture of these two fine specimens.

Then Roger found his tongue.

'What a happy family!' he cried. He opened the flap of the tent where his father lay. 'Dad, you ought to see the three baboons. Papa, mamma and the baby.'

Hal, grinning at his mischievous brother, took his new friends into the tent.

His father propped himself up on his elbow and carefully examined the big and little apes.

'Perfect. Couldn't be better. But where's the other? Roger said there were three.'

'I'm the other,' Hal said.

John Hunt laughed. 'Roger should be careful how

he calls his brother a baboon. That makes him one too. Not to mention me.'

'As a matter of fact,' Hal said, 'I don't mind being called a baboon. They're pretty smart.'

He told the story of his adventure with the three hundred baboons.

'You did well,' his father said. 'And so did they. They showed rare intelligence. They understood you wanted to help the youngster. Few other animals would have acted as wisely. Baboons can be extremely vicious, but they can also be very friendly when they know that they are not going to be harmed. I wonder what goes through a baboon's mind when he sees a man. We look more like himself than any of the other animals, so perhaps he just thinks of us as fellow baboons, only a little bigger and a good deal more stupid, because we can't speak his language and our eyesight and hearing and sense of smell are not as good as his. We can't run as fast, and we can't climb as well as he can. But he must know that there are some things we can do quite well. We can shoot fire out of the end of a stick, and perhaps we can even cure a sick baby.'

'But I never dreamed,' Hal said, 'that an adult baboon would let me bring it into camp.'

'That's not surprising. Baboons often hang around a camp and even run in among the tents and snatch food. They climb up on cars and stick their hands in through the windows, demanding something to eat. They can sometimes make themselves a great nuisance. They get angry easily, but they become affectionate just as easily. If they are in danger from other animals, they may run to the nearest village for protection. Not long ago, when a gang of men were working in Rhodesia, they heard the roar of a lion and the scream of baboons. Then the baboon troop came running out of the bush and nervously squatted along the track as near to the men as they could get. They did not return to the bush until they were sure the lion had gone away.'

'Are they easy to tame?'

'All apes are easily tamed. Of course, some learn more quickly than others. Some are clever, some stupid, just as some people are clever and some stupid. But they can be taught to do many more things than other animals, because they not only have brains but hands. I wonder if we appreciate our hands. They are marvellous instruments and much of what we do would be impossible without them. Baboons use their hands very skilfully. I'll give you an example. There's a piece of rope. Tie one end of it round the big baboon's neck and the other end to the cot.'

Hal did so. The mother baboon seemed surprised and not too well pleased. She pulled the rope tight and tried to break it. When this didn't work, she sat down, ran her fingers round her neck until she found the knot, and began picking at it. It was a tight knot; yet within a minute she had picked it loose and thrown off the rope.

John Hunt smiled. 'What other animal could do that?'

Somewhat worried by her experience with the rope, the large baboon seized her infant's hand and tried to make off, but Hal hung on to the other small hand.

'I think I'd better slap them into a cage,' he said, 'or they will walk out on us.'

'I don't believe so,' his father said. 'Let them both go, and see what they do.'

The two baboons scampered to the tent opening. When no one chased them, they turned about and looked at Hal with big soulful eyes.

John Hunt laughed. 'You are the best friend they have and they know it. They won't need a cage. You couldn't get rid of them if you tried. If you want to seal the bargain, there are some bananas in that basket in the corner.'

Hal gave each of his guests a banana. The youngster did not know what to do with it and tried sucking it. Then he saw his mother skilfully peeling her banana, and tried to do the same. He made a rather messy job of it but finally got rid of the skin.

The two sat contentedly, eating the ripe fruit, never taking their eyes off Hal.

From that moment on, they considered themselves regular members of the safari and specially appointed to wait upon Hal at all times.

He named the little one Bab and the big one Mother Bab. Bab rode on his shoulder. Mother Bab stole everything she could lay her hands on and brought it to Hal as a gift of love. Hal was kept busy returning articles to their proper owners.

Both baboons insisted on sleeping with him — a slightly difficult matter, since the narrow safari cot was not intended for three occupants. But Hal accepted the drawbacks of friendship willingly and only regretted that the day must come when his two devoted companions must be shipped away to join the American circus.

Mother Bab was terrified when she saw the two pet leopards.

Baboons and leopards are mortal enemies. A leopard would rather have monkey-meat than any other dish under the sun. Mother Bab knew this, but little Bab did not. Neither did the small leopards know it, for they had not yet eaten monkey-meat, or meat of any sort.

The leopards were tumbling over each other in a wild game when Bab first saw them. He wanted to join in the fun. He waddled over towards them, in spite of his mother's cries of warning. He made a final jump and landed on top of the two squirming bodies, and all three rolled over on their backs in the grass.

Mother Bab broke into shrill chattering and ran to Hal, looking up into his face, very plainly pleading with him to rescue her child from these horrible monsters. Hal petted the furry head and spoke softly.

'Now don't you worry, Mother Bab.'

The small baboon and the two baby leopards sat up in the grass and looked at each other. It was as if they were waiting to be introduced.

'Roger,' said Hal, 'what do you call your leopards?'

'Well, *chui* is the local word for leopard. One of these is a boy and the other a girl. So I thought I'd call them Chu and Cha.'

'All right, Miss Cha and Mister Chu, kindly allow me to present Mister Bab.'

Bab reached forward as if to shake hands with

Cha, but he was really interested only in getting his fingers into that lovely gold-and-black fur. Cha gave his hand a playful swat with her paw, then both she and Chu leaped upon the small baboon and rolled him over and over in the grass.

This was a game that both monkeys and cats understand and love. Mother Bab looked on with big, anxious eyes, but her chattering died down.

'You see,' said Hal. 'It's going to be all right.'

He was not quite so sure that it would be all right when Bab disentangled himself, leaped astride Chu's back and went careering round the camp like a jockey on a race-horse. But Chu took it all in fun and finally dumped Bab into a pail of water, from which the young ape scrambled and proceeded to use the fur of the two leopards as bath-towels.

Mischief was the chief occupation of the three play-mates and they took special delight in playing tricks on Colonel Bigg. He was afraid of all three and would wake up yelling bloody murder when Chu pounced upon him in bed, or scream when he reached into a box and Cha's small teeth closed on his fingers. When he dozed off in his camp chair, his mouth hanging open, Bab, who had seen the colonel using toothpaste, would squeeze the contents out of a tube and plaster them over the colonel's teeth.

Bab unfortunately could not read the labels on the tubes, and the colonel would wake up to find his mouth full of vaseline or shaving-cream instead of toothpaste.

He woke up in the middle of the night to hear stealthy movements in the tent. At the same time there was a very bad smell.

It must be leopards, he thought, although he had not noticed before that they had an unpleasant odour. He was afraid to get up and investigate. He buried his head under the covers.

In the morning he found that his safari boots were gone. He padded out in his bare feet, looking for them. Scorpions sometimes wandered through the camp ground, so when he felt a sharp prick on the sole of his right foot he thought he had been stung.

Shouting for Hal, he stumbled back into his tent and threw himself on the cot. When Hal came in, the colonel was foaming at the mouth.

'I'm dying,' he said. 'A scorpion got me. Bring a shot of anti-venom, quick.'

Hal, knowing that if it was really a scorpion bite it could be serious, did not stop to make an examination but rushed out to get the hypodermic, fill it, and come back on the run to the perishing colonel.

'Ouch!' gasped the colonel, as the needle plunged into his thigh. 'You were so long about it, it's probably too late now. I feel the poison creeping up my legs and into my chest. Pretty soon it will reach my heart.'

'By the way,' said Hal, 'where were you stung?'

'On the bottom of my foot. I feel very faint. I'm afraid I'm going to leave you any minute now.'

Hal studied the soles of the colonel's feet. There should be a small hole made by the scorpion's stinger. But there was nothing — nothing but a slightly brown spot like a tobacco stain.

Hal went out and looked over the ground. He picked up a cigarette butt. It was still burning. He brought it in and showed it to the colonel.

'This is your scorpion,' he said. 'You just stepped on a hot butt. I think you'll live.'

11
Hyenas Like Boots

The colonel recovered with amazing speed. Now that he knew he had suffered only a slight burn, not a poisonous sting, his pains disappeared as if by magic.

Of course, he could not admit his own foolishness. He found a way to put the blame on Hal.

'I should think you'd be red in the face,' he said, 'after a blunder like that. Young man, you must learn to think before you act. Imagine — poking a hole in me with that needle and filling me with snake dope for nothing but a cigarette burn! Scorpion, indeed! Where ever did you get that idea?'

'From you,' Hal reminded him.

'I don't recall saying anything about a scorpion. You must learn to use your head, boy, use your head.'

Hal let it go at that.

Mali came in with the colonel's boots. They looked as if sharp teeth had been chewing on them.

'Are these yours?' Mali inquired. 'We found them just at the edge of the clearing.'

'Of course they're mine, you stupid fellow. Why didn't you find them first thing this morning instead of waiting until now?'

He took the boots and turned them over, examining the tooth-marks. 'Ah-ha, I know exactly what happened. It's those cursed leopards. You let them roam all over the camp. They must have been in here during the night. Now look at the boots – they've almost ruined them.'

'Perhaps it wasn't the leopards,' Hal suggested.

Bigg raised his voice angrily. 'What else could it be? Now let me make this plain, young fellow. Those cubs must be kept in their cage at night. Why, they'll be attacking us in our beds next. In their cage, do you understand? Otherwise I leave this safari. Yes, sir, I'll leave you flat.'

Hal grinned. 'Now, Colonel, you wouldn't do that. What would we do without you?'

'In their cage, is that clear?'

To humour the touchy colonel, the leopards were put in their cage when night fell. They didn't like it much, and mewed to get out. Leopards are night animals, and enjoy playing or hunting during the hours of darkness. Chu and Cha were quite unhappy about the whole thing, and Roger sympathized with them.

'Why lock them up just to please that crusty old grouch?'

'If we don't,' Hal said, 'he'll keep on blaming them for what happens. And I have a hunch something more is going to happen.'

'What can happen? The cubs can't get out.'

'I don't believe this was done by the cubs. It must have been a bigger animal.'

'Lion?'

'Who knows? But I know how we can find out.

Would you like to stay up with me tonight and keep watch? We might have some fun, and perhaps catch something.'

Roger was more than willing. All other members of the camp turned in. The two boys sat with their backs against a tree and waited.

Roger was much excited. The mysterious jungle was talking with a hundred tongues.

'What's that?' he kept asking. Hal could not give him all the answers, though he had listened every night and had looked up the cries in his manual.

'I think that boom-boom comes from the hornbill. I know that snort — the wildebeest blasts out air from his lungs through his nostrils. Hear the zebras — there must be a lot of them — chatting like a crowd of people at a cocktail party. The jackal makes that yip-yip. Of course those way-down-deep grunts come from the hippos.'

A roar sounded not far from the camp. 'That's a lion,' Roger said confidently.

'Perhaps, perhaps not. It could have been a hyena.'

'But hyenas laugh. There's one now — what a horrible noise!'

The cry was enough to make the shivers go up and down one's spine. It did sound like a laugh.

'Tee-hee-hee-hee-hee-hee-ha-ha.'

This was followed by a sound that seemed to come from a quite different animal. It started low and rose to end in a high squeal.

'Ooooooo-wee!'

Then there came barks of dogs, yelps of puppies,

howls of wolves. Then once more the deep roar of a lion — or so it seemed.

'All made by the same animal,' Hal said. 'The hyena. They're getting closer. I think we're going to have visitors soon now.'

Roger was squirming uncomfortably. 'Weirdest noises I ever heard. They give me the creeps.'

Hal agreed. 'They sound like lost souls. The Africans think they are the spirits of the dead. They think that old men who die can come back as hyenas. Another story is that witches ride hyenas about all night and make these horrible cries.'

'Well, whatever they are, do you think they can get into the colonel's tent? He zipped up the front tight.'

'You can't keep a wild animal out of a tent if it really wants to get in. Most animals don't want to. The hyena does, and if he can't squeeze in under the side flaps he can easily tear a hole through the canvas with his claws and teeth. And what teeth! The hyena is said to have the most powerful jaws of any living mammal. His teeth will crack the toughest bones.'

'Not the bones of a really big animal, like the rhino?'

'Yes, even those. When lions bring down a rhino, they eat the flesh but leave the bones. When the lions wander off with full tummies, the hyenas rush in and crunch those big bones to bits and swallow them. They chew up the inch-thick hide as if it were so much paper, and they seem to find it quite delicious. That's why they like the colonel's boots. They are made of cow-hide and some of the animal oils are still in the leather. They eat almost anything. At the safari lodge in Amboseli they sneak up behind the cabins, upset the garbage-cans, eat the garbage, and if there is grease on the inside of the garbage-can they will almost eat the can itself — at least they crunch it so badly that it can't be used again. In Tsavo a hunter wounded a hyena, then dropped his gun and ran. The enraged hyena took the iron barrel of the gun in its jaws and twisted it into a useless wreck. Hush! Listen.'

There was a rustling in the bushes just behind the tree. A bad smell came in on the breeze.

'Hyena,' whispered Hal.

'Smells as if he hasn't brushed his teeth,' whispered Roger. He lifted the catching-rope that lay in his lap. 'Shall we nab him now? Better get him before he gets us.'

'I don't think he'll bother us. We're not dead enough for him. He likes something very dead and very smelly.'

The dog Zulu, roused from sleep by the sound or the smell, growled softly.

'Quiet, Zu,' Hal warned. 'Your chance will come later.'

A black shadow about the size of a very large dog slunk out into the camp ground. There was no moon, but the light of the bright African stars was enough to reveal the hanging head and the body that sloped from the shoulders down to the tail.

At once the animal was joined by another, just like it. Hal's spirits rose. Perhaps they could catch the two of them. His hand itched to throw a lasso. But first he would give them a chance to pay the colonel a visit. Somehow he must show the colonel that it was not the leopards who had made off with his boots, otherwise the poor little cubs would have to be locked up every night.

The hyenas sneaked over to sniff at the cage that stood near the cook's fire-place. They even walked into the cage. Now, with a quick run, Hal could have reached the cage and slammed the door shut. But he did not move.

If the hyenas knew that two boys were sitting under the tree, they paid no attention to them. Animals bold enough to crawl into a tent inhabited by a man are not easily scared by a couple of boys. They wandered over the camp ground picking up scraps of bread, meat, skin, anything edible.

Coming near the colonel's tent, they stopped and sniffed again. Would they go in or not? The boys held their breath, and hoped.

The hyenas walked slowly round the tent, pausing here and there to poke their noses under the canvas side-walls. In most places the side flaps were tucked under the ground sheet, making entry difficult. But one of the two discovered a slight gap, and by pulling at it with his teeth he drew out the canvas, then flattened himself to the ground and crawled in through the hole. The other followed him.

In a moment they came again, each holding a dark object in his teeth. Roger gleefully nudged Hal. The dark things were the colonel's boots. The hyenas settled themselves near the fire-place, where the fire had long since gone out, and chewing and smacking noises told the boys that the animals were thoroughly enjoying the colonel's foot-gear.

Hal wondered if the game had gone far enough. Should he act now and save the boots from being completely destroyed? He started up, but a mew from one of the little locked-up leopards changed his mind. No, the colonel should have his lesson.

Besides, it was hardly time yet to try to rope the hyenas. They were still on the alert, looking about constantly, ready to run at any sign of danger. The longer they were let alone, the more at home they would feel and the easier it would be to capture them.

After fifteen minutes of boot-chewing, one of the hyenas was ready for a little desert.

The pots and pans that had been used to cook dinner lay about the fire-place. They had not been washed, for the cook had been afraid to carry them down to the river in the dark. The grease of antelope steaks still covered them and nothing could appeal more to the taste of a hungry hyena.

The beast licked a heavy iron frying-pan, then picked it up and bit into it, just as he would have crunched a large bone. Soon both animals were gnawing away as if iron and copper were the daintiest of foods. The banging of the metal containers against the rocks of the fire-place woke some of the men, and heads began to poke out of tents.

'Now!' said Hal. 'Come on, Zu.'

Both boys and the dog ran forward. The hyenas, still enjoying their meal, hardly noticed. They woke up to their danger only when nooses settled over their necks.

With a howl of surprise they tried to break away. Hal stood firm, but Roger was being dragged towards the bush. Then Zu went into action. She was an experienced safari dog and knew exactly what was needed. She ran in and nipped the heels of the hyena. When the beast turned towards her, she skipped out of the way. She was not taking any chances with those grinding teeth. Roger, when the rope slackened a little, turned his end of it round a bar of heavy cage.

The other hyena, unable to escape, turned with a savage rush upon Hal. Zu lunged again. She knew the dangerous end of a hyena. She didn't make for its head, but always for its heels. The hyena, with a howl of pain, turned upon the dog, but never could quite reach her.

The Africans were coming out now, prepared to help. Their help was scarcely needed. Zu was nip-nipping her victims towards the cage. One of them rushed in, perhaps thinking there might be safety there. Zu, like a sheep-dog, kept herding the other beast towards the door. Finally it joined the first and Hal, leaping forward, slammed the door shut.

Colonel Bigg came waddling out of his tent in his pyjamas – again in his bare feet.

'What's all the noise about?' he scolded. 'Why can't you let a man sleep? What's going on here? Ouch!' – as he stepped on a sharp pebble. 'Where are my boots?'

'There are your boots,' Hal said, pointing to a sort of black puddle near the fire-place.

The boots looked as if they had gone through a meat-grinder. Heavy teeth had ground and mashed them into a black mush.

'Your leopards did that,' raged the colonel. 'I thought I told you to keep them in their cage. I'll kill those infernal little beasts.' He began searching around through the bushes.

'If it's the leopards you're looking for,' said Hal, 'look over there.'

He turned his flashlight on the leopards' cage.

Inside the cage the two cubs stood on their hind feet with their forepaws clinging to the bars, watching the excitement with big eyes that blinked in the strong light of the electric torch.

'They've been cooped up in there all night,' Hal said. 'Thanks to you.'

'Then what ruined my boots?'

Hal turned the light on the hyenas' cage. The two big spotted beasts, heads hanging, paced angrily back and forth, snarling at anyone who came close to the bars.

'They chewed your boots,' Hal said.

'I don't believe it,' retorted the stubborn colonel. 'Your leopards did it.'

'Do you think those two little cubs could chew up a frying-pan?'

'What kind of a question is that? Of course not.'

Hal's light swung to the frying-pan. It was so fantastically twisted, contorted, squeezed, jammed, crumpled, dented and smushed that it would never again fry a steak over a camp fire.

'What do you think of that?' asked Hal. 'Could a couple of baby leopards do that?'

'Very well then,' grumpily agreed the colonel, 'the hyenas did it. It's the last damage they'll do. I'll see to that.'

'Where are you going?'

'To get my gun.'

Hal blocked his way. Broad of shoulder and topping six feet, he made the blustering colonel think twice about trying to barge through to his tent. Hal spoke to the angry man as to a child. At this moment the boy nineteen years of age seemed older than the man past fifty.

'You're not going to shoot anything,' Hal said quietly. 'Remember, we're here to take animals alive, not dead. Those hyenas are worth one hundred and seventy pounds apiece to any zoo. If you don't stop firing that gun at everything you see we'll have to take it away from you. Now, go in and go to sleep. Don't worry about the boots — I'll lend you another pair. And as for the leopards, now that you know they didn't have anything to do with this, you can't object if we free them. Roger, let out the cubs.'

Roger flung open the cage door. Chu and Cha tumbled over each other in their eagerness to get out. They gambolled about through the grass, letting out little grunts and yips of delight.

Colonel Bigg, with a good deal of mumbling and muttering, disappeared into his tent.

Hal, followed by Roger, went in to their father's bed-side.

'Are you awake, Dad?'

'Of course, Hal. I wouldn't have missed this for the world. Good show.'

'Perhaps I was too rough on the colonel.'

'Not a bit of it. The sooner he knows he's not the boss of this safari, the better for him. Congratulations on getting the two *fisi*.' He used the native Swahili word for hyena.

'Well,' Hal said, 'they're worth money, but I can't say they're very pleasant animals to have around.'

'I know what you mean. The hyena has an unsavoury reputation. He makes frightful sounds and he smells bad. He eats dead bodies. People hold that against him. But has it ever occurred to you that we do the same? We eat nothing live, except perhaps oysters. It's a mighty good thing that the hyenas do eat up the dead animals. The wild-animal population of East Africa runs into millions, and every day hundreds of them die for one reason or another. Suppose all those bodies were left to rot, what a stinking jungle this would be! The hyenas are the sanitary squad. They go around and clean things up. They, along with the jackals and the vultures, are the jungle scavengers. We couldn't do without them. Suppose a lion kills a zebra — he eats only part of it, then wanders off. In come the hyenas and eat the bones. Then along come the jackals and eat the scraps of flesh lying about. Finally the vultures arrive and take whatever is left, even gobbling up the bloody sand, so that when they are all done you would never know an animal had been killed on that spot. That's a pretty good clean-up job.'

'They may be useful,' Roger admitted. 'But they look so mean.'

'They do, indeed. But perhaps they're like a lot of people — not as mean as they look. On my last trip to Africa, I saw a hyena run into camp and pick up a scrap and disappear with it into the bushes. In a moment he came back, got another bit, and off he went with it. This was repeated many times. I got curious and followed him back into the bush. There I found his mate nursing her young, and in front of her were all the scraps. The male had brought them all to her without taking one for himself. And you'd be surprised what nice pets hyena pups can be. They don't have the smell of the older animals, and they are full of fun and as affectionate as dogs. That's natural because they are a kind of dog, you know. Part cat and part dog, but more dog than cat.'

12
The Medicine Man

Dawn was beginning to grey the walls of the tent. The flaps opened and the gun-bearer Toto looked in.

'May I speak, *bwana*?'

'Come in, Toto. What's on your mind?'

'The little leopard – Chu – the male – he is gone.'

'Probably just running around in the bushes somewhere,' Hal said.

'No, I saw a man take him and run. A man from the village. I chased him but could not catch him.'

'Why should they steal Chu?'

'I think I know why, *bwana*. Last night I was in the village. The headman is sick unto death. The medicine man said only one thing could cure him. A goat must be sacrificed. It must be burned alive in front of the headman's house. The men caught a black goat and tied it to a stake and piled much wood around it. They set fire to the wood. The medicine man danced around the fire. The goat cried very loudly. The fire burned its legs and then its body, and it died. The medicine man took some of the hot ashes and mixed them with juice squeezed from the body of a toad and made the headman drink.'

'Then what?' John Hunt asked. 'Did the chief feel better?'

'No, he did not. He closed his eyes. His face showed his great pain. His body became as stiff as the trunk of a tree. His son said if he died the medicine man must also die.'

'That must have frightened the medicine man.'

'He was much afraid. He told the people it was their own fault that the medicine had not worked. It was because they did not believe. They did not have enough faith. They had not sacrificed enough. It was too easy to get a goat — they must do something more difficult. And he gave them something very hard to do.'

'What was that?'

'Their headman was no ordinary man, he said, he was their great chief, and a great man must have a great sacrifice. They must feed him the heart of a leopard. Then he would be well. If they did not give him the heart of a leopard within twelve hours, he would die.'

'He was asking the impossible. Leopards cannot be found so easily. It might take them days or weeks to find a leopard.'

'It is so,' Toto said. 'The medicine man gave them this hard thing to do and hoped they could not do it. He thought the chief would die. Then the people could not blame the medicine man. He could say, "I told you what to do and you didn't do it. If you had brought me a leopard within twelve hours, I could have cured your chief. His death is your own fault." The men turned one to the other in long palaver. Though they talked much, no one could say where they might catch a leopard. And I, weary of much listening, came back to camp.'

'I can guess what happened then,' said John Hunt. 'Someone must have remembered that we had two leopards here in camp. So one of the men sneaked down and waited his chance, and after the cubs were let out he grabbed Chu.'

Roger leaped to his feet. Already the medicine man's knife might be cutting out the heart of little Chu.

'Let's get up there in a hurry.'

Hal rose. 'Wait, Hal,' his father said. 'Take the medicine kit with you.'

Hal seized the kit, and the two boys and Toto started on the run up the hill to the village.

They heard the beating of wooden drums, shouting of men, chattering of women. The villagers must be highly excited. Above all this noise rose the howling of a single voice, probably that of the medicine man as he worked himself up into a frenzy in preparation for the sacrifice.

The three burst through the ring of huts. They had not arrived a moment too soon.

There was little Chu, standing on his hind feet, strapped to a post by his neck and his heels, his chest exposed ready for the knife. His little forepaws waved helplessly in the air. He was mewing pitifully.

Before him danced the medicine man. His body and face were painted in many colours. Strapped to his forehead was a pair of antelope horns. Tall egret feathers and ostrich plumes rose from his hair and waved wildly as he leaped about. A lion's mane had been strapped to his chin so that it looked like an enormous beard.

Hanging from his neck by a cord was a tin can with crocodile teeth dangling in front of it. Every move of his body made the teeth crash against the can, keeping up an unearthly din.

Around his throat was a necklace of hyenas' claws. His only clothing was a strip of giraffe skin round his loins. His bare legs and bare trunk were oiled with crocodile fat and he smelt to high heaven.

As he leaped, stooped, twisted and yelled, the long knife in his hand flashed in the sun, and at every sweep its savage point came closer to the frightened leopard.

Around these two central figures danced the people of the village, chanting, praying, shouting, while drummers behind them pounded on hollow logs.

Roger, seeing his pet in danger, did not stop to think of his own safety. He plunged in through the circle of dancers, jerked out his hunting-knife, cut the cords binding Chu and gathered the whimpering leopard in his arms.

Hal and Toto were at once beside him. The noise stopped abruptly. The people stared in astonishment, their mouths hanging open. They waited for the medicine man to strike these impertinent strangers dead.

The medicine man himself glared at them with a look of savage hate. He had to look up to meet Hal's eyes, for the boy was taller than he by a good twelve inches. But he had a knife, and Hal was unarmed. The medicine man screamed with fury and raised his knife. Hal seized his arm, gave it a sharp twist, and the knife fell to the ground.

'I want to see your chief,' Hal said.

The wizard looked blank, understanding no English. Toto translated into Swahili. The man replied angrily.

'He says you can't see the chief. The chief is very ill.'

Hal looked about. One hut was larger than the others. That would be the chief's home. He pressed through the crowd and entered the open door of the hut. Toto was close behind him, and Roger with the leopard in his arms. The medicine man and the villagers followed, and the hut was suddenly full.

On a straw pallet lay the chief. He raised his hand in a weak gesture of greeting.

'My friend,' he said in English.

'If we are friends,' Hal replied, 'why did you let them steal our leopard?'

'It was his plan,' the chief said, glancing at the medicine man, 'not mine. I knew nothing of it until they brought the leopard to the village. It should not have been done. We remember that you killed the man-eater that was killing our children. We are grateful.'

'It was a strange way to show gratitude,' Hal said.

'That is true,' the headman admitted. 'But my people are not so bad as you think. They wanted to save my life. That feeling was greater than their gratitude.'

'They were about to kill our pet.'

'I tried to stop them. But a chief's word is not strong when he is near death. Then the medicine man takes the power. Perhaps I did not try hard enough to stop them. After all, I wanted to live. Perhaps our medicine man is right. Perhaps eating the heart of an animal that grows strong will make me grow strong. You are a good man. You would not want me to die if I could be saved by the death of an animal.'

Hal smiled and pressed the chief's hand.

'Of course I don't want you to die. But how can you believe this nonsense? How could a leopard's heart help you? You are educated. You know the new things, you even speak English. And yet you give in to this foolish old superstition.'

The chief closed his eyes and said gently, 'Not all the old things are wrong. Not all the new things are true. You also have your superstitions.'

Hal felt like a small boy being gently reproved by his father.

'Indeed we do have our superstitions,' he said. 'We have much to learn, and we can learn a great deal from the people of Africa. Still — I *might* have something in this black box that would help you.'

'What is that?'

'A medicine kit. I'm no doctor — but we often have to doctor each other on these trips. You seem to have a fever. May I take your temperature?'

A slight nod was his only answer. But when he opened the kit and took out the thermometer, the medicine man began to jabber violently.

'He says,' Toto translated, 'that he knows this thing. It is full of poison and will kill the chief.'

The headman spoke sharply to the medicine man, then took the thermometer and put it into his own mouth.

Hal took out his handkerchief and wiped the sweat from the headman's face. He put his fingers on the sick man's pulse, watching the second hand of his watch. When he removed the thermometer and looked at the reading, he said:

'No wonder you feel uncomfortable with a temperature of 103 and a ninety pulse. How long has this been going on?'

'Since midnight.'

'And before that?'

'Headache. Chills. Shivering. I thought I would shake apart. They told me the air was warm, but to me it was icy cold.'

'And your appetite?'

The chief turned his head away with a disgusted expression on his face.

'I cannot bear the thought of eating. That is what sickened me most – the idea of swallowing the bloody heart of the leopard. I am sure it would rise again at once.'

'Do you have pain?'

'Everywhere. In every joint, every bone. I could not say where there is pain, for there is no place where it is not.'

'It sounds to me,' Hal said, 'like an acute attack of malaria.'

He took a medical booklet from his kit and turned to malaria. Then he explored the contents of the black box and picked out two bottles, one marked paludrine and the other quinine. He removed one tablet of the first drug, two of the other. He turned to the medicine man.

'Will you bring me a little water?'

The wizard angrily refused. Toto slipped out to the village well and returned with water in an ostrich shell. The chief willingly took the tablets and washed them down. He paid no attention to the excited protests of his medicine man.

'Now, try to sleep,' Hal said. 'In a few hours I'll be back. I expect you to be much better.'

'But if I am worse, my people will make you suffer. I think you had better not come back.'

'I'll be back,' Hal said, and rose to leave the hut.

The medicine man suddenly lunged forward and jerked the leopard from Roger's arms. Roger struggled to get it back.

'Leave it alone,' Hal said sharply. 'There are only

three of us. Do you want to get into a fight with forty men? What's the medicine man saying, Toto?'

'He says he will keep the leopard. If the chief recovers, the leopard will be returned to us. If the chief does not recover, the leopard will be killed.'

Worried about his pet, Roger took it out on Hal. 'Are you going to let them get away with this? What a milksop you've turned out to be! You know they'll cut that cat into little pieces as soon as we get out of the village. Why don't you do something?'

'Come on, you little hothead,' Hal replied, 'before you get us into real trouble.'

The two brothers and Toto started down the hill. A stone caught Hal squarely between the shoulder-blades. The pain made him wince, but he did not turn round. Roger, who had often seen his elder brother's courage, could not understand him now. Hal only said:

'Better a stone than a poisoned arrow. Really, I don't blame them. They're worried about their chief.'

'Well they have a nasty way of showing it,' Roger growled.

At noon the three returned to the village. Men, women and children ran out to meet them with smiles and friendly chatter.

'He must be better,' Hal guessed.

The chief was still lying down, but his eyes were bright and his greeting was warm. 'I'm all right,' he said. 'Just weak.'

Hal found that his temperature had dropped four degrees, his pulse was normal, the chills and the aches were gone.

Roger was looking anxiously about.

'Bring in the boy's leopard,' the chief ordered. A man fetched the small animal and put it into Roger's arms.

Everybody seemed very happy — nearly everybody. The only sour puss left was the medicine man.

It was a bad day for him. His people were laughing at him. His magic had failed. The sacrifice of a goat had not cured the chief. He had failed to take the heart of the leopard. Two boys had stopped him. The high and mighty medicine man, stopped by two boys! And one of these boys had cured the chief!

But the medicine man was not done. He was raving and ranting to everyone who would listen.

'What is he saying?' Hal asked Toto.

'He says the chief is not cured. He says this is only the last flash of life before death, just as a star is brightest before it drops out of sight. He tells the people that the chief will die. You have poisoned him with the small white things you put in his mouth. And the glass tube you gave him to suck . . .'

'The thermometer?'

'Yes. It had something red in it. He says it was a deadly poison. It is a poison that makes a man feel better just before he dies. But the chief will surely die. And the spirits will punish all in the village because they did not trust their medicine man. So he tells the people.'

'Do they believe him?'

'Their minds are divided. They are happy that the chief is better. But if he dies they will believe you murdered him. They will believe their medicine man was right, and he will once more be great in their eyes.'

'And I will be very small.'

'You will be nothing. They will kill you as they would kill a rat.'

'That's what I like about you, Toto,' Hal said. 'You make everything sound so jolly.'

He gave his patient another tablet of paludrine and two of quinine. There was a disturbance at the door and Mali came pushing through the crowd. Breathless from his run up the hill from the camp, he could only gasp:

'*Bwana* . . . buffalo . . . many!'

Hal did not need to know more. For days he had been watching for buffalo. Three were wanted by the London Zoo. He made his apologies to the chief.

'You will forgive me if I leave at once. But I will come back to see if you are still improving.'

'Thank you, my son.' The words, and the smile that went with them, repaid Hal for all his trouble.

As the three made their way to the door, the medicine man's voice rose shrill and harsh above the talk of the crowd. Toto interpreted his words.

'The chief will die. The chief will die.'

'I suppose nothing would please him more,' Hal remarked.

13
Charge of the Heavy Brigade

From the hill they saw the buffalo. There were about a hundred of the big black beasts.

They looked like a hundred thunder-clouds. They didn't seem to belong in this land of warmth and sunshine. They could start a storm that would be worse than any that could come out of the sky. They looked as if they were aching to do just that.

The entire herd was turned in one direction, facing the Hunt camp. They didn't seem to like what they saw. An African buffalo never seems to like anything. An elephant or a lion or even a hyena has his pleasant moments, but a buffalo always looks as if he had got out of bed the wrong side. His angry red eyes glare out of an ugly, inky-black face, and he stands with his head stretched forward as if trying to reach you with those spear-pointed horns. They are the toughest and stubbornest horns worn by any beast in Africa. A big bull will measure four feet from the tip of one horn to the tip of the other. And he has a ton on four feet ready to push those horns through anything that doesn't please him.

'If they take a notion to hit the camp,' Hal said, 'they'll flatten those tents as if a steam-roller had gone over them.'

The thought that their father, helpless on his cot, would not be able to escape such a stampede took the boys on the run down the hill.

They found the camp busy preparing for battle with the thunder-clouds on four legs. The men were busy revving up the motors of the trucks. A take-'em-alive safari, if it hopes to catch and carry many large animals, must be well equipped with cars, and there were fourteen in the Hunt outfit.

Not one of them was anything like the family car seen in city streets. They were heavy trucks and lorries, made heavier by metal rods and plates to enable them to stand the terrific banging over rocks, into holes, over ant-hills and hummocks.

The lightest of them were the heavy, solid Land-Rovers, armour-plated like army tanks and equipped with four-wheel drive to get them out of bad bogs or deep sand. Then there were the stout Ford and Chev 'catchers', intended for chasing the big animals, and the big four-ton Bedfords and Land-Rovers, each carrying one or several huge crates or cages, in which the animals would be placed after they were nabbed by the catchers.

'Our first job is to protect the camp,' Hal said. He ordered the men to drive the cars up into position facing the buffalo. There they lined up with the camp behind them. In front of them, some five hundred yards away, was the black herd. The two armies, one of metal and the other of muscle, glowered at each other.

Hal dashed into his father's tent to report on what he had done.

'That's fine,' John Hunt said. 'That ought to make them think twice. Trouble is, most of them leave the thinking to the big bulls in the front row. If just one of those bulls takes a notion to charge, all the rest will follow, like sheep. But that's the only way they're like sheep. They can be mighty mean. If they start to charge, there is only one thing to do — charge back.'

Hal ran out to instruct the men.

'If they start coming, go to meet them!'

The fourteen drivers kept their motors going. Hal hurriedly appointed others to climb aboard certain of the trucks, so that they would be on hand to help when the time came for catching and caging.

He did not forget that the whole safari numbered only thirty men, and he must leave enough of them in camp to defend it in case there was a surprise attack. For he knew the reputation of the buffalo — these beasts are as smart as they are mean. If they cannot attack you in front, they have the unpleasant habit of sneaking round and coming up on you from behind. Many hunters regard them as the most dangerous big game in Africa.

The elephant is larger, but sometimes sweet-tempered. The buffalo doesn't know what sweet temper is. Some big game, such as the rhino, cannot see very well, some cannot hear very well, some cannot smell very well. The buffalo can see, hear and smell perfectly.

You can dodge some animals. You can't dodge a

buffalo, because he is quick on his feet and will turn when you turn.

If another big animal gets you down and you play dead, he may wander away. Not so the buffalo. He isn't satisfied to have you merely dead, he wants you flat. He will trample upon you until you are as thin as a French pancake.

Roger, unwilling to be left in camp, boarded a Powerwagon. Hal jumped in beside the driver of a Ford catcher. He was not too happy to discover that the driver was Joro, the man who had sworn to kill him. But there was no time now to think of such matters.

Over the coal-black bodies of the buffalo floated snow-white egrets. Some of them perched on the broad backs, plucking out insects from the cracks in the hide. Most of them circled in the air, sharing the excitement of the animals below them.

The lovely birds, whose feathers are prized for their beauty, constrasted oddly with the ugly monsters beneath them. Here was certainly a case of beauty and the beast. The black army seemed to be waving white flags.

Usually the white flag means surrender, but it was not so this time. Pawing the ground and snorting defiantly, the buffalo had no idea of giving up or running away.

Buffalo fear only two enemies. One is the lion, the other is the gun. They did not see either lions or guns, so why should they be afraid?

They saw men. A man has no horns, and it would take a dozen men to equal a buffalo in weight and more than that to match his strength.

Hal had hoped the buffalo would be worried by the line-up of cars. But to a buffalo's eyes perhaps these things looked like horses or tents, nothing to be afraid of. And Hal himself was not so sure of victory when it occurred to him that this was going to be a contest between about thirty tons of car against a hundred tons of buffalo.

But how about noise? Many creatures were sensitive to noise. Hal put his hand on the horn-button and held it there. The drivers of the other cars got the idea, and fourteen powerful horns let out a roar that sent up the egrets in a white cloud and started the baboons down by the river chattering with terror.

Instead of turning tail, the buffalo set up a tremendous bellowing that quite drowned the sound of the horns. They howled back at the noise as a dog may howl at music. The horn-blowers gave up. The deep-voiced choir continued for a few moments, then it also fell silent.

A few of the bulls in the front line began to lose interest in the show. They started to graze on the sweet grass. They no longer faced forwards like an army about to march. Some turned broadside, and Hal began to hope that the danger of a charge was over.

Then who should run out in front of the cars but the crazy colonel! He was carrying his .470. Hal remembered that Bigg had said he wanted a buffalo head. Now he saw his chance to get one. Hal shouted:

'Bigg! Don't shoot! Come back!'

Bigg paid no attention. He raised his gun and levelled it on a huge bull, one of the leaders.

Hal leaped from the truck and ran. Before he could reach Bigg, the gun fired. Bigg turned in time to receive a smashing blow in the face from Hal's fist. The gun flew from his hands and he fell in a heap.

The herd began to bellow again, but this time they were not singing to the music of a car-horn orchestra. The bulls were roaring with rage, the cows were making loud snorts of alarm, the calves were mooing and running to their mothers for protection.

The bull that had been the colonel's target was far from dead. The bullet had torn open his forehead. The thickness of the bone had prevented it from reaching the brain. The colonel had accomplished just one thing. He had turned this animal into a devil. An animal that had been only curious was now furious. A wounded buffalo thinks only of revenge.

The bellowing bull tossed his head, flinging a spray of blood into the air from his wound, and then came on like a runaway locomotive, straight for Colonel Bigg.

A moment before, there had been a good chance that the whole herd would start grazing and walk away. Now that chance was gone. The wounded bull had not taken two strides before every adult animal in the herd was on the move. On they came, a bellowing wave of black fury.

Hal, back in the truck, nudged Joro. The car leaped forward, and so did every other car at almost the same instant. They moved just in time to save Colonel Bigg from being trampled to death by the animal he had wounded. They shot past him and closed in so that the bull could not reach him. He dizzily picked himself up, got his gun, and staggered back to camp.

Meanwhile the black avalanche he had started came on and the pounding of hooves made the earth shake. The animals in the front row could not have stopped now if they had wanted to. Those behind pushed them on. Dust rose in great clouds and through the clouds screamed the white birds.

The buffalo did not seem in the least terrified by the fourteen iron monsters roaring in to meet them. The drivers did not try to go round rocks and ridges. The trucks bounced and leaped like bucking broncos.

Roger found himself half the time in the air. At every bounce he went up and down like a jack-in-the-box. He was whanged at both ends, his head against the roof, his rear against the hard seat.

Then the two armies met. Such a roaring of motors and bellowing of buffalo and excited shrieking of baboons and birds and all other creatures within earshot surely could never have been heard before in this quiet river valley.

Heavy heads crashed into radiators, bent and twisted the metal, broke open the coils, spilled the water, and brought the cars to a shuddering halt. The horns of a buffalo join on the forehead in a boss of solid bone four inches thick, giving him a terrific battering-ram. Fenders were crumpled as if they had been cardboard, bumpers were broken, headlights smashed.

The shock of the collison threw men forward out of their seats against the wind-screens, and one wind-screen was struck even harder from the outside when a bull making a mighty leap landed on the bonnet and his great helmet of bone smashed the glass.

Four bulls concentrating on one truck pushed it backwards, slewed it sideways and toppled it upside-down. The car did not burst into flames. The quick-thinking African driver, when he saw the four black bulldozers about to crash into his vehicle, had turned off the ignition.

Vultures streamed down out of the sky. They always appeared as if by magic wherever there seemed a promise of death.

Here there was more than a promise. No man had been killed, but three of the animals lay motionless, blood streaming from their wounds. Their rock-hard heads had not suffered, but their necks or flanks had

been gouged by their metal enemies. They would never again test their strength against a truck. Others, lying stunned for a while, got unsteadily to their feet. They shook their heads, rolled their eyes, but could not make up their minds to charge again. They turned to go. The rest of the herd hesitated.

The drivers of all cars able to move were watching Hal's car, for he was their leader.

'Go ahead — slowly,' Hal told Joro. The truck inched forward. The others did the same.

It was just enough to discourage the buffalo from further attack. One after another the big brutes turned tail and began to trot away.

14
Buffalo Hunt

This was the end of the battle. But not the end of the war.

The real job was still to be done. Three buffalo must be caught and caged.

Hal shouted instructions to the drivers of the trucks on either side, and they passed the word down the line. All trucks were to return to camp except two — Hal's Ford catcher and the Powerwagon carrying Roger. Hal knew that his brother would want to be in on the chase. Operators of the other cars must stand ready to drive out at once if their help was needed. Hal called some of the extra men to ride in the rear of Roger's truck and his own.

Hal slipped out into the catcher's chair. This is a small seat *outside* the cab. It is strapped to the right front fender. The man who is to do the catching must sit in this chair.

He holds a long pole with a noose at the end. The idea is to get the noose over the head of the running animal, but this is more easily said than done.

Hal signalled Joro, and the truck set out in pursuit of the herd. At every jolt Hal thought he would be thrown out of the seat into a thorn-bush. He hung on like grim death with one hand, clutching the pole with the other.

The long grass looked as smooth as velvet, but it concealed pot-holes made by the rain, pits made by burrowing animals, boulders, stumps and logs.

Now they were actually in the herd. Like a black river, it flowed along on both sides of the car. Some of the animals were within reach of the catching pole, but Hal ignored them. He wouldn't be satisfied with just any buffalo. He wanted one of the big bulls.

Ahead, he saw one, taller by a good eighteen inches than any of the animals around him. His back was as broad as a dining-room table. From his great head the horns swept out and up, ending in points as sharp as ice-picks. On the nape of his neck an egret was taking a dizzy ride.

Over the thunder of hooves and the roar of the car, Hal shouted:

'Let's get that one.'

Joro could scarcely hear him, but he understood the pointing finger and speeded up the car. The bumper nudged the rears of some lumbering cows and they veered out of the way, leaving a fairly clear path ahead. Clear, but not smooth. The greater the speed, the rougher the ride.

It would be a miracle if the wildly leaping car did not tear out its sump on a stump or wind up against a rock with a broken axle.

A large acacia tree blocked the path. Joro threw the wheel over, the swerve nearly tossing Hal out of his seat. They barely missed striking the trunk of the tree. Joro did not turn for bushes. He ploughed straight through them. The worst were the thorn-bushes. They stood some fifteen feet high and as broad as the car, and they bristled with thousands upon thousands of thorns, each two inches long and as sharp as needles.

They did not merely scratch Hal's face and hands. They tore holes in his shirt and trousers and bloodied him from head to foot.

For a moment he wondered if Joro was giving him this treatment on purpose. But he realized that there was no help for it. If they were to catch the big bull they could not stop for bushes.

Nor even for ant-hills. The African ant-hill is a strange and wondrous thing. It may be anything from two feet to twenty feet high. Though called an ant-hill, it is really built by termites, millions of them, and every particle of the hill has passed through the body of a termite. On the way through, the clay is mixed with certain body-juices which turn it into a kind of cement.

So the ant-hill is as hard as rock, and if you attack it with a pick, all you get is sparks. It defies sun and rain and may last more than a hundred years.

It was up the slope of one of these ant-hills that the big bull rushed until he was twice as high as the roof of the car. Hal would long remember that great black body high against the blue sky. Then, instead of running down the other side, the bull leaped into space, trusting to his sturdy legs to give him safe landing.

The truck would lose valuable time if it tried to go round the hill. Joro gave the engine the last squirt of power. The truck shot up like a rocket to the top of the hill. Then it left the earth entirely and took

off into space. With bad luck, it could land upside-down. But with good luck, if you would call it that, it crashed down, right side up, into the worst thorn-bush yet.

Porcupine quills growing on bushes, Hal thought as he added to his collection of scratches.

The car ripped its way through the thorns and was once more in the open, now close to the big bull. It was too close for comfort, and the buffalo increased his speed. His hide glistened with sweat, and foam dripped from his mouth. Now both he and the truck had left most of the herd behind. The bumper of the car almost touched his flying heels. The pole extended over his back and the noose dangled above his head.

Hal tried to settle the noose in place, but succeeded only in bumping the animal's back with his pole. The egret flew up with a sharp cry of alarm. The buffalo wheeled about and went off to the right. Joro at once turned in pursuit, and the car went round the curve on two wheels.

Again it drew close. Again the bull tried to throw it off by a sharp turn, this time to the left. The heavy truck spun about and followed.

Suddenly the bull stopped dead and glared at the truck with savage red eyes. He was tired of being pestered by this smelly monster of metal and rubber.

Joro stopped the truck. The buffalo was now on Hal's side of the car. Before Hal could get the pole and noose into position, the beast charged.

If he had struck the car low down, it would have gone over in a flash, pinning Hal underneath. Instead, he crashed into the door, horns first. He pierced the door as if it had been cardboard.

He found himself locked to this strange, evil thing. He wrenched his head violently, and in doing so not only pulled his horns free but jerked open the door.

Now he could see a human being inside and his fury was redoubled. He reared up on his hind feet and thrust his head and shoulders into the cab.

But Joro was not waiting for him. There was a hatch in the roof of the catcher and it was open.

Even as the great head plunged into the cab, Joro was scrambling through the hatch and on to the roof. He was quick, but not quick enough to escape one horn, which poked him in the rear and speeded him on his way.

Hal and the men in the back of the truck could not help laughing at the way Joro shot up through that hole like a living cannon-ball.

But what happened then was still more amusing, though a bit terrifying. The huge head of the buffalo burst up through the hatch. By drawing his hind feet into the cab, he even managed to get his forefeet on to the roof.

He was mad with rage, determined that his enemy should not escape him. He swept the roof with his horns, and Joro could barely keep out of his way. The animal bellowed furiously and flung spume from his foaming mouth. His eyes were like burning coals. He struggled desperately, but could not climb higher through the hatch.

In the meantime his hind quarters and hooves were working havoc in the cab, battering the metal fittings, slashing the instrument board and smashing the windscreen.

Hal wished he had a camera instead of a catching-pole. What a sight this was! A Ford truck with a bull buffalo in the driver's seat!

Game-wardens had told him of incidents like this — buffalo, rhino, lion, leopard, bursting their way into cars. And in America's Yellowstone Park not a year went by without a report of a black bear or a grizzly breaking into a car. But it was one thing to hear about it and another to see it with his own eyes.

He was so entertained that he almost forgot to act. Then he suddenly woke up. Here was the best chance he could possibly ask for to catch a magnificent bull.

He swung his pole about until the noose was above the animal's head. This new annoyance, fluttering above like a bird, did not improve the buffalo's temper. He roared at it, tried to stab it with his ice-picks.

Hal opened the noose with a twist on the pole and lowered it. That should have dropped the loop neatly over the animal's head. But the rope caught on one of the wide-spreading horns. A part of the loop fell into the buffalo's mouth and he set out to destroy it with his powerful jaws. But a buffalo fights with his horns and hooves, not often with his teeth. His teeth are meant for grass-eating. The tough nylon cord resisted all attempts to turn it into chewing-gum.

With a sudden jerk Hal managed to pull the rope loose. The buffalo had given up trying to reach Joro. He had drawn one of his forefeet down into the cab. Soon he might withdraw his head, then back out of the car and escape. Hal realized he had only one more chance.

As skilfully as he knew how, he manipulated the pole so that the noose opened into a wide loop and dropped over his quarry's head. It settled round the great black neck. The cord ran back along the pole to Hal's hand. He gave it a yank that snugged it about the animal's throat.

The bull, with a savage bellow, tried to pull his head down through the hatch, but the rope tightened and held him fast. Hal was not trusting to his own strength. He knew his strength was no match for the bull's. He had already looped his end of the rope round the fender and made it fast.

Now it was bull versus fender. Which would prove the stronger? The fender danced and buckled and groaned. If the fender went, Hal's seat which was strapped to it, would go too. The seat bounced up and down like a yo-yo, and Hal bounced with it.

The Powerwagon was coming. Hal waved it on. Mali speeded up, and the big cage in the back of the Land-Rover rattled and banged as the car crashed over stones and holes.

Roger stared wide-eyed at this most unusual sight, a bull-headed truck. The Greeks had told stories of a centaur, half man and half horse. What would they think of this monster with an animal head, metal body and wheels?

He saw the desperate efforts the buffalo was making to back out of the trap in which he found himself. If the rope snapped, he would be lost.

'Step on it, Mali!' he urged.

He saw Hal waving to him, directing him to the other side of the Ford. In a flash he caught his brother's idea.

He called back to the men in the rear around the cage.

'Open the cage door!' Then to Mali, 'Swing round and back up.'

Now they were close enough to hear the thrashing and crashing as the big bull turned the fittings of the cab into mincemeat in his fight to get loose. A lot of repairs would be necessary. This was taking 'em alive the expensive way. It was hard on the car and it was also hard on the animal.

Mali turned out, then backed up until the open cage door was against the open door of the Ford.

'Slack away!' Roger shouted. Hal loosed the catching-rope from the fender. The bull, with the strain on his neck relieved, promptly drew down his head and began to back out of the car.

He could not see where he was going for a buffalo's eyes are planted at the front of his head, not on the sides. Before he could realize what was happening to him, he had backed into the cage.

Mali pulled forward a few feet so that the cage door would have room to swing shut, and Hal, who had already left his seat and run round to the back of the Powerwagon, closed the heavy iron door.

The animal bellowed with rage and frustration, rushed from side to side, striking the iron bars with his bony helmet and making the heavy Powerwagon rock. He might break his horns on the bars, and certainly he would bruise his flesh even through that thick hide. He must be quieted or he would destroy both himself and his cage.

Hal got out the curare gun. He watched for his chance to pump a shot into this red-eyed, foaming bunch of fury.

Before he could do so, the bull's rage suddenly simmered down. He stood with legs braced apart, dripping with sweat, blood and foam, head hanging. He was a picture of weariness and despair. Then his legs buckled beneath him and he collapsed on the steel floor.

15
Baby-Sitter to a Bull

Heart attack, Hal thought. Even a bull buffalo cannot go on for ever. This bull had been one of the leaders in the attack upon the camp, and he had probably been well battered when he had collided head-on with the trucks. Then he had been chased until he was tired by an engine that never got tired, he had undergone the unusual experience of climbing into the driver's seat and pursuing a man through a hole in the roof, he had been noosed, he had fought for liberty, and then he had tested his strength against iron bars. Now he was broken in spirit as well as in body. And Hal knew that unless he acted promptly he would have nothing but a dead animal for all his pains.

This was no job for a curare gun. The animal did not need quieting, but reviving.

Hal leaped back into the cab and got the coramine syringe.

Coramine is a heart stimulant used by catchers when an animal shows signs of dying from exhaustion, fear or shock.

To inject the drug, the syringe must be placed against the hide. But the bull lay in the middle of the cage and Hal could not reach any part of him through the bars. There was no help for it — he must join the dangerous beast inside the cage.

He opened the cage door, stepped inside, and closed the door behind him. The bull snorted angrily and struggled to his feet. Here was his enemy just where he wanted him. He feared the thing in the man's hands. It had a sharp end like a horn. But if he could get one of his own horns into the man first and push it home, he would be rid of this pest for good and all.

He threw his ton at Hal, but the acrobatic naturalist was no longer there and the horns went harmlessly through the bars. The bull drew back and charged again, and again Hal side-stepped.

This time Hal was not so lucky. He found himself pinned between the animal's right hip and the iron grating. If enough of the animal's weight was used against him, he could be minced between those iron bars like flesh in a meat-grinder.

He was smeared with the sweat of the overstrained animal and blood from its bruises. The pressure on his body was tremendous, but his arm was free and he had the presence of mind to jab the syringe into the bull's thigh and inject the stimulant. At the same instant the bull fell to the floor, his last spark of energy gone.

It would take twenty minutes or half an hour for the stimulant to act. Perhaps it had been given too late and the bull was already dead.

'Better get out of there,' Roger called. 'He's apt to rear up again any minute.'

'No,' Hal said. 'He's pooped. I just hope we won't lose him altogether.'

Hal hovered over the beast like an anxious mother. He placed his hand over the nostrils. He felt nothing and his anxiety increased.

Then there was a pulse of warmth against his hand. It was very weak, but it showed that breathing and heart action had not stopped.

Hal looked over the hide for wounds and made a mental note of them. They must be treated later — *if* the animal lived.

It was a big 'if'. The sweat on the beast's flanks had chilled. The great eyes that had glared so savagely were closed. Hal's father would not think much of him if he lost his first buffalo.

He could imagine him saying, as he had so often said before, 'Remember, you're here to take animals alive, not dead.'

He felt a sort of tenderness towards this helpless, heart-sick beast. From creases in the skin he plucked out ticks that the egrets had overlooked. He placed his hand again over the nostrils, but though he held it there for a long time he felt nothing.

Roger was peering in through the bars.

'How does it feel to be baby-sitter to a buffalo?' he laughed.

Hal was not amused.

'I only hope I'm not attending a funeral. What's the matter with that coramine? It should have acted by this time.'

Had the heart stopped? Hal was no fool as a naturalist, but he was still learning, and that was one thing he had forgotten to ask his father — how do you take a buffalo's pulse?

Another ten minutes of anxious waiting, and Hal again tested for breath. Was it just imagination, or did he feel a slight come-and-go of warm and cool? Yes, there was no doubt about it. His own heart leaped.

'He's coming through!' he shouted.

The bull came through fast. His breathing grew steadily stronger. His eyes opened and the first thing they lit upon was Hal. But in those eyes there was not the same hate as before.

Perhaps the buffalo, being a highly intelligent animal, understood that this man could have killed him but had not. Possibly he was not so bad after all. He could even be a friend. He felt Hal's fingers plucking out the painful ticks from his hide. And he could even look at the syringe with appreciation. He had been stabbed by it, and now he felt better.

He was just tired. Convinced that he did not need to fear this human, he closed his eyes and slept. Hal quietly left the cage.

'Take him to camp,' he told Mali. 'Go easy — don't shake him up any more than necessary. You'll have to give the Ford a tow. That bull dancing a jig in the cab didn't do it any more good than a bull in a china-shop.'

In half an hour the boys were after their second buffalo.

The Ford had been left in camp with a mechanic hard at work repairing or replacing the battered controls. The Powerwagon had also been left, rather than disturb the buffalo by removing the cage.

Hal had strapped his seat to the fender of a Chev catcher driven by Joro, while Mali and Roger followed in a Powerwagon bearing another cage.

The herd was grazing quietly about a mile from camp. Hal picked out a splendid bull which was wandering a little apart from the rest of the herd.

Joro drove the car alongside, and Hal neatly slipped the noose over the bull's head.

It had all been very easy up to this point. Now it began to be difficult. The bull did not take kindly to his new necklace. He tried to shake it off.

When this did not work, he went plunging away and might have broken the line if Hal had not let it out bit by bit, as a fisherman plays a fish.

Changing his tactics, the bull wheeled about, bellowed, then came on the run straight for the truck.

'Face him!' Hal shouted. 'Take him on the bumper.'

Joro didn't need to be told. He had had enough experience to know that when a buffalo, rhino or elephant charges, the car must be turned to face the charge. It cannot easily be overturned if struck in front. But if the beast manages to give it a blow on the side it may spin upside-down.

There was another good reason why Joro did not allow a flank attack. It would expose Hal to the greatest possible danger, for his small seat strapped to the fender was on the side towards the bull.

'Swing round!' Hal yelled, and accompanied the order with a swing of his hand.

Joro seemed to be trying, but there were many stones and hummocks in the way.

Then suddenly the engine went dead. Hal's heart sank. Whether the motor had stopped by accident or Joro had deliberately stalled it, Hal would never know.

But he did know that he stood a very good chance of being killed. He worked feverishly to unfasten the lifebelt that held him to his seat. The buckle was stubborn. He shouted again to Joro. Joro stepped on the starter, the engine roared, then stalled again. Joro waved his hands as if to say he could do nothing more.

A column of dust rose from the flying heels of the bull. The head was lowered, the tough forehead was ready for the crash. Joro was leaping out of the car now and placing himself at a safe distance. Hal at last pulled open the buckle and threw off the belt.

He scrambled up on to the hood just as the bull struck the very spot where he had been sitting. The chair was smashed into a pulp. The fender behind it was crushed. The heavy car toppled over on to its side. Hal slid off the hood and leaped clear.

He had not forgotten his job and was still hanging on to the catching-pole. Hot with anger, he turned upon Joro:

'Did you want to get me killed?'

'No, *bwana*,' Joro said, but the eyes seemed to say yes.

'I noticed you took good care to save yourself,' Hal said bitterly.

'All the men did,' Joro reminded him. 'Why not? It was the thing to do.'

It was so. The men in the back of the truck had jumped clear, and Hal had to admit it was the thing to do. Still, he suspected Joro.

The bull gave him no time to think about this. He was making one rush after another, trying to escape the pull of the rope. The men heaved the car back into an upright position. The Powerwagon carrying the cage had come up, and the men from both cars now undertook the dangerous job of catching and hobbling the frantic animal.

Hal had looped the end of the line round the car bumper, for a thirteen-stone man could not hold a one-ton bull.

Toto started the risky game. He dashed in and grabbed the buffalo by the tail. The bull turned sharply and tried to get at him.

But a buffalo is no cat. He cannot reach his tail. And he is no mule. He has not acquired the habit of kicking with his hind hooves. He will stamp upon his victim if he gets a chance, but kicking is not part of his act. So long as Toto could hang on, he was comparatively safe.

The bull, whirling to get at Toto, was not paying enough attention to the other men. They sneaked up on his flanks and tried to get nooses round his feet. When the bull chased them, they skipped just far enough away so that he was brought up short by the rope and could not reach them.

This worked well enough until the rope broke. It snapped close to the bumper, and the bull, trailing a hundred feet of line, went after the men in earnest.

Now there was nothing to stop him. Dragging Toto behind him, he chose to single out an African called Kenyono, who promptly made for a tree and scrambled up just one hot breath ahead of the bull.

He did not quite succeed in climbing clear. He hung from a branch and his dangling legs were within reach of the brute's teeth.

But the bull did not attack with his teeth. He had another weapon even more dangerous — his tongue. That tongue is as rough as a coarse file or wood-rasp. It will scrape off the bark of a tree or grind up thorns, twigs, sharp-edged elephant grass and tough stalks of papyrus.

The bull began licking the dangling legs. The skin came off like tissue-paper, and gobs of flesh down to the bone. In a moment both legs were streaming with blood and the African was screaming for help.

Roger did some quick thinking. He had one of the foot-nooses in his hand. He slipped it over the bull's muzzle and pulled it tight. That made him close his mouth at once.

'Hope he bit his tongue,' Roger said.

Kenyono dropped from the tree and two men helped him to a truck. The other men continued their efforts to noose the animal's feet. Time and again they barely escaped being gored by the sweeping horns.

They got a noose over the front hooves and drew it tight.

The bull stumbled, fell on his right shoulder, and threw his hind feet in the air.

Toto, the tail-hanger, had been watching for this,

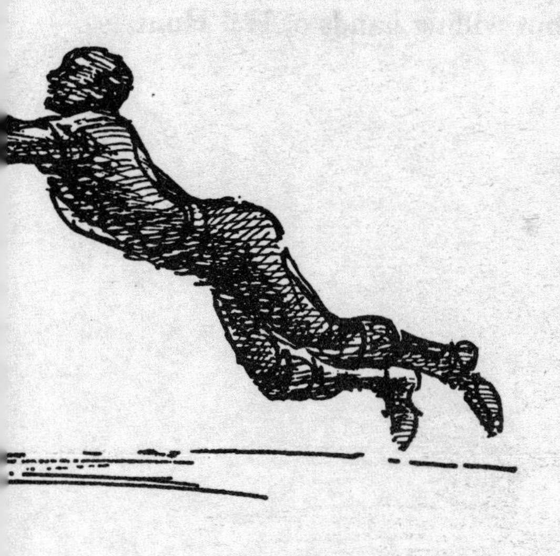

and as the feet went up he grabbed a noose from the man next to him and flipped it in place.

Bound both fore and aft, the bull lay on his side, snorting and blowing like a porpoise.

The Powerwagon rolled up with Mali at the wheel. In the back of the truck was the buffalo-size cage. The Chev took its position in front of the Land-Rover, and a cable was played back through the cage and looped round the helpless animal just behind the shoulders and forelegs.

The Chev advanced, using all its four-wheel-drive power, the cable tightened, and the squirming animal was dragged up a greased ramp into the cage.

The prize was taken to camp, and the injured Kenyono received prompt medical treatment from the not too expert but willing hands of Hal Hunt.

16
Roger Takes a Ride

'Let me snag the next one,' pleaded Roger.

Hal had noosed two buffalo. Roger considered that it was his turn.

Hal objected. His own narrow escape from being crushed between a bull's head and a steel fender chilled his blood whenever he thought of it.

'It's no game for kids,' he said.

Age thirteen looked up at age nineteen with fire in his eye.

'What's that you called me? Watch your language, you young squirt, or I'll take you over my knee and pound some sense into you.'

Hal looked at the broad shoulders and strong frame of his younger brother. The 'kid' was coming along fast. It wouldn't be many years now before the two of them would be evenly matched.

'Suppose I have no right to "kid" you,' he admitted. 'But — take a look at this chair.'

He ran his fingers over the splinters of wood and twists of metal that had once been a chair. The bits and pieces of it were plastered against the fender. No carpenter on earth could ever put it together again. Hal unstrapped it from the car and threw it away. He turned to Roger.

'Suppose you had been in that thing when the big boy arrived.'

'Do you think I'd stay in it until he got there?' Roger demanded. 'You got out, didn't you? Why couldn't I?' When his brother showed no sign of relenting, Roger added, 'Let's put it to Dad.'

They went in to their father's cot and repeated their argument. John Hunt was suffering considerable pain, but his look softened into a smile as he studied his boys.

'Hal doesn't want you to be hurt,' he said to Roger. 'I don't either. But you, Hal, must realize that this "kid", as you call him, is almost a man. We don't want to stop him from becoming one. He'll become one only if he takes his chance along with other men. Let him ride the chair.'

Roger gave a whoop that betrayed him as still being pretty much of a boy. He dashed out to the supply wagon, got another chair and lashed it to the fender of the Land-Rover that was to be used this time as the catching-vehicle. And he found himself a lasso, such as the cowboys used in the American West. He had practised with it for hours — now was his chance to see if he could use it to make a real capture.

But when Joro began to climb into the driver's seat of the Land-Rover, Hal checked him.

'You and I will go in the cage truck,' he said, 'just for a change. Mali, you drive the Land-Rover.'

Hal wanted Joro where he could watch him. He climbed in beside this doubtful fellow, who was perhaps a leopard-man and perhaps had tried to kill him only half an hour before. There were too many perhapses about Joro. But it was certain that he was a good driver and a good hunter, and he must be considered innocent until he was proven guilty.

The herd had moved into the shade to escape the growing heat of the day. Some were lying down, asleep, others slept standing up, others wallowed comfortably in a muddy marsh beside the river. All stayed close together for safety except the biggest bulls, who were so sure of their own strength that they thought they did not need the protection of the herd. They didn't want to be disturbed by the grunting of the cows and the screaming of the babies. They had strayed away, each one by himself.

Roger selected one with shoulders like a football hero's and a head as solid as the door of a safe. Surely, Roger thought, this giant must be king of the herd. He pointed him out to Mali.

The great beast moved away at a slow, dignified walk as the car approached. The walk changed to a run, and the run to a gallop.

Mali did not stop for rocks, logs or holes. Roger bounced like a rubber doll. This was his first time in a fender chair. He had never dreamed the ride could be so rough. Not trusting his lifebelt, he hung on with one hand while he held the lasso ready in the other.

Now they were close enough. Roger whirled the lasso three times round his head and let it fly. The loop settled down round a thorn-bush, and a yank on the rope might well have pulled Roger apart if Mali had not promptly ground to a stop.

Mali and the men in the back of the Land-Rover were laughing. Laughter came, too, from the following Powerwagon. Roger blushed a rosy red. A great hunter he was! Aiming at a buffalo and snagging a thorn-bush!

One of the men jumped down and pulled the loop free from the bush. Roger pulled in and coiled the rope as Mali started the car.

The bull had stopped and was looking back with a big grin on his ugly face — or so it seemed to Roger. Then with a snort and a toss of his head he took to his heels, and the chase was on again.

At every bump Roger rose several inches about his seat. Half the time he was like an astronaut, weightless, flying through space. When he did come down on the iron seat, he hit it with a painful whack. How could anyone expect a fellow to throw a lasso from this bouncing, pounding car, worse than any wild horse?

Now he was close. He would try, but he was sure he would fail. At least he would choose a spot where there were no thorn-bushes.

Seizing his chance, he snaked the nylon noose out towards the big black head.

He let out a whoop worthy of any cowboy when he saw the rope tighten round the king's neck.

The line, made fast to the fender, brought the bull up short. The men spilled out of the cars to complete the capture. Even the two drivers, Mali and Joro, joined in the struggle, for this was a real giant and would not easily be hobbled.

The bull had turned to face his tormentors and stood still like something carved out of stone, except that his blazing eyes rolled from side to side, taking in every move.

He wouldn't be half so smart if we could blindfold him, thought Roger. He loosed himself from his chair, snatched a red blanket out of the car, and made for the animal's head.

Before he could get there, the beast let out a roar of defiance, leaped straight up into the air like a black balloon, pulled the line taut and snapped it as if it had been a silk thread. Then he struck out after the nearest African, who happened to be Joro.

The men stood with their mouths agape. They could not hope to keep up with that whirlwind. Joro's oiled, black body flashed in the sun as he ran for his life.

The man and bull passed close to Roger. The boy leaped for the trailing line, grabbed it, and held on. He could not even slow down the steam-engine. He was dragged head first over humps and hollows, sticks and stones, and through elephant grass whose razor edges sliced into his face and hands.

He couldn't care less. This was his bull and it was not going to escape him.

His toboggan ride was made a little easier by the blanket which got tangled round his shoulders and took some of the jolts.

The wild race suddenly came to a halt. Roger, feeling considerably battered, raised himself on his elbow and looked. He brushed away the blood that seeped into his eyes from scratches on his forehead. What he saw made him leap to his feet and run to the assistance of the black hunter.

The bull had caught up with Joro and knocked

him flat. Now he slid his right horn under the man and tossed him ten feet in the air as lightly as if he had been a bag of meal. Joro came down on a ridge of rock with a force that would have broken the back of an ordinary man.

He tried to rise, but got up only on his hands and knees before the buffalo's head went beneath him and tossed him again, making the body spin in the air, then caught it as it came down and gave it still another skyward fling.

When the limp body sprawled to the ground, the angry buffalo stood up on his hind feet and brought his forefeet smashing down upon his victim. Joro tried to roll out of the way, but the hammer-like hooves found him again.

It was the buffalo's favourite method of attack. He would not be satisfied until he had separated bone from bone and crushed out every sign of life.

Seeing this ferocious beast at work, Roger heard a small voice telling him that he ought to be running the other way. But he ran on straight into trouble.

His brain, too, was racing. What could he do? He was no match for this huge bull. As for his blanket, he could never hope to get it over the bull's head and hold it there without any men to help him. He was sure the men were coming, but Joro would die before they arrived.

Then a crazy idea came into his head. It might work. If this bull was anything like his distant cousins in the bullrings of Spain, he would go for a waving blanket.

Facing the bull, he gripped the blanket by two corners and let it billow out on the breeze.

The bull stopped his deadly trampling. He glared at the red, flapping thing. Then with a snort of rage he charged.

When he got to where the red thing had been it was no longer there. The young toreador had flipped it into the air so that the bull passed beneath it.

The bull wheeled about. There it was again, the great red thing daring him to come on. Roger was feeling the flush of victory. If he could just keep on bamboozling this silly beast until the men got there . . . .

The bull charged. This time the wind played pranks with the blanket. It did not soar up out of the way as it was supposed to do.

The bull caught it on his horns, wrenched it out of Roger's hands, tossed it on the ground and proceeded to trample it just as he had trampled Joro. When it lay still he sniffed at it, decided it was dead, and turned his attention to Joro, who was dismally trying to get up on to his feet.

Would the men never come? Roger did not realize that what had seemed to him many minutes had only been a matter of seconds. Now he heard the men coming, but he could not wait for them. The bull was advancing upon Joro. The man would certainly be killed if he got another beating from those sledge-hammer hooves.

Roger jumped in front of the bull, waved his arms and shouted, hoping to scare him off. He might as well have tried to scare the Rock of Gibraltar.

The bull came on, horns lowered. Roger instinctively seized the horns. If he could just manage to hang on, those horns couldn't hurt him.

The bull angrily tossed his head. Up went Roger like a rocket. The first of the men came bursting through the bushes in time to see Roger in the air. His hands had been jerked loose from the horns. He came down with an ungraceful sprawl on the beast's back.

The men came pouring in, shouting, grabbing at the bull's tail, legs, horns.

This was too much, even for a king. He shook off his pursuers and took to his heels.

Roger had a free ride. He found himself half straddling the beast, gripping an ear with one hand and a horn with the other. If he slid off, this killer would take great pleasure in smashing him to smithereens with those meat-chopping hooves.

But the buffalo knew from long experience how to get rid of an undesired visitor. The lion attacks a four-footed animal by leaping upon its back. The leopard does the same. A clever buffalo, when thus attacked, looks for a tree with a low branch. He rushes through beneath it, hoping the branch will scrape his enemy from his back.

The bull headed for a low-slung mopani tree. Roger did not wake up to his danger until it was almost too late.

He had to make a lightning-quick decision between staying on board until he was brushed off or perhaps squeezed to death by a low branch, and slipping off to run the risk of being danced upon by a ton of angry bull.

He let go and landed hard on a pile of rocks.

The bull had wonderful brakes. He stopped his mad run within his own length, spun about, and

prepared to mash his enemy into the rocks. His snorting nose was within a foot of Roger's face.

Roger seized the only weapon at hand. He grabbed a heavy rock and swung it with all his strength against that great twitching nose.

He did this by instinct – without a notion that he was doing exactly the right thing. The tip of the nose is the one tender spot of the buffalo's anatomy. A good hard smash on that one vital spot takes all the fight out of him.

The bull drew back, his head swaying, his eyes popping with surprise.

Before he could collect his scattered wits, the men were upon him. Some held him by the broken lasso, some gripped him by the tail, some by the horns. As he leaped and bucked, others watched their chance and finally noosed the flying heels together, then the forefeet. The bull fell over on his right side, still puffing and snorting defiance.

The cars were brought in with some difficulty because of the thick underbrush and rocks. The first thing to do was to lay the injured Joro on the floor in the back of the Land-Rover, using as a bed the red blanket of Toreador Roger Hunt.

The captured bull was hauled up into his cage. Toto slipped in, cut the foot-nooses, slid out again and slammed shut the door before the bewildered animal could get to his feet.

Back in camp, Joro was bedded down in his tent, and Hal gave him a shot of a quarter-grain of morphine to relieve his pain. The drug acted within a few minutes. Hal went over the African's body for breaks and bruises. There were bruises aplenty, but no breaks. To the men who had crowded into the tent, Hal reported:

'His bones must be made of rubber to stand all that. He'll be all right.'

Joro was grinning from ear to ear. That was not like Joro. He was usually grim and sour.

'What's so funny?' Hal asked.

'The young *bwana*,' Joro said, looking at Roger. Then he went on to tell about the boy's exploits – the toboggan ride at the end of the lasso, his performance with the fluttering red blanket, the way he had jumped in between the bull and Joro and grabbed the animal's horns. The men roared with laughter as Joro described the boy's rocket flight, how he had come down smack on the animal's back, his wild ride until he had let go and landed on the rock pile, and then – that smash on the nose!

The African has his own sense of humour. It is tickled by stories of accidents. He thinks it very funny if someone takes a tumble – even if the one who tumbles is himself.

Roger slipped out of the tent before Joro finished. He still heard the men laughing as if they would burst their sides. He didn't like being laughed at.

Before the day was over, he found they were not laughing at him but with him. When any of them passed him, they bowed with new respect and gave him a warm smile. They were proud of him. Hal was proud of him. His father was proud of him.

He couldn't understand this, for he had only done what he had to do from one moment to the next. In a way, it had been fun. Now that he thought about it, it was even funny, and he could laugh about it too.

17
The Bag of Poison

Hal had not forgotten his promise to visit the sick chief.

It was night before he could go. Then he slipped out of the camp and walked up the hill.

The people of the village had already turned in. The doors of the mud huts were shut. The light of a flickering fire inside came from some of the small windows. Other windows were completely dark — the family slept.

Hal moved quietly. There was no reason to disturb anyone — in fact he would rather not. Especially he didn't want to meet the medicine man.

He knew the man hated him intensely. That was natural. The medicine man had failed to cure the chief. If Hal succeeded, the people would lose faith in their medicine man.

It would be better for the medicine man if the chief died. Then he could say:

'I told you so. I told you the white man's bad magic would kill him. You should have listened to me.'

Hal stopped at the chief's door. He listened for voices inside but heard nothing. He pressed open the door, slid inside, and closed the door behind him.

The place was dimly lighted by the wavering flame of a home-made, hippo-fat candle. Most of the room was in darkness. The candle lit the face of the chief, who was sound asleep.

Just what he needs, Hal thought. I won't disturb him.

He would stay awhile — possibly the chief would wake. Hal retreated into a dark corner and sat down on the mat.

He listened to his patient's breathing. It was regular and normal. There was no flush on the face, no sweat, no fever, no tossing about. The drugs administered by 'Doctor' Hal Hunt had done their good work.

Hal got to thinking about the events of the day. After a long time he found himself getting drowsy. He roused himself and looked at his watch. He had been there an hour. No use waiting longer — the chief might sleep until morning.

Hal was about to rise when he heard a slight sound outside the hut. He listened intently, but there was nothing more. He must have been mistaken. No, there it was again — a slight brushing sound as of a bare foot on the sand.

Then, slowly and silently, the door opened. Someone was edging in, being very careful to make no noise. Perhaps it was one of the chief's wives with some food. Hal was about to speak, but on second thoughts held his tongue.

The door was closed again as quietly as it had been opened. The figure slowly approached the

sleeping chief. As it came out of the dark into the candlelight, Hal recognized the medicine man.

Again he was about to speak and again he held his tongue. What was this fellow up to? In his left hand he help a small leather bag, and in his right something sharp.

He stopped and listened. He looked warily around the room.

Then he kneeled on the mat beside the chief. Now Hal could plainly see his face. Why, Hal wondered, does the face of a cruel man look so much worse than the face of a cruel animal?

Still, it was possible the man meant no harm. Perhaps he had come to wake the chief and speak with him or give him some medicine.

The man carefully studied the sleeping man. Then, before Hal could realize what was going on, he lightly touched the sharp thing against the chief's arm.

The chief did not wake. Hal guessed that the sharp thing was a *chook*. That is a quill of the brush-tailed porcupine, so sharp that it can go through the skin without being felt. It takes the place of the hypodermic needle.

But why make this tiny puncture in the chief's skin? What good, or harm, would that do?

The wizard laid down his *chook* and opened the leather bag. He inserted the tip of his finger and it came out covered with a dark paste. He was about to rub the paste into the hole made by the chook when Hal let loose.

'What the devil are you up to?' he shouted.

The words were in English but the shout was enough to do two things — wake the patient and freeze the medicine man as if he had been suddenly turned to stone.

The chief at once took in the picture — the *chook* on the mat, the leather bag, the dark smear on the finger-tip, Hal running in out of the shadows.

The medicine man leaped to his feet and made for the door. Hal grappled with him, threw him down and sat on him. Men and women came running.

All they could understand at first was that their precious medicine man was being sat upon by that meddling stranger. They pulled Hal away and the medicine man got to his feet, sputtering with injured dignity. Again he started for the door.

'Don't let him go,' the chief called. 'Bring him here.'

Men blocked the door. They hesitated to lay hands on the wizard. Some of the more courageous seized him and brought him to the chief's side.

'Release my friend,' commanded the chief. Hal, suddenly free, came to stand beside the man.

A hush fell over the crowd. It was like a court with a judge about to pronounce sentence.

'The man you hold,' the chief said quietly, 'was about to end my life. You see this *chook*. As I slept, he used it upon me. You see its mark on my arm. Force him to show you the middle finger of his right hand. You see that dark stain. Search among his claws and feathers and you will find the bag from which it came.'

The bag was found. One of the elders opened it. He picked up a small stick and dipped the end of it into the bag. It came out covered with a black, sticky paste like tar. It was the same as the stuff on the medicine man's finger-tip, the stuff he had been about to rub into the cut on the chief's arm.

'You all know what this is,' said the chief.

'Except me,' Hal said. 'Is it a poison?'

'It is.'

'I guessed that it might be — that's why I stopped him.'

'You did well,' the chief said. 'If you had not, my people would now be making ready to bury me.'

'It acts so fast?'

'It kills in a few minutes. We use it on our arrow-heads. It is made from the sap of the mrichu tree.'

Hal, as a student of animals and plants, knew the tree.

'I have often see it,' he said. 'We call it the acocan-thera. The ground under it is covered with bees and beetles and humming-birds — all dead.'

'Yes. They drink from the purple flowers of the mrichu and they die of the poison.'

'How do you make this paste for the arrows?'

'We boil the bark for many hours. So we get a thick, black syrup. We add to it the venom of snakes, the poison of spiders and the roots of deadly weeds. A live shrew is thrown in and we boil it all again.'

'How can you tell when it is strong enough to kill?'

'We make a small cut in a man's arm near the shoulder and let the blood trickle down the arm. We touch the lower end of this trickle with a little bit of the poison. Its touch makes the blood turn black. The blackness goes up the trickle of blood towards the cut. We wipe it away just before it reaches the cut. If the black climbs slowly or stops, we know the poison is too weak. If it climbs fast we know it is strong.'

The medicine man broke out into a torrent of argument. When he had finished, the chief said to Hal:

'He says this is not poison, but only good medicine. Very well, we will test it.'

He gave an order to the elder who had opened the bag. The elder took up the *chook*. In spite of the medicine man's angry protests, the elder made a slight incision in the medicine man's upper arm, just enough to draw the blood.

A tiny stream of blood ran down the arm to the elbow.

The old man touched the blood at the elbow with the end of the paste-smeared stick.

The blood at once turned black. The blackness

climbed the arm with amazing speed towards the cut.

The medicine man was wrenching and twisting now, trying to get away from the men who held him and crying like a terrified child. The chief spoke to him firmly.

'I am telling him,' the chief said to Hal, 'that he will be a dead man in three minutes unless he makes a full confession. He must admit that he was trying to poison me, and he must say why.'

The blackness had now gone up like a snake halfway to the cut.

The medicine man, pale-faced, eyes popping with terror, broke out into a rapid babble. Up went the black snake. Just before it reached the opening through which it would have gone its killing way into the bloodstream, the chief gave a sharp order. The elder wiped the medicine man's arm clean.

'We have saved his life,' the chief said, 'though he does not deserve it. He has made full confession. He was jealous of your power to heal. With all his magic he could not cure me, and then you cured me with a few small white things. The people were laughing at him. He wanted me to die so that he could say your medicine had killed me. For this evil he should be burned. But we of this village are not cruel. He shall live, but he must leave this village and trouble us never again.'

The sentence was carried out at once. The would-be murderer was allowed to collect a few of his personal belongings and was sent out into the night. Hal returned to camp.

He did not sleep well, for he had an uneasy feeling

that this was not quite the end of the story. If he understood the evil gleam he had last seen in the medicine man's eyes, the Hunt family and Hal in particular could expect more trouble, soon.

18
Killers' Pledge

The night was dark, and the medicine man's journey through the country where a lion, elephant or buffalo might be lurking behind any bush was not too pleasant.

At every step his bitterness and his passion for revenge grew. He would show that white magician and his brother and father that it was dangerous to get in the way of a clever medicine man.

He was not aimlessly wandering about. He knew exactly where he was going and what he was going to do. After some five miles of winding trail he saw lights shining between the tree-trunks of a patch of woodland.

He stopped at the edge of the woods. The sound of voices told him that many men were gathered in conference beneath the trees.

He knew who these men were. He was one of them. But no one may walk into a meeting of the Leopard Society unannounced. If he should try it, he would get a poisoned arrow in his chest before he could come out of the shadows.

The medicine man made the peculiar cry of the leopard. It was a good imitation. The leopard has a number of ways of expressing himself. He can growl, and he can roar, and he can scream. But usually he saws wood, just as the medicine man did now.

It sounded quite like a coarse saw going through a log. After each 'saw' the breath was noisily drawn in. So every time there was a double sound. It was something like 'Saw-ah! Saw-ah! Saw-ah! Saw-ah!'

Immediately the talking stopped. Then someone came swinging a lantern. He held the light up to the medicine man's face.

'Ah, it is you, great one. We are honoured that you have come.'

He led the way back to the lighted circle. The medicine man took his place on slightly higher ground with the leaders. A leopard costume was brought to him and he put it on.

Here was a strange sight — twenty men all clothed in leopard skins, masks over their heads, curved iron spikes like leopards' claws projecting from their fingers, leopard pads strapped to their feet so that wherever they went they would leave the track of a leopard.

It seemed like a fevered dream. But the Leopard Society is no figment of the imagination. It is to be found throughout Central and West Africa. The police have forced it back into the hills, but there it still exists. Different branches of it go under different names, the Idiong Society, the Ekpe Leopards, and so on. Within three years, in one small area of West Africa, 196 men, women and children were murdered by the leopard-men.

Why? The reasons vary from place to place. Sometimes the purpose is to punish a village that has become too rich and powerful. Sometimes the killing is prompted by hate of whites. Often the human leopards kill other humans just to get the heart, the eyeballs, the tongue, the ears or some other members which are supposed to have magic powers as medicine or charms.

Make no mistake about it – most Africans are kind and good. Every year more of them go to school. Every year some of the old superstitions die. But there is a long way yet to go. Think of it – when the Congo became independent of Belgium, this great African nation, eighty-eight times as big as Belgium itself, had only sixteen university graduates.

There are still millions of Africans who have never spent one day in school. Without education, they still believe strange things – that a leopard-man can turn into a leopard, that the heart of a strong man will make you strong if you eat it, and that no white man can be trusted.

One of the leaders spoke.

'Chief, among us is the friend who has just come. Let him speak that we may obey.'

The medicine man rose. Here was a man whom even the leopard-men feared, for he could work dark and dangerous magic. They listened in respectful silence.

'There is one among you,' he began, 'who has not kept his pledge. He solemnly promised to kill and has not killed. His name is Joro. I call upon him to stand.'

Joro slowly got to his feet. Dressed as a leopard-man, he looked quite different from the Joro of the Hunt camp. Besides the leopard skin on his back and the steel claws on his hands, his chest was spotted with strange colours and his face painted to make him look more like the savage beast he was supposed to represent. But now he hung his head like a guilty schoolboy.

'A week ago,' the medicine man said, 'you, Joro, performed a sacred ritual and made a pledge. What was that pledge?'

Joro looked helplessly about him. 'I pledged,' he said in a low voice, 'I pledged to kill three men of my safari.'

'And who were they?'

'A father and two sons. Their name is Hunt.'

'And have you fulfilled your promise?'

'I tried. The three were with me in a canoe. There was a hippopotamus in the river and many crocodiles. The hippo attacked, and I held the canoe so that he could strike it, and the canoe was smashed, and I left the three at the mercy of the crocodiles. The father was nearly killed but the others saved him. Even now the father lies helpless between life and death. I could do no more.'

'And was that all?'

'No. I tried again. The elder son was in the catching-chair. A bull buffalo charged. I held the car in its place so that the buffalo would crush the man. The buffalo destroyed the chair — but the man was not in it. He escaped. He was too quick for me.'

'Two failures,' the medicine man said grimly. 'Anything else?'

'The younger son. I planned that a buffalo should kill him.'

Joro hesitated.

'Go on,' demanded the medicine man. 'Did you carry out your plan?'

'Instead, it was I who was nearly killed. It was the boy who prevented my death. If it had not been for him, I would not be standing before you now. He was very brave. He is but a boy, but he is a man. All three are good men. I cannot kill them. I beg you to relieve me from this pledge.'

'That cannot be done,' said the medicine man fiercely. 'If you do not carry out your pledge you must die.'

The threat did not seem to frighten Joro. He lifted his head and looked back at the medicine man with an air of defiance.

'Do with me as you will,' he said. 'Better one death than three.'

'It will not be one death,' replied the medicine man. 'You have a wife and four children. If you do not fulfil your oath, all six of you will pay with your lives.'

Joro's head sank again on his chest. He was a picture of sorrow and defeat. His companions watched him and waited. They were so still that they seemed scarcely to be breathing. The medicine man was also content to wait, a savage glint of victory in his eye. He knew he had won.

At last Joro spoke, but without lifting his head. His voice was low and very sad.

'I will try again,' he said.

19
Tallest Animal on Earth

'GIRAFFES!'

Mali broke into the Hunt tent to make the announcement as it was just beginning to get light. Hal and Roger, with a hard day behind them, would have liked to sleep longer. But this was exciting news.

'Where?' Hal asked sleepily.

'Just outside the camp. Five of them.'

John Hunt spoke. 'Wish I could help you, boys. Nailing down a giraffe is a real job. Try to get two if you can – a male and a female. The Rio Zoo wants a pair.'

'Will they pay enough to make it worth while for me to get up?' grumbled Roger.

'Would you get up for six thousand pounds?'

Roger's eyes opened wide. He and his brother leaped out of bed and pulled on their clothes in such a hurry that Roger got his trousers on hind side before and Hal broke a bootlace.

One would have thought they were money-mad. They were not – usually. But this kind of money was hardly to be made every day. In two minutes they were out of the tent.

There they were, only a few hundred yards from the camp, five handsome giraffes. Four were full grown, one was a baby. But what a baby! A giraffe on the day it is born is six feet tall.

They were all looking at the camp with the greatest curiosity. It is said that curiosity killed a cat. If curiosity kills, then all giraffes would have been dead long ago. There is no animal on earth more curious about things, more anxious to see what is going on.

Hal remembered the local story about the giraffe's curiosity. In the beginning, God gave them normal necks but long legs. Their long legs raised them so high that they couldn't see beneath the trees. So they tried to see over the tops of the trees. They stretched and stretched and stretched their necks, and the higher they stretched the better the view, and so they stretched some more. And now they stand twenty feet high and can look over the usual flat-topped acacia tree. And if they keep on getting taller some day they will be able to look straight into heaven, so say the tellers of tales.

In the early morning sun the golden hides looked very rich with their dark-brown spots.

'What I want to know,' Roger put in, 'is how he ever pumps blood up that skyscraper neck.'

'Just by having a big pump. His heart is forty times as big as yours. It weighs twenty-five pounds. He has the world's highest blood-pressure. The jugular vein in his neck is nearly two inches across, and blood shoots up it like water through a fire-hose.'

'But when he puts his head down to the ground,

what then? All that pressure would blow his head off.'

'No. He has a fancy set of valves that slow down the blood. Don't worry. Nature has done a good job on him.'

A snort behind them made them look round. There was Colonel Bigg with his gun.

'What do you kids know about the giraffe?' he said sarcastically. 'I'll tell you about the giraffe. He's the silliest thing on earth. Look at those long, skinny legs — what good are they? One crack with a cricket bat and they'd break like pipe stems. And that neck — you could tie a knot in it. Giraffes eat nothing but leaves. They can't even growl. They're not dangerous. Tell you what I'll do.' Colonel Bigg was feeling bigger every minute. His efforts so far to prove himself a great hunter had failed. Now he had his chance — he was sure he was more than a match for this flimsy, absurd imitation of an animal. He had heard that the giraffe was as timid as a mouse. 'If you're going to hunt 'em, I'm going with you. I'll show you how easy it is to tackle one of those walking telegraph-poles.'

'If it's so easy,' Hal said, 'you won't need your gun. I'll take it.'

Reluctantly, Bigg parted with the gun. He set his hat at a jaunty angle. He was very proud of that hat. It made him look like an honest-to-goodness professional hunter.

'Who wants a gun?' he growled. 'All I need is my bare hands and a bit of rope. Come on, lads, I'll show you how it's done in a real safari.'

The boys and Bigg, with plenty of other helpers,

climbed into a Land-Rover and a Bedford lorry. The lorry was a big four-ton job and carried a cage especially intended for the tallest of all living animals. The sides of the cage were fifteen feet high, but there was no roof — the last five feet of the bean-pole beast could project upwards into space.

'Run in on them fast,' Bigg told Mali, who was driving. But Roger ventured to correct him.

'No. Go easy. Don't scare them.'

Mali could choose between these two contrary orders. He evidently thought Roger's idea more sensible, for he made the Land-Rover crawl as quietly as possible towards the inquisitive beasts. When he got within fifty feet of them and they began to show signs of nervousness, he stopped.

Now Roger could study them closely. Perhaps Bigg was right — they certainly looked very gentle and harmless. Their great brown eyes were as beautiful and tender as a girl's. Their eyelashes were long and lovely and a glossy jet black.

'Look as if they used mascara,' Roger said.

They were the Baringo type, the so-called five-horned giraffe. And there were the five horns — but they certainly didn't look dangerous. They were just stubby nubbins a few inches long and covered with hair. Roger asked Mali about the horns.

'Just decoration,' Mali said. 'He doesn't use them for fighting.'

'He's not a fighting animal,' Bigg put in.

Mali smiled. 'You'd be surprised. He uses his head — and not just for thinking. He strikes his enemy with the side of his head, not with his horns. And because his neck is so long he can give that head of his a terrific swing. I've seen one kill a leopard with a single swat.'

'A tall story,' Bigg said scornfully. 'They wouldn't hurt a fly. See that one with his mouth open. Why, he has no upper front teeth.'

'That's right,' Mali admitted. 'But he has plenty of big grinders back where you can't see them. Look at that one feeding on the thorn-tree. He has to have good teeth to grind up those thorns.'

'And a tough tongue,' Roger said, amazed to see a tongue a foot and a half long flick out and draw in the four-inch thorns where they could be crushed by the molars. Here again the giraffe was unusual. The whale had a longer tongue; but no land animal except the giant ant-eater could beat the giraffe.

'Another thing about these silly animals,' Bigg said with an air of superior knowledge. 'They can't make a sound.'

'I beg your pardon,' Mali objected. 'A lot of people think that – but it isn't so. The giraffe came make a moo or a grunt.'

Bigg snorted. 'A fine thing, that! An animal twenty feet tall and all he can do is moo or grunt! Even a jackal can make more noise than that.'

Mali turned and looked at Bigg gravely. 'Perhaps the giraffe doesn't need to make much noise. Animals are like people. Sometimes it's the people who talk the most who do the least.'

Bigg glared at him. 'I'll ask you to keep a civil tongue in your head. Remember who you are, you black scum. And if you think I talk too much and don't do anything, I'll show you.'

He opened the door and slid out into the catcher's

seat. Roger was disappointed. He had hoped to do the catching himself.

'Let's go,' cried the colonel.

'Strap yourself in,' Mali suggested.

'Don't need to. We won't bump much. These creatures are as slow as molasses. Step on it. Go after that big one.'

Mali stepped on it. The bull giraffe cocked his head to one side and studied the car with his great brown eyes. Then he turned slowly and began lumbering away.

It was a very awkward lumber. The front feet went forward together, then the back feet came forward together outside the front feet. It was a sleepy, slow-motion kind of gait. The creature moved like a lazy rocking-chair. Bigg laughed.

'Clumsy fool! We'll catch him in no time.'

Roger watched the speedometer. It touched ten, then climbed to twenty, went up to thirty, and the giraffe was still rocking along well ahead of the car. The colonel was bouncing like popcorn. Now he tried to strap himself in, but could not.

'Hey!' he cried. 'Let up.'

But Roger nudged Mali, and Mali, with a grin, stepped a little harder. The speedometer showed forty miles an hour.

Now they were alongside the giraffe. He showed no signs of tiring. Every movement took him a good twenty feet. Bigg tried to unlimber his lariat, but he had to hold himself to his seat with both hands.

Suddenly a wall of heavy underbrush blocked the giraffe's path. He found himself trapped. He tried to cross in front of the car to more open country on the other side. He didn't quite make it. There was nothing for it but to leap over the car, and this he tried to do.

Bigg screamed with terror when he saw the great golden-brown body soaring over him. He would never have believed a giraffe could look so enormous. He cringed in his chair, expecting to be mashed to a pulp.

The flying giraffe, more than twice as tall as the car, easily rose above it. But his leap was not quite long enough, and one foot came down on the roof.

It was a stout steel roof, and Bigg would never have thought it possible that one of those skinny, weak-looking legs could go through it. But what he had never realized was that this creature which looked so thin and frail actually weighed up to two tons.

When a foot with two tons of push behind it struck the roof, it went through like a knife through butter.

The colonel had left his precious hat on the seat beside Roger. The great hoof, a foot wide, was just the right size for that hat. It came down upon it squarely and turned it instantly into a brown pancake.

The foot had no sooner come down than it went up again, getting a few scratches from the torn metal, and the giraffe came to earth on the far side of the car and floated away.

Mali turned the car to follow him. The speed was forty and the ground was rougher than ever. Roger looked out and could see no colonel. He had bounced off.

Mali stopped the car and backed up. Bigg got

unsteadily to his feet. He did not try to get back into the catcher's chair.

'Come, boy,' he managed to say, 'don't expect me to do all the work. It's your turn.'

Roger gleefully got out into the catcher's chair and firmly strapped himself in. Bigg climbed into the cab and surveyed his pancaked hat with amazement.

If he had stopped to think it out, he would not have been so surprised. After all, this two-ton weight on his hat was equal to that of twenty-five men each weighing twelve stone. And twenty-five men sitting on a hat would not be too good for the hat.

With many a leap and bounce the speeding car pursued the smoothly gliding giraffe.

But suddenly the big fellow veered off to avoid something that had been concealed in the long grass. That something turned out to be a pride of five lions. (A group of lions is called a pride — why, don't ask me.)

The lions took off after the giraffe. Lions as well as humans find giraffe meat very tasty.

The lion is the one dangerous enemy of the giraffe. A single lion doesn't dare attack — but a whole pride of lions rushing in at once may sometimes turn a giraffe into a good dinner.

The big bull giraffe was tiring. The lions streaking through the grass came up around him.

'Now you'll see,' Bigg declared. 'They'll turn him into mincemeat in ten seconds.'

One lion leaped for the giraffe's back, but it was too high a jump and he fell back sprawling on his rear end. Another leaped for the throat. The giraffe swung his sledge-hammer head and caught the airborne lion in the stomach and sent him flying with all the wind and half the will knocked out of him.

Two attacked the front legs. Up went the great twelve-inch hooves and came down with a savage chopping effect that evidently caused severe internal injuries, for both the marauders slunk off, feeling very sick.

But it was the hind hooves of this magnificent, mild-mannered fighter that really took the cake. They flew out with such a powerful two-ton thrust that one lion died at once of a dislocated neck and another was knocked head over heels and lay on his back waving his feet in the air.

The Land-Rover rolled up, and the big cats that were still able to move crawled away. The giraffe was still watching them warily. That gave Roger his chance. He flung the lasso and the noose settled over the bull giraffe's neck.

The big bull began to lay about him furiously, and Hal, who had come up in the Bedford, feared for his brother's safety. He came running with the curare gun and fired the drug into the animal's thigh.

The medicine was given time to have its quieting effect. Then, without too much difficulty, the animal was led up into the cage, the cage door was closed, and the car driven back to camp — very slowly so that the hide of the magnificent beast should not be bruised by the iron bars.

The conquest of the female giraffe, the one with the six-foot baby, was more easily accomplished. The baby presented no problem at all. When he saw his mother in the cage, he promptly followed.

So the boys had a good report to make to their

father. They not only had the big male and female, but a baby as a bonus.

'But I suppose it's not worth much,' Roger remarked.

'Don't you believe it,' said his father. 'It will bring just as much as a grown-up, perhaps more. I think Rio will be very happy to get the little fellow along with the others. Giraffes are enormously strong, as you found out, but their nerves are very delicate. The adults are apt to be much worried on this long trip to Rio and might even get sick, but the little fellow won't mind a thing so long as he is with his mother. He's really the best bet of the three. By the way, while you were gone Toto bagged a python. You'll see it in the snake cage. It's a beauty and ought to be worth almost as much as a giraffe, if only we can get it to a zoo alive. We have enough animals now for a shipment. The cargo ship *Kangaroo* will be arriving in Mombasa at the end of this week. I think that tomorrow morning we should start our animals to the coast, so that they'll get there in time to be put aboard that ship.'

20
The Deadly Whiskers

The boys found the python getting his dinner.

The great snake was nineteen feet long and as big round as Roger. It was as colourful as a rainbow, as graceful as a girl, and as mad as a hornet.

Ten men were with it inside the cage. One held its head, one its neck, and others gripped its body all the way down to the tip of its tail. They tried desperately to keep it straight, and it tried just as hard to whip loose, wrap its body round one of these pestiferous humans, and squeeze the life out of him.

Facing the big snake was Toto, who was trying to force large chunks of meat down the creature's throat, using a broom-handle as a poker. A newly captured python is too nervous to eat. He must be force-fed, otherwise he may starve to death.

Toto was performing a dangerous job. True, the python is not poisonous. He does not sting. But he can bite, and his savage teeth slant inwards, so that when they once get locked on your hand or your foot they hang on grimly until the snake is killed.

Therefore Toto, when he slipped a chunk of meat into the mouth, had to be very careful not to get his hand caught between those vicious jaws. Then he poked the meat back into the throat with the broom-handle. Gradually he pushed it farther back through the gullet, while the angry, wriggling snake tried to spit it out.

To prevent it from being thrown out, a rope was tied round the throat just in front of the bulge of meat. Then hands massaged the food back until it reached the snake's belly. Another tourniquet was tied just in front of the stomach to prevent the food from shooting out like a ball from a cannon.

The same ticklish business had to be repeated with each chunk of meat. The first tourniquet was opened to let it pass, then closed, the food was stroked down the body, the second tourniquet opened to let it move into the stomach, then the tourniquet once more pulled tight.

And all the time the men were pushed from one side to the other by the squirming body until it looked as if they were performing some strange, barbaric dance.

When the feeding was completed, the neck tourniquet was removed, but the stomach tourniquet was kept on for another ten minutes, until the powerful gastric juices had begun their work upon the meat and it was no longer likely that the food would be thrown out by the excited snake.

Pythons love water — so the cage was equipped with a large water-trough, and as soon as the men had gone the python slid into it.

There he lay quiet at last, enjoying the cool bath, only his head above water.

The boys went on to inspect the giraffes. They too

were having a meal. Their dinner tables were fifteen feet high!

They were not exactly tables but boxes, strapped inside the cage near the top and full of acacia leaves.

Why so high? Giraffes are used to feeding from the top of thorn-trees. They spend much of the day feeding. If they had to bend their necks down all this time to eat, the strain would be too great and they might sicken and die.

The hippo was happy, at least as happy as a hippo can be without a river to wallow in. Palm leaves had been placed over the top of the cage to protect him from the sun. Tick birds had wriggled through the bars into the cage and were busily digging their dinner out of cracks in the hide.

Then there were the three buffalo cages. Two of the buffalo were as savage as ever, but the one Hal had cared for greeted him with friendly grunts.

The hyenas paced back and forth in their cage with heads down as if deep in thought.

The baby leopards, Chu and Cha, needed no cage and tumbled about the camp head over heels in wild games with the dog, Zulu, and little Bab, the baby baboon.

Mother Bab sat and watched. When her baby played too roughly, or when he got into mischief among the cook's pans and dishes, she walked in and swatted him and said to him in very plain baboon language:

'Mind your manners.'

Every day the three hundred baboons of her tribe came to the edge of the camp. They seemed to argue with her.

'Why don't you come back with us to the trees and the river?'

But she politely refused. She would stay with the friends who had saved her young one's life. The other baboons could understand, for they also had come to look upon the men of the camp as friends, and the many bits of food that were thrown to them cemented the friendship.

In smaller cages were many little beasts and birds that the men had caught in their spare time – mongooses, honey badgers, jackals, bush babies, wart-hogs, pelicans, storks and secretary-birds.

Altogether it was a good collection. It had meant hard and sometimes dangerous work, but it was worth it.

The boys sat down to dinner with the contented feeling that they and their African friends had really done a job. They were all the more pleased because their father had been able to hobble out of his tent and join them at the table.

As they waited to be served, Hal noticed Joro half hidden behind the tents talking with a black stranger. They seemed to be arguing violently. The stranger drew his knife and made such threatening gestures that Hal almost rose from his seat to go to Joro's assistance. Then he decided to wait and see what happened.

His father and Roger had their backs turned towards this little drama. Hal alone could witness what was going on.

The stranger seemed to win the argument. Joro at last threw out his hands in a gesture that appeared to mean, 'Very well. I will do as you say.'

Then he went to the supply wagon and disappeared inside. In a few moments he was out again and wandered over to the open fire, on which a pot of gazelle meat was simmering – the stew that would very soon be brought to the table. The cook was busy preparing other food. Joro stood with his back to the pot and his hands behind him.

Could it be that he was dropping something into the pot?

Presently he wandered away, his head down, his shoulders slumped. Whatever he had done, if he had done anything, he was not happy about it.

The cook had brought fruit to the table. Roger and his father were eagerly devouring bananas and mangoes. Hal did not eat.

'What's the matter?' Roger asked his brother. 'No appetite?'

'Something funny is going on,' Hal said. 'Don't look round.'

The cook ladled the gazelle stew out of the pot. He brought the steaming dishes to the table and set them before the three hungry Hunts. Roger was about to dig in when Hal said sharply:

'Wait!' Then he turned to his father. 'Dad, do you see anything wrong with this stew?'

'Why should there be?'

'It may be all right. But I thought I saw Joro put something into it.'

'It certainly smells good,' John Hunt said. He dipped up a spoonful and examined it carefully. 'No sign of any poison.'

'Hal is just imagining things,' Roger put in. 'Let's eat.'

'Hold it,' his father warned. 'What are these tiny bristles? They look like bits of stiff hair – chopped up.' He studied them for a moment. Then he said unhappily, 'I would never have believed Joro would do this.'

'Do what?' demanded Roger, impatient to get on with his meal.

'I'll explain later. Just now, I want to test Joro. I'm sure he's a leopard-man, but I still can't believe he would let us die. Act as if nothing was wrong. Pretend to eat — but don't.'

He stirred the fragrant stew, then took up a generous spoonful and raised it slowly to his lips.

'*Bwana!*' It was a sharp cry, and it came from Joro. He strode over to the table.

'What is it, Joro?'

'Two more hippos! They are on shore — not far away.'

'Don't bother me now,' John Hunt replied. 'After dinner we'll take a look at them.'

'But they will go into the river. Then it will be very hard to get them.'

'We can do better after we've had some food,' Hunt insisted. 'This smells mighty good.' He again made as if about to take some of the stew. Joro stopped him.

'No, no. It is *not* good. The cook made a mistake. He used bad meat. It is spoiled. It will make you sick.'

'Nonsense!' said Hunt. 'This gazelle was fresh-killed this morning. It's perfectly good.'

Joro grew more excited. 'I beg you — don't eat it.' But the three ignored him and bent over their dishes. Hysterically, Joro seized Roger's dish and emptied the contents on the ground. Then he did the same with the other two dishes. The cook came hurrying over to see what was wrong. Joro broke down, shaking and sobbing.

'I did it,' he confessed. 'The cook is not to blame.

I did it. I put death in it.' He was trembling as if attacked by a violent fever.

John Hunt rose and put his hands on the man's shaking shoulders.

'Pull yourself together, Joro. We understand. I know you are a leopard-man. I guessed it that night in the woods. I know how the Leopard Society works. They made you promise to kill us. Now it's all right — we didn't swallow any of the whiskers — so stop worrying.'

'Whiskers?' exclaimed Roger, staring as if he thought his father had gone off his head.

'Yes, whiskers. Joro, bring the leopard skin here.'

Joro hesitated. Then he went to the supply wagon and came back carrying the skin of the man-eating leopard that Hal had drowned on that first night of the safari.

John Hunt took the head in his hands and turned it so that the boys could look full into the beast's face.

'Do you see anything wrong?'

'It doesn't look quite natural,' Hal muttered, 'especially round the mouth.'

Roger guessed what made the difference. 'The hairs,' he said, 'the stiff white hairs round its mouth — they're all gone.'

'Exactly. And you notice they weren't cut off. They were pulled out by the roots. Then they were chopped into small bits and put into the stew.'

'But how could a few bits of hair hurt anybody? Are they poisonous?'

'Not at all. But they kill just the same. They don't dissolve in the stomach. They pierce the stomach wall and cause cysts. These become inflamed and lead to peritonitis. The Africans don't know the disease by name, but they do know that people die in terrible agony some time after swallowing leopards' whiskers.'

Hal saw Joro looking off into the bush. He followed his glance and spotted the black stranger. The man's face was full of anger and evil. Then he turned and ran.

Hal told his father what he had seen.

John Hunt said, 'He will probably report to the Leopard Society. He will tell them that Joro failed to carry out his pledge.'

'Then what will they do?'

'I don't know. One thing is certain. They'll do something, and whatever it is we're not going to like it. Keep your eyes skinned. If you see any sign of trouble, let me know.'

21
Night Attack

It was an anxious afternoon.

The boys were busy preparing the cage trucks for the trip to the coast. But no matter how busy, they could not get rid of the uneasy feeling that they were in great danger. They watched warily for any strangers lurking in the bushes. Roger hunched his shoulders.

'Any minute I expect to get a poisoned arrow in my back.'

Hour by hour they worked, and waited. The sun finally went down in a blaze of glory. There was a deep quiet over the plain, the woods, and the river. The birds peeped sleepily, a wart-hog sniffled, and the breeze made music in the long grass.

'Reckon nothing is going to happen after all,' hoped Roger.

'All the same,' Hal said, 'we'd better keep watch tonight. You bed down in the bushes at that side of the camp, I'll take the other.'

Roger went outside the ring of tents and made a nest for himself in the long grass. He tuned his ears to catch the slightest sound of approaching footsteps. This was rather exciting. He liked the idea of standing guard — especially if you could stand guard lying down.

An hour went by, and another hour, and he began to get drowsy. Then he slept, and dreamed.

He was standing guard on the battlements of a castle. Poisoned arrows were whizzing by him on all sides. It was not exactly a whizzing sound, more like a crackling — the crackling of fire. Then the castle, though it was built of solid stone, burst into flames. Roger woke.

There *was* a crackling. He stood up. There was fire in the woods. The wind was carrying it towards the camp.

He heard another sound besides the crackling. It was the peculiar sawing voice of a leopard. It was joined by others. Now the sound came from all sides. The camp seemed to be completely surrounded by leopards.

Roger ran to his father's tent and found Hal already there, reporting on what he had seen and heard.

'They aren't leopards,' John Hunt said. 'They're the leopard-men. I'm afraid we have the whole Leopard Society moving in on us. And they're counting on the fire to help them. We may lose all our animals if that fire reaches them. Rouse the men. Have them drive the cage trucks over to the side of the camp away from the fire.'

'Do you think our crew will help us fight the leopard-men?' wondered Hal.

'Who knows? They're scared to death of leopard-men. Tell Joro to come here.'

A few moments after the boys had left, Joro entered.

'Joro,' John Hunt said, 'the time has come for you to decide whether you are with us or against us. If you help the leopard-men, you may save yourself and your wife and children. If you help us, they may kill both you and your family. I can't advise you what to do. But whatever you do, do it quickly.'

Joro did not answer. He turned and left the tent.

Motors were roaring. The cars were being moved to the safer side of camp. The entire woods were a sheet of flame and a steady wind brought it on towards the camp.

The leopard voices were now very close, and by the light of the fire leopard-clad figures could be seen coming out of the shrubbery. Roger was glad that at least they carried no bows and poisoned arrows. But he caught the flash of fire-light on their long steel claws.

Of course they would not use arrows, for they considered that they had changed into real leopards. And a real leopard would use only his claws and teeth.

As they came rushing into camp, their smell came with them — the sour smell of a leopard. For they had greased themselves from head to foot with leopard fat.

One of them came straight for Roger, claws outstretched. When he was within five feet he leaped, as a leopard would leap upon an antelope.

Possibly he thought the boy would be an easy victim. But Roger, large and strong for his age and acquainted with some of the tricks of Japanese judo, flipped the flying body so that it came down with a whack on the stony ground. There the man who had thought himself a beast lay badly stunned. For a while at least he would give no more trouble.

Roger saw Hal, his face streaming with blood from the scratches of steel claws, fighting three of the man-beasts. Roger plunged in to help him. He tripped one of the attackers so that he fell face down and Roger promptly sat on him. He could hardly stand the strong leopard stink that rose from the man's slippery hide. He saw that Hal had discouraged one of his assailants with a punch in the solar plexus and the other had run off to find an easier victim.

What about the safari men? They were not doing too well. Some fought half-heartedly, the others stood to one side, shaking with fear. To them, these creatures with the voices of leopards *were* leopards, or evil spirits, or both. But Joro — Joro was fighting tooth and nail. He, himself a leopard-man, was not fighting with the leopard-men.

He stood squarely in front of John Hunt's tent and barred anyone who tried to enter. Skilfully he avoided the flashing claws and hurled back every opponent until he had a wriggling pile of them on the ground before him. And all the time Joro shouted to the other safari men, urging them to fight with him.

The tent flaps behind him opened and John Hunt came out. He was weak and unsteady and in no condition to fight. Joro roughly forced him back into the tent.

Another would-be fighter appeared, Colonel Bigg with his gun. He fired two rounds, but his aim was so poor that he nearly got safari men instead of leopard-men. At the first scratch of steel claws he howled with pain and dashed back into his tent.

But Hal, Roger, Joro and two or three faithful safari men could not hope to stand up to twenty steel-clawed devils.

Then help came from an unexpected quarter. Three hundred screaming baboons fled before the fire straight towards the camp. The humans who had helped them before perhaps would help them now. Driven mad with fear, they poured into the camp ground.

But there they found the creatures they hated and abhorred more than any others on earth. Their nostrils were assailed by the sickening stench of their most deadly enemies, the leopards. The horrible spotted hides were all about them.

Every leopard skin drew the attack of a dozen baboons, twenty, thirty, as many as could get their teeth into it.

The leopard-men ran for their lives. But wherever they ran, there were more baboons.

One of the now badly frightened human leopards noticed the open door of an empty elephant cage on one of the big Bedfords. He leaped through the door and was promptly followed by the other leopard-men.

Hal saw Joro running towards the cage. Was he going to join his leopard companions after all? But Joro had no such idea. He seized the cage door and swung it shut. Its automatic lock snapped.

The safari men, seeing twenty leopard-men behind bars, suddenly became very brave. These men or

beasts or spirits could not have such magical powers after all, if iron bars could hold them. They crowded round the cage, shouting taunts and flinging pebbles at the prisoners.

The fire died out at the edge of the bare, stony camp ground. Tongues of fire licked on around the camp, terrifying the caged animals so that they gave out a wild chorus of screeches, snorts, hoots, croaks and roars.

Their tumult died away when they found that they were safe from the flames, which raced on before the wind and would keep going until they reached bare sand or a river.

Joro went into the master's tent. Hunt's electric torch revealed torn clothes, bloody skin and a happy smile. Joro looked as if the weight of the whole world had been lifted from his shoulders.

John Hunt felt a tide of affection for this man who had suffered and dared so much and had come through at last with flying colours. Here was a real friend if ever there was one. Hunt had a lump in his throat and did not trust himself to speak. Silently he reached up and gripped the former leopard-man's blood-stained hand.

22
Elephant

Dawn saw the cage trucks on their way to the coast. Hal went along to superintend loading on to the ship.

The imprisoned leopard-men would be handed over to the police at Kampala.

At the same town the safari would see the last of Colonel Bigg and his gun. Probably he would brag to the end of his days about how he had fought off twenty devils single-handed and captured a magnificent collection of wild beasts.

The men not needed on the trip to Mombasa stayed in camp with Roger and his father.

'We'll have a surprise for Hal when he comes back,' said Hunt. 'Ever hear of the Mountains of the Moon?'

'Who hasn't?' exclaimed Roger. 'Land of the giants. Where flowers are as high as trees and even the worms are three feet long!'

'And elephants grow as big as mastodons,' Hunt added.

Roger saw the sparkle in his father's eye. 'I'll bet that's what you're after. Elephants. How soon do we start?'

'As soon as your brother comes back.'

So both Roger and the reader must wait a bit until Hal returns. The adventures of the Hunts in pursuit of the biggest of all land animals will be told in *Elephant Adventure*.

OTHER BOOKS BY WILLARD PRICE

If you enjoyed these two adventure stories why not read some of the other Willard Price books published by Red Fox

Amazon Adventure

Underwater Adventure

Volcano Adventure

South Sea Adventure

Arctic Adventure

Elephant Adventure

Safari Adventure

Cannibal Adventure

Diving Adventure

Gorilla Adventure

Lion Adventure

Tiger Adventure

RED FOX STORY COLLECTIONS

Are you wild about animals?
Do you go bonkers over ballet? Or are you an adventure addict?
Whatever you're into, there's a **RED FOX STORY COLLECTION** just for you! So go ahead and take your pick!

COMPLETELY WILD STORIES
ISBN 0 09 926584 2

THE ADVENTURE COLLECTION
ISBN 0 09 926592 3

ANIMAL STORIES
ISBN 0 09 926583 4

THE CHARLIE MOON COLLECTION
ISBN 0 09 926699 7

DOCTOR DOLITTLE STORIES
ISBN 0 09 926593 1

COOL SCHOOL STORIES
ISBN 0 09 926585 0

BALLET STORIES
ISBN 0 09 926582 6

Tales of Redwall

BRIAN JACQUES

'Not since Roald Dahl have children filled their shelves so compulsively' *The Times*

An award-winning, best-selling series from master storyteller, Brian Jacques. Discover the epic **Tales of Redwall** *adventures about Redwall Abbey - and beyond!*

- **Martin the Warrior** 0 09 928171 6
- **Mossflower** 0 09 955400 3
- **Outcast of Redwall** 0 09 960091 9
- **Mariel of Redwall** 0 09 992960 0
- **The Bellmaker** 0 09 943331 1
- **Salamandastron** 0 09 914361 5
- **Redwall** 0 09 951200 9
- **Mattimeo** 0 09 967540 4
- **The Pearls of Lutra** 0 09 963871 1

Tales of Redwall by Brian Jacques
Out now in paperback from Red Fox priced £4.99

THE RUNTON WEREWOLF

Ritchie Perry

'I suppose I ought to mention one minor fact about myself - I'm a werewolf. Yes, that's right, I'm a werewolf. So is Dad, and my mum is a vampire...'

By day Alan's a normal schoolboy. But at night his 'gronk factor' kicks in - and suddenly, he's not your average kind of guy...

THE RUNTON WEREWOLF
When a legendary werewolf is spotted running through Runton, Alan uncovers an amazing family secret - and suddenly his hair-raising bad dreams begin to make sense...

THE RUNTON WEREWOLF AND THE BIG MATCH
Alan's just got to grips with being a Gronk (a nice, friendly werewolf) only to discover that a couple of mad scientists are hot on his trail. Poor Alan - it looks like it's all over...

THE RUNTON WEREWOLF by Ritchie Perry
Red Fox *paperback*, ISBN 0 09 930327 2 £2.99

THE RUNTON WEREWOLF
AND THE BIG MATCH by Ritchie Perry,
Red Fox *paperback*, ISBN 0 09 968901 4 £3.50

He's super-friendly, SQUEAMISH and... veggie! Meet everyone's favourite tomato-juice-drinking TRANSYLVANIAN: Count Alucard. Or is that... D-R-A-C-U-L-A?!? *Aaaaah!!!*

Manic vampire Alucard and his buddy Henry Hollins star in the HORRIFYINGLY HILARIOUS and seriously unspooky VAMPIRE series, written by Willis Hall with wacky illustrations by Tony Ross and Babette Cole.

Bite into the **VAMPIRE** series - it's fangtastic!

THE LAST VAMPIRE ISBN 0 09 922102 0

THE VAMPIRE'S HOLIDAY ISBN 0 09 922112 8

THE VAMPIRE'S REVENGE ISBN 0 09 922122 5

THE VAMPIRE'S CHRISTMAS ISBN 0 09 922132 2

THE VAMPIRE VANISHES ISBN 0 09 922142 X

VAMPIRE PARK ISBN 0 09 965331 1

VAMPIRE books by Willis Hall
Out now in paperback from Red Fox, priced £3.99

GO SADDLE THE SEA

Action-packed adventure, high-tension drama and heroic swashbuckling!
Join dashing hero Felix Brooke as he boldly embarks upon the journey of a lifetime...
Here's a taster to tempt you!

'Ye've run yourself into a real nest of adders, here, lad,' Sammy whispered.

'I know they are smugglers,' I began protesting. 'That was why the fee was low. But I could take care of my — '

'They are worse than smugglers, lad – they are Comprachicos,' he breathed into my ear.

'Compra — c-comprachicos?'

At first I thought I could not have heard him aright. Then I could not believe him. The I *did* believe him – Sam would not make up such a tale – and, despite myself, my teeth began to chatter.

THE FELIX TRILOGY by Joan Aiken from Red Fox

Go Saddle the Sea	£3.99	ISBN 0 09 953771 0
Bridle the Wind	£3.99	ISBN 0 09 953781 8
The Teeth of the Gale	£3.99	ISBN 0 09 953791 5

FOX ALSO IN RED FOX ALSO IN RED FOX ALSO IN

THE SNOW-WALKER'S SON

Short-listed for the WH Smith Mind Boggling Books Award

Some say he's a monster, others hope he is dead, and no one has seen him for many, many years. Until now...

'I'm sending you to live with my son,' the Jarl said.

For a moment they couldn't realize what he meant. Then Jessa felt sick; cold sweat prickled on her back.

Thorkil was white. 'You can't send us there,' he breathed.

'Hold your tongue and let me finish.' Ragnar was looking at them now, with a hard, amused stare.

'Call it exile, and think yourselves lucky. At least you'll have a sort of life. You leave tomorrow for Thrasirshall, at first light.'

Jessa saw Thorkil was trembling. She knew he couldn't believe this; he was terrified. It burst out of him in a wild despairing cry.

'I won't go! You can't send us out there, not to that creature!'

Out now in paperback from Red Fox at £3.50

1 THE SNOW-WALKER'S SON, ISBN 0 09 925192 2

2 THE EMPTY HAND, ISBN 0 09 925182 5

3 THE SOUL THIEVES, ISBN 0 09 953971 3

By the creator of the award-winning THE ANIMALS OF FARTHING WOOD

Incredible animal adventures starring furry felines, Sammy and Pinkie...

'Don't stray into Quartermile Field. Any animal with sense avoids the spot,' warns Sammy's mother. But Sammy is curious - about the Field, and about his father, the fierce, wild father he's never met.

Then one day Sammy discovers that his father has returned. And determined to track him down, Sammy sets off towards the strange, wild land of Quartermile Field - and into a very different and dangerous world...

THE CITY CATS SERIES by Colin Dann
in paperback from Red Fox

KING OF THE VAGABONDS
ISBN 0 09 921192 0 £3.50

THE CITY CATS
ISBN 0 09 921202 1 £3.50

and coming soon!
COPYCAT ISBN 0 09 21212 9